Books by Patricia Bellomo

In the Louie Morelli series:
Louie Morelli's Mistress
Stella di Mare
Louie Morelli's Daughter
The Prince of Mafia Princes

Author online:
www.patriciabellomo.com
Patricia Bellomo on Facebook

The *Prince* of Mafia *Princes*

A Thriller
by

Patricia Bellomo

Libreria
PUBLICATIONS

The Prince of Mafia Princes

Copyright © 2015 by Patricia Bellomo

Book Cover Design by KarrieRoss.com
Author photo by Sieloff Studios
Book interior by Jera Publishing

Libreria Publications
Mt. Clemens, Michigan
www.libreriapublications.com
books@libreriapublications.com

Printed in the United States of America

ISBN: 978-0-9846305-8-5
ISBN: 978-0-9846305-9-2 (ebook)

Library of Congress Control Number: 2014921629

For the real prince.

To my readers:

This is the fourth novel in my Louie Morelli series. As always, Louie likes the good life and dines at some of this author's favorite restaurants. With the exception of Mizu Café, located inside the fictitious Ocean Breeze Hotel, the restaurants named in this book are actual places and provide great backdrop for my scenes.

If you happen to dine at any of the restaurants mentioned in *The Prince of Mafia Princes*, tell them I sent you.

Chapter One

LOUIE MORELLI HAD A FONDNESS for all things Italian. Thus, when his daughter decorated his Boca Raton office, she acquired his inlaid walnut desk in a showroom on the Via Montenapoleone. Louie's mahogany-leather executive chair and shorter-backed guest chairs had been imported from the same Milanese designer, and his buffed travertine floor, with its swirls of bronze and amber, was carved from an ancient quarry once favored by Michelangelo. Louie himself was Sicilian, and with his dark good looks and impeccable sense of style, he could pass for an Italian movie star. But his cadence was New Orleans working class, and sitting at his beautiful desk with the glare of the Florida sun diffused by the tinted, impact-resistant glass on the arched windows behind him, Louie looked immensely rich and unmistakably American.

Louie sat facing his door. In front of his desk were two of the aforementioned chairs, one of them occupied by the beefy, red-faced man who had delivered the purchase agreement Louie held in his hands. Less than a minute had passed since Brian Chapman had presented his offer, but there was only one line on a real estate contract that mattered, and Louie determined instantly that Chapman's clients were never going to own the Fort Lauderdale property he was selling for ten million and change. Other investors took offense at lowball offers, but Louie was merely amused, his dark eyes glinting with silent laughter as he regarded Chapman from over the tops of his narrow readers. Louie's gaze lingered to the point where Chapman began to squirm, and then he tossed the contract onto his desk and said, "Jesus, Brian, you've got to be kidding me."

Chapman blushed. He looked out of place with his rumpled suit and scuffed loafers, his battered briefcase set on the floor beside him. In contrast, Louie's tropical-weight gray suit was cut from the finest Italian wool and blended with silk, its sleek, tailored lines impeccably fitted to the contours of his slender body. Louie's apricot-colored neck-tie and pocket square had a scrolled paisley design in midnight-blue. Louie wasn't crazy about the tie, but the woven silk duo was a gift from his wife, and he'd worn it to please her.

Louie's secretary had left his door ajar, and noises from the exterior office drifted in, phones ringing, the whir of a printer, a brief discussion between two male voices about a property on Jupiter Island, and then one of the voices said, "Hey, Emily, is *he* in today?"

Louie's secretary said coolly, "If you are asking if Mr. Morelli is in his office, the answer is yes. If you are inquiring whether or not he is available, the answer is no."

Hearing Emily get up from her desk, Louie half expected her to poke her head into his office; instead, his door was pulled shut, muffling the rest of the conversation. Keeping his eyes on Chapman, who shifted uneasily, Louie said, "Brian, this deal is garbage. You know better than to bring me something like this."

Chapman coughed once and said, "You could at least look at it."

Louie waved dismissively at the paperwork. "I saw enough. It's Los Olas Boulevard. You can't get any better than that, not in Fort Lauderdale."

Chapman said, "I know the offer's low. But my client's good for the money. If you would read the terms—"

Louie took off his reading glasses and laid them on the desk beside his two cell phones. One of the mobiles was smart and sleek, the other a prepaid flip-top, its number printed on a label and taped to the back. He said, "Who cares what the terms are, if they're not willing to pay for the building?"

Chapman had misrepresented the deal on the phone, leading Louie to think there was more to it. But from the moment he stepped into Louie's office, he'd stopped talking. Louie's rejection further deflated him, and Chapman sighed loudly, his eyes skipping away from Louie's and looking beyond him, to the row of arched windows that gave view onto a courtyard. Tinted glass emitted a soft light that accentuated the silver in Louie's hair and glinted on the burnished frames of family photos arranged on his desk. Rolled blueprints were stacked on a side table, next to a scale model design of an award-winning shopping mall Louie had developed in Naples. Framed prints showcased similar achievements, depicting coastal high-rises, along with golf-courses and upscale shopping centers, even a couple of instantly recognizable Gulf Coast casinos.

Louie had been doing business with Chapman for years and remembered a time when he was a hustler. But Chapman was in decline, his hand trembling as he lifted the blue-rimmed cup of coffee Emily had set before him, his eyes inadvertently darting to the granite-topped bar where bottles of blended Scotch whiskey, aged bourbons, and premium vodkas glinted invitingly.

Taking pity on him, Louie said, "Brian, you want a drink?"

Chapman blotted his forehead with the lace-edged doily Emily had left on his saucer, and said weakly, "No, no thanks."

"I know you drink, Brian. Help yourself."

Chapman looked relieved. "I guess I'll have a nip," he said, rising from the burnished-leather chair. Casting a sheepish glance at Louie, he mumbled something about "the hair of the dog," as he shuffled self-consciously toward the bar.

Chapman went for the Kentucky bourbon, pouring two fingers worth into a tumbler etched with the logo for L&M Enterprises, the name of the company Louie had founded years ago in New Orleans. Chapman tossed back half the drink in one gulp, and then breathed a sigh of relief, exhaling so profusely that Louie caught a whiff of bourbon from clear across the room.

A closet was to the right of Louie's door, a bathroom just beyond it. The bar was to the left, where Chapman stood, his back to a sitting area that was squared off by a mahogany-leather couch. Hanging on the wall was a sleek LED. Lifting the remote control, Louie aimed it at the panel. Fox News came on, blaring, and he lowered the volume. Chapman tipped the bottle, adding another inch of bourbon to his glass. He walked back to the desk, where Louie gestured dismissively at the contract. "Brian, this deal is a no go."

"I know it's weak, Lou. That's why I wanted to present it in person. I was hoping maybe you'd counter."

"I'm expecting another offer tomorrow."

Chapman's face fell. Louie suspected he really needed this deal. He'd seen a lot of that in recent years. He said, "I have a building in Pompano—"

"My buyer wants Las Olas. It's where the action is."

"Then your buyer needs to come up with a lot more money."

Chapman knew he was being dismissed, but he wasn't leaving before he finished his drink. For a minute there was silence between them, punctuated by the low murmur of the television. Chapman's gaze returned to the glossy-framed photos on Louie's desk. He said, "Is your youngest boy still at Florida Atlantic?"

"Michael flunked out. I sent him to New Orleans."

"He going to school there?"

"Michael's working for me. You know, I do a ton of business in my hometown. Plus I own a coffee company there, in partnership with my cousin."

"Yeah, I remember. Crescent City Coffee—you gave me some coffee once. The wife liked it. She gets it at Winn Dixie." Chapman swirled the bourbon in his glass, eyeing it appreciatively. "It's good liquor, Lou." He glanced back at the pictures. "What's your daughter doing these days?"

Louie smiled. "Stella shops."

Chapman snorted, tilted the glass to his lips. He was down to an inch. "I didn't see Tony when I came in. Is he still working for you?"

"Tony's my acting VP."

Chapman nodded, brow furrowing as he considered this. "Did he get divorced?"

"Tony?" Startled, Louie looked at Chapman, his eyes widening. "Not Tony. In fact, his wife just had another baby. That's three boys in five years." Louie pointed at a recent picture of Tony and Gina, taken with baby Thomas on his christening day.

Chapman eyed the photo. "Nice looking kid," he observed. "Another grandson for you, eh, Lou? That's got to make you feel good." He drained the last of the bourbon, smacking his lips. "I saw Tony at Mizu Café week before last. You know, that's that sushi joint in the Ocean Breeze Hotel, in Lauderdale?"

"I know the place. You ran into Tony there?"

"I didn't talk to him. I was in the bar." He chuckled and set the glass down on Louie's desk. "Tony was with a blonde."

Louie blinked. "Not my son. Tony's straight as an arrow."

"I guess he doesn't take after his old man then." Chapman bent to retrieve his battered briefcase. Straightening, briefcase in hand, he said, "It was dark. I was drinking. It might not even have been Tony."

Louie escorted Chapman to the door, stepping out with him into the anterior office where Emily Myers sat on a swivel-backed chair behind her desk. Emily had a fifteen-inch computer monitor, but she was hunched over the side arm of her desk, typing a form on an old IBM Selectric. Emily treasured her typewriter and kept five years' supply of replacement ribbons, as she feared the manufacturer would quit making them.

Emily was Louie's age, but it was obvious she'd lived a much quieter life than he had. She was married to a man who spent all of his spare time fishing and had an adult son who still lived at home. The son made good money but his personality was zilch. Louie suspected Emily's sole source of excitement was her job.

Louie had hired Emily when he relocated to Florida, before he'd even built the building that headquartered his real estate development and investment company. During the interview it was established that they were both Catholic. This meant a lot to Emily, who kept a small statue of the Virgin Mary on her desk. Living in Boca Raton, Emily's previous employer had been Jewish. "Not that I have anything against the Jewish people," she'd said. "Mr. Berman was a wonderful man, very devoted to his family, as I'm sure you are. But it will be nice to work for a man who shares my faith."

Emily nearly quit her first week, when she learned that the sultry-voiced woman who called Louie every afternoon was his mistress. Victor puzzled her, too. "What exactly does Mr. DeAngelis do for you?" she'd asked, upon catching Victor snoozing on the couch in Louie's office, his Beretta on the floor beside him.

Looking up from her typewriter, Emily adjusted her eyeglasses and smiled pleasantly at Chapman. She was round-faced, with a pear-shaped figure that reminded Louie of Hillary Clinton's. She had a hairdo like Clinton's, too, except Emily's brown hair was streaked with gray. Save for a pale shade of pink lipstick, she wore no makeup.

Emily's desk faced a wall of glass, providing her with a view of posh corridors, modern workstations, and interior offices inhabited by the independent contractors who worked for Louie. Several agents were roaming about with cell phones pressed to their ears while staff diligently attended to their needs. Louie was on a first name basis with all of his agents, although he employed a broker to manage them.

Emily's nose wrinkled as Chapman walked past her desk. She said, "Have a nice day, Mr. Chapman," waiting until he stepped into the hall before she looked inquisitively at Louie. "He smells like booze."

Louie said, "He needed a drink."

"My goodness, it's rather early for *that*."

Louie glanced at his Girard Perregaux watch with its band of black crocodile leather and white-gold case. It was simple, unpretentious, and remarkably expensive. The time was ten-thirty. He said, "Do I have any more appointments?"

"Mark wants to go over some figures with you on the Rosemary development."

Louie had assigned the West Palm project to Tony. Surprised that Tony had delegated it to an assistant, Louie said, "Why is Mark handling it?"

"It's my understanding that Tony asked him to." Emily stood, smoothing her brown polyester slacks, which were stretched taut against her hips. She reached for the Coach bag Louie had given her on her birthday. "Mr. Morelli, I'm going to take my break. Would you like something from the café, perhaps a croissant or muffin?"

"No, thank you. I'm waiting for Victor. We're doing an early lunch on account of the fact that he's cooking for the family tonight."

Emily softened. She'd been invited to some of Victor's meals before. She said, "Mr. DeAngelis was in quite a lot of pain yesterday. I hope he's well enough to cook for your crowd."

Returning to his office, Louie glanced at the television, where Lauren Simonetti was reporting for Fox News from the floor of the NYSE. Seeing that the markets were heading south, he muted the audio and placed a couple of calls. Then Mark came in and they went over details for the development, which took about twenty minutes.

As soon as Mark left, Louie snagged a bottle of San Pellegrino from the fridge beneath the bar. He twisted off the cap and poured the mineral water into a glass. Taking a drink, he strolled to the column of windows behind his desk and gazed absently at the courtyard. Fan-palms bordered the brick-paved walkway, and a two-tiered fountain was spouting water, upper basin cascading into lower. Across the courtyard a trio of tables shaded with green-canvas umbrellas were clustered outside the building's café. The tables were noticeably devoid of people. It was mid May, and a hot, muggy heat was keeping everybody inside.

The black kid who worked at the café was bussing one of the tables, flicking crumbs to a family of waiting sparrows. Behind him a paunchy, pony-tailed man in faded denims and leather sandals emerged from the café's revolving door. The man looked like an aging hippie, but Louie knew Dick Weinstein was attached to the tony law firm that leased space in the building.

Louie sipped water, watching Weinstein without really seeing him. Louie's mind was on Tony, as it was beginning to occur to him that his firstborn was having issues. Busy with his own life, Louie hadn't paid much attention when Tony took off Tuesday, claiming a nasty stomach bug. He'd shown up yesterday, but he'd been evasive with Louie. Tony was not in the office this morning, but Louie knew he had a meeting in Deerfield Beach and wasn't expected until noon.

Puzzled by Tony's recent behavior, Louie reconsidered what Chapman had said about seeing Tony with a blonde at Mizu Café. This was so out of character that Louie had dismissed the comment. While Louie did not discuss his private life with his son, Tony was aware of his father's indiscretions, and he'd been critical in the past, declaring that he'd never cheat on his wife.

But life could change on a dime, and maybe Tony's life was changing. He'd seemed preoccupied lately, but Louie put it down to the stress of a new baby. Yesterday, after his sick day, Louie asked Tony if everything was okay at home, and Tony said everything was fine. But now Louie didn't think everything was fine at all.

Absorbed in his thoughts, Louie paid scant attention to the people entering and exiting through the café's revolving door until Emily and the blonde stunner from the temp agency stepped out. The stunner's name was Adriana McIntyre. She was a leggy beauty with shoulder-length hair and violet-blue eyes, and she'd been working at L&M Enterprises for two months, although it wasn't until last Friday, when Louie discovered Adriana sitting in the chair at the side of Emily's desk, the hem of her skirt hugging her thighs, that he'd actually met her. She'd looked up, almond-shaped eyes sparkling like amethysts, and given Louie a wide-eyed look that was both innocent and knowing.

Fortunately, Emily had been away from her desk, and Louie lingered, discovering in the space of a few minutes that Adriana was thirty-two years old and had a nine-year old-daughter with her soon to be ex-husband. He learned that her husband had been having an affair with their babysitter. Worse, he'd made some bad investments, and they were essentially broke. Adriana had left their Vero Beach home and moved into her mother's house in Boca. She told Louie she was grateful for her job because she really needed it.

On Monday Adriana entered his office seeking Emily, who was conveniently out to lunch. At Louie's invitation she stayed to chat, revealing a little more of her circumstances while alluding to a newly discovered preference for "older men." That evening Louie took Adriana to Trattoria Romana, where she confessed her infatuation over calamari and Baby Amarone. From the restaurant on Palmetto to the Boca Raton Resort and Marina off of El Camino it was five minutes, tops. Thus, before the wine buzz wore off, Louie had Adriana in the stateroom of his eighty-foot Hatteras, the *Stella di Mare*.

Louie hadn't seen Adriana since he'd kissed her goodnight in the parking lot of the marina. Now, watching her cross the courtyard with Emily, he noted how her height and slender curves contrasted with the older woman's middle-aged spread. Next to Emily's polyester pantsuit, Adriana's sleeveless white dress was refreshingly elegant. Trimmed with black at the neck and hemline, it had a pleated skirt that was billowing in the breeze, exposing shapely, suntanned legs with well-muscled calves.

Adriana and Emily looped around the fountain, walking directly toward Louie's side of the building. The women were talking, Adriana laughing at something Emily said, her golden curls gleaming in the sunlight. Her fake Louie Vuitton, so obvious as to amuse Louie, hung in the crook of her arm, and she carried a cardboard cup-carrier with three iced-coffee drinks and a pastry bag. Beside her Emily was balancing a hot cup of coffee and a box lunch.

The buzzing of Louie's smart phone distracted him. Turning away from the window, he walked to his desk and snatched it up, saw Victor's name flashing. Dragging his finger across the screen to answer, he said, "Hey, how you doing?"

"I'm done." Victor DeAngelis had gone for a root canal this morning—his voice sounded thick. "I'm filling a prescription at Walgreen's. I should be at the office in half an hour."

"Are you in pain?"

"Christ, Lou, they got me all numbed up. I'm drooling like a baby. You should have seen the size of the needle they jabbed into my gum. I can't feel anything now, but when the Novocain wears off, it's going to hurt like a mother."

Louie smiled. Victor's tooth had abscessed a week ago, and they'd put him on antibiotics to bring the swelling down. He'd been complaining incessantly, and Louie was glad he'd finally had the procedure. He had a brief flashback to a time when Victor had extracted a man's tooth with a pair of pliers. It was a long time ago, and he wondered if Victor remembered.

"Okay," said Louie. "Get your prescription filled and then come in."

"They don't have one person in this pharmacy that speaks English. You should see this rag-head—hey, hold on, Lou. Angie's calling me."

Idly, Louie wondered what his wife was calling Victor about. He drank San Pellegrino, waiting for Victor to come back on the line. Louie heard a beep, and then Victor said, "Lou, you there?"

"Yeah. What did Angie want?"

"She wanted to see how I was, asked if I was up to making the sauce tonight. Like a little old toothache is going to keep me away from the kitchen. I told her not to sweat it."

Louie took a swig of his mineral water. "Victor, I'll see you when you get here."

"Wait a minute. Tony called—texted me, actually. I was in the chair and couldn't get to my phone. He said he made the meeting in Deerfield, but that he's sick. He's not coming into the office today."

Louie felt a flicker of alarm, followed swiftly by annoyance. He was used to people approaching him through Victor. Everyone did it, even his family. But *texting* Victor showed cowardice.

Louie paused, digesting what Victor had told him. Finally, he said, "Did you call Tony back?"

"I figure something's going on, Lou. I wanted to run it by you first."

"Jesus," said Louie.

"I can drive by his house if you want. Talk to him."

"No. Come straight to the office. I'll call Tony."

Louie hung up with Victor. He scrolled through his contacts and found Tony's number. Tony's phone was powered off—the call went to voicemail. Louie said, "Tony, what's going on with you? Call me."

Then he tossed his phone onto his desk and stood, staring blankly out the window, not seeing the people going about their daily routines. With a father's instinct Louie suddenly comprehended that Tony was in trouble, and he reproached himself for not seeing it sooner. He felt a nagging sense that something was seriously wrong, and he sat back and waited for Tony to return his call.

Chapter Two

TONY DID NOT CALL BACK. Annoyed, Louie halfheartedly returned to his tasks. He was lounging with his feet propped on his desk while studying a set of blueprints when a knock sounded on his door. Without bothering to look up, he called a quick "Come in."

Expecting to see Emily, Louie was pleasantly surprised when Adriana opened the door and stepped in. She was carrying the cup container, minus one of the three iced drinks he'd glimpsed, and the pastry bag, holding it aloft and nudging the door shut with her shoulder.

Louie's shoes hit the floor. He hopped up, coming around the desk to greet her. "Hi, baby," he said, a warm smile breaking on his face as he slipped his arm about her waist, drawing her to him in a half hug.

Adriana stood five-ten in her heels, giving her a two inch advantage over Louie. Looking down at him, her high cheekbones shimmering with bronze blusher, Adriana handed him the cup carrier. "I bought you and Victor an iced café au lait. I remember how you told me you get them at the Café du Monde, in New Orleans."

"Baby, that's so sweet of you." Louie lifted the cardboard container from her hands. "What's in the bag...beignets?" he asked facetiously, knowing the café did not serve the powdery pastries indigenous to his hometown.

"I wish." Adriana tossed her head. "They're molasses cookies, for Victor. He told me they're his favorite." She turned, scoping his office. "Is Victor here?"

"On his way. He had a dental appointment this morning." Louie had a feeling she already knew this. He gave her a little smile, his gaze automatically sweeping her, a gleam of appreciation in his eyes as he observed the outline of a lace-edged bra visible beneath the thin fabric of her dress. Even more enticing was the fact that her breasts were reacting to the cooler temps in his office.

Louie said, "Baby, you look good."

She smiled coyly and moved toward his desk, setting the pastry bag on it. Louie placed the cup carrier beside the bag, and then reached for her hand. Giving a little squeeze, he said, "Did you have a good time the other night?"

She blushed, and he recalled how she'd gone shy in his stateroom, her passive-aggressiveness puzzling him. Louie sensed that she'd played the sophisticated divorcée to impress him, and he wondered why she had tried so hard. Not that he particularly cared about her feelings. His instincts were purely primal, his gaze wandering from her lips to her eyes and back. Adriana ducked her head, and Louie tilted her chin up with his finger. "Don't go shy on me now, baby."

He pressed his lips to hers, and she sighed against his mouth. Kissing her lightly, Louie tasted coffee and raspberry lip gloss. He said, "Mmm," and drew back, regarding her with eyes that were narrowed and burning. His smile was gentle. "I want to see you again."

She laughed softly, if not a little nervously. "I had a great time the other night. It's been years since I went on a real date. You're the first man I've been with since Kevin and I separated."

Louie wanted to make sure he was the second. "Come by the marina today," he said. "I'll be at the *Stella* at four. I'll leave word at the gate for them to admit you."

"I have to check with my mother. She babysits my daughter every day. "

Louie had forgotten she was a mother. This cooled his ardor a bit, and he perched on the edge of his desk, one foot flat on the floor, the other dangling above it. He said, "I'll be there. I'd love to see you … if you can make it."

Adriana sat on the chair Chapman had favored and reached for one of the iced-drinks, poking a straw into the lid before handing it to Louie. He took a sip, and then said, "Someday, when you have more time, I'll take you for a boat ride. Would you like that?"

"Gosh, yes."

"Maybe a trip to Bimini or Nassau. Have you ever been to the Atlantis Casino?"

"No, I've been married for ten years to a very dull man. The only exciting thing Kevin ever did was to take me to Red Lobster. It was our standing date every Friday. Now he takes our babysitter there."

Louie smiled. "Hang with me, and I'll take you to a lot of exciting places." He took another drink of iced café au lait, rattling the cubes in his plastic cup. His eyes slid over her, drawn like a magnet to her breasts, her silky-sheer dress barely concealing the provocative bra. There was nothing subtle about Adriana's perfume either, a sultry fragrance that hinted of warm, female skin.

Adriana was stunning, if not beautiful, and she'd shown herself companionable to him. On the physical level they clicked, but he was getting mixed signals, sensing vulnerability beneath the facade of the blasé divorcée. Currently without a mistress, Louie was on the lookout for a companion with the right combination of beauty, charm, and character.

In other words he wanted a woman who liked sex as much as he did. Overall, Louie had discovered this wasn't difficult to find, but he treated his girlfriends well, and they invariably fell in love, which was the ultimate spoiler, resulting in tearful demands and heartfelt declarations. Only one of Louie's affairs had been long term, lasting eleven years, but Mercedes had been cut from a different cloth. Louie already knew that Adriana was not of this same cloth, but this didn't preclude him from judging her favorably.

Of course, women always wanted to please him, but the fakers didn't last. Adriana's passion had been genuine, and she'd seemed a little embarrassed by it. Now, leaning forward, his eyes holding hers, Louie said, "If I take you down to the islands, you'll have to be able to get away for a night or two. Will traveling be a problem?"

"Umm, no. I can make arrangements, as long as I have ample time to plan." Adriana twirled a strand of golden hair around her finger, her eyes darkening imperceptibly. She touched her tongue to her lips. "It was good between us, wasn't it?"

"The best, baby."

Adriana smiled. "When I started here, Emily told me you were a charmer and forewarned that if you ever called me 'baby,' I was to remind myself you are a married man and that you've been married for longer than I've been alive." She glanced at the photos on his desk, her eyes fastening on one of him and Angie dressed in formal attire for Stella's ill-fated wedding. She said, "You have an attractive wife. Emily says she's a lovely woman."

"She is," he said curtly.

Adriana looked up, eyes hardening. "Does it ever bother you to cheat on her?"

Louie set down his café au lait and looked warily at her. This probing question diminished her potential as his girlfriend, revealing an insecure and possessive nature. After all, she'd gone to bed with him in full knowledge of his marital state, and now, abruptly, she was showing discomfort with it. At this point Louie desired her, but she was not important to him, and he wanted no complications. Gently, he said to her, his voice silky smooth, "It doesn't bother me, honey, but if you're having second thoughts about going out with a married man, I understand. We don't have to continue as lovers. We can still be friends."

Taken aback by the cavalier speed with which he was willing to dismiss her, Adriana's eyes flashed. "I don't *want* to be friends. How can you say such a thing? Is that what you want?"

"Darling, you're a beautiful woman. Of course, I don't want to be 'just friends'. But it's important to me that you don't do anything you're uncomfortable with or might regret later."

His eyes, glinting, held hers. He saw her waver, then soften. "I don't think you're the type of man who has platonic friendships with women," she said flippantly. "So I guess I'll have to settle for being your lover."

Chapter Three

I F VICTOR HAD ONCE PUZZLED and intimidated Emily, she'd long since gotten over it. Victor was one of Emily's favorite people. In fact, he was the only man in her life who paid any attention to her, flattering her with little gifts and tidbits of gossip. Today, Victor brought Emily a Snickers bar, which Louie knew she loved. He heard her playfully admonishing Victor for ruining her diet, and then Victor opened Louie's door without knocking, his big, muscled frame filling up the space before he stepped in, exhibiting a gracefulness that was peculiar for a man of his size.

Victor came in whistling, a Walgreen's bag dangling from his hand. His mercurial hazel eyes twinkled as he looked from Adriana to Louie and back. Of course, Victor assessed the situation immediately and understood it at a glance. Single all of his life until he had married last year, Victor had a keen appreciation for women. His gaze skimmed over Adriana, and Louie knew he was seeing the same things Louie had, and Louie smiled with amusement when Victor said, "Hey, doll, look how pretty you are. That's some dress. It must have cost a fortune."

"Not at all. I got it on sale at Stein Mart."

Approaching the desk, Victor set down the bag, and said, "No kidding. It looks like a designer dress to me. A Versace or something, like maybe you got it in South Beach."

Adriana looked unaccountably pleased. Before she could reply to this, Louie said, "Victor, look how you rate. Adriana brought you an iced café au lait and cookies."

"Doll, you're a real sweetheart," said Victor, patting Adriana on the shoulder.

Louie could tell by looking at Victor's bushy-brown hair that the humidity was off the charts today. Victor was clean-shaven and sporting a suntan, although the tropical sun was starting to take its toll on his skin. Beneath his lavender linen sport coat Victor wore a purple shirt, opened at the collar, no tie. The jacket hung a little heavy on one side, clueing Louie to the fact that Victor had not bothered with a shoulder holster today.

Victor opened the bag, extracting the *Palm Beach Post*, which he handed to Louie, who was still sitting on the edge of his desk. He said, "I figured you already got the *Sun.*"

He meant the *Sun-Sentinel*, the Lauderdale paper which Louie preferred. A smaller, paper bag inside the larger one held Victor's prescription. He ripped it open, snapping the cap off the bottle and shaking two pills into the palm of his hand. Adriana said, "Are you hurting?"

"No, but the numbness is starting to go away. I figure I'd better get a jump on it." He reached for the plastic cup of café au lait, popped the lid, and, lifting it to his mouth, swallowed both pills.

Adriana said, "Are you sure you're supposed to take two? They might make you sleepy."

"I'm a big guy, doll." Victor touched the lower left side of his jaw, where it was slightly swollen. "Have you ever had a root canal?"

"No, but I worked for an oral surgeon when I first got married. I quit after Darcy was born. Kevin was making good money then, and I could afford to stay home. Hmpf." Her voice hardened. "That didn't last long."

Victor sat in the chair beside her and reached for the pastry bag. "What happened, doll? Things get tough for you?"

"Yeah, you could say that. Kevin's a house painter, and we got hit hard by the recession. Plus, he was hiding money from me, putting things in his name because I guess he was planning to dump me all along."

"I don't understand. What kind of a man treats a beautiful woman like you that way? Can you figure it, Lou?"

Louie's eyes met Adriana's, holding hers for a second, a little smile flitting across his face. "It's beyond my comprehension."

Victor said, "The guy's a bum, that's for sure."

"Huh, you don't know the half of it. Kevin was having an affair with our nineteen-year old babysitter."

"Jeez, that's low. I feel for you, doll. It's got to be hard. How long were you married?"

"Ten years. My divorce will be final next month, on our anniversary."

Victor reached into the bag and pulled out a large molasses cookie. He glanced appreciatively at Adriana. "Doll, you're a nice girl. You know how I can tell? Only a nice girl would bring a tough guy like me a cookie. It's sweet of you to remember that I like molasses."

"I don't think you're such a tough guy," said Adriana. "You seem like a bighearted guy, a real pussycat."

"I don't know about being a pussycat, but I admit to being tenderhearted," said Victor, taking a bite out of the cookie and giving a moan of appreciation.

Louie turned at the sound of his phone. It was his landline, ringing through from Emily, and he got up and walked around his desk. Answering, he missed Victor's witty repartee, but Adriana laughed, her perfume mingling with Victor's Polo and the sweet smell of molasses and brown sugar.

Louie's caller was a contractor he was using on a development in Bradenton. Louie sat at his desk, swiveling his chair so that he presented his back to his guests. The contractor had a question about a minor issue, which Louie answered quickly, finishing up as Adriana came to her feet. She said, "If I don't get back to work, Emily's going to come in here and drag me back."

Victor swallowed a mouthful of cookie. "If she gives you a hard time, doll, you let me know."

Adriana looked expectantly at Louie. Standing, he came around the desk, set a light hand on the small of her back. He walked her to the door. Just before he opened it, she gave him a smoldering look and said softly, "I'll be at the marina at four."

Louie felt a quick thrill. "What about your mother?"

"I'll tell her I have to work late."

He kissed her lightly, saw her eyes turn smoky. This time, when she gazed at him, there was no mistaking her desire. Before he could take advantage of this, Adriana yanked open the door, startling Emily, who looked up, eyes narrowing with suspicion. Emily gave Louie a sharply disapproving look. He shut the door before she could comment and returned to his desk, where Victor was starting on another cookie. "What was all that about?" Victor asked.

Louie sat in his chair and extended his legs. He locked his knuckles together behind his neck, stretching his upper arms and shoulders. "I have a date with her this afternoon."

"She's some looker."

"Emily's laying a guilt trip on her."

"She would, wouldn't she? I don't know why women can't mind their own business. The way I figure is that Adriana really likes you. Otherwise, she wouldn't make a fuss. That could be a problem."

"Isn't it always?" Louie looked at his watch. It was a quarter of twelve. "I'm getting hungry."

"You want to go to Max's Grille for lunch?"

"Sure, but I'm not eating heavy. I haven't forgotten that you're cooking tonight."

Emily knocked and then opened the door, stepping in with the mail. It was no coincidence that she'd chosen this moment to intervene, although her manner was purely professional. Tapping the top envelope with her fingernail, Emily said, "Mr. Morelli, we've received a Chapter Eleven notice for See-More Studios. I've faxed the information to Abraham Mischcoff's law office, but it's doubtful that you'll be able to collect on your investment while Albert Seymour's studio is in bankruptcy."

Emily said *studio* with disdain. See-More Studios was an adult film studio, and Emily did not approve. Louie lifted the envelope from the pile and opened it, skimming through the legal jargon. He thought of the personal loan he'd given Albert Seymour, the one Emily didn't know about—a verbal contract, paperless. He *would* collect on that loan.

"Thank you, Emily." To Victor, he said, "Let's go to lunch."

Emily looked as though she wanted to say something else, but at that moment Louie's phone started vibrating, and she reluctantly retreated. Louie saw Tony's name flashing on the screen and snatched it up. He unlocked the device and said, "Yeah, Tony, what's going on?"

Tony cleared his throat. "Nothing, Dad. Just feeling a little under the weather."

Tony didn't sound sick, and he hadn't looked sick yesterday, either. Again, Louie felt a flicker of alarm. He said sharply, "What's wrong, Tony?"

"Can't I take a day off without getting the third degree?"

"Are you sick?" When Tony did not answer, Louie said, "You don't sound sick."

"I'm not … I mean, I'm tired. I've got a few issues … personal things … I need to take care of."

"Anything you want to tell me?"

"Not at this time."

"Tony—"

"Dad, I'm fine. I just need some space. In fact, I'm going to take tomorrow off, too. I'll be in on Monday."

Today was Thursday—that gave Tony Friday plus two. Louie said, "You're sure I can't help?"

"No."

Louie hesitated. "Okay. I'm here if you need me."

Tony gave a short derisive laugh that Louie did not like. He said, "Yeah, sure, Dad," and hung up.

Chapter Four

LOUIE HUNG UP WITH A sigh, and Victor said, "What's going on with Tony?"

"He won't say. He's not sick."

"I didn't think so. You figure he and Gina are having problems?"

Louie shrugged. "You've got to consider it's a possibility." He related what Chapman had said about seeing Tony with a blonde. When Victor expressed surprise, Louie said, "Tony's always been so damned straight-laced. You know how self righteous he is about everything. He swore he'd never dishonor his wife by playing around on her."

Victor said, "Yeah, but we all start with good intentions. I know I did."

This restored some of Louie's humor, and he couldn't help laughing. "Victor, you've only been married a year." He sat back in his chair, his stomach forgotten. "Tony doesn't even call in sick when he's sick." He looked at Victor. "Something's wrong, really wrong. I can feel it."

"The problem with Tony is that he takes himself too serious."

"He always did, even as a kid." Louie drummed his fingers on his desktop, irritated now, Tony's sarcasm lingering. He looked at Victor, swilling the last of his café au lait, and said, "Get Carmen in here. I want to talk to him."

Carmen was Louie's nephew by marriage, the only child of Angie's worthless older sister. Angie's sister hadn't been a good mother, and Carmen had spent his childhood summers with Louie's family. He was Tony's age, so this worked out well. The cousins were close, and Louie reasoned that if Tony confided in anybody, it would be Carmen.

Carmen was from Tampa, as all of Angie's people were. Upon graduating from college he'd floundered around, not finding any direct path until Louie put him in charge of his property management division. Carmen was at his desk when Victor summoned him, and he arrived in Louie's office a few minutes later.

Carmen was a round-faced, husky guy with soft brown eyes and a polite, respectful manner. Despite his parent's fuckups, or, perhaps, because of them, Carmen had turned out surprisingly well. He was a thoroughly decent young man, and Louie was very fond of him, treating him like one of his own sons.

Carmen came in looking a little frazzled, as though Louie had taken him from something pressing. His shirt-sleeves were rolled to his elbows, his blue-and-yellow striped tie hanging askew. He wore navy slacks and brown loafers, and Louie couldn't help but notice that his curly hair was starting to thin on top.

Greeting Louie with a smile, Carmen said, "Hi, Uncle Louie." He nodded at Victor. "Hey, how's the tooth?"

This was a mistake. Victor launched into a detailed explanation of the procedure he'd had, as though he was the only person to ever have a root canal. But now Louie saw that Adriana might have had a point about Victor taking two pills because his eyelids seemed a little droopy, and he stifled a yawn. "Aw, heck, kid, sit down. You don't want to hear about my tooth," calling Carmen a "kid," even though he was only about a dozen years older.

Carmen sat in the chair beside Victor. He eyed the open pastry bag, with its one remaining cookie. Victor slid the bag to him. "Help yourself."

"Don't mind if I do." Snatching up the cookie, Carmen took a healthy bite. "Mmm, it's good."

Louie said, "Adriana brought them for Victor."

Carmen's head jerked up. "Adriana … the blonde?" His tone carried a trace of disbelief. "No shit. She's hot, but stuck-up. I tried being friendly with her, but she wouldn't give me the time of day."

Louie said drolly, "Well, she likes Victor." He watched Carmen take another bite. "Victor, get Carmen something to drink."

Victor got up and walked to the bar. He didn't offer booze, but opened the mini-fridge and said, "Coke, Diet Coke, ginger-ale, mineral water—"

"Coke is good."

Victor brought him the can with a glass. He set the glass in front of Carmen, popped the tab, and poured soda. Finishing the cookie, Carmen brushed the crumbs from his fingers and nodded at Victor. "Thanks."

Louie said, "You're coming over to the house tonight, right? Victor's cooking."

"Are you kidding? I've been waiting all week. I wouldn't miss one of Victor's meals for anything." He looked at Victor. "You cook better than anybody I know, even Nonna, although I don't dare tell her. What are you making?"

"*Frutti di mare.*"

"Fruit of the sea. I'm in heaven already."

Dispensing with the small talk, Louie said, "Carmen, you're close with Tony. Tell me what's going on with him. Do you know?"

Carmen's eyes widened. "I'm not sure," he said abruptly, looking away from Louie.

His quick evasion told Louie that he did know. While Louie appreciated Carmen's loyalty to his cousin, he felt that the young man's first loyalty was to him, and he said sternly, "Tell me what you know."

Carmen hesitated, letting the silence stretch out. Victor patted him on the arm. "Look, Carm, we know there is something going on with Tony. He's not acting right—not even coming in to work. Lou's worried about him—hell, Tony's shutting out his own father. Now, if you know something, anything, it would help—"

Carmen looked at Louie. "I don't know everything because Tony's shutting me out, too. I do know that he and Gina are having problems. I guess it's not easy having a baby, but Gina's been a real bitch. She's nagging Tony all the time. She put on weight with Thomas, and she isn't even attempting to take it off. Not that that's the reason he's unhappy—it's just that she's so miserable. And it isn't as though Gina has it tough. I mean, Tony provides a lot of domestic help for her."

Victor said, "She's probably got those postpartum blues they talk about on women's shows. Dr. Oz had somebody on—"

"Yeah, Tony thought so, too. He took Gina to the doctor, and they got her on some meds, and her mood has improved. I visited with them on Sunday, and I could really see the difference. But now it's Tony who is falling apart."

"How so?" asked Louie.

"It's my fault," said Carmen, pausing to take a drink of cola. "You see, a couple of months ago Tony was really fed up. Uncle

Louie, you know how he is—he wants to do everything right." Louie nodded, and Carmen continued. "Well, Tony was constantly complaining to me, and I said it sounded like he needed to get laid, and he admitted that he and Gina weren't having sex, and I gave him the phone number to a girl I know—"

"You set him up with somebody?"

"No, nothing like that. Irina's a … friend. Somebody I see from time to time. Nothing serious."

Louie was starting to get the picture. He said, "Is Tony involved with this girl?"

Carmen shrugged. "He won't really say. He seems embarrassed. I mean, she's not a bad sort."

"What sort is she?"

"Uncle Louie, she's a Russian girl. She's a hot looking chick, but not exactly the type you want to get involved with. I wouldn't want to date her seriously or anything."

Louie said, "You're telling me my son is involved with a prostitute?"

There was a hard edge to his voice, and Carmen flushed. "I don't know the extent of Tony's involvement. I was kind of surprised when he started seeing Irina regularly. You know, it was like he was keeping everything in control for so long that once he let loose … well, he sort of went wild."

Victor said, "Did you talk to Tony about this?"

"Yeah, I tried talking sense into him. Told him to cool it, you know? I mean, Gina's starting to give him a hard time about never being home. And I can't say that I blame her. And now I don't think Tony's even seeing Irina. I guess things were getting a little hot, and Irina brought in a girlfriend. Tony's been going down to Miami to see this other girl. He didn't tell me her name, but I know she hangs at Franco's."

Franco's was a Miami Beach hotspot, a nightclub that Louie was part owner of, although he was a silent partner and most people assumed Franco Santia was the sole proprietor. If Tony was seeing a working girl who hung at Franco's, Louie would have no problem finding out who she was. He exchanged looks with Victor, seeing some of his own amazement reflected in his friend's eyes.

Louie's phone buzzed. It had rung twice before, and he'd ignored it, but now he saw that Stella was calling him, and he answered it, saying, "Hi, Princess."

"Daddy, are you busy?"

"A little bit, baby. What's up?"

"Gina and the boys are over."

"How are the kids?"

"Holy terrors, but they're having a ball with Michael." Louie's youngest son was visiting for a few days, which is why they were doing the big dinner tonight. Stella said, "Little Louis and Anthony are going to spend the night."

"Great. That'll give Gina a break." Stella hadn't mentioned Tony, and Louie didn't ask. Stella hesitated, and Louie knew she hadn't gotten around to the reason for her call. Louie worried about Stella. She'd lost her husband eighteen months ago and was still vulnerable, staying with Louie and Angie since. He said, "Are you okay, baby?"

"Fine, Daddy."

"How's Isabella?"

"She's happy as can be, playing with her cousins."

"Give her a kiss for me."

"You can give her one yourself, when you come home. You *are* coming home tonight, aren't you?"

"I'll be there, baby. Victor's cooking tonight. Did you forget?"

"Umm, it slipped my mind."

Victor got up and went into the bathroom. Louie heard the exhaust fan click on. Stella said, "Daddy, I scheduled the caterers for the fourteenth of June. It's a Saturday. I told them a hundred, but it looks like we might have more people. Mom knows about the party—there's no way I could plan it without her knowing. I'm going to do a pink theme, and we'll have pink champagne and pink roses. Is that okay with you?"

Louie had learned early on in his marriage that Angie's birthday, falling on the tenth of June, was a momentous occasion. In the past he'd bestowed lavish gifts and dinners, but this year Stella had suggested the party and Louie had gone along with it. He should have known that Stella would plan it on a grand scale. Her own wedding had cost an easy million. Louie hadn't minded paying, but the marriage had been a complete disaster.

Louie said, "Whatever you want, Princess." He heard water running in the bathroom. Carmen got up, carrying his glass to the sink and dumping what was left of his cola. Louie glanced at his watch. "Listen, baby, I have to go—"

"Daddy, I want to talk to you about Chester. He's here. He brought Mom flowers—orchids, if you can believe it."

Chester Morgan was an older gentleman who belonged to Angie's garden club. Louie strongly suspected Chester was a fruit, but Angie flattered herself that Chester was "sweet" on her. Louie didn't begrudge his wife much, indulging her whims. That she had an admirer was a source of amusement for him, but Stella's next words made him realize that the situation might not be so innocent after all.

Stella said, "Chester told Mom he lost all of his money to that Madoff man. Is this true?"

"I don't know, baby. Why do you ask?"

Victor popped out of the bathroom, paper towel in hand. Stella said, "Because Chester told me he bought his flower shop with money he had from an inheritance, and he seemed to sort of contradict himself, and I got a feeling he was making things up. I think he's a phony. But I didn't say anything to Mom. Don't let on that I called you, either."

"I'm glad you brought it to my attention."

"I don't want to make an issue out of it—Chester *is* very nice to Mom. And she does so enjoy his visits."

"You did the right thing by telling me." He glanced at Carmen, waiting patiently. "Baby, I have to go. I'll talk to you more about this later."

Stella said good-bye, and Louie hit the End button. He looked at Victor and Carmen, shaking his head to clear his thoughts. "Sorry," he said, his mind coming back to the more immediate problem of Tony and his prostitute. It was not the sex that was bothering him. No, what bothered Louie was that Tony and Carmen were *paying* for sex.

Louie said, "Carmen, I don't get it. You're young, good looking... Hell, you and Tony are handsome guys. How is it that neither of you can get a girl?" He thought of the women he'd known, girls like Adriana. Nice girls, lonely and bored, looking for a man to show them a good time, take care of them.

"Uncle Louie, it's not that easy," said Carmen. "I want to get married, but I just don't seem to have much luck with women. I even tried an online dating service—"

Victor said, "Carmen, there's more pussy in South Florida than anywhere. You're telling me you can't score?"

"No... not too often. Girls are particular nowadays. You take them out to dinner, and they spend the whole night texting their girlfriends. They ask me outright how much money I make. With a girl like Irina it's convenient, you know what I mean? You don't have to pretend. No small talk or nothing."

Personally, Louie had nothing against prostitutes. In fact, he sanctioned an escort service in New Orleans, and he'd known a lot of working girls, but he'd never messed with them, never even felt attracted to them, and some of them were downright gorgeous. He'd always sensed their vulnerabilities, pitied them in a way he'd never attempted to analyze.

Of course, Louie's affairs cost him plenty. Women were his greatest indulgence, but the thought of paying for the actual act offended his pride. But he could see that he'd embarrassed his nephew, and he said, "Don't sell yourself short, Carmen. You have a lot to offer a girl." He glanced at his watch, remembered that he was hungry. "So you think Tony is in love with Irina's friend?"

"Yeah," said Carmen. "That's what I'm worried about."

"You mentioned Miami: Is this where Irina operates?"

"No. She operates in Lauderdale. I used to meet her at the Holiday Inn on Broward, but the last time it was at the Ocean Breeze Hotel—"

"You mean over near A1A and Oakland?" asked Victor. At Carmen's nod, he continued, "It's not the type of place you'd expect to go to with a girl like Irina. It's a tourist place—"

"Yeah, but it's discreet. They have a decent bar. Irina said she has a friend who leases a unit—some of those places are privately owned. She said he lets her use it."

Chapter Five

LEAVING THE OFFICE, LOUIE AND Victor said good-bye to the classy receptionist who presided at the front desk, and stepped out and into the building's atrium lobby. Skylights flooded the area with sunlight, nourishing the green, potted plants that enclosed the small sitting area. Next to the main entrance was a desk where a thick-bodied uniformed guard sat. Sighting them, he bobbed his head in acknowledgement, even as his focus moved beyond them to the couple standing this side of the bronze-door elevator. Nobody else was in the lobby.

Louie followed the guard's gaze and observed Adriana talking with Dick Weinstein. She was leaning over his arm and peering at a file Weinstein held upright. The lawyer was explaining something to her, talking in a low-pitched voice, but as soon as Victor let go of the door, it closed with a loud whoosh, and Weinstein broke off and looked at them. Adriana turned to see who had disturbed them, and spotting Louie, she grew visibly flustered. Taking a studied step back, Adriana said, "Thanks, Dick," her eyes going apprehensively to Louie, as though she expected him to fault her for talking to Weinstein.

Through the building's smoked windows, Louie saw dark clouds moving in. It rained daily this time of year, quick, midday showers that swept across South Florida like clockwork. A rumble of thunder sounded. Noting this, Victor said, "I'll get the car, Lou."

Weinstein's gaze flickered between Louie and Victor, and then between Louie and Adriana, who was suddenly anxious to distance herself from him. She approached Louie, regarding him with a hint of her previous shyness. She said timorously, "Mr. Morelli, this is my attorney, Dick Weinstein. Mr. Weinstein is with Sawyer and—"

Scowling, Weinstein stepped forward, gave Louie a brief nod. His eyes were cool and impersonal, and Louie, inclining his head in acknowledgement, said, "We've met."

Victor pulled open the door and warm, gusty air blew into the lobby. Adriana said, "Dick...Mr. Weinstein is handling my divorce."

Louie looked at Weinstein. He would never hire an attorney who had a ponytail and wore hippie sandals. His eyes moved back to Adriana, standing there in her white dress, with the lace-edged bra visible beneath the sheer fabric and her sultry perfume altering the chemistry in the air. Her cheeks were flushed, eyes smoky with a hint of the desire he'd seen earlier.

Feeling the sexual attraction between them, and knowing that in a couple of hours she'd be in his bed, Louie's gaze softened, a languid light in his eyes as he regarded her, his lips curving in a tender smile. He saw Weinstein watching them, a flash of resentment flitting across his face. Snapping the file shut, Weinstein said, "Adriana, call me if you have any questions."

Adriana glanced at Weinstein. "For sure, Dick. Thanks so much. I really appreciate you taking the extra time to help me."

"Don't mention it," said Weinstein, a note of irritation in his voice.

Adriana's gaze reconnected with Louie's. She smiled, and then started for the door he and Victor had just exited, where L&M Enterprises was emblazoned on a brass nameplate in bold script. Louie watched her walk away, admiring the view she presented from behind, and then he turned and caught Weinstein studying him.

The hair in Weinstein's ponytail was half gray. He wore an open-collared short-sleeved green-plaid shirt; his eyes were pale blue and unblinking as he regarded Louie, who said, "I thought you only did criminal law."

Weinstein said, "Adriana's brother is a client, and he asked me to help. She was married to a real jerk—the guy's challenging her for custody of their daughter. Not that it is any of your business, or is it?"

Louie ignored the challenge, tinged as it was with a trace of hostility. Hearing another crack of thunder, he turned toward the door, where Victor was pulling his black XTS to the curb. The security guard rolled back his chair and stood. Louie gave Weinstein a cool smile. "Have a nice day."

Weinstein's pale eyes held his. "You're a long way from home, Morelli."

"Excuse me?"

Weinstein smirked. "A friend gave me a book called *Gulf Coast Mob Dynasties*. Ever read it?"

"I haven't had the pleasure."

"You should check it out. It's rather enlightening—particularly the part about your old man Tony Morelli. The author insists that Tony made a deal with Lee Harvey Oswald, and while I'm not quite sold on his theory, I must admit he did have some intriguing facts to back it up. Jack Ruby was your father's man, too, or so the author claims."

Outside, the rain came down in a sudden rush, and Victor's headlights popped on. Louie said, "I don't believe in conspiracy theories."

"The author puts forth a convincing argument. Not that I'm a believer, mind you. I was more interested in the chapters he devoted to you. The Prince of Mafia Princes, he called you. A true Dapper Don, discreet and deadly."

"Don't believe everything you read, Weinstein."

He strode toward the door. Weinstein snickered, but Louie did not turn around. The guard opened the door, stepping out in the rain to hold it for Louie. Nodding his thanks, Louie walked briskly across the sidewalk and got into the car where Victor's defrosters were blasting cold air. Looking at Victor, he said, "That damn Jew is a smartass."

Chapter Six

THE DIGITAL CLOCK ON THE dashboard of Louie's Mercedes read 7:07 when he signaled the gate at the foot of his driveway. Pulling up the short, winding drive, Louie had the feeling he was late for his own party, as the motor court in front of his Mediterranean-style villa was jammed with the vehicles of his family and friends. Indeed, Victor's XTS blocked his entry to the garage, and he parked outside the front door, preparing to exit the car when his phone rang.

Louie took the call—he'd been waiting for it. He listened tersely, not liking what he was hearing. Sitting in the car, he eyed the creamy walls of his villa, the tall, lead-paned windows reflecting pink from the orange shadows of the late-day sun. Potted hibiscus trees, red blooms fat and heavy in the heat, framed the entry.

Louie got out of the car, smelling the sea as soon as he stepped out, the windows on his S-Class Mercedes filmed with salt. Tangled bougainvillea vines crowned the walls surrounding his property, and in the side garden Angie's trellised roses flamed purple against the house. A hot breeze was blowing, palm fronds rustling. Already,

Louie could hear the surf, although the slow moving traffic on A1A was louder, with the roar of a motorcycle splitting the air.

Louie's house was located just outside the seaside village of Delray Beach, along that magnificent stretch of beachfront road that hugged the Atlantic shore and where the super rich built their homes, hiding them behind stone walls and impenetrable hedges. Some homes, newly built, were more lavishly displayed, staggering the imaginations of the curious on A1A. Louie's villa was not so ostentatious, but he valued his privacy, and only the tree-lined sweep of his drive and red-barrel tiled roof were visible from the highway.

With the information Louie requested fresh in his mind, he said good-bye to his caller and went to join his family. Inside, the vaulted entry was cool, the thick walls and limestone flooring holding the heat at bay. For a minute as he stepped in, the silence was amplified, the elements shut out with the click of the door. Then he heard men's voices and sniffed the rich, mouth-watering aroma of warm bread and simmering sauce, and he moved into the colonnaded foyer, past the seldom-used parlor and into the dining room, where Angie's two maids were setting the table, one of them looking up and giving Louie a shy smile. Attached to the kitchen by a walk-through butler's pantry, the dining room held an ornately carved table with a dozen tall-backed chairs, its wide sweep of windows drawing Louie's eye toward the palatial columns surrounding his turquoise-tiled pool and beyond, to the stone wall shielding his property.

Because Louie's house was built on a high elevation to protect it from the storm surges of Atlantic hurricanes, he had an unimpeded view beyond the walls, to where the dune grass flattened to sand and the sea shimmered beneath the fading sun. He could see people on the beach, including two small boys and a little girl in a pink-skirted bathing suit. These were Louie's grandchildren.

Nodding a greeting at the maids, who alternated between calling him "Senor Morelli" and "Don Luis" he moved into the kitchen, where Victor presided over the six-burner range, one large skillet steaming, a pot bubbling, the counter littered with utensils and bowls, bottles of olive oil and cooking wine, a cutting board with shaved garlic. Having changed into cargo shorts, his massive biceps straining the armholes of his T-shirt, Victor was in top form. Circling his feet were Angie's buff-colored toy poodle, Gigi, and Stella's two Pomeranians. Gigi and one of the Pomeranians had pink bows attached to their ears, while the male Pom, slightly larger than its twin, wore a jaunty blue scarf around his neck.

Carmen and a young man Louie recognized as a friend of Michael's sat on high chairs at the peninsula, and Michael, wearing hip designer jeans and a black silk shirt, was leaning against the counter with a bottle of Stella Artois in one hand and his Samsung Galaxy in the other. Michael was looking at his phone but as soon as he saw his father, he slipped it into his shirt pocket. Doubtless, he was recalling the last family dinner when Louie had ripped the phone out of his hand, carried it outside, and flung it into the deep end of the swimming pool.

Though he was taller than his father, Michael looked the way Louie had thirty years ago, slender and dark, with his father's ink-black eyes. He had acquired Louie's mannerisms, as well as his love of women. He rotated girlfriends, alarming his mother with some of his choices. Tonight, he'd invited his buddy, a nice young man whose name evaded Louie. He was dressed similarly to Michael, and Louie assumed they were going into town after dinner. Carmen was in shirt-sleeves and tie, although he looked visibly more relaxed than he had earlier and was sipping from a glass of red wine when Louie walked in.

An *antipasti* of green olives, paper-thin prosciutto, and Reggiano was on a platter, and the young men were digging in. Adjacent to the kitchen was the family room, where the sleek screen hanging above the limestone fireplace was blasting a Marlins game. Through the row of French doors, Louie saw Angie sitting at the custom-tiled table on the terrace, her spry, aging mother on one side of her, Victor's pretty wife, Diana, on the other. He did not see Gina or Tony, though he hadn't expected to see Tony.

After greeting the others with handshakes and hugs, Louie kissed Michael. He said, "Is your brother here?"

Michael said, "Gina said he's in Miami. You missed Gina— Carmen and I just got back from driving her and the baby home."

At the mention of Miami, Louie's eyes sought Victor's. Louie said, "Didn't Gina want to stay for dinner?"

Victor said, "She was pretty tired, Lou. I made sure she ate good before she left. Little Louis and Anthony are here. They've been playing down on the beach, but look—" Victor glanced out the window, nodding in the direction of the water. "They're coming up now."

Through the wide expanse of thick, impact-resistant glass Louie saw Stella open the gate at the rear of his property, her yellow sarong fluttering in the wind. Stella was lithe and slender, her small breasts cupped in a yellow bikini top, her glossy black hair tucked into a ponytail. Isabella and the two boys trailed her, with the athletic-looking nanny, the one who looked like a volleyball player, bringing up the rear.

The nanny wore denim shorts over a black maillot. Her arms were filled with towels and beach bags. Each of Louie's grandchildren carried sand pails and shovels, and Louie watched, amused, as three-year old Anthony hefted his orange plastic shovel and walloped his older brother on the back. Little Louis responded by decking him, and an all-out brawl ensued. Dropping her load, the nanny intervened, separating them and scolding Anthony, who began bawling at the top of his lungs. On the terrace Angie's chair scraped back, and she hopped to her feet, already moving toward the fracas.

Angie looked good for her age, a medium-boned woman with a short, layered hairstyle, tinted auburn. She wore white cotton capris with a sleeveless turquoise blouse and wedge sandals. Though she used sunscreen diligently, Angie had acquired a sort of permanent tan, the way olive-skinned people do in tropical climates. Unmindful of her summer whites, Angie rushed into the melee, instilling order where the nanny had failed. Taking Anthony by the hand, Angie led him to the beach shower attached to the bath house where Stella was rinsing sand from Isabella's feet.

Carmen asked Louie if he wanted wine, which Louie did not. He did snag a couple of olives, popping them into his mouth. Michael and his buddy were debating the merits of an NFL player the Saints had picked up in the draft. Gigi barked, the Pomeranians joining her, and Victor said, "Somebody get these dogs out of here."

Carmen called to the dogs, but it was Louie who shooed them away from the stove, leading them to the French doors and letting them onto the terrace. Stepping out after the dogs, Louie greeted Diana and his mother-in-law, Maria. Angie was still attending their grandsons, and Stella and Isabella were cutting across the patio. The water in the long, rectangular pool was flat as glass, the spa bubbling like champagne. Tall columns gave the terrace an exotic feel, as though it was a Roman villa on the edge of the Mediterranean. Stone planters bursting with red and purple flowers enhanced this feeling, as did the cushioned loungers, angled to face the pool and sea. Above the ocean the sky was lavender; puffy clouds were bunched on the horizon, a caravan of sailboats passing.

A pitcher of lemon water was on the table, the ladies with their own plate of olives and cheese. Diana, a short-haired brunette, was wearing sunglasses, though she didn't need them beneath the overhang of the terrace, where the ceiling fans were twirling at high speed. A glass-door refrigerator and wine-cooler was built into the counter, and an overhead television was on, Brian Williams anchoring the evening news.

Isabella saw Louie and ran to him, arms outstretched. "Papa," she called, her bare feet slapping the pavement.

Unmindful of her damp swimsuit and the stray particles of sand that clung to her feet, Louie swung her into his arms, showering her upturned face with kisses. Isabella was four years old, and the spitting image of Stella with her glossy black curls and sparkly eyes. Secure in her grandfather's affection, she looped her arms about his neck and began prattling about her day, telling Louie she'd jumped into the deep end without her life vest on. Louie knew she was taking swimming lessons, but he feigned alarm. "Bella, baby, I don't want you going in the deep end."

"Mama said I can, as long as there is an adult in the pool. I don't really need the life vest anymore. It's for babies."

"Bella bambino." Louie kissed her on the forehead. "You're my baby."

Isabella giggled delightfully, squirming in his arms. He stooped to let her down, but she wrapped her legs around his waist, clung tighter to his neck. "Hold me, Papa."

He resettled her in his arms. Speaking a mixture of broken English and Italian, Maria commented that he was spoiling "*la figlia.*" But it was useless pointing this out. Louie knew he was spoiling Isabella shamelessly, the way he'd once spoiled Stella. It was what he did best, spoiled little girls and big girls, provided the big ones were pretty and he was having sex with them. He thought of Adriana—she'd clung to him, too, body trembling, eyes wide with surprise. "You make me feel so special," she'd said.

Stella came abreast of them, and Louie turned his head so she could kiss him, his eyes meeting hers, which were as dark as his own, thick lashes fluttering over them. Knowing the damage her late husband, Johnny, had inflicted on her, Louie looked at Stella cautiously, wondering at her mood and knowing she was still conflicted about Johnny—tender and grieving some days, angry and bitter on others.

Today, there was none of the sadness in Stella's eyes that Louie sometimes glimpsed, only the joyous contentment of a young mother who had spent the day playing on the beach with her daughter. Looking at him, Stella said, "Daddy, it's about time you got home."

"I'm sorry, baby. I had a meeting that ran late."

"Well, I'm glad you're here. Me and Isabella both." She gazed fondly at her daughter. "You adorable little angel, you. Let's go and get you out of this wet bathing suit."

Stella reached for her daughter, but Isabella burrowed her head on Louie's shoulder. "I'm staying with Papa."

Louie laughed. Knowing she had said something cute, Isabella turned adoring eyes to him. Stella opened the door and all three dogs darted into the house, the Pomeranians yapping in unison. With only a trace of annoyance in her voice, Stella said, "Daddy, bring her in. She has to change."

Louie turned back for Angie. Seeing that she was still supervising their grandsons, he followed Stella inside. The dogs raced into the kitchen and dashed to the stove. Victor said, "Not you three again." Then he looked at Louie. "Ten minutes, Lou."

Arms weighted with Isabella, Louie walked into the colonnaded hall, lit by the medieval chandeliers Stella had found in Tuscany. She went up the grand staircase before him, her hand lightly skimming the iron banister. Three-quarters of the way up was a landing with a tall window overlooking the front courtyard. Two narrow-backed chairs were on either side of the window. An oil painting by a protégé of Raphael's hung above a Florentine console table. On the table was a round vase filled with green stems and dark purple orchids. Stella pointed at the flowers. "From Chester," she said.

Louie set Isabella down. Ordinarily, the orchids would have amused him. Now, knowing what he did about Chester, he was unaccountably annoyed. He yanked the small card out of its holder. Seeing that it was signed: *To my angel, Chester,* Louie said, "He's got a lot of nerve."

Stella laughed agreeably. "Daddy, we need to talk about Chester." She took Isabella's hand, leading her daughter up the last few steps. At the top, she paused and looked at Louie. "You should have heard the line of BS he was giving Mom."

Louie was anxious to hear, but at that moment his grandson and namesake, Louis, careened into the hallway and called out to him. Louie yelled down a greeting, and the boy bounded up the steps. The child had not bothered to dry off, and his swim trunks dripped puddles. When he reached the top of the stairs, Louie kissed him on the forehead and ruffled his damp hair.

Eyes big with excitement, Louis said, "Papa, I saw a shark."

Louie said, "Did you? When, today?"

Stella rolled her eyes at Louie. "Louis thinks he saw a shark."

"I *did* see one."

"Tell Papa about it at dinner," said Stella. "You're dripping everywhere. You need to change into dry clothes."

Young Louis rushed off toward the nursery. Watching him, Louie said, "Did he see a shark?"

"He thinks. I'm pretty sure it was a porpoise. But we're humoring him." Stella leaned in, sniffing suspiciously at Louie's collar. "That must have been some meeting, Daddy. You're wearing *Desire*."

"What?"

"It's *Desire*, by Dolce and Gabbana." She turned away in a huff, called back over her shoulder. "You better change, too, Daddy."

Chapter Seven

VICTOR'S *FRUTTI DI MARE*—**SHRIMP, TENDER** chunks of lobster, clams and mussels—was served with linguine in a light tomato sauce. For a precursor, there was romaine lettuce with hearts of palm, sweet peppers, and chilled octopus.

Conversation at the table was lively and punctuated by outbursts from the children, who were tired and cranky. Toward the end Stella and the nanny hustled the kids up to bed, and Angie helped the maids clear the table. By the time Stella returned, Maria's almond-cream cake was being served with coffee. At Angie's inquiry, Stella said that Isabella had "gone out like a light."

Victor had Monte Cristos for the men, and they headed out to the terrace to smoke. Louie took Stella by the hand and escorted her into the library, a seldom used room with comfortable reading chairs and the requisite bookshelves lined with leather-bound classics that nobody read. Angie was the only reader in the family, favoring trashy paperbacks and the badly written romances she downloaded on her Kindle, preferring to do her reading beneath the beach canopy.

Plantation shutters were closed over the windows. There was no television in this room, but a handsome writing desk held a flat-panel monitor. A sidebar was stocked with a few preferred brands, which Louie availed himself of, pouring two fingers of Famous Grouse into a glass. Swirling the blended Scotch whiskey that he favored, he said to Stella, "Do you want a nightcap, baby?"

Stella declined. She sat on the armchair and put her feet up on the ottoman. She wore flat, leather sandals with a toe-strap. She'd recently gone for a pedicure, and her toenails gleamed with a fresh layer of coral polish. Louie sat on the couch, turning to face Stella. "What is it that you wanted to tell me about Chester, Princess?"

"Daddy, I don't want to begrudge Mom her friendship, but I've had it with that phony."

"What did he do, baby?"

"Well, after I called you today, I went back into the parlor where Mom was entertaining Chester, and he was giving her a line of bull—laying it on thick. I think he's creepy."

"Creepy how?"

"He's way overboard. Telling her how beautiful she is, and how he'd give anything to be with her. Mom's not used to men flirting with her, and she was acting silly, giggling like a girl."

Louie did not like the image this conjured. He thought about Angie being made a fool of and felt a rush of anger. He said, "I found out today that Chester is a charlatan. He has a history of conning wealthy women. He even served time for it."

"Oh no, Daddy," Stella looked horrified. "I hate to tell you this, but Mom's been giving Chester money. I saw her hand him a check. It wasn't for any charity thing either because I distinctly heard her ask Chester if it was enough."

———— ⊙ ————

After his guests left, Louie went upstairs to his room. He washed his face and brushed his teeth, and then he crossed the sitting room to Angie's bedroom and pushed open the door.

Angie sat on the side of her painted, Venetian bed in a lace-trimmed nightgown sprigged with pink flowers. Young Anthony lay propped on pillows, his ragged teddy bear tucked under his arm. His lids were at half-mast, big brown eyes peeping through dark, spiky lashes. Curled into a ball at the foot of the bed, Gigi snored softly. Angie held a child's book, with a frog painted on the cover. She was reading to Anthony.

Looking at Louie, her brown eyes luminous in the lamplight, Angie said, "Here's Papa. Can he read to you?"

Anthony nodded. Louie walked in and sat on the opposite side of the bed from Angie, placing their grandson between them. Her room was softly lit, decorated with creams and blushes and pinks, with a crystal chandelier and tinkling crystal lamps, the furniture custom-made and exquisite, reflecting Angie's femininity and her love for all things Venetian.

Louie took the book from Angie. Freddy the frog was pictured on the cover, crouched on a giant lily pad. Sliding closer to his grandson, Louie said, "Ah, this must be Freddy."

Anthony said, "Read it."

Louie read the first couple pages aloud. Freddy had a frog friend named Lester, which made Louie think of Chester. He'd come in here to discuss Angie's ardent suitor, but reading to Anthony took precedence. Louie read until Anthony's eyes closed. They thought he was out but as soon as Angie made to rise, the little boy sat up and started crying.

Angie pulled Anthony onto her lap. "Shush," she said. "It's okay. Nonna's here."

Softly, Louie asked, "Why is he crying?"

"He misses his mother. It's hard on him with the baby...it's an adjustment. Really, Louie, you know I don't like to interfere with your business, but these long hours Tony is working are awfully hard on his family. At a time like this, with the new baby, I think you should lighten Tony's workload. Poor Gina. She was worn out today—frazzled to tears."

"I'm sorry to hear that." Louie stroked his grandson's forehead—the boy was quieting, fighting to stay awake.

"You should be," said Angie, her voice subdued. "I mean, what is going on at that hotel in Miami that requires so much of Tony's time?"

"What hotel?"

"The Walker Hotel. Is there another hotel Tony owns half-interest in? Louie, I didn't say anything at the time, but when you formed a partnership between Tony and that girl...Tara, well, I wasn't thrilled. I understood, but I wasn't happy about it. I never said a word though, did I?"

Although it was brief, Louie's affair with Tara had been very hot, their feelings for one another profound. When Tara became pregnant, it was Louie's friend, Nathan, who chivalrously stepped forward and married her. It was then that Louie deeded his interest in the hotel, dividing it between Tara and Tony, forming the partnership Angie was so critical of—not that Angie knew the details. Somehow, she'd assumed that Tara had already been a majority owner, and Louie had allowed her to think this. Not wishing to discuss any of it, Louie said wearily, "Angie, what is this about?"

"I think Tony is having an affair with Tara."

Louie looked at her, and, with a certainty that made her mouth turn down, he said, "That's not possible."

He spoke too loudly. Anthony's eyes popped opened, and Angie said, "Shush." She laid Anthony down between them, drawing the sheet up to his chest. He gazed sleepily at his grandmother, and then his lids fluttered shut. "He's overtired," she whispered.

Louie watched his grandson, listening to his deep breathing, his small chest rising and falling as sleep overcame him. At the foot of the bed Gigi repositioned herself, resting her muzzle on her paws. Louie's gaze returned to Angie, who said softly, "Why isn't it possible? She's that type, isn't she?"

"What type?"

"The type who goes for married men."

"Angie, she's *married* to Nathan. They have a family."

"Tony shouldn't be working down there so much with the new baby." Angie whispered furtively, keeping an eye on Anthony.

Louie plumped a pillow with his fist and leaned back with a weary sigh. "I agree," he said. "I'm going to Miami tomorrow. I'll talk to Tony; get him to take some time off."

Chapter Eight

WHEN LOUIE WOKE, THE SUN was trying to penetrate the blackout shades on Angie's windows. He'd slept in his shorts on Angie's bed with little Anthony's head nestled on his shoulder. It was half-past seven, and his wife and grandson were still sleeping.

As soon as Louie slipped from the bed, Gigi stood, looking expectantly at him, and he picked her up and set her on the rug. She followed Louie into his room, where he changed into his bathing trunks. Then she trotted down the steps beside him and beat him into the kitchen, where Maria was making coffee.

Maria had been given the first-floor guest room off the back hall. An early riser, Maria always had coffee made when Louie came down. But Louie never drank coffee before his swim, and after taking a small glass of juice, he let Gigi out on the side lawn. He waited while the dog did her business, and then he let her in and went out to the pool for his swim.

Louie swam the length of his pool back and forth forty times each morning. If the weather was really bad—and it sometimes was—he rode his stationary bike or jogged on the treadmill.

Occasionally, if he was feeling ambitious and had a slow day planned, he did both. Today he was not so ambitious. He stepped into the shallow end.

Louie's saltwater pool was set to a perfect temperature in the cooler months. Now, on the verge of summer, it was downright hot. Louie made a mental note to tell the pool man to add cool water, and then he started his swim, moving at an unhurried pace, relishing the luxuriant warmth of the water on his body, like liquid silk. He swam his laps, thinking of his day ahead, planning it.

He was nearing the end of his swim when Angie stepped onto the terrace, her eyes shielded by a white sun-visor, her legs tan below the hem of her blue cotton shorts. Angie wore a loose fitting white T-shirt and rubber sandals, which Louie knew she would remove before hitting the beach for her morning walk. Treading water in the deep end, Louie called out, "Hold on, honey. I'll go with you."

He dunked himself under water and swam to the shallow end. Climbing out, he grabbed the thick, terry towel he'd left on a lounge chair and wiped the saltwater from his eyes. Angie stood, waiting, and Louie said, "Give me a minute, baby."

He crossed the terrace and stepped beneath the shaded shelter of the canopy. Opening the glass-door fridge, he grabbed a bottle of water. Louie unscrewed the cap and drank half the water in one swallow. A steady breeze from the ceiling fans lifted the humid air around him. The overhead television was tuned to Channel 7 News. They were finishing the weather report, which was totally predictable, high-eighties, high-humidity, afternoon showers. WSVN's camera cut to a live traffic shot showing congestion on I-95. Even more predictable than the weather, thought Louie.

He lifted the phone on the counter and called Victor. It was their morning routine, and Victor answered on the first ring. "No hurry today," said Louie. "We're going to Miami."

"I figured that. You want to take the *Stella?* It might be hard to hustle the crew on such short notice—"

Louie said, "No. Have Sam drive us. Pick me up at ten." Louie paused to take a swig of water, wiping his mouth with the back of his hand. "Call Tara. Better yet, call Nathan and let him know we'll be calling on Tara at the Walker."

"Tara," said Victor, surprised. "Why Tara—?"

"Gina's crying over how much time Tony's spending down there. Angie thinks he's fooling with Tara, if you can believe that. She read me the riot-act for making Tony work so hard with a new baby at home."

Louie hung up and reached for the gauzy shirt he used as a beach jacket. He put it on, leaving it unbuttoned. Then he drank the rest of the water, set the bottle on the counter, and crossed to where Angie was waiting. He opened the gate and they walked single-file on the narrow trail that led through the dune grass. The sun was still ascending, and the sky was streaked with orange, the sea dazzling. Louie squinted, wishing he'd remembered to bring his sunglasses. Angie didn't have hers either, but the visor shaded her eyes.

There were always beach walkers in the morning, a few joggers. It was a solitary, sacred time, and the people they saw gave polite nods or called a quiet good-morning. Gulls circled and swooped, their shrill cries piercing the air. Out at sea a huge cargo ship was crawling south. Luxury homes dotted the beach, several under new construction. Passing an elderly couple, they exchanged greetings. Further down the beach a man stood on shore while his black lab frolicked in the surf. Louie noted that the waves were much higher today than yesterday.

They walked about half a mile, trekking toward the public beach in Delray. A few families were already at play, small children lugging sand toys. Louie and Angie kept to the track of packed earth just above the surf line, their heels squishing in the wet sand. Bits of driftwood, crushed shells and clumps of seaweed littered the beach. They strolled leisurely, and Angie said, "I usually walk faster than this."

Louie said, "Baby, I want to talk to you about Chester."

He said it with enough brevity that she stopped walking and looked at him. "What about Chester?" When Louie did not immediately reply, she said, "You're jealous. You are, aren't you?"

"Baby, it's not about me."

"Hah, of course it's about you, Louie. It's *always* about you. I know you're jealous of Chester. I saw how you looked at me last night, when I mentioned that he'd brought me flowers. I realize Chester is a bit…ardent, but he's really a nice man. I feel sorry for him. Do you know that after Chester lost all of his money to Bernie Madoff, his wife committed suicide?"

Taking the high road, Louie did not tell Angie he'd discovered her gallant suitor had never been married and that he had a preference for young men. Chester had changed his name, too, from Fred Schroeder. He'd also done a three year stint for defrauding a widow. Louie said, "Look, Angie, I realize Chester may have had some difficulties in his life, but I think he's becoming too attentive to you. I'd appreciate it if you could cool it with him."

Angie turned and resumed her walking. "You really have your nerve. You, of all people, objecting to my friendship. Hah, Chester's never even made a pass at me. He's not…it's not like you, with your women. He's respectful."

Louie said, "He's a *finocchio*."

She halted, glaring up at him. "You have no way of knowing that. Just because a man owns a flower shop and likes to garden, it doesn't make him gay. You're such a homophobe."

The fact that Louie was amused and didn't try to hide it accelerated Angie's indignation. She dug her toes into the sand. "How dare you."

"Come on, baby, don't be sore. Did you think I'd let him squire you about—all those little luncheons and garden parties—if I didn't think he was an old queen?"

Tears sprang to her eyes. "Leave me alone, Louie. Let me finish my walk in peace."

"Baby, don't be upset. I don't mind you having a good time. Chester seems okay, but what do you really know about him?"

"I know he's had a tough time, and he's grieving for his wife. She committed suicide, Louie. That's not easy to deal with. And he's *not* gay, despite what you might think. He told me he's staying faithful to the memory of his wife." Her voice hardened. "You wouldn't know anything about that, seeing as how you can't even stay faithful to your living wife." Her chin lifted defiantly. "Some people do have higher moral standards."

"Well, being that Chester is so high minded, I don't have to worry about him taking an unfair advantage of you. What a relief."

"You're such a hypocrite, Louie. How dare you criticize—?"

"Please. I was agreeing with you."

"If you don't mind, I'd like to finish my walk without you."

Angie flounced off, her heels kicking up sand. Louie turned and retraced his steps, walking back with the sun in his face. When he arrived at the house, he went into the library and sat at the desk. Angie kept the household bills here, the paid receipts filed in the bottom drawer, the unpaid in an untidy stack on top. Angie's checkbook was in the top drawer, and Louie drew it out and opened it. The account was in Angie's name, funded by Louie on a monthly basis.

Angie's expenses were typical. Nieman Marcus, Saks, Nordstrom's, spa treatments, yoga classes, and charitable donations.

Yesterday, she'd written a check for two thousand dollars to Green Gardens Floral Shop, which was the name of Chester's business. Louie went back a month, saw that Angie had given Chester two thousand on the fifth of May. The same denomination was given in April. During the month of March Angie had scribbled Chester's name in the register, conveniently leaving off an amount, and Louie wasn't sure if this meant she had given him money or not.

Assuming that she had, he did not bother researching any further. He'd seen enough, at least six thousand dollars in three months. Stunned by how easily his wife had been swindled, Louie returned Angie's checkbook to the drawer. He went up to his room and showered, putting on a suit that was the color of crushed oyster shells, selecting a solid royal-blue tie with a contrasting polka-dotted pocket square. Then he picked up his cheap, prepaid phone, the one he rotated frequently and used for select calls, and stepped onto his balcony to call his cousin Anthony, in New Orleans.

The balcony ran the length of the master suite, accessible from both bedrooms and the sitting room. A bistro table and colorfully cushioned chairs and loungers were strategically placed to capture the sea breezes, not to mention the stellar view. Planters of begonias, geraniums, and Confederate jasmine added splashes of color. Walking to the edge of the balcony, Louie leaned against the balustrade and called his cousin. He stood facing the sea, saw shadows and shapes swirling beneath the surface as clouds floated over the sun. There was nobody on the beach except for Angie, coming through the gate. She gathered her sandals, stopping to bathe her feet at the shower. She looked up, spotted Louie, and quickly averted her gaze.

Louie talked to Anthony for about ten minutes, discussing minor matters of business and providing the advice he knew Anthony required but was too proud to ask for. But Louie had always been a sort of father figure to his cousin, whose own father had gone to prison when he was a kid, and Anthony was grateful for his counsel.

When Louie hung up with Anthony, he stepped into his bedroom. From the marble-topped nightstand next to his bed he took his P250 sub-compact pistol, tucking it into the nylon gun belt he wore beneath his jacket. Then he picked up his smart phone and called his daughter, Ceci, who was also in New Orleans.

Ceci was the love child Louie had had with his former mistress, Mercedes. After ending their affair several years ago, Mercedes married a young man named Robert. Unfortunately, Robert's ex-fiancée fatally shot Mercedes, leaving Ceci without a mother. Already attached to Ceci, Robert had legally adopted her. In what was one of the most difficult decisions of his life, Louie had granted permission, relinquishing his parental rights.

Because he'd never been a full-time father to his daughter, Louie's relationship with Ceci remained unchanged. He visited frequently and spoke with her several times a week. Today, Ceci answered on the first ring. "Hi, Papa Louie," she said, her voice achingly sweet. "I knew you would call—I was waiting for my phone to ring."

"And I was waiting to hear your voice," said Louie. "How's my little girl this morning?"

"I got my period yesterday. That means I'm officially a woman."

Detecting sadness in her voice, Louie said, "How are you feeling, baby?"

"I'm staying home from school today because I have cramps. Anjolie made me some herb tea, but it tastes awful."

"I'm sorry you're not feeling good."

"Yeah. Me, too. I don't like being grown-up—it's no fun."

She sounded so dejected Louie had to smile. He thought of Mercedes—she had certainly liked being a woman. He said, "You'll get used to it, honey. You have to grow up eventually."

She said, "I had a bad dream about Uncle Victor. Is he going to be okay?"

Ceci's dreams were often prophetic. She was gifted, but there was some confusion, and she'd been tested for schizophrenia without any diagnosis other than "eccentric" being applied to her. Her premonitions were nothing to scoff at, and Louie felt a flicker of alarm at this latest one. Reassuringly, he said, "Sure, baby. Victor's fine."

"I miss him."

"He misses you, too. We'll see you next week. I'll take you somewhere special, okay? Wherever you want to go."

"I just want to be with you."

Aw, Jesus. She sounded on the verge of tears. Louie said, "What's wrong, Ceci? Are you having problems at school again?"

"I got in trouble for reading Tarot cards in my math class."

"Maybe you shouldn't be telling fortunes in school."

"Some of the girls are starting to ask me things. I usually tell the truth but people don't always like that. They only want to hear good things." She paused, and then said, "I went to a party yesterday. A girl at school invited me to her birthday party."

"Did you have a good time?

"Not really. Everybody was nice to me but nobody likes me."

Ceci frightened kids, and she was so beautiful even grown women despised her on sight. Louie said, "I'm sure that's not true," even though he knew it was.

He told her he had to go, and she said, "Bye, Papa Louie. I love you."

"Gosh, baby. I love you, too."

He clicked off and sat there staring at his phone, still hearing Ceci's voice, like a ghostly whisper in his ear, her presence enveloping him. After a minute he called Robert, the young man he treated like a son, whom he admired and respected and tried not to resent. He also tried not to interfere, and he was grateful to Robert for letting him voice his concerns. Afterward, Robert said, "Louie, Ceci's okay. She's a little moody because she's starting to have her monthlies. I'm going to take her over to my parents—she likes to spend time with my mother."

Mollified, Louie's next call was to Emily. Louie informed her that he would not be in the office today, and to call him on his cell if she needed to get hold of him. Then he told Emily to have flowers sent to Angie. She perked up at this. "Certainly," she said. "Is there a special occasion?"

"Do I need an occasion to send flowers to my wife?"

"No, sir. I'll do it right away. Any particular type of arrangement?"

"No orchids. Anything else is fine. I also want you to send flowers to my little girl in New Orleans. Use that florist on St. Charles—the one whose number I gave you. See if they can add something to the bouquet, maybe a charm bracelet or necklace, something for a young girl. I want it delivered today."

"Yes, of course." Emily cleared her throat. She wasn't comfortable with Louie's indiscretions, but once she recovered from the shock of his double life, she'd fully embraced Ceci. Cautiously, she said, "How is Ceci?"

"She's growing up, and she's not happy about it."

Emily permitted an awkward silence before saying what Louie sensed she'd been dying to tell him. "Mr. Morelli, I hate to bring this up, but I think you should know that the temp agency called to inform me that Adriana McIntyre quit."

"What?" Adriana had been fine last night. In fact, she'd been more than fine. "What happened?"

"Well, my contact at the agency didn't say. They seemed quite surprised, as I am. I was hoping you could shed some light on the situation. I know you and she are a bit ... friendly."

"Friendly" wasn't quite the word Louie would have used to describe Adriana's affection. Smiling at the memory of yesterday's rendezvous, he recalled that he'd been stranded at the marina by Victor and had relied on Adriana to drive him back to the office so he could retrieve his car. As luck would have it, Weinstein, who was standing outside of a silver Jeep Cherokee and conversing with the driver, spotted them the moment they turned in.

Louie hadn't paid much attention, his Mercedes being parked several aisles away. Adriana expressed annoyance at being seen by her attorney but it hadn't stopped her from kissing Louie good bye. But now Louie recalled the things Weinstein had said to him yesterday, and he wondered if he'd spouted off to Adriana, frightened her away.

Louie said, "I'm not aware of anything that would cause Adriana to quit. But please give me her phone number. I'd like to call her."

"Don't you have her number?"

"I never got around to asking for it."

"Mr. Morelli, I don't have a personnel file on Adriana. The agency doesn't provide us with her contact information."

"Okay," said Louie. He'd have to get his guy on it. "Let me know if she calls."

Louie ended the call. He wondered if there was a full moon because he was certainly having an unusual morning. It was ten o'clock. Victor and Sam were waiting downstairs, and he hadn't yet had breakfast. And he still had to make up with his wife.

Chapter Nine

LOUIE'S DRIVER, SAM, WAS A seventy-year old widower. Sam kept himself on call for Louie, who liked the convenience of a driver when he went to Miami or across state to Naples or Tampa. Miami was fifty miles from Delray Beach, but on a bad day it could take two hours or more to get there.

Sam always drove the black Town Car that was registered to L&M Enterprises. He maintained the vehicle, keeping it cleaned and gassed. Though they frequently got caught in South Florida's notorious traffic jams and were sometimes delayed for appointments, Sam was never late when he picked up Louie. Today, Sam was as prompt as ever, but it was an hour before Louie was ready to leave. Despite the delay, Sam had them in Lauderdale before noon.

Louie's first stop was the building on Commercial Boulevard where Albert Seymour's company, See-More Studios, was located. Seymour was a car buff, and when Louie saw the yellow Ferrari Daytona convertible parked in the first non-handicapped space in the lot, he knew Seymour was in. The building was two floors—a squat rectangle with smoked glass. A graphic design studio and insurance company were on the first floor. See-More Studio's occupied all of the second.

There was an elevator, but Louie and Victor opted to use the open-sided staircase. From the way the carpet was wearing on the steps, Louie deduced that most visitors to See-More Studios chose the same option. At the top of the stairs was a vestibule, onto which the elevator opened. The first door off the hall was the entrance to See-More Studios. This door was locked, and Victor rapped loudly. After a minute, when no one answered, he knocked a second time.

The door was opened by Seymour's assistant, Sophie. Pressing a red-tipped fingernail to her mouth, Sophie said, "Quiet. They're filming."

Sophie's skin was the color of dark chocolate. She had large, expressive eyes accentuated with bright green eye-shadow. She was Louie's height, but he guessed her weight was about equal to Victor's. She was wearing a loud purple caftan and matching turban that Louie judged an improvement over the leggings she'd been wearing the last time he visited. Victor said, "Hey, doll, you're going native."

"Ssshh. You'll disturb the actors."

Louie didn't care who he disturbed. He and Victor stepped in. The large, open space supported two stage sets. One set was a generic living room, complete with couch, entertainment center, and phony window with a curtain. A well-built actor sat on the couch. He was naked, except for a hand towel draped over his lap. Beneath the towel he stroked himself. His eyes were closed, his face pinched tight as he concentrated.

The other set—the one where they were filming—was made up to resemble a bedroom. Two cameras were perched on tripods, a third hefted onto a ladder and trained on two young women who were having sex on the bed, while the entire trio of camera-men was filming. One girl had a wild mane of blonde hair, her oversized breasts bursting like cantaloupes. Kneeling beside her was a girl with jet-black hair and a back covered in red and green tattoos. The aggressor was nuzzling the blonde's fake breasts, and the blonde was responding with loud, panting moans.

Sitting off to the side of the set was the make-up artist, a skinny redhead in white pants, and a nerdy-looking tech guy who was fiddling with video equipment. Albert Seymour was standing at the edge of the stage, holding a director's board. Seymour wore black, rectangular eyeglasses. He was in his late forties, and his sandy-brown hair was streaked with gray. He was thickset, with a ruddy complexion and a scruffy goatee.

Glancing over his shoulder, Seymour barely registered their presence. At that moment the black-haired girl lifted her head, and called out, "For God's sake, isn't that dick hard yet?"

Seymour yelled, "Cut." He glared at the girl. "Jasmin, was that necessary?"

With an exasperated sigh, the pervert on the couch tossed his towel onto the floor and stood. "Dumb bitch. If you gave a decent blowjob, it wouldn't take so long."

"Fuck you, loser." Jasmin yelled. "You can't get it up."

Seymour said, "Stop. Both of you. At this rate, we'll be here all day."

He set down his director's board, and turned to Louie, acknowledging him with an irritated scowl. "Lou, I'm kind of busy here. This is not a good time."

"It's a good time for me, Albert." Louie's eyes scanned the group. The black-haired girl was sitting on her haunches. Sophie and the skinny redhead were talking quietly, the nerdy tech adjusting his equipment. The actor, genitals shaved as smooth as a baby's bottom, was strutting around as though he was fully clothed, his sex hanging down between his legs. Louie looked at Victor, who was shaking his head in disgust. He said, "Jesus, it's a freak show."

Seymour glared at him. "This is a film studio," he said. "These are artists."

Victor laughed outright, and Louie said, "Come on, Albert. Who do you think you're talking to?"

Giving way to pressure, Seymour let out a weary sigh. He turned to his crew. "All right, people, let's take ten minutes." Brushing his palms on his jeans, he walked over to Louie. "Most people make appointments when they want to see me."

The camera lights shut off. The girls scrambled off the bed, the blonde saying, "Christ, I could use a smoke. Who has my cigarettes?"

Victor said, "Albert, let's go in your office."

Seymour was abrasive, but he wasn't stupid. He led the way to his office, which was at the front of the suite. The door to Seymour's office was open, and they walked in. The office was a cluttered mess, full of metal filing cabinets, their drawers ajar. Stacked on the desk were files and DVD's and piles of paper and unopened mail. It was such a pigsty, full of discarded fast food wrappers and empty soda cans, that it took a few seconds before Louie noticed a young man sitting on a chair in the corner. He could have been a good looking kid, a stunner, but his sun-bleached blonde hair was shaggy, his face thin and pinched. Louie put his age at thirty, with a year or two on either side of it. His clothes were youthful—faded denims and a long-sleeved purple shirt that played up his dark blue irises, giving his eyes a gray-violet tint. Circled by dark shadows, his eyes had the hollowed-out look of a junkie, and Louie felt a sudden pity, the way he always did when he encountered addicts.

As soon as he saw Louie and Victor, the young man's eyes widened with alarm, and he abruptly stood, his jeans hanging on his skinny frame. He was seriously underweight, angular jaw protruding, sharp elbows jabbing through his sleeves. He looked at Louie with confusion, eyes flickering with fear. For a minute, Louie had a sense of déjà vu, as though he'd seen this kid before and couldn't place him. He said, "Have we met?"

The young man shook his head. "N-no," he said, his eyes darting to Victor, who acknowledged him with a curt nod.

Seymour said, "Fuck, Molinsky, I forgot you were waiting. I told Sophie to pay you."

Molinsky said, "She said to see you."

Seymour held up his hands. "Refresh my memory. How much do I owe you?"

Looking away from Louie and Victor, Molinsky said, "It came to eighty-nine dollars and ninety cents."

Seymour winced. "I'm short today. If you come back tomorrow—"

Molinsky looked stricken. "I already paid for the developing," he said. "I really need the money, Albert."

Louie was betting he needed a fix. He exchanged a look with Victor, who said, "Albert, are you stiffing this kid for ninety bucks? You cheap bastard. You ought to be ashamed of yourself." He turned to the young man. "What kind of work do you do, kid?"

"Uh ..." he gulped, looking apprehensively at Victor. "I'm a photographer."

Seymour snorted, "Molinsky takes pictures of pussy."

Louie strolled over to the window, stepping around mounds of paper. Parting the blinds, he looked down at the yellow Ferrari convertible. He said, "What do you do with the pictures, Albert?"

"They're for advertising. You know, shots of the girls." He inclined his head toward his studio. "Teasers. For magazines and DVD covers."

Victor leaned against a four-drawer file cabinet, propping one arm against it, a casual, relaxed posture, yet somehow menacing.

He unbuttoned his sport jacket, letting it gap open. Following his boss's lead, Victor was wearing a shoulder holster, the black butt of his Beretta impossible to miss. His eyes went to Seymour, who was clearing newspaper off of his desk chair. Victor said, "Albert, pay this kid. I don't want to see you stiff anyone. It's bad business."

The sight of Victor's gun seemed to accelerate Molinsky's fear. His eyes flashed desperately from Victor to Seymour. The latter dropped a pile of newspaper onto the floor, gave Victor an aggrieved look, and then promptly dug out his wallet. Opening it, he extracted two fifties and handed them to Molinsky.

"Thanks, man."

Molinsky started fumbling in his pocket for change, and Victor said, "Keep the change, kid."

"Uh, thanks." Molinsky took one last look at Victor's gun, his Adam's apple bobbing up and down, and then bolted from the room without a backward glance.

Victor said, "The kid's all hopped up."

Seymour sat in his chair. "Yeah, he's got a habit. It's a fucking shame because he's got talent. Hell, two years ago he was working for a tony magazine in Miami, heading for the big leagues, and then he starts using. Now he's doing odd jobs, scraping the bottom of the barrel to feed his habit."

"He looked scared to death."

"Molinsky's paranoid. It doesn't help that he's got some kind of bench warrant issued for him. Ten to one he thinks you're a cop."

Victor said, "I look like a cop?"

"Not to me. But he thinks my bookkeeper is a CIA agent, so who knows?" Seymour's gaze drifted to Victor's Beretta. He kept his expression neutral. "I guess it's the gun," he said.

Victor moved to the door and closed it, slipping the lock. Seymour's eyes registered alarm, and he began nervously rearranging the piles of paper in front of him. Victor grabbed the chair Molinsky had been sitting on and dragged it to the desk. Louie walked to the chair, hitched up his trousers, and sat. Seymour's iPhone blasted Mick Jagger's voice, and Louie said, "Shut your phone off, Albert. I want to talk to you."

Seymour rejected the call, and then powered his phone off. He looked distinctly uncomfortable. Louie said, "Albert, I'm concerned about the way you've mismanaged my investment. I had faith in your ability to run a studio. You approached me with your fancy credentials and your Hollywood references, but now I'm wondering if you might have taken advantage of me. After all, it's only been a few months, and you're already in Chapter Eleven. And from what I'm seeing of your operation, it stinks. You're using skanky actors—the girls look like streetwalkers to me."

"Personally, I wouldn't touch them with a ten-foot pole," said Victor. He was back to leaning against the filing cabinet. "You want guys to get turned on watching your flicks, you better get girls that look good—the kind men would want to fuck, if they could."

Seymour said, "One of those girls is Dana Starr. She's been in a lot of porn movies—"

"She looks used up. Don't you think, Lou?"

"I wasn't impressed." He fixed a steady gaze on Seymour. "It's time for you to make a payment, Albert."

"Look, Lou, I'm sorry about the Chapter Eleven thing. I'm not going under—I just need to reorganize my finances. You won't lose out on your investment. It's just going to take a little longer to realize a return."

"I don't like that, Albert. What about my personal loan, the thirty G's I lent you?"

"I'll make it good, Lou. If you can give me extra time, I'll repay you. I mean ... I'll be honest ... things are tougher than I thought.

I'm doing my best—it's why I declared bankruptcy, so I could catch my breath, get a better handle on things."

"That's not good enough, Albert."

"I don't know what to say. It's the way things are. I can't change that, although I'd like to. You think I'm happy I got myself in this mess? Hell, I've got other investors relying on me, too. Men who really need their money."

"Hmpf." Annoyed by the implication that his trust could be violated, Louie leaned back and crossed his arms. "So you think that, because I'm rich, you don't need to pay me back?"

"Come on, Lou. I didn't mean it that way. It's just that you've got so damned much money—everybody knows you're loaded. I heard it cost forty grand just to fill up the *Stella di Mare.*"

"Not quite forty," said Louie.

A knock sounded on the door. Sophie said, "Albert, the crews getting restless."

"Start the scene without me." Seymour looked at Louie. "I've got to get back. They'll fuck it up, if I'm not there."

Victor said, "What if your star can't get a hard-on?"

Seymour flushed at Victor's needling tone. He said smartly, "We'll improvise."

Louie said, "Albert, let me get this straight. I invested fifty thousand in See-More Studios. That's subject to delay because of the bankruptcy proceedings. Am I correct?"

"That's right. But I'm not going under, Lou. You're going to make money on your investment—"

"Yeah, I get it," said Louie. "But it will take time, that's what you're saying, right?"

"Of course. That's what I'm telling you."

"What about the personal loan, the thirty G's? That's not subject to bankruptcy law, is it, Albert? In fact, that's subject to *my* law.

Believing that you were a man of honor, I handed over the cash on a handshake."

"I *am* a man of honor."

"You haven't made a payment in weeks. You can make one now, if you like. What was your monthly principal? Victor, do you remember?"

"Yeah. Thirty G's at eighteen percent juice—we have Albert on the twenty-four month plan, don't we? Let's see, that's fifteen hundred, Lou."

Louie gazed steadily at Seymour. Angry splotches of color were turning his ruddy complexion even redder. Louie said, "Do you have fifteen hundred to pay me today?"

"No, I'm sorry. I can give you eight hundred—that's all I've got in the office here, in my safe."

"Not good enough, Albert. We need to work out another solution. You see, I'm not feeling too confident. Despite your eagerness to assure me of my sound investment, I'm not optimistic. Quite frankly, I think you're going to fail." Louie brushed lint from his sleeve, and then looked up and gave Seymour a cold smile. "I'd like to attach some collateral to my loan."

"Fuck. I'm mortgaged to the hilt. But if you want to put a lien on my house, be my guest. I can't stop you."

Louie said, "I know you have clear title on the Ferrari."

Seymour's expression registered horror. "Come on, Lou—you're joking." Louie's demeanor did not reflect humor, and Seymour's left eyelid twitched. "How do you know I don't have it financed?"

"Don't take me for a fool," said Louie. "It's not listed among your personal assets. Besides, you've boasted enough about your cars, telling Victor they're free and clear." Louie inclined his head toward the window. "How much did you pay for the Ferrari?"

"Lou, don't … please. I didn't say anything before, but I'm in negotiation with an investor—he wants me to make movies for him. It's an under-the-table type thing. There's some risk, and I told him no, but I can call him, get things in motion."

"Don't lie to me, Albert."

"Lou, it's a classic—a 1971 Daytona convertible."

"I've never had a classic car. Have you, Victor?"

"Nah, I'm a Lincoln or Cadillac man myself. But maybe I'll try a little sports car." He looked at Seymour. "It's got to be good for scoring with women, eh, Albert? What happened to the '67 Vette?"

"I sold it—traded it for the Ferrari."

"I think I liked the Vette better. I don't care for the yellow—what did you get for the Vette?"

"One-ten."

"A hundred and ten G's. Is that what I'm hearing? Christ, I didn't know these cars were worth that kind of dough. Did you, Lou?"

Louie shrugged. "It's all new to me. I'm not much of a car buff. So what's the Ferrari worth?"

"More than the Vette. It's got five hundred horse power—"

"Put a number on it, Albert."

"One ten, maybe one twenty."

"Well, that's more than enough collateral. I'll tell you what … do you have the title here? Before you say no, consider that Victor has a power of attorney that you can assign to him for duplicate title. There's a notary downstairs at the insurance company. So, you see, Albert, we've come prepared."

Seymour's eyelid was twitching nonstop. He wiped sweat from his brow, his eyes flashing to Victor's open jacket, the Beretta an unspoken threat. He dropped his head into his hands, massaging his temples. He looked up with a groan. "That's extortion."

"You're insulting me. I'm merely proposing an amicable solution. What I'd like for you to do, Albert, is to sign the title over to Victor for ninety thousand—no, make it eighty, we'll factor in the tax and juice. Not to mention my inconvenience."

Seymour's head snapped up. "I can't sell it for less than a hundred. It's worth—"

"Don't be difficult, Albert. You've already sold it to me for eighty. The title's a mere formality—a paper trail."

"You're robbing me."

"Yes, but I'll give you time to recoup your prized Ferrari. In fact, Victor will put it in safe storage for you. We'll hold the title, but we won't record it. I'll give you twelve months. If I don't see a return on my investment in the next year, then Victor sells the car and we're even. No hard feelings."

"Are you kidding me? Jesus effing Christ. What if I say no?"

Louie shrugged. "That's your prerogative."

"Yeah right. You come in here with your guns, and you tell me I have a choice. What a joke."

Louie shook his head. "Albert, you're offending me with these inferences. Do you honestly think I'm threatening you? That's not my way at all." Louie's smile was chilling. "As you said yourself, I'm a rich man. I carry for protection. Several years ago a man jumped me. It's a good thing I had a gun because I didn't hesitate to use it. In fact, I only meant to injure the man, but I killed him. I'm not sure what his motive was—I don't think the New Orleans police ever determined motive. I believe they ruled it a case of mistaken identity. But it was clearly self-protection. I felt a little bad about killing the man, but what choice did I have?" Louie shrugged, his palms upturned to indicate his helplessness. "So, you see Albert, my carrying a weapon has nothing whatsoever to do with you, and

I would hate to think that you might be intimidated by it. That's certainly not my intention." His eyes bore steadily into Seymour's. "You have every right to refuse me, of course."

Seymour's forehead was beaded with sweat, his body emitting an unpleasant odor. Louie gave him an encouraging smile. "Take your time, Albert. If you want a couple of days to think it over—"

"I have the title," he said, voice cracking. "Here, in my safe."

Chapter Ten

VICTOR HADN'T DRIVEN A STICK shift in years so it fell upon Sam to drive the Ferrari to a storage unit on Federal. Once the sports car was locked away, Sam drove them to Morton's, where they ordered chopped salads and grilled rib-eyes with a premium Napa Valley Cabernet. Louie and Victor had the Cab, Sam settling for iced-tea. The lunch was a pleasant respite in an otherwise busy day. It was five o'clock by the time they hit I-95, driving south during the late afternoon commute.

Traffic was heavy. Ensconced in the back seat, Louie rested his head against the Lincoln's plush leather. Setting his day aside, his thoughts returned to Tony. Last night, Victor had gotten a little more information from Carmen, and it sure sounded like Tony was in love. Carmen had confided to Victor that Tony was actually thinking of divorcing his wife.

This stunned Louie. He'd always been contemptuous of men who cast aside their families. It was incomprehensible to Louie that men actually fell in love with women who sold their bodies, even left their wives for them. Louie was no stranger to extramarital affairs, but he'd never had trouble separating sex from love. Even when he was romantically involved with a woman, as he had been with Mercedes and, more recently, Tara, he'd never contemplated leaving Angie. Not once. And he'd gone with Mercedes eleven years.

How is it that Tony, getting his first taste of unconventional sex, had gotten involved to the point where his marriage was in trouble? How could he be so damned foolish?

The more Louie considered Tony's behavior, the more irritated he became. His mood worsened when Angie called. Not because she was calling—they'd declared a truce this morning, and Louie was glad to hear her voice. She said, "Thanks for the gardenias."

So, Emily had sent gardenias. Louie said, "Better than orchids, eh, baby?"

"They're beautiful."

"Enjoy them. I hated to upset you this morning. Are you feeling better?"

Angie was. She gabbed about her day. Two of her sisters were coming in from Tampa, and they were planning dinner and a show. Gina had stopped by with the baby. Here, Angie's voice grew tense, as she explained that Gina had expressed concern for her marriage. Angie was still under the illusion that her beloved firstborn was in Miami at Louie's direction, and without divulging too much information, Louie assured his wife that he was on his way to see Tony. "He'll be home tonight," he said. "Or first thing tomorrow morning."

Then he hung up and fielded a number of calls, conducting business in the back seat of the Town Car as they came into Miami, the downtown skyline glossy and golden in the late day sun. Twenty-five miles separated Fort Lauderdale from Miami, but the air seemed sultrier, the sky softer, the women stunningly beautiful. The waters in Biscayne Bay were streaked with the colors of the Caribbean, turquoise when viewed from the windows of the Lincoln as they crawled along the MacArthur Causeway, arriving in south Miami Beach in a flood of traffic. It was, after all, Friday night.

Louie's phone rang as they came into South Beach. He saw the number flashing on the display and answered immediately. His caller was his aging Swiss banker, ringing Louie from his glass tower in the Caymans. Louie's banker was a genius, moving money received from questionable sources through corporations and shadow corporations spread across the globe. Too efficient to bother with small talk, Louie's banker said, "Louis, some changes will be necessary. When can I expect you?"

A summons from his banker was sacrosanct, given top priority. Immediately, Louie shifted his schedule. He said, "I'm free tomorrow afternoon."

"Three o'clock, in my office."

Louie ended the call, sticking the phone back in his pocket. He said, "Victor, we're going to the Caymans tomorrow. Arrange for a twelve o'clock flight."

As an alternative to jet ownership, Louie paid an annual fee to a company that provided private jets for hire. This way he had the convenience of being able to fly anywhere, at any time, on his schedule, with their pilots and crew. Since Louie was a frequent visitor to the Caymans and travel was sometimes required on a moment's notice, he and Victor always carried their passports. Thus, tomorrow's flight was arranged in less time than it took for Sam to drive the last stretch of mile to The Venezia Tower, where Louie kept a condo on the edge of South Pointe Park. He'd built the building in partnership with another developer. It was one of the newer high-rises, with wide, sweeping terraces and blue-glass windows. The lobby and resort style pool had a Venetian theme, reminiscent of a Vegas hotel.

Louie had sold off all of his units except for four. Three of these he leased, and one he kept for himself, making it available for family and friends. For a while Tara Roth had lived here before she was married to Nathan, when she'd been Louie's girl. It had been a couple of years, and Stella had redecorated the condo with a lighter, cooler touch and an Island flavor. Nevertheless, Louie always thought of Tara when he stepped in, his mind automatically recalling the tender moments they'd shared here.

The floor plan was spacious, with sliding glass-doors providing stellar views of Fisher Island. First-time visitors always stepped onto the terrace to admire the scenery, but Louie and Victor stopped in just long enough to refresh themselves and change into more casual attire. Then they were back in the Lincoln, and Sam was navigating the bumper to bumper traffic on Collins.

Sharing the same stretch of magnificent beach as the Fontainebleau and Delano Hotels, the Walker was an Art Deco classic and Miami Beach icon. For a while, after Franco Santia lost the hotel to him, Louie had been the exclusive owner. He'd met Tara on the day he took over the hotel. A year later, when Tara was pregnant with Louie's child and newly married to Nathan, he'd deeded sixty percent ownership to her and forty percent to Tony.

Victor had spoken with Tara earlier. Because of this Louie knew Tony was camped out in one of the Walker's guest suites. Reluctant to say anything bad about anyone, Tara had hemmed and hawed in reply to Victor's questions. Now, greeting them in the Walker's splendid lobby, Tara seemed conflicted. Of course, she and Louie rarely met these days, and though he treated her with the friendly respect accorded the wife of a friend, there was always that initial awkwardness, born of their previous involvement.

Leaning forward, Louie kissed Tara on the cheek, saw her green eyes soften. Then he stepped back, observing with the reserved manner of a stranger the affectionate hug Victor gave her. "Doll, you get prettier every time I see you," Victor said, lifting her off of her feet and giving her a twirl before setting her down. "How are those kids of yours?"

"Gosh, Victor, they're getting so big."

Tara had the face of the girl next door, with wide-spaced eyes and Irish cream skin. Her chestnut hair was shorter than it used to be, cut above the shoulders. She wore a blue knit dress, the fabric clinging to her voluptuous curves in ways that stirred the imagination. But then, she couldn't hide those curves behind a burlap bag. It didn't much matter what Tara Roth wore.

Although Louie and Victor clearly knew the way, they followed Tara into her office, which overlooked the infinity pool and the columns of palms that ran to the edge of the beach. The sky was fast approaching dusk, but there were plenty of people lounging about the pool. The large desk chosen by Louie's flamboyant predecessor faced the door, with two white visitor's chairs placed in front of it. On the desk was an 8x10 family photo of Tara and Nathan with their two boys. Picking up the glass-framed picture, Victor gave a low whistle, causing Tara to flush with pride.

Louie thought she looked a little nervous when he took the picture from Victor. He studied it somberly. The eldest boy was six, with a crop of curly blonde hair and blue eyes. Joey was Tara's nephew, whom she and Nathan had adopted, rescuing him from an abusive situation. The younger boy was three, the same age as Louie's grandson Anthony. He looked like Anthony, too. In fact, he looked exactly like Michael had when he was that age.

It was obvious the boy was Louie's son, physically, at least. But, unlike Ceci in New Orleans, this child would grow up thinking Nathan was his father, and rightly so. Lewis Roth, they'd named him. Tara had told Victor it was Nathan's idea to name him after Louie, and it was she who altered the spelling.

Louie could do nothing for this child. He'd been cut out of the boy's life even before he'd been born, which is why he'd deeded the hotel to Tara, providing a legacy in lieu of child support. Feeling a pang of regret, Louie set the picture on the desk. He looked at Tara, and saw that she was watching him anxiously. Humbled by the moment, Louie cleared his throat, and said, "He's beautiful, Tara."

Her eyes moistened with unshed tears. She managed a tremulous smile. "Lewis is a very active boy. He's … Nathan's really good with him—with both boys. You know how patient he is."

Louie nodded. He knew exactly how patient Nathan was. He turned away from the desk and strolled toward the window, looking out at the people frolicking in the pool. It was Victor who drew back one of the white chairs and, taking a seat, said, "Doll, what's going on with Tony? You mentioned that he's been staying here off and on for a few weeks now."

"Yes." She glanced at Louie, and then sat in the big chair behind her desk. "At first, I didn't think too much of it. I know Tony frequently has business in Miami, and as long as we're not booked solid, there is always a room available for him. But this time it's different. Tony has practically moved into a suite up on the eighth."

"Has he got a girl up there with him?"

"Not today, at least not that I'm aware of. Tony's been secretive, particularly with me. I don't know if you're aware of it, but we've become good friends. Tony and Gina's boys are the same age as ours, and they get along great. I know Gina's been having a rough time—she had some postpartum depression." She paused, thinking, gnawing nervously on her lower lip. "I'm worried about Tony. I tried to talk to him, but he told me to mind my own business. That's so unlike him."

Victor said, "Lou's worried about him, too. Doll, you've seen him with this chick … do you know anything about her?"

Tara said, "She's a Russian girl. Lena says she hangs at Franco's. Have you talked to Franco?"

"Not yet."

"He's the one to ask about her."

"Lou's worried that Tony might give up his marriage for this girl."

Tara sighed. "There's more to it than that, Victor. I think you should know that Tony took twenty thousand out of yesterday's deposit." She caught the flash of surprise on Louie's face. "He told me he intends to pay the money back, but I've never known Tony to be short on cash."

Chapter Eleven

A DISCARDED ROOM SERVICE TRAY WAS on the floor outside of Suite 811, and Victor scooted it aside with his foot. He rapped loudly, competing with the television blaring on the other side of the door. Immediately, the volume was lowered, and they heard movement in the suite, bare feet tracking across a wood floor. A scratching sounded on the other side of the door as Tony peeked at them through the peephole.

Looking directly at the peephole, Louie said, "Tony, let me in."

Tony cracked the door about an inch, peering at them through the narrow slot. He said, "Dad, it's not a good time—"

"Don't piss me off." Louie put the flat of his hand on the door and gave a little shove. Tony jumped back, admitting entry, although he looked anything but pleased. Favoring Angie's side in looks, Tony was taller and broader than Louie, with his mother's soft brown eyes.

The whites of Tony's eyes were bloodshot. His jaw was thick with stubble, his coarse, curly hair tousled and uncombed. His khaki shorts looked as though he'd slept in them, and his black T-shirt was crusted with mustard stains. Regarding his father with nervous trepidation, Tony's broad, handsome face was shiny with sweat.

Normally, Tony greeted Louie with familial affection. Today, he backed off, crossing his arms over his chest. He refused to meet his father's eye, and with a defeated slump of his shoulders, he led the way into the suite, standing off to the side as his visitors appraised the scene.

Tony was health-conscious to the point of being fanatical, religious about his exercise and diet and never missing an opportunity to hop on his mountain bike and clock a few miles. He drank in moderation, if at all. So Louie was surprised to smell whiskey on his son's breath; even more surprising was the half-empty fifth of Canadian Club on the glass-and-stone coffee table in the suite's sitting area. The booze startled Louie almost as much as the bundles of cash spread across the surface of the table. On the floor beside the coffee table was a nylon gym bag. A tumbler with melting ice and watered whiskey sat on the edge of the table next to a note pad and pen.

The suite comprised one large room divided by a half-wall designating bedroom and sitting area. An unmade bed faced the wall of windows, where a sliding door opened onto a balcony. Although the sun had not yet set, filmy drapes were pulled across the windows, obscuring the ocean view. The padded-leather bench-style couch and chrome-legged chair were to the right, where a wall unit held a built-in-television and small refrigerator. The television was tuned to a Seinfeld rerun. Spotting the remote on the couch, Louie picked it up and killed the picture.

On the desk were glasses and a silver ice-bucket, the trash can beside it overflowing with empty water bottles and Styrofoam take-out boxes. Closed up all week, the suite smelled of stale sweat and booze and the lingering traces of a dozen hastily eaten meals.

Louie surveyed the scene, mouth instinctively turning down. Victor said, "Hey, kid," patting Tony on the shoulder as he walked to the sliding door. He yanked apart the drapes and slid the door back on its tracks. Instantly, balmy heat blew in, the smell of tropical air and saltwater chasing stale odors from the room.

Looking at Louie, Victor said, "You want me to stay?"

At Louie's nod, Victor took off his sport coat, draping it over the back of the chair. He still wore his gun belt. Beneath it his powerful muscles stretched the silk of his slate-blue T-shirt.

Eyeing the bottle of booze, Victor plucked two glasses from the desk, added ice, and then carried them to the coffee table where he poured a couple of inches of whiskey into each. He set Louie's tumbler on the opposite side of the table from Tony's cash. Then he sat on the chrome-legged chair and crossed his ankle over his knee, his big hand cupping the glass.

Louie's gaze drifted from the cash to Tony and back. All day he'd been worried that Tony was going to leave his wife, worried that he'd disgraced himself with some two-bit whore. But the money told a different story. Louie felt a sinking sensation in his stomach. He sat on the edge of the couch and reached for the glass of whiskey. He took a small sip, his mouth flooding with heat.

Gesturing to the space beside him, Louie said, "Tony, sit down."

Reluctantly, bare feet shuffling, Tony moved forward and sat where Louie instructed. He glanced sullenly at Louie, and then hastily turned away, leaving Louie to wonder what had become of the young executive he was so proud of. Louie said, "Do you want to tell me what's going on?"

"No, not really." Tony sounded like a spoiled frat boy rather than a married father of three. He was still refusing to meet Louie's eye.

Disappointed, Louie said, "What did I pay you last year?"

"Dad—"

"I paid you five hundred thousand dollars, plus bonuses. And you're raiding Tara's cash box?"

"My money's invested. I needed cash…I don't have piles of money sitting around in safety boxes like you do."

Ignoring the barb, Louie said, "What's going on, Tony?"

Tony breathed noisily, his throat working. Finally, he inhaled deeply, and said, "I'm being blackmailed."

Louie's eyes shot to Victor's. From the moment Tara had mentioned money, he'd expected this. But now he felt a slow, creeping anger. "You're being blackmailed, and you didn't come to me, your father? What in God's name is wrong with you?"

Tony laughed shortly, his lips curling with contempt. "As if you'd understand."

Victor said, "Tony, your dad is worried about you. Why don't you show him some respect?"

"Maybe I'm not feeling too respectful."

"Come on, kid, how bad could it be? Nothing is going to surprise your old man."

But something did surprise Louie. It was the photos Tony showed them on his high-tech tablet. First, he reached into the duffel bag and removed his iPad. He touched the tablet, fingers gliding expertly across the screen the way they did when he showed Louie pictures of his kids.

Except this time there were no images of little Louis or Anthony or baby Thomas. What Louie saw were shots of Tony, taken while he was lying naked on a bed with his hands bound behind his back. Two blondes, dressed alike in leather bustiers and thigh high lace-up boots, were playing dominatrix. The pictures faded and a video began, the screen showing erotic acts, none of which were particularly flattering to Tony. The camera caught him at all angles, which made Louie consider that there must have been more than one camera in the room. It was quality work, too—it looked as though somebody had taken time to edit the video, as one scene flowed flawlessly into another.

Louie was not impressed with the girls. They looked cheap, reminding him of the porn stars he'd seen this afternoon in Seymour's studio. The taller of the two had a hard, used-up look. She was too thin, her mouth too large, her jaw sharp and jutting. Louie suspected this was the blonde Chapman had seen. Her companion was petite, with curves instead of hard angles. Behind the false eyelashes and heavy shadow, her eyes were flat and expressionless. Her bleached hair showed dark roots, revealing that she was no blonde at all.

Louie handed the tablet to Victor, who took one look and said, "Aw, Jesus, kid...you let them tie you up."

"It was a fantasy."

"Did you ever think you could be putting yourself in danger?"

Tony did not answer. He gulped his watered-down whiskey, draining the glass. Louie said, "What happened to the Boy Scout who was never going to cheat on his wife?"

"Yeah, well...I'm not perfect."

"None of us are, kid." Victor set the tablet down. "You could have picked a couple of nicer girls. You should have come to me when you were looking to get laid. I would have set you up with some quality piece of ass."

Tony said, "It was going to be a one-time thing. You know...just sex. Gina and I were going through a rough patch—"

"Carmen's worried you're going to leave Gina," said Louie. "How involved are you with these girls?"

"Oh, you talked to Carmen."

Tony reached for the bottle, pouring two fingers worth of whiskey into his glass. Victor said, "You want ice?"

"No." Tony shook his head. He looked at Louie, really looking at him for the first time. Louie saw how devastated he was and felt a rush of pity. Then he thought of the responsibilities he'd carried at Tony's age and his sympathy cooled. Tony said, "Dad, I fucked up. What do you want me to say?"

Louie said, "You're too hard on yourself. You always had to be perfect." He took a sip of whiskey. It was smoother now, the ice melting. The filmy drapes gusted into the room, hung suspended in midair, and then fell flat against the glass as the wind receded. "So what's the story with you and Gina? Is your marriage in trouble?"

"You mean, does Gina know about this?" Tony gestured at the iPad. "No. She thinks I'm down here working. But I don't see how I'm going to be able to keep a lid on this much longer. The pictures and video were e-mailed to me at the office. But look—" he picked up the tablet and showed Louie a picture of Gina retrieving mail from the mailbox at the foot of his driveway, saying bitterly, "They know where I live."

Tony told them the story. He'd been seeing both girls, sometimes apart, sometimes together. With Irina, the girl Carmen had turned him onto, it was just sex. With Natasha there was some affection. She was a nice girl, and he felt a little sorry for her. But he certainly wasn't planning on leaving Gina for her, if that's what Louie was worried about. But Gina might very well divorce him because this wasn't the first time they'd blackmailed him. He'd already paid them ten thousand dollars.

Before Louie could recover from the shock of this, Victor said, "Any idea who 'them' is?"

Tony explained. About a week after the playacting scene, he received the first e-mail, with the picture and video attachment. The message was brief: Ten thousand dollars to be delivered to a mailbox at a UPS store on Oakland Park Boulevard in Lauderdale.

"Not too far from the Ocean Breeze Hotel," Louie observed, knowing this is where Tony's trysts had occurred.

Having confirmed that he'd met the girls there on several occasions, Tony said that Irina and Natasha shared the studio with a couple of other girls. They were careful not to be too conspicuous, alternating between the Ocean Breeze and a few other hotels in the area. Both girls mentioned boyfriends, but they refrained from sharing details. Having conducted a title search on the apartment, Tony was aware that the owner was an eighty-five year old man. The unit was leased, although Tony did not know the name of the lessee.

Victor was familiar with the hotel, as well as its owner, a connected guy from Jersey. He stopped in Mizu Café from time to time, liked to eat sushi at the bar. He used to date a girl who had a condo in a neighboring building and reported that the hotel was decent and catered to family people. "I'm surprised somebody's running an operation like that over there and getting away with it," he said.

Tony started to say something, but overcome with sudden emotion, he stopped, his eyes flooding with tears. He hung his head in shame. "I'm sorry, Dad."

Louie studied him dispassionately, a little coolly. This display of weakness repelled him, and he had no comforting words to give his son. His eyes grazed Victor's. Thinking of the obstacles he'd overcome, sometimes by shedding blood, Louie said abruptly, "Why did you pay them?"

"Why? You saw that video. My God, they could ruin me. I just want the problem to go away."

The room was fading into shadows, and Victor leaned over and snapped on the floor lamp. "These things have a way of escalating when you give in," said Victor. "That's why the United States doesn't negotiate with terrorists when they kidnap our people. So you paid ten grand, putting it in a mailbox in a UPS store. How'd you get the key to the box?"

"They e-mailed me the pictures and a note, saying ten grand, no cops. Told me the location of the UPS store, and advised me that a key would be mailed to me the next day. And it was. I paid them because the e-mail instructed that after I paid, the pictures and video would be destroyed."

"But they weren't, were they?"

"Everything was good for a couple of weeks. I quit seeing the girls. At least, I quit seeing Irina, but I came down here and met Natasha a few times. She swore to me that she had nothing to do with the blackmailing. She thinks it's Irina and her boyfriend, and I ... well ... I believe her. She's not a bad person, Dad. She's sweet."

Tony wept again, silently, and Victor got up and refreshed his drink, patting him on the knee for encouragement. After a few minutes, Tony blotted his eyes with tissue. Louie said, "How did they approach you the second time?"

"Same way. By e-mail." Tony leaned over and lifted his iPad, tapping his finger to his mail icon. He selected the item and opened it, tilting the tablet to show Louie. The message read: "$50,000 or wife gets video. Do not call cops. You have three days."

Tony said, "It's been five days. I e-mailed back, asking for more time, but I've received no confirmation. I'm scared to death Gina's going to get a package in the mail. Or that they'll upload it to YouTube or something."

Louie glanced at the cash. "So you're trying to put together fifty thousand?"

"Yeah, without Gina getting suspicious. We have joint accounts. If I start pulling out large sums, she's going to notice. So I'm taking a little from here and there."

"Jesus, Tony, I'm really having a hard time with this. You're *my* son, for God's sake. Why in the hell didn't you come to me?"

"I didn't want you thinking badly of me. Besides, I don't want any blood vendettas."

"They're threatening the sanctity of your family. Doesn't that piss you off?"

"Hell, yes, it makes me mad. But I'm more worried about Gina finding out. She's not like Mom—she's not going to tolerate my playing around. If she finds out, she'll divorce me. And she'll take everything."

Louie didn't understand how some men lived in fear of their wives, allowing them to dominate them completely. Appalled, he said, "You're going to have to get things straight with Gina. You can't let a woman control you."

"Huh, that's easier said than done."

"You can't pay attention to everything a woman says," advised Victor. "Women are emotional. They think with their heart. You've got to humor them once in a while, let them think you're interested in hearing what they have to say. You know, play along to get along, and then you go out and do your own thing."

"Look," said Louie. "It's a tough time with the new baby. Do yourself a favor and don't have any more kids. And quit telling your wife everything. You're not helping yourself."

Tony dropped his head into his hands and groaned. "You think I'm a real fuck-up, don't you? I know what you're thinking. You hate weakness, and you think I'm weak."

Louie said, "Tony, I'm your father. I'm on your side, even when you fuck up, as you've clearly done. What do you want me to say? I can forgive anything except cowardice. And you've been a coward by avoiding your problems at home, and a bigger coward by paying blackmailers. It was a cheap stunt, and you fell for it. And I'm really, really, angry that you didn't come to me. Now put your money away and go take a shower. You stink."

Tony started to say something in his defense, but Louie made a dismissive gesture. He got up and stepped out onto the balcony. Night had fallen on Miami, and a full moon was rising over the ocean, luminescent rays shimmering on the sea. Eight floors below him floodlights illuminated the pool deck. People strolled on the boardwalk and lovers gathered on the beach as the moon began a glorious ascent.

For a moment, Louie felt almost nostalgic. Then he heard Victor talking to Tony, and his mood hardened as he considered his son's dilemma. He was stunned that *his* son—*his father's grandson*—had paid money to blackmailers.

Inside, Tony was saying to Victor, "I would have come to you, if I didn't think you would tell him. Do you know how ashamed I am?"

"You're going to have to pull yourself together, kid. Come on, now, go take a shower. Put some cold water on your head. You've got to start thinking clearly."

Victor coaxed and talked, and after a couple of minutes Louie heard Tony go into the bathroom. When the sound of the shower reached him, Louie reentered the suite. Victor looked at him and breathed out a sigh. "He'll be okay, Lou."

"What's wrong with him, falling apart like this? Does he need a doctor?"

"I don't know. He's a little young for a mid-life crisis, but that's what this looks like to me."

"Christ." Louie pointed at the iPad. "Let me see that tablet. Get those pictures back on the screen."

Victor complied, finding the pictures and turning the tablet to Louie, who said, "What the fuck is wrong with him? Look at these chicks, posing. They knew that camera was there—both of them. Can't he see that?"

"I guess he's got a soft spot for the little one."

Louie snickered. "Call Chucky Lane. Get this shit forwarded to him. Tell him I want him to start on it right away. Tonight, if he can."

The Walker's in-house restaurant, Abby's, was not renowned for its food. Their specialty was burgers, mahi-mahi sandwiches and grilled chicken salads. Anything requiring more culinary skill subjected the diner to risk; nevertheless, Louie ordered Tony a New York strip, and then he sent Victor in the kitchen to supervise so that when Tony's steak came, it was medium rare and tender, his plate pink with juice.

They sat on the terrace, amidst tables filled with vacationing Germans and Argentineans. Tara was nowhere to be seen, but Nathan had arrived while they were upstairs, and he came and sat with them.

Nathan was in his early forties, with brown hair that was thinning on top and deep, dark eyes. He had the body of an elite warrior, keeping himself in shape with an exercise regimen he'd adopted while working for Israeli military intelligence. Nathan had never divulged why he'd quit, but upon emigration to Miami, he'd started a security business, although Louie knew he still did contract work or what he termed as "side jobs" for his former employer and, on occasion and in secrecy, the CIA.

Nathan was second to Victor in holding Louie's confidence and friendship. Nathan had met Tara through Louie, and while he must have fallen for her immediately, he'd never shown his feelings. When Tara revealed that she was pregnant, Nathan stepped in and proposed. And in the end, frustrated and helpless, Louie had given his blessing.

Louie found Nathan's presence comforting, although it wasn't until after they dined on grilled mahi-mahi sandwiches and discussed everything from baseball to current events that Louie and Nathan stepped away from the table. They headed toward the beach, stepping up onto the boardwalk where a woman was filling several plastic bowls with cat food.

The woman was an environmentalist type, wearing a bandana and tie-dyed T-shirt. She carried a bag of Purina Cat Chow, and several ragged alley cats were already converging. There were not as many people on the boardwalk as Louie had noted earlier, when he'd viewed it from Tony's balcony. The beach, however, remained the domain of lovers, who sat in pairs, gazing out at the sea, where moonlight glittered and danced on the waves.

When they were out of earshot of the cat lady, Nathan said, "What's going on?"

Louie told him. While Nathan showed a flicker of surprise at Tony's behavior, he offered no judgment. He did say, "I don't think you'll have too much difficulty tracking down the blackmailers. From what you've told me, they're not pros."

"No," said Louie. "I didn't think so either. I'm going to have Franco set up a meeting with Sergei Szarnakov. The girls are Russian—"

"Watch yourself with Szarnakov."

Louie smiled grimly. "Sergei owes me a favor."

"Hmm. That's your business. Personally, I don't trust the Russians. And Szarnakov is being watched. He's been selling arms to the Syrians, who are acting as middlemen for the Iranians." He looked at Louie, head cocked, as though debating how much to tell him. "It's a fact that Szarnakov is providing missiles and rocket launchers to Hezbollah and Hamas," he said. "One way or another, he's going down. Remember that."

Louie said, "Well, I won't ask you to join us. You're likely to spook Szarnakov. But then, all I want is information about a couple of whores. It shouldn't be too complicated."

"With the Russians everything is complicated," said Nathan.

Chapter Twelve

LOUIE WALKED TONY TO HIS Range Rover, which was parked on the beach side of Ocean Avenue, opposite the News Café where they'd had breakfast. It was Saturday morning, and the tourists were just starting to emerge from their hotels. In Lummus Park joggers shared the walkways with scantily clad young women on roller blades. T-shirt vendors were setting up, hauling tables across the sidewalk. Rain clouds were gathering, a low rumble of thunder sounding in the distance.

Tony had called Louie at sun-up, arranging to meet him at the News Café at eight. Now, on the street, Louie told Tony to take a week off. "Spend time with your family," he said.

"Okay, sure." Tony nodded, trying to act nonchalant, but Louie could see he was still embarrassed.

Louie said, "Are you sure you don't want to see a doctor? Stella had that therapist—"

"Stella quit that therapist. Do you know why she quit? It's because we're a fundamentally flawed family. We have secrets we can't share, not even with our shrinks."

Annoyed, Louie said, "Why do you have to be a smart ass? Victor says you're depressed—"

"What, Victor's a psychiatrist now?" Seeing the way Louie's eyes hardened, Tony gave an exasperated sigh. "Look, Dad, I'll be okay. Give me a chance."

Tony was freshly groomed, his hair curling in the heat. After last night's dishabille, his clean shirt and khakis inspired confidence. But Louie was not convinced Tony was okay. Nodding thoughtfully, he said, "Call your mother. She's worried about you."

Tony flinched. "You didn't tell Mom—"

Louie set a reassuring hand on Tony's back. "Of course not. This is our secret. We keep it between us."

"Thanks, Dad."

"Now go home to your wife and kids and quit worrying. In a few days this will all be over with." Louie leaned in and kissed Tony on the cheek, and then he drew back and patted him in the same spot. "And stay away from Russian girls."

Tony got in the SUV, and Louie stood there until he pulled out, driving north on the picturesque street, the old Art Deco hotels fronting the avenue. Filtered through a thick canopy of trees, the light in the park was tinted green. Traffic on Ocean Avenue was always heavy, but at nine o'clock on a Saturday morning it was crawling at a snail's pace, and Louie walked back across the street to the café, where Victor and another man were sitting at a table on the edge of the sidewalk.

The man with Victor was Frankie Adamo, an old time bookmaker. Louie didn't quite know how old Frankie was, but he knew for a fact he was over eighty. He had small, dark eyes that were bright and quick, and a mane of shaggy gray hair that curled against the collar of his silk shirt. The shirt was black, with a white-scrolled design, his top three buttons undone. He was clean-shaven, his skin tanned and weathered.

Frankie had never been a big guy—he was about Louie's size, a little stoop-shouldered in his old age. He had a dozen kids and was currently on his fifth wife, who was forty years' his junior. Frankie had been on the street his whole life and had seen it all, reminiscing about the old days while they ate, entertaining Victor with tales that seemed fanciful by today's standards. But Louie knew they were true.

Louie reclaimed his chair, listened to Frankie complain about the perils of modern bookmaking. "I've got good people, and I don't have too much trouble. But some of my guys let their bettors get out of hand. I tell them to settle weekly. A guy doesn't pay, you don't let him bet. That way you don't run into problems. It's not the like the old days, when you could shake a guy down, break a leg or two."

Victor, who'd broken a couple of those legs for Frankie, nodded agreeably. Then he looked up, signaling the waiter. The guy came over, and Victor said, "We need coffee. And bring me a bread pudding." He glanced at Frankie. "They've got a good bread pudding with vanilla sauce. Lou, you want anything?"

Louie declined, but Frankie liked the sound of the bread pudding, and Victor ordered two. The waiter hustled off. Facing the building, Frankie watched people going in and out of News Café's bookstore and convenience shop. Nodding his head in the direction of the door, he said, "Get a look at this."

Louie and Victor looked. Two women were entering the store, one in short white shorts and a black tank top. Not bad at all, except her girlfriend was stunning. Louie caught a flash of a white bikini, string dangling on a slender, sculpted back, and then the high-cut bottoms, exposing enough prime ass to drive a man crazy.

"Damn," said Frankie. "That's a perfect ass."

"Hell of a body," said Victor.

Louie noted the girl's height, marking that she was tall. She had short, black hair, flipped up at the neck, and wore a red ball cap. Too busy checking out her figure, he didn't notice anything familiar about her, but five minutes later, when the waiter was delivering the bread puddings, the girl in the white bikini emerged from the store, and Louie looked up and recognized her.

Her name was Rachel Richards. She was the former girlfriend of Buddy Schuler, the conservative talk radio king, but she'd been too controversial for Buddy, and when he learned of her checkered past, which included a number of years as an exotic dancer, he'd bolted. Louie had met Rachel in the company of Buddy on several occasions, but the very first time he'd ever laid eyes on her was in a mutual friend's condo, and she'd been wearing less than she was now.

Rachel spotted Louie at the same time that he noticed her and made a beeline for his table. She looked just as good from the front as she did from the rear, her full breasts covered by triangular patches held in place by a string. She was lightly and fashionably tanned—the type of girl who didn't have tan lines. Her dark blue eyes, set in a face with a cute, upturned nose and a faint splattering of freckles across the bridge, sparkled mischievously.

Rachel was forty, but looked ten years younger. She was the only woman at the News Café in a bikini, which might have been prohibited, but nobody was telling her to leave. Taking full advantage, Rachel strutted toward Louie as though she was parading on a stage. Toned and tight with muscle, nothing jiggled except for her breasts, trying to escape the confines of their triangular patches.

Every man on the patio was her audience, and Rachel loved it, arriving at Louie's table with dramatic flourish, one arm extended in greeting. "Louie Morelli, you bastard," she said playfully, dropping the latest edition of *Elle* onto the table.

Grinning, his eyes sweeping over her, Louie stood to greet her. They were the same height, although her wedge sandals gave her the advantage of a couple inches. Louie gave Rachel a proper kiss on the cheek. She pressed her near naked body against him, and he slipped an arm about her waist, resisting the urge to palm her backside, which is what he would have done if they'd been alone. Louie said, "Hi baby, what a nice surprise. What are you doing in Miami?"

"Jolene won a cruise to the Bahamas. We just got back last night—it was one of those three day cruises. Jolene," she turned, beckoning to her friend, who stepped forward. Taken on her own, Jolene was an attractive girl, with straight brown hair and gray-green eyes. Her short shorts showcased muscular legs, the body of a girl who surfed or rode bicycles.

"Jolene's my cousin," said Rachel.

Introductions were made, with Victor getting up to kiss Rachel. He offered his hand to Jolene. "Nice to meet you, doll."

Victor placed Jolene in Tony's vacated seat. Seemingly embarrassed by her cousin's wanton exhibitionism, Jolene smiled gratefully at Victor, who waved over the waiter, requesting another chair. Louie offered his chair to Rachel, but she preferred to stand, posturing and teasing until management squeezed the requested chair to the table. At last Rachel sat, bare cheeks slapping the wooden slats. She crossed her legs toward Louie, her knee brushing against his. "Fancy meeting you here," she said. "I was just telling Jolene all about you, wasn't I, Jo? Did you bring the *Stella di Mare* down?"

"Not this trip."

"Too bad. I'd love a boat ride. Jo, Louie's got a kick ass boat. It's a fucking yacht. It's like a hundred feet—"

"It's eighty feet," corrected Louie.

"Whatever." Rachel rolled her eyes. "It's awesome." She looked at Louie, pushed out her lower lip. "I'm mad at you, Morelli."

"How can you be mad at me? What have I done?"

"You know damn well what you've done. You haven't called me. Not once. And don't tell me you're staying true to your wife because that is absolute BS. I know you, Louie Morelli. I know you like your pussy."

Jolene gave an exclamation of disgust. Glaring at her cousin, she said, "For God's sake, Rachel. Can't you be civil?"

Victor's and Frankie's expressions registered amusement, but three women at the next table, overhearing, gazed at one another in shock before shooting venomous looks at Rachel. Louie said, "Baby, let's not make a scene."

But Rachel was all about making scenes. She twisted and bounced in her chair, and after the waiter set down her coffee, she got up and leaned over the table, deliberately jutting her ass at Louie while she reached for the cream. Victor said, "Doll, all you had to do was ask."

Frankie, eyes roving over her, said, "Honey, you've got a hell of a body."

"I'm glad *you* noticed." She glanced sideways at Louie, giving him a deliberately provocative look. "This man pays no attention to me. He's completely indifferent to me."

Louie said, "Not indifferent, baby. Not with you. A man would have to be dead not to notice you."

"Then why haven't you called me?"

He gave her a little smile. "Honey, you're too complicated for me."

"Bull. How can you say such a thing? I'm perfect for you, and you know it. Victor, don't you think I'd be the perfect girl for Louie?"

"Doll, you sure got the right equipment."

"And I know what to do with it, too." She pouted, blue eyes glinting with a devilish light. "Don't forget, Louie, I don't spit. I swallow."

Chapter Thirteen

TWO HOURS LATER, WHEN LOUIE boarded a Gulfstream G450 at Kendall-Tamiami, Rachel Richards clambered up behind him, her raven hair still damp from her shower.

Louie had issued the invitation impulsively, eliciting excited squeals from Rachel and Jolene. With no time to spare, the girls abandoned their breakfasts before they arrived, rushing to the nearby Colony Hotel to primp for their outing. Sixty minutes later, when Sam picked them up in front of the hotel, the short shorts and string bikini had been replaced by sleeveless summer shifts and elegant sandals.

By this time it was raining, and the girls stepped gingerly around the puddles before sliding into the backseat with Louie. As soon as they got in the Lincoln, Victor said, "You girls have your passports?" and when Rachel confirmed they did, Sam headed for the airport.

They were on the runway by twelve-fifteen, and in the air at twelve-thirty, the girls sipping mimosas. "Don't get drunk," said Louie, watching Rachel slurping thirstily. "We have a long day ahead of us."

"I'd never embarrass you by getting drunk, love. I'll be a proper lady, I promise. God, you look good." She fingered his pale-blue silk sport coat. "I love a well-dressed man. Buddy couldn't dress worth a damn. Every time we went out, I'd have to go over to his house and pick out his clothes. All he ever wore were polo shirts and golf pants." She dropped her hand to Louie's thigh, feeling his tropical-weight trousers. "Buddy never wore pants like these, that's for sure."

Rachel prattled on about Buddy's wardrobe while she continued to examine the plane's amenities, including the delicate glass her mimosa had been served in. She determined that it was "real" crystal, and then, spotting the lone flight attendant at her forward station, she said, "I can't believe we're the only people on this plane. The steward told me it seats eighteen."

"Mmm." Louie reached for the *Miami-Herald*, skimming the headlines.

"Can I take pictures of the plane?"

"Yes, but no pictures of me or Victor."

"No problem." She looked across the aisle, to where Victor and Jolene were sitting. Jolene was telling Victor about her life. Louie could hear snatches of their conversation. Jolene was an ER nurse at a big hospital outside of Orlando, and she was dating a deputy sheriff named Wayne who made her pay for her own dinner when they went out to eat.

Wayne had thrown a fit when she told him she was taking Rachel with her on the cruise. Cheap ass Wayne had expected Jolene to take him. But wait, he'd actually proposed marriage. Jolene wanted to get married—she was almost thirty-eight, but Wayne was a controller, and he had a mean temper.

Rachel, who was listening along with Louie, said, beneath her breath. "Wayne's a creep. He's a stalker, following her around.

Telling her she can't go to the Bahamas with me. Who the hell is he to tell her what she can and cannot do? The asshole won't even buy her dinner. I told her to break up with him. That's what she's been trying to figure out on this trip. I think she wants to call it off, but she's afraid to be alone." Rachel leaned close, whispering. "Jolene's a little square. When I told her Victor was married, she freaked, almost declined to come. Do you believe it?"

Louie said, "Mmm," barely listening, his attention returning to the headlines.

Rachel nudged him with her elbow. "Victor just kissed her. I bet they get it on. What do you think?"

"I think Victor knows how to take care of a woman."

"I love Victor. He's the sweetest guy I've ever met. I'd go for him if I couldn't get you." She turned in her seat, looking behind her. "What's back there?"

Louie shrugged. "The rear cabin. Another lavatory, some seats."

"Show me."

She stood, holding out her hand to him. Louie set down the paper and got to his feet, feeling the engine vibrating beneath him. It had been raining in Miami, but above the clouds the view from the windows showed blue sky. They walked to the rear cabin, divided from the front by a narrow partition.

The lights in the aft cabin were dimmed. Four executive seats faced a large video screen, their rounded backs to the aisle. Rachel said, "I want to sit here."

She chose one of the chairs, and then patted the seat beside her, beckoning Louie with a smile. As soon as he sat, Rachel lifted the armrest dividing her seat from Louie's and scooted over, her hand dropping to his trousers, touching him again, in a different spot.

———————◉———————

Louie's driver dropped the girls off in front of the designer shops in George Town before taking him and Victor on to the bank, where Louie moved money around the globe, protecting it from encroaching governments and volatile markets.

Louie spent a couple of hours with his banker, returning to pick up the girls by late afternoon. They'd done some damage; both girls were toting shopping bags. Rachel was even wearing a new dress, a dark blue skintight sheath that accentuated the color of her eyes. The cousins were waiting outside one of the jewelry stores, and Louie went in and bought Rachel a pair of diamond ear studs. He then purchased tennis bracelets for Angie and Stella, a necklace with a heart-shaped, diamond-studded pendant for Ceci, and a small, gold locket for Isabella.

By dusk they were at Blue by Eric Ripert, the award-winning restaurant in the Ritz Carlton named for the renowned seafood chef. Chucky Lane and his girlfriend, a frizzy-haired blonde in a red, strapless dress, were waiting for them in the lounge. Chucky was a former jewel thief and self-described nerd who could hack his way past firewalls and complicated passwords. Louie had relocated Chucky to the Caymans to get in on the online gaming action, but since the feds police offshore gambling, Chucky chose to start a website design and SEO company. Louie had bankrolled Chucky, an investment that was paying off, as Chucky was becoming a millionaire in his own right.

Chucky looked the way Ron Howard would look if he had not lost his hair, with the same sort of "Aw, shucks," apple-pie look, his red hair fading to gray. Since moving to the Caymans, Chucky's wardrobe had improved, but even with his stylish white blazer and handsome new saddle shoes, Chucky looked like a computer programmer. He'd grown up in north Florida—an original Florida cracker—and retained his southern accent.

Beholden to his benefactor, Chucky dropped everything for Louie. He had news for him, too. From the e-mail Victor had forwarded from Tony's iPad, he'd been able to trace the IP address and had hacked into the sender's computer, creating what he called "nuclear havoc" with the files. The images of Tony and the damning video weren't going anywhere, unless the blackmailer had backed up the file to a cloud or old-fashioned DVD or USB flash-drive, in which case the backed-up file could be reloaded onto a new computer and everything set in motion all over again. But Chucky hadn't encountered any encryption or sophisticated firewalls, and he didn't think the sender was too proactive.

He'd also gone ahead and researched Tony's e-mail account, examining the first e-mail from the blackmailer. It was the same sender; that is, the sender's email address was identical, but a different IP address had been used, indicating a separate location. At this point Louie got a little fuzzy, and he said to Victor, "Do you understand what he's talking about?"

They were standing at the end of a rounded bar, where low-hanging pendant lights cast an ambient glow. The girls sat on low-backed cinnamon-colored suede chairs clustered together near a cocktail table on an expanse of blue tile, admiring each other's dresses in that phony way peculiar to women. Rachel was wearing her new earrings. As Louie watched, she touched her left lobe, fingering the sparkling diamond, and then she looked over and gave him a big smile.

They shared a lingering look, Louie's mind flashing to the obscene act she'd performed so capably on the plane. She seemed to guess his thoughts; her eyes sparkled mischievously. Reluctantly, Louie broke eye contact, returning to the conversation. Victor, savoring a taste of Woodford Reserve, looked up, frowning. "I think Chucky's trying to tell us there's more than one person involved."

Chucky said, "I suspect there is more than one person involved. But there may not be. Remember, the sender's e-mail address is the same. What I've determined is that the first e-mail originated from an IP address in Hollywood. The second e-mail was sent from an IP address in Palm Beach County. I'll get the physical addresses to you tomorrow."

Louie said, "Get them to Victor."

"Sure." Chucky nodded, continuing. "What this means is that you have one person utilizing two computers, say a work site and a home site. Or two people working together from two different locations."

"That's not so good," said Louie.

"No, but I scrambled up both systems, crashed them completely. They'll have to get new computers. I've started extracting information from the files, and I can tell you that the Hollywood computer is owned by a woman."

Victor said, "How do you know that?"

"She shops. A lot of it is lingerie and sex toys. I've got credit cards in nine different names, and several shipping addresses, including Fort Lauderdale, Hollywood Beach, and Sunny Isles Beach. I'm going to look at it again tomorrow and compile a list. I think the cards are stolen."

Louie said, "Were any of those names Russian?"

"Yeah, now that you mention it, a couple of them were."

"I want the names."

"I'm trying to determine which ones are false. I know she's been playing this game for a while—there was an extensive library. Maybe twenty or thirty guys in pictures and videos like the ones they took of Tony. The early pictures were terrible, grainy, from hidden cameras, maybe cell phones. But somewhere along the way our girl got a pro—it's high quality photography."

"We noticed that, too," said Victor.

"Another thing," said Chucky. "You have to consider that they've used digital cameras and recording equipment, so they may be able to recreate the photos and video all over again. If they put them online, I can find them. But you really have to get to the source. All I'm doing is giving them headaches."

Louie nodded. Glancing up from his glass of blended Scotch whiskey, he watched the elegant maître d' approach him. "Mr. Morelli," the man said, in a posh British accent. "Your table is ready."

The girls rose in a flurry of chatter and bright dresses. Louie savored a final sip of his Scotch, and then set the glass on the bar. Victor stepped forward, holding his arm out to Jolene. "Come on, doll, let's go eat."

Louie made to follow, but Chucky held back, extracting a folded slip of paper from his pocket and handing it to Louie. "Here's the information on Adriana McIntyre that you requested. You were right, all the records were in Vero Beach, but I found her for you. She's in Boca Raton, at her mother's place. I wrote the address for you."

Louie put the slip of paper in his pocket and didn't touch it again until he was on the Gulfstream, in the dimly lit cabin, where a muted video screen was tuned to CNN. It was past midnight, the sky black beyond the drawn shades. Across the aisle Victor reclined in his chair, snoring softly. Beside him Jolene lay with her head snuggled against his shoulder.

Louie's chair was in a recline position, the armrest dividing his seat from Rachel's lifted, as it had been on the incoming flight. Curled on her side, and with an airline blanket covering her, Rachel slept, her chest rising and falling with her soft, even breathing. They were all tired from feasting on ceviche and sea scallops and yellowtail, with a variety of wines from Alsace and the Piedmont region: A wine for each taste, a tease of the palate, with a fawning sommelier and waiters spreading thick napkins across their laps.

When Louie first got on the plane, he'd closed his eyes, expecting sleep. But he had not slept, his tired brain refusing to shut down. It was then that he remembered the slip of paper Chucky had given him, and he dug it out of his pocket and looked at the address: NE 5th Avenue, in Boca Raton.

Louie smiled at Chucky's neat, square writing, as precise as a draftsman. He'd written Adriana's name at the top of the paper. There were two phone numbers with the address, and he'd even drawn a small map, showing a grid of streets between Federal and Dixie Highway. Not a high rent district.

Louie had been too busy to think about Adriana, but now he wondered why she hadn't shown up to work, why she hadn't even called. She'd been a bit of a mystery—cool, sophisticated blonde on the outside and coy little girl on the inside. He hadn't imagined her passion either.

Louie liked Adriana, but she wasn't worth worrying about. There were too many other beautiful women, like the one sleeping beside him, for Louie to concern himself with the one who got away. He refolded the paper and put it in his pocket, and then he looked at Rachel and saw that she was awake and watching him. She smiled dreamily, and Louie reached out and brushed a wayward lock of hair off of her cheek. She sat up, the blanket folding across her waist. "The plane's descending."

"Fifteen minutes," said Louie.

"To the Caymans and back in one day. God, what a life."

Louie smiled. "Have a good time?"

"The best, ever."

"You're a knockout, baby." Louie's dark eyes, gleaming, gazed steadily into hers. "Are you seeing anybody?"

"I haven't been with a man since Buddy, and that's the honest to God's truth. It's been a year."

Tracing the curve of her jaw with his forefinger, Louie said, "I don't want you seeing other men when you're with me. Drinks or dinner is fine, but you only have sex with me."

Her eyes flickered. "I have a girlfriend I get it on with once in a while. She's married … she married an old fart, so she's not getting any sex either. Is that okay?"

He liked the sound of this, his imagination already seizing it. "Yeah, that's okay," he said.

Rachel put her head on his shoulder. "Does this mean I'm your girl?"

"Hmm. Maybe … let's see how it goes. You may not *want* to be my girl."

"Are you kidding me? Everyone wants to be your girl."

"Baby, I can't offer you anything except for a good time. No permanent commitments. And I'm going to be brutally honest. I know a lot of men say they don't love their wives and that they stay married out of a sense of obligation or for financial reasons. But that's not the case with me. I genuinely love my wife, and we do have a relationship." His eyes held hers, saying it the way he always did, putting his cards on the table. "I'll never leave my wife."

Chapter Fourteen

LOCATED NEXT DOOR TO THE Walker Hotel, Franco's was one of Miami Beach's premier hotspots, popular with celebrities, sports stars, and beautiful women. When Louie took over the hotel, an outdated steakhouse had been on the property, but he'd demolished the existing structure and built the glittering two-story club in its place, naming it after Franco Santia, the Walker's former proprietor.

Some people found it unusual that after throwing Franco out of the Walker, Louie had elevated him to business partner, putting him in charge of the nightclub. But Franco had been born and raised in Miami, and he knew everyone who was anyone, and because he'd gone broke and Louie saved him, he was beholden to Louie in much the same way that Chucky Lane was.

But Franco wasn't anything like Chucky. He was good looking, with black hair and dark blue eyes, dressed in tight Versace jeans, a blue silk shirt, and white Gucci loafers when Louie and Victor walked into the club at half past five on Sunday afternoon.

The nightclub had not officially opened for the day, and staff was hanging around the main floor lounge, waitresses dressed in black shorts and fishnet stockings. A couple of bartenders were behind the bar, prepping for the night ahead. Most of the lights were on, the doors to the patio flung open. A handful of patrons were sitting at the outside bar.

Greeting Louie and Victor, Franco welcomed them with affectionate hugs. Then they went upstairs, circumventing the velvet ropes and taking the broad stairs to a private lounge that overlooked the first floor. Glass doors accessed a wide gallery set with high-tops. The view was to the ocean, looking out over the Walker's beach. A mezzanine level held a VIP room, another set of velvet ropes prohibiting access. During peak times burly bouncers were on alert.

Franco's office was at the end of a hall, past the restrooms and elevator. They went in here first and discovered Franco's petite, redheaded girlfriend lounging on the red leather couch behind his desk. Kimmie looked up, green eyes languorous, and gave them a little smile. Her hair was tousled to the point that Louie wondered if she'd been doing something other than napping prior to their arrival. She got up, yawning, and smoothed her hair. She was wearing very thin and very snug black leggings and a black sports-bra with crossed straps on her back.

Pictures of Franco's wife and kids were on his desk, and they spent a few minutes inquiring after one another's families. Then Franco pulled out his ledgers, and he and Louie went over the books while Victor and Kimmie chatted. Kimmie had put herself through law school working at Franco's. She'd recently started at a downtown law firm and complained to Victor that she'd made more money serving cocktails than she did as an attorney. "Go figure," she said.

Franco was ADHD. Their conversation was distracting him, and he turned with a frown, saying, "Kimmie, why don't you see if they've got the VIP lounge ready for Lou?"

She strutted off, haunches moving beneath the thin leotards, drawing their eyes like a magnet. Louie said, "She looks good, Franco."

"She wants to fuck all the time."

"That's not so bad, is it?"

"It is when your wife expects you to perform twice a week."

They had a good laugh, and then tucked their noses back in the books. After a few minutes Victor went out. Ten minutes later he returned and said, "Lou, that Russian chick is here."

Louie followed Victor out to the lounge. A young woman in a silver-metallic mini-skirt sat on a high chair at the bar. The chair was glossy chrome with a white leather seat and padded back, the only one at the long, rectangular bar that was occupied. The girl's legs were crossed, revealing bare skin and thigh. A black-velvet corset with silver lacings hugged her torso and pushed up her breasts. She was fair-skinned, her brown eyes heavily lined, her cupid's mouth red with lipstick. Louie noticed that her black lace-up boots with the platform heels were the same ones she'd been wearing in the video.

Definitely the same girl, the one Tony had identified as Natasha. She looked a little better in person, but this was probably because she'd restored her hair to its natural shade of brown. It was shoulder length, worn in a center part without bangs. Natasha was small and curvy. She sat facing the glass doors, an oversized shoulder bag plopped on the chair beside her.

Behind the bar Kimmie poured Parrot Bay into a glass and squirted cola with the syrup-gun. She added a sliver of lime and set the drink on the bar in front of Natasha. She looked at Louie and Victor, and then at Franco, trailing them. "Do you guys want anything?"

"Water for me," said Victor. "Get Lou a Pellegrino."

Kimmie got Victor an ice water, and then she grabbed a Pellegrino from the cooler and set it on the bar with a glass. Natasha swiveled her chair sideways and regarded Louie and Victor with interest. Looking at Louie, she offered a smile, her hand dropping to her thigh, her red-tipped fingernails toying with the hem of her skirt. Franco said, "Natasha, these are the gentlemen who asked to meet you."

Franco made a "let's-go" gesture at Kimmie, and she walked down the bar and ducked out through an opening. She headed back toward the office. Franco went in the opposite direction, toward the stairs. Louie poured mineral water into a glass and stepped closer to Natasha, claiming the chair beside the one her purse sat on. She looked archly at him. Her eyes slid to his Girard Perregaux watch, flickered over his black silk-knit shirt and crocodile-leather belt. She said, "You want to have date with me?"

Her English was heavily accented, harsh in the vowels. Natasha evoked no ardor in Louie. She was too young—barely out of her teens—and too contrived, trying desperately to be sexy. She didn't have one-tenth of the sex appeal that Kimmie had, but girls like her seldom did. In Louie's eyes, Natasha was one cut above a street-walker. His disappointment in Tony flared anew, and he thought dismally, *is this the best he can do?*

Louie glanced at Victor. Casually, Victor set a one hundred dollar bill on the bar near Natasha's rum and coke. She looked at it and made a disparaging sound. "I guess you no want to have date with me."

Victor slapped another Ben Franklin on the bar. "Five minutes," he said. "All you have to do is talk."

Her eyes flickered, showing a glimmer of fear. "Are you police?"

Louie said, "Tony Morelli is my son."

There was a spark of recognition, and then Natasha looked pointedly away. She managed an indifferent shrug. "I don't know this name." She stirred her drink with the cocktail straw. Looking at Louie, eyes narrowing with suspicion, she said, "You want date or no?"

Louie said, "You're blackmailing my son—"

"You crazy. This is big lie—"

"Who's behind this scheme?"

Natasha reached for her handbag. She started to rise, but Victor set a hand on her shoulder. "Not so fast, doll." He patted her. "Sit back and relax. No one is going to hurt you. All we want is a little information."

Natasha dropped her purse and reached for the glass, sucked rum and coke through the straw. "For another hundred I tell you."

Louie said, "I'm not playing that game." He kept his voice neutral, his manner nonthreatening. "I've seen the video you and Irina starred in. So don't lie to me, okay? I want to know who set this operation up—"

She took the two bills off the bar and slipped them into her handbag. "I can't talk to you," she said. "I go now. If you try to stop me, I scream. Franco knows me—he knows I'm not troublemaker. He'll make you leave."

Victor said, "Doll, do not get out of that chair. We're being nice here, asking you politely. Who made that video of Tony? We want the camera, the hard drive it's stored on and all the copies. You pass the word on to your friends. Tell them the game's over."

"Fuck you, mister." She got up, glared defiantly at Victor, and then hoisted her heavy handbag. She started for the stairs, looking back over her shoulder as though daring Victor to stop her.

But Victor made no move to halt Natasha. By this time it wasn't necessary. The sound of men's voices filled the stairwell, sounding louder as they ascended. Franco was in the lead, followed by a couple of halfbacks in shiny suits and pointy-toed shoes. They had rough faces and mean eyes. One man had a puckered scar that sliced an eyebrow in half, giving his face a disjointed look. He sized up Victor and Louie. His eyes grazed Natasha's and she suddenly looked worried, made a beeline back toward the bar. She reclaimed her chair and sucked another quarter of an inch of rum and coke through the straw.

At the top of the stairs the suits divided, scar-face standing like a sentry while his companion strutted forward, eyes flickering around the bar. Behind them Sergei Szarnakov and a handsome blonde man stepped onto the landing. The blonde man was speaking Russian and gesturing with his hands in a manner that was almost Italian. But the only thing Italian about him was his clothing, as there was no mistaking the Slavic cut of his jaw and Nordic blue eyes.

Szarnakov looked like a hatchet-faced Soviet-era KGB agent. He was a squat man, with a barrel-shaped chest and an acne-pitted face. He was sixty years old, and the clipped, shoe-polish black hair on his massive head looked unnatural. But there was nothing silly about Sergei Szarnakov. Though he stood a full head shorter than the Viking beside him, he radiated a powerful life force that diminished his friend's golden good looks. Both men were dressed casually, albeit expensively. Szarnakov wore white linen slacks and a brown silk sport-shirt with white piping on the front, and his companion had on tan trousers, a beige button-down shirt, and brown leather sandals. Behind them was an entourage comprised of six men and three women. The women were young, attractive, and scantily dressed. The men were of varying ages and, Louie suspected, nationalities. Two bodyguards trailed the group, unremarkable from the first set by dress or manner, although one of the guards had alopecia. His bald head shone as though it was waxed. He was without eyebrows and eyelashes, his cheeks smooth and milky white, without even a shadow of a beard. His pale eyes were hard and unblinking, and his swagger slightly more pronounced than that of his comrades. Lastly, trailing the bodyguards, were several of Franco's wait-staff, including two bartenders.

Franco came over to Louie and said, "The VIP room is all set for you."

Louie said, "Put out some shrimp and oysters. Do the oysters Rockefeller. Some steak-bites, too. Tenderloin."

Franco sped off to do Louie's bidding. Szarnakov spoke Russian to his friend, and then he turned, his frosty gray eyes seizing on Louie. He smiled with genuine affection and moved toward Louie with outstretched hands. Speaking English with a slight accent, Szarnakov said, "Louis, my friend, it is good to see you."

Standing, Louie took a couple of steps toward Szarnakov, narrowing the distance between them. "Hello, Sergei." He extended his hand, and the bodyguard with the split eyebrow sprang forward like a Doberman. The bodyguard intended to pat Louie down but before he could lay a hand on him, Szarnakov reprimanded him in Russian. The man jerked back as though burned.

Szarnakov gripped Louie by the elbows and embraced him Russian-style, planting a kiss on each cheek. He offered Victor his hand, and the bodyguard's eyes narrowed as he observed this gesture. He wasn't alone in eyeing Victor with distrust. Equal in size with Victor, all of the suits were uncomfortable with him, knowing, instinctively, that he was carrying a weapon.

Szarnakov introduced the dapper man at his side as Dimitri, saying, "Dimitri is my money man, my advisor."

There was more handshaking and polite "How do you do's." None of the entourage was introduced, nor did they expect to be. They hung back like groupies, talking among themselves. One of the girls giggled. The bald bodyguard gave Natasha the evil eye, looking at her in a way that suggested he knew her. She shifted uneasily in her seat and refused to make eye contact. Her hand trembled as she lifted her glass.

Louie's meeting with Szarnakov would be private, which meant Victor and Dimitri were included. Szarnakov's bodyguards stepped into formation, two in front and two in rear, although it was obvious by now that the danger to their boss was minimal. Sensing an opportune moment to escape, Natasha reached for her handbag. Victor put another hundred on the bar. "Stick around, doll. We've got a date."

In the VIP room French doors led to a private terrace. The view through the glass was of the Walker's riveting stretch of beach. Striped umbrellas dotted the shoreline. The water was turquoise, shot through with streaks of darker blue. In the corner of the VIP room was a bar. Plush couches formed an open, three-sided square, with enough space between the couches for a man to walk through. A large, flat-panel screen hung on one wall. Functioning as a television, it was also hooked into a camera that panned the first floor entertainment and dance floor. Today, the screen was blank.

Szarnakov and Louie sat on one couch, Victor and Dimitri on another. Two bodyguards stood outside. Two more came in, examined the room and the balcony, and then stepped out, flanking the door like soldiers. A striking black barmaid entered, long legs showcased by fishnet stockings and high heels. She wore short black shorts and a sleeveless, fitted, Tuxedo-style top with a red bow tie. She served them from a silver tray; Imperial Premium Vodka on the rocks for Szarnakov, Johnny Walker Blue for Dimitri, and Kentucky's finest for Victor. Louie had his blended malt whiskey. She set down cocktail napkins and glass bowls filled with nuts and then departed, giving Louie a smile as she went out.

They spent a few minutes exchanging pleasantries. Szarnakov told Dimitri that Louie was the man who'd sold him the warehouse on the Miami River. "First I deal with a Jew, who wants me to pay twice as much for a smaller building. Then someone tells me to call Lou, and I do. He gives me a fair deal."

Dimitri smiled agreeably. He had a polished veneer, projecting a Continental charm which seemed somewhat affected, and the smile he gave Louie was both patronizing and amused. His English was superior to Szarnakov's, with barely a trace of an accent. Louie had met several of Szarnakov's people before, and he wondered what had become of Dimitri's predecessor. Louie had heard a rumor, unsubstantiated, that Szarnakov caught him stealing and had cut off his hand. Szarnakov's wealth was so enormous that Louie imagined it might be easy to think you could steal from him.

Most of Szarnakov's money had been made in the international arms trade by brokering deals with rogue regimes. He consistently did business with Iran and Syria, selling them Chinese and Russian-made munitions. Previous clients included North Korea, the former Libyan and Iraqi dictators, and a fair number of so-called friendly states.

Szarnakov owned ten houses, favoring his mansion on Biscayne Bay because his wife despised the heat and his mistress did not. He told Louie he would be moving to his villa on Cyprus for the summer, casually extending an invitation for Louie to visit. Louie said this sounded good, as he'd never been to Cyprus.

Louie told Szarnakov what was going on with Tony, alerting him to the personalities involved and asking if he could look into the matter. "My son disappoints me," he told Szarnakov. "He pays these blackmailers instead of coming to me. They got greedy and now they want more from him. You understand that I don't care about their operation. What I want are the actual videos and hard-drives this stuff is stored on."

"Say no more," said Szarnakov. "This will be fixed for you, my friend." He ate a handful of nuts, washing them down with vodka. He spoke Russian to Dimitri, who got up and went to the door. Opening it, he summoned the bald guard with one word: "Grigori."

The bodyguard came in. Dimitri returned to his seat, a little smile hovering on his lips. Szarnakov said, "Grigori, you know that girl out there?"

"Which girl is that, boss?"

Grigori spoke English as though it was his first language. Clearly, he'd learned to speak it in Brooklyn. He sounded like a gangster in a B movie. Apparently, Louie wasn't the only one who noticed how he'd looked at Natasha. Szarnakov's eyes narrowed. "You knew that girl at the bar: Natasha. Get her."

Grigori's eyes shot to Louie, then Victor. He nodded and backed out. As soon as he had gone, Dimitri said, "Sergei, Natasha is one of Cyrus's girls."

A subtle, nuanced shift occurred as Szarnakov contemplated this. Turning to Louie, he said, "Cyrus is my cousin's son."

Blood had the potential to complicate things, but Szarnakov had given Louie his word, and there was nothing worse for a Russian than to lose face. Louie felt Dimitri's eyes on him and glimpsed the faintest shadow of a smile, understood that the whole thing greatly amused him. The barmaid entered and refreshed their drinks, retreating just as Grigori returned with Natasha.

Later, Franco's staff would tell Louie that Grigori yanked Natasha off the bar chair and cussed her in English and Russian, the bartender reporting he called her a "thieving bitch." This fit, as she came in trembling and terrified, her eyes darting around the room. The imprint of Grigori's hand flamed red on her upper arm, and she rubbed at this spot.

Szarnakov said something to her in Russian. His tone was kind, and it seemed to Louie that he was reassuring her. He pointed at the third couch, the one where nobody was sitting, and she moved awkwardly to it. She sat on the far end, setting her purse on the floor by her feet.

Switching to English, Szarnakov said, "Do you know who I am?"

She nodded vigorously, "Yes, yes. You are big boss."

"How do you know my bodyguard, Grigori Buzeczki?"

She glanced at Grigori, who was still giving her the evil eye, and shuddered involuntarily. "He's friend of Cyrus," she said, in a low, quaking voice.

"Does Cyrus know you extort money from the men who pay you for sex?"

Natasha hung her head, looking down at the toes of her shiny, high-heeled boots. When she did not answer, Szarnakov said, "You take pictures and movies of men having sex with you, and then you threaten to send the pictures to their wives and mothers. Is this how you do business, a girl like you?"

"No...I..." Her voice broke. "Cyrus does not know." She looked at Szarnakov, her eyes pooling with tears. "I make big mistake. I listen to Irina—she tells me it's for extra money. She asks me to do it and I go along."

Grigori gave a contemptuous snort, and they all looked at him. Szarnakov said, "What do you know of this?"

"Nothing, boss. I know the girls turn a lot of tricks. It's possible they're cheating Cyrus. If you ask me, he gives them too much freedom."

Szarnakov took a drink of vodka. He turned to Dimitri. "Call Cyrus. Tell him to come and see me tonight."

Dimitri was looking at Natasha, his dark blue eyes gleaming cold as he studied her. It occurred to Louie that he was enjoying her discomfiture. Smirking, he reached for his phone and got up. He walked over to the French doors and placed his call. Szarnakov swung back to Natasha. "Who took the videos?"

She blanched, her eyes showing sudden panic. "I do not know camera man. He's friend of Irina."

The lie was obvious. Grigori's jaw hardened, and Louie suspected he knew more than he was admitting. It was pointless to browbeat the girl. She was terrified as it was, and he was sure worse things awaited her. Louie said, "I want the hard copies and files. The camera my son was filmed with."

Szarnakov said, "And you will have them, my friend."

He studied Natasha, and then sighed, gave a dismissive wave. Natasha seized her purse and bolted upright. She gave Louie a sideways glance. "I'm sorry, mister. Your son ... Tony ... he's nice."

She rushed for the exit, stumbling in her platform heels. Grigori reached out and caught her by the wrist, and she gave a frightened squawk, wincing as his fingers bit painfully into her flesh. It didn't take a genius to figure out that Grigori was more than just a friend of Cyrus and that Natasha was seconds away from a beating. Grigori hustled her to the door. Flinging it open, he shoved Natasha ahead of him. She tripped and fell, landing on her hands and knees.

Grigori yanked Natasha up by the hair. She shrieked, and then Victor was on his feet and moving toward the door, getting there just as Grigori stood Natasha upright. Nudging his way in between them, Victor clamped his hand on Natasha's shoulder and said, "Sorry, buddy, she's with me."

"The fuck she is."

Ignoring Grigori, Victor propelled Natasha through the door. "Come on, doll. Let's go."

Grigori started to go after them and Szarnakov barked out one harsh, guttural word, and Grigori halted in mid-step. He turned sulkily, gave Louie a hard look. Szarnakov saw and disapproved, his mouth forming a grim line.

Perceiving the whole thing as entertainment, Dimitri said to Louie, "Your friend is sentimental, but he needn't be. Every now and then these whores need a beating to keep them in line."

Chapter Fifteen

LOUIE LEARNED NOTHING ELSE FROM Szarnakov. In fact, the entire subject was dropped, transitioned easily when the food arrived. Franco's waiters laid it out on the buffet table, and Szarnakov's entourage was let in, his guards taking positions around the room. Franco and Kimmie came in to assist with the serving.

Two of the young women, one of whom was Oriental, sat on either side of Szarnakov, crossing their legs toward him. The third girl squeezed herself into the narrow space next to Louie and gave him an inviting smile. She was blonde with a tanning-bed tan and oversized breasts. The rest of her was too thin, bony hips emphasized in a tight red skirt. Her eyes were bright and manic, the tip of her nose reddened, as though she had a cold. She told Louie she was a "wild girl," and liked to have "a good time."

She amused him for a few minutes. Dimitri came over, smiling. He held a small plate spread with cocktail sauce, Gulf-sized shrimp, and tangy bites of tenderloin. He sat on the couch to the left of Louie and set his plate on the coffee table. His eyes slid over the girl's body. They were both blonde, hers streaked with different shades of yellow and gold, Dimitri's more natural. She stiffened at his presence. "Don't look at me like that, Dimitri."

"Why not? You're a slut—you've said so yourself." He smiled, but his eyes were cold. "My offer still stands."

She laughed shortly. "It's too bad you're such a fucking pervert, Dimitri. You're really a good looking man. But in case you don't know by now, I'm not into pain. I just like to fuck."

The girl got up and walked over to the buffet table, where her friends were gathering. The room was fragrant with food. Somebody opened the door to the balcony, and a warm, scented breeze blew in. Dimitri dipped shrimp into the cocktail sauce and put it in his mouth, wiping his fingers on a napkin. He chewed and swallowed, and then said, "Sergei tells me not to underestimate you, but he doesn't tell me why." Again, he gave Louie a chilly smile. "My sources tell me you're a dangerous man."

Louie said, "It's possible your sources are wrong."

Dimitri laughed. "No, they're never wrong." He bit into another piece of shrimp and chewed it. His teeth were very white. "I lived in Palermo for a few years," he said. "I understand Sicilians." He looked at Louie, studying him. "You're American, but blood is blood. And people tell me you're Sicilian."

Louie laughed. He asked Dimitri about living in Sicily. He was not surprised to learn that Dimitri had worked in the "heroin" trade. He'd also been fleeing a bit of trouble in Moscow, assuming a new identity while in Italy. He admitted that his old enemies knew where he was, though they didn't dare touch him while he was under Szarnakov's protection. His candor surprised Louie. With an amused glance at the party girl who had flagrantly rebuffed him, Dimitri told Louie of a recent visit to Istanbul where he'd purchased a girl at a private auction. With a calculating smile, he recounted that the entire experience, particularly the training, was "exquisite."

Louie had a feeling things had ended poorly for Dimitri's concubine, and he was glad when Victor returned. Stepping up to the bar, Victor accepted a drink from the barmaid, and then he wandered over to the couch, claiming the open space on the other side of Dimitri, who said, "I hope you got something for your trouble, my friend."

From across the room Grigori's pale eyes burned holes in Victor. He was staring so hard at Victor that somebody could have held a gun to Szarnakov's head and he wouldn't have noticed. His attitude was getting to Louie. When Dimitri got up, Victor slid into his vacated spot and told Louie that Grigori was from Brighton Beach, born and raised in the Russian community. He was more than a friend of Szarnakov's cousin; they were business partners. "Drugs and women," said Victor. "He's Natasha's manager, hers and Irina's."

Later, Victor would tell Louie that Grigori lived in Fort Lauderdale. He got nasty when he drank, sometimes beating Natasha but most often Irina, who was considered "his girl." Grigori knew all about the blackmailing operation because he'd implemented it, choosing victims by their wealth and vulnerability. He particularly liked when the girls catered to a john's fantasies, as they had done with Tony. Rich guys were always willing to pay to make those kinds of pictures go away. The caveat here was that Grigori never hit a guy up for more than five or ten grand. He knew better than to push it. Surprisingly, Natasha admitted that she and Irina, along with an unnamed "friend," decided to approach Tony a second time, thus, they double-crossed Grigori, which was a dangerous thing to do.

Natasha told Victor she was certain Cyrus didn't know any of this. Cyrus was a creep but an honest one, with a large stable of Eastern European girls and a reputation to uphold. He'd never been overtly cruel with them, but now Natasha worried that he would hurt them badly, maybe even kill them. And if he didn't, Grigori was certain to.

Victor got everything out of Natasha except the one thing Louie wanted, the equipment and videos. "Natasha told me she didn't know the camera-man, said Grigori arranged it all. But I got the sense she was lying to protect someone, probably the third member of her blackmailing party. She's pretty shaken up and scared. I offered her a way out, told her I could make a few phone calls, get her someplace safe and out of the life, but Natasha said she had to warn Irina while there was still time."

Victor would tell this to Louie in the car on the drive back to Delray Beach. In the VIP room with Szarnakov, Louie could only speculate. But Szarnakov knew more than he'd let on, and he certainly disapproved of Grigori's attitude even more than Louie. In fact, at one point, disgusted with the hostility his bodyguard was projecting toward his friends, Szarnakov got up, walked over to Grigori, and slapped him.

Activity in the room instantly ceased. The barmaid froze in her duties, the waiters stared. The chatter of the young women halted, their male companions cringing outright. Even Dimitri's self-satisfied smile faded. Anticipating trouble, the other three guards edged closer, one of them drawing his gun and pointing it at Grigori, who stood white-faced, fists balled impotently at his sides.

Szarnakov said something in Russian and Grigori's pale, lashless eyelids twitched. Thrusting a hand into Grigori's unbuttoned coat, Szarnakov lifted his gun from its nylon holster. He removed the clip, sliding it into his own pocket. Then he tossed the gun onto the coffee table, where it landed noisily on a tray of oysters, scattering spinach-topped shells in all directions. Szarnakov said something to the guard holding the gun, who then gestured at Grigori, and he and another of Szarnakov's bodyguards led him toward the door.

Szarnakov returned to his seat, apologizing to Louie for his man's insolence. Louie assured him it was no problem. Looking up, he saw Grigori staring at him with unbridled hatred. Then he saw him make eye contact with Dimitri, saw some silent communication pass between them. A second later the guards hustled Grigori out.

Everybody went back to what they were doing, the noise level returning to a civilized buzz. One of the servers started to clean up the oysters, some of which had splattered onto the floor. Szarnakov picked up his drink. "He offends me."

Louie said, "I found him rather unpleasant myself."

He looked at Grigori's gun, observing that it was a Walther PPK. Louie had never owned a Walther, but this didn't stop him from admiring it. Dimitri, amusement restored, leaned over and picked up the weapon. He flashed Louie a smile. "It's a nice weapon, isn't it? I've always admired German ingenuity. In fact, Adolf Hitler killed himself with a Walther PPK."

Chapter Sixteen

ARRIVING HOME THAT EVENING, LOUIE walked into a houseful of women. Two of Angie's sisters were visiting, along with one niece and two great-nieces. Grouped around the kitchen table, the adults were alternately playing cards and gossiping about the family members who weren't present. The little girls had a Barbie house set up on the family room floor. Pizzas topped with sauce and grated Parmesan were cooling on the counter. Louie eyed the pizzas with sudden appetite, his mouth watering at the combined smells of Maria's sweet sauce and homemade dough, the crust thin and crisp, browned along the edges.

Louie greeted his family. He devoured his first slice of pizza while standing at the counter. Maria made a place for him at the table by shooing away one of the nieces. *"Mangia, mangia,"* she said, bringing him an ice-cold Peroni before admonishing Angie for failing to execute even this smallest duty.

Louie sat in a sea of chattering women. Isabella climbed onto his lap, snuggling into the crook of his arm. Stella snapped a picture of him and Isabella, passing her phone around the table so they could all view it. Angie's sisters flattered Louie. Angie was one of five daughters. None of her sisters had married men who did particularly well for themselves, and through the years Louie had advanced down payments, contributed to college funds, sent his nieces and nephews on trips, paid for weddings and funerals. Jealous of Angie's wealth, the sisters might be spiteful with her on occasion, but they were always gracious to Louie.

It was getting late. Stella took Isabella upstairs, but the little girl wouldn't go to bed until Louie kissed her goodnight. He went upstairs and watched fondly as she and Stella knelt on the floor by the bed and said a little prayer. When mother and daughter rose, Louie walked in and sat on the side of the bed. Wearing a white nightgown embroidered with pink rosettes, Isabella perched on his knee. Taking her in his arms, Louie called her *"bella principessa,"* his beautiful princess.

She beamed and kissed him on the cheek, her small arms looped about his neck. "I love Mama best, then you, then Nonna."

It was after two when Angie pattered quietly into Louie's room. Having given her own bed to her sisters, she'd planned on sleeping with Louie. He woke when she slid beneath the sheets.

Louie got up and went to the bathroom. When he returned, Angie was propped on pillows, Gigi snuggled against her side. Louie had fallen asleep watching the Military Channel, and on the screen the London blitz was being reenacted in black and white. Using the remote, Angie lowered the volume and then held up her wrist, her new bracelet gleaming in the gray light. "Thanks for the bracelet, Louie. It's lovely."

He crawled into bed, drawing the covers over him. Angie smelled of expensive face cream and lavender-scented talcum. Louie said, "Did you have a good time with your sisters?"

"Umm, yes. Vera never stops talking." She looked over at him. "Are you still mad at me about Chester?"

"I don't recall ever being mad."

"He wanted to take me to lunch tomorrow, but I declined. Does that make you happy?"

"Immensely."

She laughed softly. "My God, you *are* jealous."

The television flickered, the light in the room going bright, and then blinking into darkness. Angie resettled herself, curling her body towards him. "Tony and Gina stopped by this afternoon. Tony seemed a little subdued. He said he's taking a week off. They're going to Cape Hatteras with the kids."

Louie closed his eyes. Gigi's small body pressed against his leg. Angie said, "Are you going to tell me what's going on with Tony? And don't tell me he's fine because I know there is something wrong. I'm worried about him."

"Don't be worried, baby. Tony's going to be okay. He had a little problem, but I took care of it for him." Louie rolled onto his side, his arm going about her waist. "Go to sleep. Everything's fine now. You have nothing to worry about."

Chapter Seventeen

BY THE TIME LOUIE GOT up on Monday, Angie's family
had left and Angie was at yoga class. He called Victor
and told him to take the day off, and then he went out
to the pool for his swim. Angie returned as he was finishing his
laps. They cleaned up and went for a late breakfast at Poppies in
Delray Beach. Afterwards, they drove over to The Little Gym on
Jog Road and watched Isabella flit around in a white tutu with a
dozen aspiring ballerinas.

Louie popped in the office around four. After making a dozen
calls, he signed the documents Emily put in front of him. Then he
looked at the results of the property search he'd requested on the
studio apartment at the Ocean Breeze Hotel. As he'd learned from
Tony, the unit was owned by one Theodore Jones. No surprise
here. The eighty-five year old regularly rented out the studio. Two
months ago a six-month lease had been assigned to A.J. Molinsky.

The name threw Louie. He'd been expecting that Cyrus Panatev
or even Grigori Buzeczki would have rented the apartment. But

Molinsky was the name of the drugged up photographer he'd met at Albert Seymour's studio, and, suddenly, Louie knew who had taken the pictures and video of Tony.

Louie was about to call Victor and reveal this startling bit of information when Victor phoned him. Louie related his news about Molinsky's name being on the lease, and Victor said, "No shit. The dumb kid was all hopped up. I don't think he has two nickels to rub together, so he's obviously fronting for the Russians. I assume they're supplying him. I'll call Seymour and see if I can get the rundown on Molinsky."

Before hanging up with Louie, Victor told him Chucky had provided the physical addresses that corresponded to the IP addresses used in the threatening e-mails. Victor intended on checking them out tomorrow. He did not relay the locations to Louie.

Emily's light was blinking on Louie's desk phone. Saying a quick good-bye to Victor, Louie pressed his intercom button and said, "Yes, Emily?"

"Mr. Morelli," Emily cleared her throat, giving a loud, "Ahem," and Louie knew she was not pleased. "Miss Richards is here to see you."

"Who?"

Immediately, Louie heard Rachel say, "My God, he knows who I am. He better not play that game with me."

Louie couldn't stop the smile that sprang to his lips, and he said, "Emily, tell Miss Richards to come in," his tone conveying amusement.

Rachel had the door opened before Louie could get out of his chair. Then he forgot his manners and sat back, watching her strut toward him in the tiniest pair of pink shorts he'd ever seen. They were made of a cheap stretch-knit fabric, slung low beneath her belly and cut high on her thighs, exposing almost as much ass as her bikini had done. She'd paired the shorts with a white scoop-necked tank-top with spaghetti straps and a cropped waist, revealing a good three inches of skin between the top and shorts.

The tank had a built-in support bra, but it didn't quite do the job, and Rachel's breasts threatened to spill over. Her black hair was flipped up at the neck, her long bangs swept to the right side of her forehead. She wore the diamond ear-studs he'd bought her in George Town, and a dozen silvery link-bracelets, equally divided between her wrists. High-heeled sling-back sandals and a wallet-sized clutch completed her attire.

"Wow," Louie let out a low whistle. "Jesus, baby, what are you wearing? My granddaughter has shorts bigger than yours."

"Pooh," she waved an airy hand, making her bracelets clink. "What's the point of doing those dreadful butt-busting exercises if I can't show off the results? I know I have a nice ass."

"It's better than nice." Louie's eyes slid over her. "It's outstanding."

She came around the side of his desk, pirouetting, so he could get a better look at her treasured derriere. Louie slid back his chair, turning it sideways to face her. Rachel stepped between his feet. Leaning forward, she balanced her hands on his shoulders. "I'm so happy I'm your girl, Louie. You're not mad I stopped in, are you?"

He slid his hands up the backs of her thighs, fingers poking beneath the thin layer of fabric. Then her ass was in his hands and he gave a little squeeze and said, "Mmm." Her breasts were pressed against his face, and he smelled vanilla-scented skin. Now his blood was hot, and he smacked her playfully on that magnificent ass. "Baby, you're killing me."

Rachel drew back, giving him an enigmatic smile, eyes twinkling. "You can spank me if you want," she said. "I'd love it if you took me over your knee—"

She'd left the door ajar, but now, suddenly, it closed with a violent thud. Rachel looked at Louie, startled, and he said, "You're going to get me in trouble. What are you doing here anyhow?"

"I was in the neighborhood and thought I'd drop by."

This was a lie. Rachel lived in Boynton Beach. Not terribly far, but not quite like "being in the neighborhood." Her eyes swept his office, alighting on the couch. She'd been to his office before, briefly, but Louie hadn't been alone with her. She said, "Have you ever had sex in here?"

"I'm not in the habit of entertaining women in my office."

"Maybe you ought to try." She straddled him, her knees resting on the outside of his hips, pelvis thrusting forward. She reached her hand down between them, touching him. Her eyes opened wide. She said, "Ah, you're hard," and drew in a quick, ragged breath. "I love when a man gets big. With Buddy, I always had to wait for the Viagra to kick in." She had both hands between them now, unbuckling his belt and tugging on his zipper. "I'm going to the best girl you ever had."

Louie preferred leisurely sex. What he had with Rachel was what most people call a "quickie." He didn't mind at all, thought the element of danger added a certain spark. Afterward, she purred contentedly, pouring them both a drink. She sat on the side of his desk, sipping vodka and water, and told Louie the real reason she had stopped by. "I don't want to be an alarmist," she said. "But Jolene had a problem with Wayne."

"Wayne." Drowsy from sex, Louie did not remember who Wayne was.

Rachel rolled her eyes. "Jolene's boyfriend," she said. "Remember, she was talking about him on the plane. His name is Wayne Rawlins, and if that doesn't tell you he's a redneck, nothing will. He's a deputy sheriff in Osceola County, and it's like his dream job, let me tell you. He gets to carry a gun and harass people. He's such an ass. Do you know when Jolene got home last night, Wayne was waiting for her?"

"How would I know this?"

"Well, you wouldn't. But Jolene should have expected it. Wayne busted in on her and started accusing her of cheating on him. She told me being with Victor helped her make the decision not to see Wayne anymore. She said Victor was sweet with her, and she realizes that's how a man should treat a woman. So she broke up with Wayne, or tried to … he was furious and went berserk. Jolene was terrified he was going to kill her. Thankfully, her neighbors called the police."

"Is Jolene okay?"

"He beat her up—she has a black eye and some bruises. This morning she went over to the court and applied for a restraining order against him. The bad thing is crazy Wayne went through her purse and found the card Victor had given her."

"What card?"

"Victor gave Jolene a business card so that she could get in touch with him. So Wayne knows Victor's name, and he knows that he works here. He accused her of having a long-standing affair with Victor, which Jolene denied. But Wayne's convinced Victor is the reason Jolene broke up with him, and he's making a lot of noise about it. In fact, Wayne told Jolene he was going to shoot her lover. If that's not bad enough, Wayne didn't show up for work today. He's on the afternoon shift—he was due in at three. The sheriff was alarmed enough to call Jolene about it."

Louie was not a computer aficionado, but even he'd had to learn how to navigate the Internet, and after Rachel left, he powered up the glitzy laptop that was more frequently used by Victor to check horse racing stats. Louie did a Google search and discovered that Sheriff Warren of Osceola County was fifty-four years old and had been re-elected to a second term last year. Sheriff Warren's picture was on the screen. Years ago all Southern sheriffs had looked like hard-asses. Nowadays they tended to resemble high school football coaches, and Sheriff "Duke" Warren was no exception.

Louie called the sheriff directly, giving his name to the desk clerk. He was not surprised to find that he was patched through immediately. The sheriff came on the line; "Warren here," he said crisply.

Louie said, "Sheriff Warren, this is Lou Morelli. I'm a real estate developer—"

Warren might have been short on patience, but he was not discourteous. "I know who you are, Mr. Morelli."

"Sheriff, it's just come to my attention that one of your deputies has stated his intention of shooting one of my employees—"

Again, Warren interrupted Louie. "I'm aware of the situation, Mr. Morelli. Wayne Rawlins suffered a setback and overreacted. He's been put on temporary leave pending an investigation—"

Now it was Louie's turn to break in. "I understand Rawlins was scheduled for the afternoon shift and didn't show up for work. Was this before or after you placed him on leave?"

Warren's tone hardened. "It was decided before his shift that Rawlins would be placed on leave. I wanted to talk to him in person."

"Have you spoken with him?"

"Do you think I don't know how to do my job? I sent a car over to Wayne's house to check on him and relieve him of his weapon. The situation has been defused, Mr. Morelli."

"I meant no disrespect, Sheriff. And I'm glad to hear you're proactive. Obviously, I'm concerned. I don't want an enraged deputy down here shooting at my employee—"

"Does DeAngelis work for you?"

"Yes."

"Well, thanks for filling me in. I heard he was an enforcer for a New Orleans syndicate."

"It sounds like you've been misinformed, Sheriff."

"Mr. Morelli, I appreciate your concern. I really do. Let me reassure you that Wayne Rawlins is being disciplined for his actions. He has some anger management issues and the department is providing counseling for him. I'll even go one step further and promise you that I'm personally keeping an eye on Wayne. I've spoken with him, and he has expressed remorse. Mr. DeAngelis has nothing to fear from Deputy Rawlins, and this is not the time to take matters into your own hands. I would caution you to remember that this is a law enforcement issue."

"Indeed, that's why I called you. I'm a law-abiding citizen, Sheriff."

Chapter Eighteen

LOUIE CALLED VICTOR TO APPRISE him of Deputy Rawlins's threats. Victor had his thirty-eight footer, *Happy Hour*, docked at The Sands Patio Bar in Pompano and couldn't discuss the details of Rawlins's obsession on account of the fact that he was having dinner with his wife.

No matter. Louie delivered his message. He felt a nagging sense that, despite Sheriff Warren's assurances to the contrary, he hadn't heard the last of Rawlins. Still, he wasn't overly concerned. It wasn't as though Victor couldn't take care of himself. But a hotheaded deputy sheriff could pose unwanted complications, and it was best to be forewarned.

With these thoughts in mind, Louie gathered his mobile phones and prepared to leave his office. It was now six-thirty, and the blaze of sun outside his windows had faded to a soft, mellow light, with a light breeze rustling the palm fronds in the courtyard. Stepping out of his office, Louie was surprised to see Emily at her desk.

Emily never worked past five. True, she didn't appear to be working, as she was absently rubbing an emery board over a fingernail. Her Coach bag was placed in front of her on the desk, signaling intent to leave. A small cardboard box held magazines and coffee cups, along with a bud vase and a picture frame.

Louie saw the jumbled contents of the box without identifying any of it. He was more concerned for Emily. "What are you still doing here?" he asked.

"I'm waiting for Wanda to pick me up." Wanda was Emily's sister. "It's movie night," explained Emily. "We're going to the theater at Mizner Park."

"What are you going to see?"

"It's Wanda's pick tonight, so I'm not sure. There are several contenders." She set the emery board in her top drawer, and fixed a discerning eye on him. "Mr. Morelli, please forgive me for saying so, but your reputation suffers when you receive women like Miss Richards. "

By Louie's reckoning Emily was only about fourteen years older than Rachel, but the gulf between the two women seemed generational. Louie said, "Emily, I can forgive anything you say to me. I'm sorry Rachel Richards offended you. Was it something she said?"

"She told me her business with you was personal."

Louie grinned, and Emily said huffily, "I was quite disturbed by her lack of modesty."

Louie thought the discussion of Rachel had gone far enough, and he gestured at the box, saying facetiously, "Is that why you're packing?"

Emily gave Louie a stern look. "Actually, it's Adriana McIntyre's personal effects." She caught the look of surprise on his face and added, "I can only imagine how distraught she must have been not to return to work on Friday. I *know* she needed this job. Look," she leaned forward, lifting the picture frame from the box and presenting it to Louie. It was a cheap, double plastic frame, with the photograph on the left showing a young girl in a First Communion dress. The child was blonde and blue-eyed, obviously Adriana's daughter. The picture on the right showed the girl posing beside a Golden Retriever.

Louie took the frame from Emily, briefly studied the pictures, and then returned it to the box. He felt a sense of disquiet, a nagging feeling that Adriana had quit a job she badly needed because of him. Apparently, Emily was of this same opinion, for she smiled grimly at his discomfort. "Adriana has a lovely little girl. I'm sure she must regret parting with such precious pictures, so I'm going to drop the box off at the employment agency in the morning. This way Adriana will be spared further distress."

Louie caught Emily's eye, saw she was judging him unfavorably. Emily said, "Mr. Morelli, Adriana is going through a difficult divorce. Did it ever occur to you that she might be at a particularly vulnerable point in her life?"

Fifteen minutes later Louie pulled up to a pink-bricked ranch on NE 5th Avenue. Unlike Naples's chic 5th Avenue shopping district, Boca Raton's version was an older residential street tucked between Federal and Dixie Highways. 5th Avenue ran parallel to Federal, the first street on the right after Louie turned into the sub, easily designated on Chucky's map by the landmark Boca Raton Plaza Hotel.

Louie guessed the house dated from the sixties. The gray, shingled roof was new, but the asphalt on the driveway was fragmented with cracks. A jacaranda tree decorated the front yard, and giant orange daylilies were planted on both sides of the front step. The narrow, single-car garage was attached to the house on the right, its door closed, but Adriana's Ford Fusion was in the drive and Louie knew he had the right house.

Honey bees were buzzing over the lilies when Louie stepped onto the porch. From inside the house he heard the sound of the television, and then he rang the bell and a dog began barking. A woman said, "Down Trixie," in an aggrieved tone, and then the door opened, and he was looking through the screen at Adriana's mother, Margaret Peterson.

Louie knew the property owner was listed as Margaret Peterson, and he assumed this was Adriana's mother because the resemblance was striking. It was the way Adriana would look at sixty, if she cut her hair short and added bleached highlights. Mrs. Peterson wore frameless eyeglasses, squinting suspiciously at him through the lenses. Her face was sun-damaged, with dark pigment splotches.

Mrs. Peterson wore a white-mesh cover-up over a pink-checked swimsuit. She was busty, but otherwise slender. The Golden Retriever pressing her muzzle to the screen beside her was the same one Louie had seen in the photograph. Trixie was not much of a watchdog. The barking had ceased as soon as Mrs. Peterson opened the door. Now the tail was wagging, the dog regarding Louie as a potential playmate.

Standing there with Emily's cardboard box tucked under his left arm, Louie said, "Mrs. Peterson?" At her nod, he continued, "I'm Lou Morelli. I was hoping to have a word with your daughter. Is Adriana here?"

Holding Trixie's collar with one hand, Mrs. Peterson opened the screen door with the other. "Come in."

He stepped into a small foyer. A full wall was on Louie's left, with a round mirror centered above a console table. A living room was to his immediate right. The décor was dated, the white laminate end tables straight from the eighties. Mauve carpet covered the floor, with the floral-print couch and chairs reflecting this color. A forty-inch flat screen was set on a TV stand, the screen flashing images of one of the Kardashian girls with an overweight rapper.

As soon as Louie stepped in, Mrs. Peterson allowed the screen-door to slam shut. She let go of Trixie's collar and closed the entry door, shutting out the thick, summer heat. Inside, it was pleasantly cool. Louie held the box toward Mrs. Peterson. "Adriana left some personal things at the office. My secretary was particularly concerned lest Adriana lose pictures of her daughter. She felt certain these would be missed."

Mrs. Peterson took the box from Louie and set it on the floor. Trixie circled his legs, sniffing, and Louie patted her on the head. Mrs. Peterson said, "I'm Adriana's mother. You can call me Maggie."

"You look like a Maggie."

"My first husband used to call me Meg, but that was a long time ago." Maggie gave him an appraising look. "Adriana told me you were good looking. You're a confident man, too. I can tell."

Maggie had the air of a woman who was comfortable with men, but in a practical, no-nonsense way. Gesturing to Louie, she said, "Come on in and have a seat. Adriana just stepped into the shower, but I'll let her know you're here."

A glance down the carpeted hallway revealed three open doors and one closed. From behind the closed door came a faint sound of running water. Louie followed Maggie into the kitchen, where a dining area was split from the workspace by a Formica-topped counter. A combination sunroom and family room was off the kitchen, and it was here that Maggie led him.

The floor was tiled in white ceramic. Windows overlooked a backyard full of scrub-grass and overgrown bushes. A green velour couch sat on the back wall, facing an entertainment center. A computer desk was in the corner. Here Adriana's daughter sat, her blonde hair plaited into pigtails. She turned away from the monitor, her blue eyes studying him curiously. Like her grandmother, she was wearing a bathing suit. Hers was green and white, a two-piece style with a long top, what Angie called a "tankini."

Maggie said, "Darcy, this is Mr. Morelli. He's a friend of your mother's."

Louie said, "Hi, Darcy."

She looked away without saying anything, returning to her computer. Maggie said, "Darcy, where are your manners? Say hello to the gentleman."

Darcy looked up shyly. "Hi." Then she turned to Maggie, and pointing at the computer, said, "Grandma, I can't get online."

"I can't do anything about that now, Missy. It'll do you good to walk away from that thing."

"Can we get a new computer?"

Maggie didn't answer but turned back through the kitchen and went into the hallway. Louie heard her knocking on the bathroom door. Loudly, speaking above the shower, she said, "Adriana, shut off that water. Your friend is here."

The water shut off, pipes screeching. "What friend?"

"Morelli. From that job."

"What?" Adriana sounded panicked. "He doesn't know where I live."

"Well, he's here. He wants to talk to you."

"Mom—"

"I was just going to take Darcy swimming."

Louie looked at Darcy. "You're going swimming, huh?"

"Yeah. We go to the hotel on the corner. They got a nice pool. There's a gate that opens to the parking lot, so we can sneak in. Nobody ever notices."

Stepping further into the room, Louie walked to the sliding door and looked out at a concrete slab. "Do you like to swim?"

"It's my favorite thing to do. Sometimes we go to the beach."

Maggie reentered the kitchen. "Darcy, get your shoes on so we can go. And don't forget your towel."

Darcy looked at Louie and grinned. She stood, bare feet hitting the tile. "Grandma, Sally posted pictures of her kitten, and I can't even go online to see them. We have to get a new computer. Can we?"

"Heavens, no. You'll have to wait until your uncle comes around. He'll know how to fix it."

"I don't think so," said Darcy. "Besides, Adam doesn't come over anymore."

Darcy gave Louie a final look and then walked through the kitchen, heading the opposite way, toward a back hallway. Louie turned to Maggie. "If this is not a good time—"

"She's coming," said Maggie. "Give her a few minutes. You want some lemonade? I make mine from scratch, the old-fashioned way."

"Lemonade sounds good."

The kitchen appliances were gleaming white. Stacked on the counter next to the sink were dirty dishes from the family's last meal. Louie watched Maggie open the refrigerator and reach for a pitcher. Trixie walked up to Louie, and he looked down and patted her.

"She's a pest," said Maggie. "Always looking for attention."

Louie smiled. "Don't they all?" He gave Trixie another pat. "I like dogs."

Louie's phone vibrated in his pocket, and he took it out and looked at it. Angie's name was flashing on the display pad, and he returned the phone to his pocket without answering it. He studied the room he was in, noting some quality prints on the walls, including an acrylic painting of a secluded stretch of beach at Spanish River Park. The play of light and water evoked a feeling of serenity. In the bottom right hand corner of the painting the artist had signed: Adam.

Maggie came back into the room with a glass of lemonade. She said, "My son painted that when he was eighteen."

"He's very talented."

"Oh, yes. Adam's gifted. His first love is painting, but he got a free ride at Miami International University of Art and Design. Got a master's in Fine Arts."

"You must be very proud of him."

"Well...yes." Her hesitation was palpable. She handed Louie the glass. "Here's your lemonade."

Louie took a sip, nodding his approval. "It's good. Not too tart."

He sat on the green couch, setting his glass on the coffee table in front of him. Next to the couch an end table showcased a variety of family photographs. Maggie selected one, handing it to Louie. It showed two tow-headed children with a tall blonde man. "That's Adriana and Adam with my first husband, Walter. You knew Adriana was a twin, didn't you?"

"No, I didn't," said Louie, noting the resemblance between the children in the photo.

"That's the last picture with their dad. Walter died in an accident soon after it was taken. The twins were seven at the time."

"How awful," said Louie.

"What can you do? We had a rough time, but I met my second husband a few years later and eventually remarried. No kids with the second marriage, though." Louie handed the picture back to Maggie, and though he had not asked, she said, "Jack died three years ago." She sighed. "I'm sixty-two years old, and I've buried two husbands."

"I'm sorry for your loss."

Darcy walked into the kitchen with a beach bag. "Grandma, I'm ready."

Louie said, "Enjoy your swim."

Maggie nodded. "Adriana should be out any minute." She set the picture down and moved toward her granddaughter, swiping a straw handbag off the kitchen counter and turning back to say, "Nice meeting you."

They left through a back door. Louie heard the garage door whirring as it opened. Louie sat in the sunroom with the dog. Maggie had neglected to turn off the television in the front room, and Louie heard ABC's *World News* starting. Louie drank some lemonade, and then pulled out his phone and called Angie.

"Hi," she said, answering.

"You called."

"Mama's making pepper steak. She said you told her you'd be home for dinner."

"I will be home in about thirty, forty minutes."

"Okay, we'll wait for you."

Adriana rounded the corner, stepping from the hallway and into the kitchen. Louie said, "Angie, I have another call. I'll see you when I get home."

He tucked the phone back into his pocket, rising as Adriana came into the room, her hastily combed wet hair tucked behind her ears. She wore jean shorts and a yellow T-shirt with flip-flops. She'd managed some lipstick, and a dusting of bronze blusher sparkled on her cheeks, a faint smell of Dove soap clinging to her. Staring aghast at him, Adriana said, "Louie, what are you doing here?"

"Was it something I said?"

"How did you find me?"

"It wasn't too difficult." He touched her gently on the arm. "Look, I'm sorry to bust in on you like this. I would have phoned if I thought you would have taken my call. Can we sit a minute and talk?"

They sat on the couch, an awkward space between them. Trixie perched on the floor by Louie and put her head on his knee. He stroked her between the ears. "She likes you," said Adriana.

"Trixie's a nice dog." Louie turned to Adriana. "I came to see if you were okay, offer my apologies—"

She sank back onto the couch, deflated. "You didn't do anything wrong. It's me. I was…am…confused."

"I realize that. Emily made me aware that you're at a vulnerable point in your life. I feel as though I took advantage of you."

"Hah." She snorted. "I led you on. I wanted you to notice me." She gazed out the window, looking at the overgrown yard. "I wanted to be cool and sophisticated. Men play around, and I thought, why shouldn't I? But the other night—it was really good." Her voice cracked. "My husband wasn't that attentive to me, and I could see myself falling for you, and well…I can't put myself through that."

"I understand." Louie sipped lemonade, let the silence stretch out. "I know you really needed your job. Do you want it back?"

Adriana shook her head. Her hair was curling, turning glossy gold as it dried. "No." She cast her eyes downward. "I couldn't work for you. Not after all this. The agency is sending me to Office Depot next week. They have something available at their headquarters. It could be permanent."

"If it doesn't work out, give me a call."

"Thanks, Louie." She gave him a tentative smile. "I'm sorry…you must think I'm a nutcase."

Louie patted her hand. "No apologies." His phone was vibrating, and he pulled it out of his pocket: Angie. He took a drink of lemonade, gave Trixie a friendly rub, and stood. "I have to go."

She walked him through the kitchen and into the living room. When they reached the front door, Adriana said, "Dick Weinstein told me you're all mobbed up. That's how he said it. Mobbed up."

Louie said, "My father was connected back in the day. Those rumors have been following me my whole life."

Chapter Nineteen

WHEN LOUIE ARRIVED HOME, TONY was sitting at the kitchen counter, nervously clutching a bottle of Pellegrino. He was in shorts and sandals, his blue-plaid shirt opened at the collar. He looked better than he had on Friday night, but Louie saw the undisguised tension in his face. Tony was talking to Maria, who stood at the stove, peppers and steak simmering in a cast-iron skillet. Maria was wearing one of Victor's big aprons over her housedress, the hem of which nearly touched the floor.

Five places were set at the oblong table in the breakfast nook, including one place setting with a Disney Princess for Isabella, and Angie was adding a sixth for Tony, laying down a ceramic plate as Louie entered. She signaled him with her eyes, and he went over and kissed her. The dogs were in the kitchen, converging on Louie as they smelled Trixie. For a few minutes everything was normal, and then Louie set a hand on Tony's shoulder and said, "Let's go in the library."

Tony had been trying to behave as though nothing was wrong in front of his mother and grandmother, but now, plopping down on the armchair in the library, he turned anxious eyes to his father.

Louie said, "What's wrong, son?"

"Dad, it's awful. I saw it on the news...they didn't say it was her, but they showed the body—"

"You're going too fast. Slow down and tell me what happened."

"I put the news on after dinner. The body of an unidentified female was found in a drainage ditch in Dania Beach. They didn't give too many details except to say that the victim was blonde and appeared to be in her early twenties. The police said the body has a distinctive butterfly tattoo on the navel." Tony paused, looking nervously at Louie. "Dad, Irina has a butterfly tattoo on her navel. The police are asking for help in identifying her. Do you think I should—?"

"No," said Louie abruptly. "I don't think you should do anything, least of all talk to the police."

"I can't shake the thought that it's her. She was beaten to death. If I can give a positive identification, it might help the police solve her murder."

"And what are you going to say? You were her john, and she was blackmailing you? For God's sake, Tony, start thinking with your head."

"So I'm supposed to go about my life and forget Irina was murdered?"

Louie said, "I have a pretty good idea of who killed her."

Tony's head snapped up. "What?"

"Look, I made some inquiries about your situation. I met with Sergei Szarnakov yesterday—"

"The Russian gangster? You *know* him?"

Louie didn't say anything because he was trying to figure out how he had raised a son this clueless. He stepped over to the bar and poured an inch of Famous Grouse into a glass. He looked at Tony, "Do you want anything?"

"Not Scotch."

Louie swallowed back the malt whiskey, located Victor's bottle of Kentucky bourbon and poured Tony a shot. Handing it to him, he said, "I met your friend Natasha last night. She told Victor some things. Do you know anything about a bald Russian named Grigori, talks with a Brooklyn accent?"

Tony downed his shot, wincing as the whiskey burned his throat. He shook his head. "The only Russians I know are women."

Angie tapped on the door and then opened it, poking her head in. "Mama has the food on the table."

"Go ahead and start without us," said Louie. "We'll be there in a minute." He waited until she closed the door, and then he turned to Tony. "I don't want you to do a damned thing about this. Do you understand me? No phone calls to the police or scared little hookers. You keep yourself out of this—"

"What if the police find the video of me?"

"I don't think you need to concern yourself with that. I know who the photographer is. I'll get to him before the police."

Tony's eyes widened. "Dad, I don't want anyone else dying because I was dumb enough to let myself be compromised."

Louie said, "Now you're insulting me. If anybody else dies, it's not going to be by my hand. And I'm glad you've admitted to your stupidity. Now, let's go to the table."

"I can't eat."

"I want you to behave like there's nothing wrong. Your mother doesn't need to be worrying about you."

"Dad—"

"Look, I know this is difficult for you. But you have to trust me. I want you to get up tomorrow and take your family on vacation as planned."

"Dad, how can you—? Doesn't the fact that a girl was killed because of me bother you?"

"Don't assume she was killed because of you."

"She's dead, killed brutally. Doesn't that bother you?"

"It bothers me more than you think. But my main concern is for my family. Don't forget, it's *you* I'm protecting, Tony. You and *your* family."

Chapter Twenty

LOUIE DIDN'T CARE FOR THE town of Lake Worth. True, it bordered South Palm Beach and had a historic district with ancient trees and a quaint Spanish feel, but Lake Worth had always been a hard luck town. Competing for tourists' dollars the downtown area had a smattering of bakeries and pubs, with some New Age type shops and art galleries. A large Hispanic community was comprised of Guatemalans, Mexicans, and Hondurans. There was also a prominent Haitian presence, but on a muggy Tuesday morning the people on the sidewalks in the historic section were heat-weary tourists and sun-damaged hippies.

Although the town slumbered in the heat, Victor had to circle the block a couple of times before a parking spot opened on Lake Avenue near Green Gardens Floral Shop. Victor was a pro at parallel parking and had his black XTS backed into a spot in no time, much to the relief of the sanitation truck driver who was waiting for the street to clear.

Stepping onto the sidewalk in his light summer suit, Louie felt the cloying heat instantly, remarking to Victor that it felt like New Orleans in August. Just a few miles inland, and there was no sea breeze, the air wet and sodden. Mercifully, the sky was banked with clouds, but every now and then a piercing sun broke through.

It was the kind of weather that stressed air-conditioners; nevertheless, Louie expected to feel some relief when he pushed open the door of the flower shop, but he was out of luck. A pedestal fan was circulating the air, slowly rotating back and forth. The shop smelled like a greenhouse and had more potted plants and garden statuary than fresh-cut flowers. A woman with darkly tanned skin, wearing a floppy hat and ankle-length dress was standing in front of the counter with her wallet in one hand and a loosely held leash in the other, a terrier-mix sprawled on the floor beside her. The dog perked up, ears lifting as Louie and Victor walked in. Behind the counter, Chester Morgan, who was in the process of bubble-wrapping a ceramic turtle, looked up and froze.

Chester nearly dropped the turtle. To his credit, he composed himself quickly, showing none of the apprehension that must have swept him at the sight of Louie. And, as Louie and Victor politely stepped aside, exhibiting no outward impatience, Chester went back to his task without further interruption.

Chester had a Donald Trump do, although his hair was white-gray. Despite the fact that he'd told Angie he was in his upper seventies, Louie knew he'd just turned seventy. He was good-looking in a debonair way, reminding Louie of a TV movie host, like someone who would wear smoking jackets and velvet slippers. He was of an average height, soft and thick in the middle. Today, Chester was wearing pink-plaid pants and a raspberry-colored polo shirt.

Louie knew Chester's attire was in keeping with a certain preppy look fashionable among Palm Beach elites; however, it only took Louie one glance to ascertain that he was a *finocchio*. How Angie had not been able to discern this was beyond him. Louie exchanged an amused glance with Victor, who was looking around as if he might actually be interested in something, peeking through a dusty paned-glass door at a tiny courtyard filled with flowering shrubs and statues. A spiral staircase ascended to an upper level, a shadowy form moving in front of the balcony door as Victor craned his neck to look.

Victor's hair was frizzing. He wore a cream-colored sport coat and tan slacks, strutting around the flower shop like a city inspector as he opened walk-in-coolers and peered into the back room, spotting another set of stairs. Chester eyed him warily but said nothing. He finished packing the turtle, taping up the outside of the box. He handed over the box with a polite smile. "Here you go, ma'am. I hope you enjoy it."

"I'm sure I will." The woman put her wallet back in her shoulder bag before reaching for the parcel. Then she gave a slight tug on the leash. "Come on, Felix, time to go."

Felix got up, stretched and farted, and the woman said, "Oops. Say excuse me, Felix."

Looking a little smug, Felix and his mistress ambled to the door. Victor got there first and opened it, saying "So long, Felix," and grimacing, waving a hand in front of his face as they went out.

The door whisked shut, the bell atop it jingling. Victor strode to the counter and regarded Chester with a slight smile. After a few tension-filled minutes, he said, "How you doing today, Chester? Or should I call you Fred?" At the look of alarm on Chester's face, Victor smirked. "I'm a little confused. Mrs. Morelli tells me your name is Chester Morgan, but I've got sources who say it's Fred Schroeder. Which is it?"

Chester watched apprehensively as Victor walked around the counter, coming to stand beside him. "What do you want?" he asked tremulously.

"Right now I'd like to know your name," said Victor.

"It's Chester," said Chester. "I changed my name."

"Yeah, I guess you might have had to. After all, you got busted and sent down for swindling old ladies while using the name of Fred Schroeder. It makes sense to change it, especially since you've gone back into business. Same game, different name."

"That's not true."

"Isn't it?" said Victor.

He moved behind Chester, thereby putting Chester between him and Louie, who was standing on the opposite side of the counter. Chester was aware of this ploy and acutely uncomfortable with it, eyes zigzagging between them. Then his gaze slid to a drawer beneath the cabinet and, as he seemed to be debating something, Louie pointed at the cabinet. "Victor, open that drawer."

Obligingly, Victor slid out the drawer. It was papers and pens and spools of pink and yellow ribbon, and a snub-nosed .38. Lifting the gun from the drawer, Victor said, "Lou, we've got a nice little revolver here." Pressing his thumb to the release, Victor popped open the barrel and extracted six bullets from the chambers. "Fully loaded, too," he said, scattering the bullets onto the floor behind him. He dropped the gun back into the drawer and slammed it shut. "The first gun I ever owned was a Smith and Wesson Revolver, a .38 long barrel. Nice weapon, Chester. Have you ever fired it, besides at the range, that is?"

"No," said Chester.

"Lucky you. I bet you carry it when you're cruising for boys. Some of them young hustlers are fickle, aren't they?"

Above them a floorboard creaked. Again, Victor poked his head into the back room. Eyeing the staircase, he said, "Who's upstairs?"

"Nobody," said Chester nervously.

Victor's eyes narrowed. "Maybe I should go up there and take a look."

"I have a friend up there, visiting."

"A boyfriend, huh?"

"What is it that you want?" asked Chester testily, his nerve coming back to him.

Victor slammed the door to the back room, and Louie stepped forward. Looking at Chester, he said, "I don't like you taking money from my wife."

Hitherto, Louie sensed that Chester had deemed Victor the greater threat, but as Louie spoke, the blood drained from Chester's face. It was not just Louie's words, but the softly menacing way in which he'd said them that made Chester go pale. He swallowed hard, his Adam's apple bobbing. "I told Angie I'd pay her back."

"Funny, she failed to mention that to me," said Louie, who hadn't discussed it at all with Angie. "I wasn't too happy when I learned that you took an unfair advantage of her. In fact, it really pissed me off, Chester. I had to give myself a couple of days to calm down because I certainly didn't want to confront you in anger. There's no telling what I might have done. You see, I'm really protective of my wife."

Chester heaved a sigh, glancing dubiously at Victor before turning back to Louie. "I'll pay Angie back."

"Sure you will." Louie glanced casually around the store. "I can see you might be struggling here. I'm not unsympathetic, believe me. I'm assuming your credit sources are tapped out. If you were seeking a loan, you should have come to me. I'm always happy to lend to friends, and seeing how gallant you were to Angie before you decided to con her, I might have worked out a special arrangement. But, no, you had to give Angie some cock and bull story about being ripped off by Bernie Madoff and having your wife commit suicide. As if you ever even had a wife. You're a liar, Chester."

"I'm sorry."

"I don't really think you are. I'm more inclined to think you're sorry you were found out. But don't look alarmed, Chester, we're going to clear this up, work out something. I'd like to give you a word of advice, though, if I may." Looking punch drunk, Chester barely nodded. Louie said, "The next time you plan to steal from a woman, you might want to consider what type of man her husband is. You know, I'm Italian, a little old-fashioned about things. Another type of man might be more forgiving, but I'm not really the forgiving type."

"I…uh…yes, see what you mean," said Chester, eyes darting apprehensively to Victor.

Louie studied him coldly, the faintest suggestion of a smile touching the corners of his mouth. "Lucky for you, Chester, I'm a nice guy. So I'm going to suggest that I loan you the money to pay back my wife."

"What?"

"You heard me. I want to loan you the money to pay back Angie. We don't even have to tell her, you and I. We'll keep it between us, and let her think you came into a stroke of good fortune. That way, we don't abuse her feelings."

"I see. That's er…uh…chivalrous of you."

"Yes, I like to keep my wife happy. Now, how I'd like to do this is to give you the money straight out, in cash. Then I set you up on a monthly payment plan, and we'll charge a little interest, nothing too outrageous, say fifteen percent."

"That seems high to me."

"It's better than a credit card. If you don't like it, I can go to eighteen percent. You know, in the old days, I sometimes loaned money with interest rates as high as thirty or forty percent. But times change, don't they?"

"I … I guess." The fan wafted over them, the breeze lifting the wing of Chester's comb-over. His face was pink and shiny with sweat. They were all perspiring in the heat, and Louie longed for the cool comfort of Victor's car. But, just as he was about to close the deal, two elderly women entered the store.

Chester greeted his customers with a sour smile, but it was Victor who chatted with them, playing the role of savvy merchant. The ladies wanted a bouquet to take to an ailing friend, and Victor directed them to the walk-in-cooler, suggesting they pick the one with the smiley-face painted on the vase. "That always does the job," he said, confounding Chester because he made the sale in about two seconds flat.

Still, it was another five minutes while the ladies selected a card, and then Chester rang them up and put the vase in a support-box, fussing with tissue like an old maid. This time it was Louie who opened the door, ushering them out. Then Louie walked back to the counter and said, "Chester, let's get this done. I can give you the cash today, and then we start the payments on the first of next month. Victor, set it up."

"That won't be necessary." Chester looked at Louie. "I'd rather not be beholden to you, Mr. Morelli. I'm doing a big wedding this weekend. If you can give me until then, I'll pay Angie back in full."

Chapter Twenty-One

VICTOR HAD PARKED HIS CADILLAC in front of the bakery two doors down from Green Gardens. Emerging from the flower shop, Louie and Victor were surprised to see a small crowd gathered around Victor's car. A police cruiser was pulled alongside the vehicle.

Felix and his owner were standing on the sidewalk along with patrons from the bakery. A cop was in the process of jotting down Victor's license plate. All four of Victor's tires were punctured and flattened, his headlights were busted out, and the side panels gouged with key tracks.

"He might have done more damage, but Felix saw him and barked." The woman in the floppy hat told Victor. It was she who had called the police, providing the description of a man in a ball cap and dark sunglasses.

"He was wearing shorts and a black T-shirt," she said helpfully. "I'm afraid I didn't get a look at his face. His back was to me."

Louie glanced up and down the street, looking for surveillance cameras. The art gallery on the corner had one, but not the bakery and certainly not the stationery shop next to Green Gardens.

The cop, ascertaining that the vehicle was Victor's, seemed impatient to finish his report and return to his air-conditioned squad car. He said to the woman, "Young guy, old, black, white?"

"Oh, a white man, most definitely. As I didn't see his face, it's hard to say what age he was, but I'm assuming he was fairly young. He was well-built, kind of muscular. He had the cap pulled down around his ears, but I didn't see a lot of hair."

"He was bald?" asked the cop.

"Maybe."

"Hmpf." The cop grunted. "What happened after you spotted him?"

"Well, it wasn't really me. It was Felix. We were coming out of the bakery, and Felix barked. I guess that scared him because he started walking away real fast."

"Did you see which way he went?"

"Just to the corner. He went down the side street—"

"Was he on foot the whole time?"

"Well …yes, to the corner. I didn't follow him."

It was too hot for Felix on the sidewalk, and the woman walked him back to the shade beneath the bakery's awning, where a bowl of ice-water was waiting. An elderly man said he was fairly certain he'd seen the suspect get into a black pick-up truck at the corner. "He was driving," the man said. "I saw him pull out into traffic."

This witness hadn't been able to get a license plate or provide any better of a description than Felix's owner. In fact, this man wore thick sunglasses and confided to Louie that he had cataracts, which were scheduled to be removed later in the week.

The cop called it in, started writing his formal report. The small crowd dispersed, and Lake Avenue went back to sleep. Felix and his owner got into a nearby Subaru and drove away. Louie and Victor went into the bakery and bought a couple of waters and some pastry. They sat at a bistro table in the corner. After guzzling half the water in his bottle, Victor called his insurance company and arranged for a tow. Then he called the Cadillac dealer and talked to someone who agreed to have a rental sent to him immediately.

This was all done very matter-of-factly, as it took more than a keyed car to rile Victor. But it was obvious Victor's vehicle had been deliberately targeted. The cop said as much when he came into the bakery to give Victor his license and registration back. "Somebody got a personal beef with you, Mr. DeAngelis?" he asked.

The cop's shirt was sticking to him, the fabric beneath his armpits ringed with sweat. A younger, fresh-faced cop was at his side. After telling the girl behind the counter to get the officers something cold to drink, Victor said, "As far as I know, I haven't made any enemies lately."

The cop, who by now had talked to his station chief, seemed to have acquired a bit more knowledge about Victor and Louie. He eyed them suspiciously but asked no questions. He mopped at his brow with a stack of paper napkins and accepted a bottle of soda from the girl, tilting it toward Victor in acknowledgement.

After the cops left, Chester entered the bakery. He'd peeked out during the height of the commotion and knew it was Victor's car that had been vandalized. Now, spotting the two of them at the bistro table, Chester smirked and said smartly, "Gee, it couldn't have happened to a nicer guy."

Emily said the exact same thing to Louie, but in a much different tone when she learned of their difficulties. But this was after they reached the office, and just before Louie went into a meeting and Victor took off, heading to the gym in his rental car. Victor was more annoyed than angry by what had transpired this morning. By this time he'd called Jolene and learned that Wayne Rawlins wore a short buzz cut, pumped iron at Gold's Gym, and drove a black Ford F-150. Briefly, Victor and Louie had considered Grigori Buzeczki as being the vandal, but it didn't fit. Buzeczki might try to kill Victor, but it was doubtful he'd waste his time puncturing tires. So that left Rawlins.

Having pinpointed their main suspect, Louie told Victor to watch his back. He did not bother calling Sheriff Warren. It was obvious the sheriff's surveillance had gone awry and that his so-called counseling had failed. This told Louie that they'd have to deal with the out-of-control deputy on their own.

Checking in with Louie after his workout, Victor told him that he was heading home to shower, and then he planned to investigate the addresses Chucky had provided. He also informed Louie that Szarnakov's man, Dimitri, had called to let him know that "they had nothing to do with the dead whore."

Apparently, Cyrus the pimp was innocent as well, although the Fort Lauderdale police had identified Irina and connected her to him. They were questioning Cyrus, who supposedly had an airtight alibi. Szarnakov had sent counsel to advise his cousin. Victor had called his source in the department and was waiting to hear back. He promised to check in with Louie later.

Three hours later Victor called back. He was at the Ocean Breeze Hotel. "I'm at the bar, talking with the barmaid," he said. "It's a long shot, but I thought I might find Natasha or Molinsky here."

Victor also reported that his contact in the Fort Lauderdale Police Department was off today, so he had no new information about Irina's murder. Victor had heard from Chucky, who had noticed a discrepancy with one of the addresses he'd provided.

"What kind of a discrepancy?" asked Louie.

"I don't know. Chucky wants to double check something—some kind of coincidence he missed before. He's going to call me back."

"Keep me informed," said Louie. "What about the hotshot deputy? Any sign of him?"

"Maybe. I had an F-150 tailing me on the way here, but I lost him pretty quickly."

Chapter Twenty-Two

THAT EVENING WHEN LOUIE AND Angie drove into Delray Beach, the sky was electric with lightning. The seaside village slumbered in the dusky heat, the shade trees bordering the avenue hanging motionless. The approaching storm all but guaranteed them a parking spot in front of Tramonti's Ristorante on Atlantic Avenue.

Tramonti was minus its usual crowd. Despite this, almost all of the street-side tables were full. Louie never ate on the patio, even in cooler weather, when it was much pleasanter. He preferred the comfort of the dining room, and it was blessedly cool when they stepped in, Tramonti's maître d', Glen, greeting them warmly. "Do you want a table tonight, Lou?" he asked, but Louie spotted a man he knew at the bar and moved toward it.

Tramonti's bar curved gently along one wall. Many of the high chairs at the bar were occupied, with most of the people sitting there eating. Shaded, pendant lights cast a warm glow, adding to the restaurant's ambiance. Tramonti was Louie's favorite restaurant in South Florida, and he came here often.

Louie's acquaintance was dining with a woman he introduced as his wife. They exchanged polite greetings, and then Louie and Angie claimed the last two seats available at the bar. As soon as they sat, one of Tramonti's two male bartenders stepped up to greet them. The young man knew Louie's drink preferences, and after ascertaining that Louie wanted wine, he poured a Chianti Classico Riserva for him and a Pinto Grigio for Angie. When the wine was served, they resumed their conversation with the other couple.

They sat at the foot of the bar, with their backs to the patio. Tramonti's glossy bar was streaked with shades of tan and brown and cream, its padded lip providing a comfortable surface for Louie's forearms. He set his smart phone on the bar. Sitting with their backs to the patio, Louie and Angie missed the jagged streaks of lightning flickering over Delray Beach, but the loud cracks of thunder made Angie jump. Nervous diners began trickling inside, the open doors emitting a swell of warm, rain-scented air.

Louie did not bother with a menu and ordered *profumi mediteranei*, a baby octopus salad. Cloth napkins were spread on the bar in front of them, and a wire basket of warm, crusty bread was delivered with butter and olive oil. Tramonti's owner, entering the bar, came over to shake Louie's hand.

Their antipasti arrived. Angie squeezed lemon juice over the salad while Louie buttered his bread. He was relishing his first taste of tender octopus when his phone rang. The name on the screen flashed "Unavailable" and Louie almost didn't answer. But on second thought he picked up, sliding his finger across the screen and saying, "Yes," a bit abruptly.

The dining room hummed with activity as waiters resettled patrons, the noise level suddenly accelerating as the storm broke overhead, but the crisp, authoritative voice on Louie's phone was perfectly audible. "Lou Morelli?" a man asked.

Something in the man's voice made Louie sit up taller. He said, "Yes, this is he."

"This is Sergeant West with the Fort Lauderdale Police Department. I'm calling to tell you there's been an accident."

"What?"

"I'm sorry to inform you that Victor DeAngelis has been shot."

Louie's heart plummeted. Shoving his plate aside, he stood abruptly, causing Angie to look up with alarm. Louie said, "How bad is it?"

"Pretty bad. He's being transported to Broward Medical."

Without thinking, Louie signaled the bartender, gesturing at the food. Louie said, "Can you tell me what happened?"

"We're investigating. It was called in about fifteen minutes ago. We identified DeAngelis at the scene. I'm giving you a heads up."

"Thank you, Sergeant. I'm on my way. You said Broward—"

"Yes, Broward Health Medical Center, over on South Andrews. Somebody from the department will meet you there."

Chapter Twenty-Three

LOUIE TOSSED A HUNDRED DOLLAR bill onto the bar. Angie was looking at him, uncomprehending, and Louie took her by the arm. "Let's go," he said, "Victor's been shot."

They hit the worst of the storm, and for a few minutes, after pulling away from Tramonti's, it was like driving in a hurricane. Water choked the roads and traffic lights swayed wildly over the intersections. Debris flew through the air, a spinning tree branch nearly striking Louie's Mercedes. It was impossible to see more than a few feet ahead, and Louie gripped the steering wheel, focusing on driving while Angie called Diana.

Fortunately, Diana's mother, Susan, was visiting and happened to answer the phone. Counseled by Louie, Angie explained that Victor had been in an accident, alerting Susan that they would pick her and Diana up in a few minutes. Victor's house was on the Intracoastal in Highland Beach, just a few miles south of Delray, but it took twelve minutes to get there in the battering rain. As soon as Louie pulled into the drive, the garage door lifted and Diana and Susan rushed out, ducking their heads beneath one umbrella. The wind tore at the umbrella, turning it inside out, and in the short distance they travelled they got wet, their clothes splotchy and damp as they climbed into the backseat. White-faced and trembling, Diana's voice shook as she asked Louie what had happened.

He gave a condensed version of what Sergeant West had told him. There'd been an accident, and Victor had been transported to Broward Medical. He did not mention that Victor had been shot or that West had said Victor was "pretty bad." He did not reveal the terse way in which West had told Louie that someone from the department would be waiting for him at the hospital, indicating that Victor might possibly be dead.

Louie stayed calm, and he was able to convey this calm to Diana, preventing full-scale panic, but this didn't mean he wasn't filled with dread at the thought of what awaited them at the hospital. It helped that Diana's mother was visiting. In fact, Susan had been scheduled to fly home that evening, but her flight had been cancelled due to weather. A plus-sized woman with short blonde hair, Susan was dressed for traveling, wearing navy slacks and a tunic patterned with pink flamingoes. Diana wore gray sweat pants and a blue T-shirt. She'd obviously dressed hastily. She was without make-up, her hair flattened on one side, as though she'd been lying down when Angie called.

The storm was sweeping inland, leaving a trail of destruction. Torn leaves carpeted the pavement and stuck to the windshield. Power outages took out traffic lights and a section of I-95 was closed due to flooding. The good news was that the storm moved off fairly quickly. By the time they hit Pompano the worst was over. In Lauderdale it wasn't even raining, although whole neighborhoods were without power and parts of Davie were washed over, necessitating one-lane traffic, which further delayed them.

At Broward the paramedics who had transported Victor lingered in the emergency area, filling out their reports. Louie knew they had attended Victor by the way they looked up when he mentioned Victor's name, their eyes touching briefly on Diana, who was now weeping as the enormity of the situation hit her. A female doctor came over to greet them. Speaking bluntly, she told them Victor's condition was grave. He'd been shot multiple times and had been rushed into surgery. She was scant on details, but after ascertaining that Diana was Victor's wife, she hastened to assure her that Broward was a Level One Trauma Center. "Mr. DeAngelis," she said, "is receiving the best care available." She confiscated an intern, asking him to escort them to the waiting room on the second floor.

Alerted to their arrival, a surgical coordinator met them in the lounge. Introducing herself as Jan, the woman offered her sympathy and apologized that the surgeon would not be able to meet with them until later. Echoing the doctor, she stressed that Victor's situation was "critical." He'd sustained four gunshot wounds. Shots to the shoulder and upper left arm were non-threatening. Unfortunately, Victor had been shot in the chest and had a collapsed lung. If the surgeon was unable to repair the damaged tissue, Victor would have to undergo a lobectomy, or, in layman's terms, a partial removal of the lung. Finally, as if this news wasn't grim enough, Jan informed them that a wound to Victor's upper thigh had hit his femoral artery, causing massive blood loss. All shots had been to the left side of his body.

Victor was already in a state of hypovolemic shock when the paramedics arrived on the scene, although first responders reported that he was able to tell them his name. Quick response by attending paramedics had probably saved Victor's life; they were able to stabilize and transport him. Surgery had commenced immediately, with a cardiothoracic and vascular surgeon attending. Jan said she would keep them posted throughout the operation.

They huddled in the waiting area. Except for another unfortunate family whose relative had been the victim of a car accident, they were alone. Stunned, her eyes wide with fear, Diana wondered aloud why anyone would want to kill Victor. After a year of marriage Diana was still somewhat naïve concerning her husband's lifestyle and had incorrectly assumed that he was the victim of a crime, perhaps a robbery gone astray or a carjacking.

Louie's mind raced. He had no answers as to how or where Victor had been shot. Despite what Sergeant West had told him, nobody met them at the hospital. Piecing together what had happened was Louie's first priority. He was prepared to call the police department and ask for West, when two detectives walked into the waiting area. They wore plainclothes, but Louie knew immediately that they were cops. They zeroed in on Louie, and he rose to meet them.

Their first questions were directed at Diana. Had Victor told her where he was going tonight? "No," said Diana. She hadn't even known Victor was in Fort Lauderdale. Was she aware of anyone who had recently threatened her husband or wished to do him harm? Confused, Diana shook her head. "Everybody likes Victor," she said. "Who would want to hurt him?"

The detectives turned to Louie, their eyes suspicious and alert. Both were clean cut, one middle-aged, his partner on the verge of it. The Fort Lauderdale police weren't taking any chances by sending novices. Louie allowed them to draw him away from the group, preferring to speak without the ladies present.

They sat at a round table in the narrow cafeteria adjacent to the surgical waiting area. A handful of tables were lined in a column, but the coffee urns and single buffet table were shut down,

everything wiped clean and gleaming, smelling faintly of indus-
trial cleaner. Nobody was about, not even hospital personnel. The
younger cop, the sideburns of his buzz cut glinting with gray, said,
"Victor DeAngelis works for you," stating a fact.

This cop had introduced himself as Detective Bartlett. He had
an athletic look, his skin weathered from too much sun exposure.
Bartlett's partner, Detective Holbrooke, had considerably more gray
in his military-style cut. Behind the lenses of his frameless glasses,
his eyes were gray. He said, with a trace of baiting sarcasm, "Let
me get this straight. DeAngelis is your executive assistant?"

"Yes," said Louie, meeting Holbrooke's steely gaze. A surgeon
entered the lounge, and he tensed in anticipation of bad news, but
the doctor veered toward the other distraught family. Louie looked
at the detectives. "Could you tell me what happened, please?"

"We're trying to piece together a scenario. Any idea what Victor
was doing at the Avondale Inn?"

"What?" Louie blinked, genuinely bewildered. "I have no idea.
I don't even know where it is. Is this where he was shot?"

Bartlett said, "It's a spring break motel, a block north of the
Hilton, between Sunrise and Las Olas. Victor was shot in the parking area behind the motel."

Louie nodded. "I know the neighborhood. I've torn down some
of those old places."

"It's a busy area," said Bartlett. "But that end of the property is
secluded. There are some low rent efficiencies back there."

"I'm sorry," said Louie. "I have no idea why Victor was there."
He wondered if this was one of the addresses Victor had gotten
from Chucky, recalling abruptly that Chucky had mentioned some
kind of discrepancy to Victor.

Aware that the detectives were awaiting his reply, Louie said,
"I wish I had more answers for you, but I'm puzzled myself. When

I spoke with Victor earlier, he was at Mizu Café in the Ocean Breeze Hotel."

"What time was that?"

Louie shrugged. "About half-past six. I'd just gotten home."

"Do you know what he was doing at Mizu Café?"

"He was in the bar getting a bite to eat."

Bartlett said, "Was he alone?"

"Yes." He saw Holbrooke staring at him. "What happened at the Avondale?"

"It appears Victor was walking back to his car when he was hit. There's a good chance he knew the shooter."

"How do you figure?"

"Victor was carrying a fully loaded weapon, a 9mm handgun," said Bartlett. "He never drew his weapon. It appears he may have fumbled for his gun, but he was already down by that time."

Louie shook his head, perplexed. "Excuse me, Officer. I'm having a hard time with this. Were there any witnesses?"

Holbrooke said, "We have a couple of tourists who were in the courtyard of the motel and heard the gunshots. They called it in. We're still canvassing the neighborhood—there are a lot of mom and pop places, efficiencies, and small apartments in the area. We're hoping somebody saw something." He checked his notes, skimming back a couple of pages. "Why was Victor driving a rental car?"

"We had a problem in Lake Worth this morning," said Louie. By his calculations he figured they already knew this or should have. He explained what had happened, giving the police their suspect in the person of Wayne Rawlins. The crazed deputy seemed a likely culprit, although Victor would not have been taken off guard by him.

Louie told this to the detectives. "Victor's not the type of guy to be taken unawares. If Rawlins was coming at him, Victor would have drawn his weapon."

"There are some tall bushes around there. The guy could have been hiding, waiting for Victor to come out. Remember, he was walking *back* to his car. The shooting was done at a fairly close range. At least one of the bullets went clean through—we were able to recover a .380 at the scene."

Louie digested this, thinking. Genuinely puzzled, shaking his head, he said, "I have no idea what Victor was doing at the Avondale. Did you check with the motel?"

Bartlett said, "We're in the process of doing that right now."

Holbrooke gave Louie his card, asking him to call if he thought of anything that might be relevant. The cops pushed back their chairs, ready to go to work now, at quarter to eleven in the evening. Louie stood with them. Tucking his notebook into the pocket of his blazer, Holbrooke said, without a trace of his earlier attitude, "Mr. Morelli, the FBI considers you the official head of the Morelli Crime Family in New Orleans. Is there any chance that Victor's shooting could be some kind of mob hit?"

Louie smiled coldly, "Detective, the federal government brought numerous charges against me, none of which were ever proven in a court of law. I'm surprised these rumors persist."

Chapter Twenty-Four

AFTER THE DETECTIVES DEPARTED, LOUIE used his prepaid phone to call Anthony, advising him that Victor had been shot. Victor's parents were dead, but he had a sister in Gretna, outside of New Orleans, and Louie asked Anthony to call her. Then he called Nathan, who did not answer. Louie did not leave a message and hung up.

He used his smart phone to call Michael. Scrolling through his contacts, it occurred to Louie that the police had Victor's phone and were probably scrutinizing his calls. That made him think of Chucky, and after relaying his bad news to Michael, Louie called him. The connection was bad—the Caymans were being battered by a tropical front. Louie said, "You gave Victor some addresses. Was one of these at the Avondale Inn in Lauderdale?"

"No. One was in Hollywood, the other in—"

There was a burst of static and the connection was dropped. Irritated, Louie clicked off. His pre-paid was ringing, and he answered. "Yeah?" he said.

"What's up?"

It was Nathan. Louie told him about Victor. "Are you in town?" he asked.

"I will be. I'm on a plane, over the Ozarks."

"Call me when you get in," said Louie.

Angie walked over to Louie. She had her phone in hand; she'd called Stella. Wearing a sleeveless silk dress with a square-cut emerald pendant, her Chanel bag dangling from her shoulder, Angie looked distinctly out of place in the hospital waiting room. Shivering in the brisk, artificial air, Angie hugged her arms to her chest, and Louie removed his sport coat and draped it over her shoulders. He kissed her on the forehead. "How is Diana holding up?"

"As best as can be expected. I'm glad Susan's here." She drew the ends of the coat close against her midsection. "Come with me to the chapel. I want to say a prayer for Victor."

"Let me call Tony first. He's the only one I haven't spoken to yet."

Tony was on the deck of the beach cottage he'd rented in North Carolina. He expressed dismay upon learning that Victor had been shot. "Do you want me to come home?" he asked.

"There's nothing you can do here," said Louie. "I'll keep you posted."

"Dad, does this have anything to do with my situation?"

"I don't know." Louie was annoyed that Tony would ask this on the phone. "The police are investigating."

"Maybe I should have called them—"

"Tony, shut up. I'll call you if Victor's condition worsens."

He clicked off before Tony could commit another faux pas. Alarmed, Angie said, "Why are you so angry with him?"

"He's stupid."

Her nostrils flared. "Our son is *not* stupid. How can you say such a demeaning thing? You're being very hard on Tony. Don't think I haven't noticed how you've been treating him."

Louie did not answer. He called Nathan back. "I don't know who shot at Victor but I'm not taking chances. Get one of your men over here to guard him." Nathan owned a security firm, and his man would have the proper credentials to satisfy the authorities.

Louie made one more call, to his managing broker, Martin. Louie had a meeting in the morning, and Martin would have to sit in. Louie apprised him of the situation. Then he put his hand on the small of Angie's back, escorting her to the elevator. Had Louie been alone, he would have walked down one flight, but Angie was wearing heels, and she'd already complained to Louie that her feet were hurting. They stepped onto the car, devoid of people at this hour.

Angie tugged at the lapels of Louie's coat. "Your jacket is heavy."

"There's a gun in the inside pocket, on the left."

"I'm aware of that."

"It might be better if you wear it. Put your arms in the sleeves." Angie complied, and Louie buttoned the jacket, his hand patting the gun. "Better?"

"I guess."

"You should keep a sweater in the car."

The elevator door slid open and they stepped into Broward's atrium lobby. Soaring three floors, the upper level balconies overlooked the lobby with its gazebo-styled reception desk, sitting stations, and potted greenery. A Starbucks had prime space off the lobby, with a McDonald's and Subway tucked around the corner. Angie remarked that the hospital reminded her of a Holiday Inn, and Louie said, "When was the last time you stayed in a Holiday Inn?"

Louie escorted Angie through the lobby, where only a few people lingered, sitting quietly and talking. They walked past the gift shop, which was closed. Peering absently in the window, Angie said, "My feet hurt."

"You've never worn sensible shoes."

"I wasn't planning on walking tonight."

The chapel was tucked into the corner near the gift ship. Bouquets of flowers had been left on the altar, where a thick Bible was opened. The Star of David was etched into the glass on the bay window behind the altar, and a tablet of the Ten Commandments was on display, along with a crucifix and an American flag.

Designed to accommodate all faiths, the chapel lacked the statues and stained glass that Louie associated with holy places. Without adhering to the principals of Catholicism, Louie preferred its aesthetics. He was a New Orleans Catholic, accustomed to the gilded altar of the cathedral and the stunning Gothic beauty of St. Patrick's. Not that Louie prayed in these churches, but they instilled a restful feeling in him. As for prayer itself, he'd abandoned it years ago, after his father died and his enemies challenged him.

They were alone in the chapel. Angie slid into the front pew, scooting over so Louie could sit beside her. She crossed herself and knelt, bowing her head into her hands as she prayed. Louie leaned against the back of the pew and closed his eyes. Now, in this quiet moment, he faced his fears, admitted to himself that he was afraid of losing Victor.

Angie finished her prayer, saying "Amen," and crossing herself again. She sat on the pew beside Louie and reached for his hand. Her fingers were cold.

"Did it help?" asked Louie.

"It feels like it. I don't know that I've a right to ask God to spare Victor. Despite what Diana thinks, he hasn't exactly been a saint. I was thinking of Johnny," her voice quavered, "and that other man."

Louie let the Johnny comment fly by. "What other man?"

"Years ago. From my art class, remember?"

Louie smiled faintly. "I don't remember."

"You're a liar. Remember how the kids loved Victor? He used to play ball with Tony and his friends. Just like a boy himself. He wasn't like any of your other men. And then you sent him to take care of my friend. I was shocked beyond belief—"

"If I recall, your friend died in a boating accident."

"Yes, you arranged it that way. That's when I really began to understand who you were…what you were capable of. It seems incomprehensible now, almost like the memory of a bad dream, but you really did kill a man for flirting with me."

Without attempting to deny her accusation, Louie said quietly, "My dear, you're distraught—"

"That's what you said then. What shocked me the most was that you used Victor." Her voice broke. Angie snapped open her purse, extracting a small packet of tissue. She pulled one free and dabbed at her eyes, then blew her nose with a snort. "Tonight, I prayed for Victor, and I prayed for you."

"Thank you, baby. I need all the prayers I can get."

She sniffed. "You shouldn't joke—"

"I wasn't joking."

"It's hard to imagine our lives without Victor."

Louie put his arm around her, pulling her against him. "He'll make it, baby. He's strong."

She laid her head on his shoulder. "I'm scared he might die."

"I know, baby. I'm scared, too."

They sat quietly for a moment, and then the chapel door opened and an elderly black man stepped in. Louie looked at him, wondering who he was praying for. He patted Angie on the arm. "Let's go back upstairs. We've been gone too long."

They shuffled out, Louie nodding somberly at the old man. In the brightly lit lobby it was like another world, although at this hour it was deserted. Louie took Angie's arm, retracing their steps to the elevator. Going up one floor, the door barely closed before the car stopped. Waiting for the door to slide open, Angie leaned against Louie and said, "I don't know why I love you so much, but I do."

Chapter Twenty-Five

THEY HAD MISSED THE UPDATE, which amounted to the fact that Victor was alive and in surgery. He was said to be "doing well."

The night lengthened, and they settled in to wait. Shortly after midnight one of the attending surgeons came out to tell them that the artery in Victor's leg had been successfully repaired. They were concentrating solely on the lung.

At Diana's anxious inquiry, the doctor reassured her that Victor was stable. It helped that Victor was in excellent physical shape, he told them, before disappearing back into the sterile corridor from which he had emerged. Contrary to expectations, the lounge got busier, with family members of accident and trauma victims trickling in, some clearly panicked and distraught.

One of Nathan's security guys showed up, bringing fresh coffee from the Starbucks in the lobby. But by then they were jittery from fatigue and caffeine, and Louie merely sipped at it. After an hour he sent the guard home with orders to come back in the morning. He paced, waiting. Angie and Susan alternately chattered and dozed. Diana never moved, except to go to the bathroom. Finally, at three in the morning, after five and a half hours of surgery, the cardiothoracic surgeon came out to inform them that Victor had successfully withstood the operation. While they had not performed a full lobectomy, they had done a wedge resection, which was the removal of a small, wedge-shaped portion of the lung. There'd been extensive tissue damage, he explained, justifying the procedure. Victor's chances for a full recovery were promising.

Diana wept with relief. Louie thanked the doctor, marveling at the stamina of the surgical team. An hour later they were given a peek at Victor, which brought renewed fears, seeing him hooked up on a ventilator, with tubes running in and out of his body.

They got home at five, with light trickling on the edge of the ocean when Louie fell into bed. He slept till nine, awoken by the ringing of his phones. He took Anthony's call first. "Michael and I are flying in this afternoon," Anthony told him. "With Ceci."

"Ceci," said Louie. He thought of what she had said to him last week, asking if Victor was going to be okay, and a chill ran up his spine.

Anthony said, "She's pretty adamant. I guess she's been dreaming about Victor. Robert's going to call you."

Robert did call Louie. He said he tried to talk Ceci out of coming, but she was convinced Victor needed her. So he'd reluctantly granted permission. "I'd bring her myself, but I can't get there today."

Ceci was such a special child that her un-childlike requests were almost always granted. Louie assured Robert he understood and clicked off, placing his next call to Emily, who'd heard about Victor from Martin and was weeping. Louie instructed her to reschedule his appointments. He'd stay in touch throughout the day.

Louie hung up and sat on the edge of his bed with his head in his hands. Intuitively, without second-guessing his instincts, Louie sensed that whoever had shot Victor was connected to the dead prostitute Irina and the Russians. His primary candidate was Grigori Buzeczki, but there was a spider web of connections in the Russian émigré community, and it could be that Buzeczki was the only visible suspect. Louie did not suspect the jilted deputy, although he hadn't completely ruled him out, and he'd been happy to steer the police in this direction.

Most people, upon learning that their loved one has been the victim of a crime, are anxious for the police to catch the criminals. Not Louie. He didn't want the police to apprehend the shooter because it would deprive him of the ability to deliver his own retribution, which was certain to be fatal. He thought of Buzeczki, whom he'd already marked without initiating any action, and he felt that his complacency had caused Victor to be shot. He regretted this the way a field commander laments a wrong tactical move—an error in judgment that costs lives. Anger burned in him, fueling a desire to retaliate, but his enemy was faceless.

For the first time in a decade, Louie questioned his decision to move to Florida. Undoubtedly, it had been beneficial for his family, and he'd gotten immensely richer in South Florida, but if Victor had been shot in New Orleans, there was no doubt the cops would apprehend the shooter and bring him to Louie. Victor had contacts with the Fort Lauderdale police, but the ties of blood and family and favors were not prominent, and Louie would have to play the game by their rules, improvising as he went along.

Louie started out by calling Chucky, but the satellites were still not transmitting. Then he turned on the television and saw that the tropical front which had hit the Caymans had been upgraded to a Cat 3 Hurricane. Officially, the season didn't start for another week, and the media was sensationalizing this early freak storm. Forgoing his swim, Louie showered and shaved. He dressed in casual, lightweight slacks and a cream silk shirt. He was sitting on the edge of his bed checking his gun, when a news bulletin made him stop and look at the TV.

The local ABC affiliate, WPLG, had burst into the morning talk show to report that alleged mobster, Victor DeAngelis, had been gunned down near the Fort Lauderdale strip last evening. DeAngelis had been taken to Broward Medical Center, where his condition was critical. A picture of Victor flashed on the screen—an FBI surveillance photo from the archives, showing a younger Victor. Unbelievably, an outdated photo of Louie popped up next, with the usual garbage about "alleged mob boss."

Louie aimed the remote at the wall above his dresser, killing the picture before they finished the hack piece. He walked back into his closet and selected a lightweight beige sport coat, with the reinforced interior pocket on the left side for his gun. This was an option for times when he eschewed the gun-belt, perfect for his compact P250. He thought of the .380 they'd found on the ground near Victor, recalled Buzeczki's Walther PPK, and abruptly remembered that they fired .380's

Louie slipped his phones into his front pocket and then walked through the sitting room and gently pushed open Angie's door. He expected to find her sleeping, but she was propped on pillows, Gigi curled against her side. The window shades were drawn, the room in a false twilight.

Louie walked to the bed. "Baby, what are you doing up? I thought you'd be sleeping."

"Gigi needed to go out."

Louie sat on the side of Angie's bed and leaned over to kiss her. He held her chin between his thumb and forefinger, lightly tracing the outline of her jaw with his thumb. "Thanks for being there for me last night."

"Are you kidding me? Louie, where else would I be?"

He planted another kiss on her forehead. "It meant a lot to me that you were there."

"Have you heard from the hospital?"

"Victor's stable. He's in intensive care. They told me on the phone, family only, but if they think that's going to prevent me from seeing Victor, they have another think coming."

"I'll come later, with Stella."

"Go back to sleep."

He started to rise, and she took his hand. "Tony called me."

"Oh?"

"He wanted to see how Victor was." Angie hesitated, and Louie saw anxiety flicker in her eyes. "Tony's a little … emotional. I gather he didn't sleep too well. He—" she twisted her mouth, chewing the inside of her lip. "Tony alluded to the possibility that Victor's being shot might have something to do with him—that bit of trouble you mentioned. That's why you were so abrupt with him last night. You blame Tony, don't you?"

"Baby, I'm not blaming anyone except the person who pulled the trigger." He stood, looking down at her. He knew she wasn't satisfied, but she'd been married to him too long to persist with questions he would never answer. He said, "Get your rest. I'll call you from the hospital."

Downstairs, Stella gave him a wordless embrace, looking at him with searching intensity. Sensitive to the mood of the adults around her, Isabella also provided a heartfelt hug. She had been told that Victor was hurt, and she asked serious questions about him. Louie sat at the counter, and she climbed onto the chair beside him.

Maria served him a grapefruit half and poured him a mug of coffee. It was about the time Victor would usually arrive, bringing Louie's newspaper and a box of pastry, whipping up a fluffy omelet or hotcakes with cinnamon and powdered sugar.

Having missed dinner last night, Louie was very hungry. Maria scrambled eggs, crumbling in tiny bits of sausage. She buttered toasted Italian bread and set Louie's plate in front of him. His phones started before he even took a bite. Friends, associates—people were hearing about Victor on the radio and TV. The man from Philadelphia, who had a place in Boca and a fondness for Victor, called to express his sympathy and offer his assistance, should Louie desire it. Louie thanked him and hung up. He quit answering his phone so he could eat his breakfast.

Before leaving the house Louie asked Stella to call Emily and have her arrange a hotel room near the hospital for Diana and Susan. "It's going to be a rough few days," he said. "I'd rather they didn't have to battle traffic going to and from the hospital."

Chapter Twenty-Six

LOUIE DROVE DOWN TO THE Fort Lauderdale strip. Despite the passing of last night's storm, dark clouds were still bunched over the Atlantic as though for an encore. He thought of the hurricane battering the Caymans. The media was already hysterical about its potential path, forewarning of possible calamity and providing frequent updates.

Heading south on A1A from Sunrise, the beach appeared on Louie's left, packed with vacationers despite the threatening skies. The ocean was still and flat, hazard flags hanging limply. Louie spotted the Avondale Inn and realized he'd seen it a hundred times without noticing it. He signaled and turned onto Viramar Street, which ran south of the property. At first glance Louie could see that the Avondale had swallowed up its adjoining neighbors, incorporating them under its banner. There were three distinct designs, with property dividers and individual pools, indicating there had been three different motels at one time. Now Avondale claimed them all, with the choicest rooms at the front.

In the southwest corner of the property the old efficiencies were dated, the back lot gone to gravel—a place where college boys crashed after a day on the beach. Fort Lauderdale Beach was fairly safe, its problems confined to pickpockets, drunken brawls, and reckless swimmers. Victor's shooting was big news. A satellite truck emblazoned with the logo for a local TV station was leaving the scene as Louie turned in.

A small group of spectators had gathered at the corner. An SUV from the Broward Sheriff's Office was backing out of the lot, and a police cruiser was parked alongside an unmarked sedan. Louie spotted Holbrooke talking with one of the uniformed cops. He turned the corner and parked his Mercedes along the street. A block from the beach, Louie was in the heart of Fort Lauderdale. He wondered what had prompted Victor to come here.

If there had been any incriminating evidence left at the shooting site, last night's storm had washed it away. The lot was strewn with sand and debris, the bushes shielding the courtyard stripped of leaves. Heels crunching on gravel, he walked to Holbrooke, who was wearing reflective sunglasses, his face flushed with heat. Nodding cordially at the patrol cop, Louie turned to Holbrooke. "Good morning, Detective," he said. "Any news?"

"As a matter of fact, there is," said Holbrooke. He pushed his sunglasses onto his head; his eyes were gray and absent of warmth, narrowing slightly as they regarded Louie. "We picked up that deputy from Osceola."

"What?"

Happy to convey this, Holbrooke grinned. "One of the witnesses recalled seeing a black pick-up racing away from here right after the gunshots. The person she described as the driver matched the description provided by witnesses in Lake Worth. We did a little checking, found out Rawlins flew the coop yesterday. Boca detained him this morning—he'd checked into the Best Western on Federal."

His eyes narrowed, gazing intently at Louie. "Not too far from your office. My partner just left to get him."

Louie nodded. It fit, and then it didn't. He surveyed the hotel, all doors and windows facing inward, with a view to the courtyard. As though reading his mind, Holbrooke said, "Maybe he was hooking up with a girl here?"

"No. Not here. It's not his style."

There were dozens of places in Lauderdale Victor would take a girl. He'd never brought one here. Looking at the hotel, Louie recalled the detectives telling him that Victor was walking toward his car. The building's back cinderblock wall was painted sky-blue. Louie noticed there were no windows fronting the parking strip. A walkway led onto the property, with the wall on one side and a privacy fence on the other. Tall shrubs that had been blown apart by the storm hugged the fence. Entering the premises, you had to take a sharp turn to the left.

Louie turned away from Holbrooke, following the walkway. The first room off the corridor was a utility room, with a coin-operated washer and dryer, the dryer tumbling and emitting heat. Guest rooms back here were secluded. It wasn't the Ritz—these places were used and used hard. But you get what you pay for.

Cheap patio furniture was scattered around the courtyard. Several Harleys were parked alongside the building, and Louie spotted three bikers sitting at an umbrella-shaded table, their women lounging on beach chairs. One biker chick, frizzy blonde hair bleached shockingly white, looked directly at Louie. She said something to her companions, and then she got up and walked toward him.

Her face was aging, her body well-toned and baked brown from the sun, her nose peeling. Her eyes were blue. She wore a bikini patterned after the stars and stripes and nothing else, not even a pair of a sandals. "Hey, you're the mob guy," she said. "I saw you on TV."

Louie said, "I'm Lou Morelli. It was my friend who was shot here last night."

"Yeah, yeah. I called it in. Lisa and I—" she gestured at the group, indicating another bleached blonde. "We were sitting out here and heard the shots—pop, pop, pop. Lisa said it sounded like firecrackers, but I live in Cleveland, and I know what gunshots sound like. I was like, what the shit. I had just seen your friend leave—"

"Where was he coming from," asked Louie. "What room?"

"That one." She pointed behind him. Louie noted that it was the first room next to the laundry. Room 38.

"Did you see him come out of the room?"

"No. I saw him enter the courtyard and go up to the door and knock. He knocked a few times, but no one answered, and then he turned around and left. I noticed him right away. I thought he was a good-looking guy—I like a big man, myself."

She gave Louie a meaningful smile. Louie said, "Do you know who's staying in the room?"

She shrugged. "Beats me. We've been here three days, and I never saw anyone go in or out of there. I knew someone was staying there because they had the Do Not Disturb sign on the door yesterday. But, you know, we're on vacation. Who's paying attention?"

Louie nodded. "You've told this to the police?"

"Oh yeah, a couple of times. Last night and again this morning." She caught his eye, studying him. "Did I screw it up by talking to the fuzz?"

Louie smiled. He liked her spunk. "Not at all," he said. "So, you watched Victor leave. How long after before you heard the shots?"

"Maybe a minute or two. Not long. Seems to me like somebody was waiting for him out there. I told that to the cops, too."

"Are you the one who saw the black pickup truck?"

"Huh? No, that wasn't me. Lisa said she saw a gray Jeep pull out, but that Jeep was here before—I guess it belongs to one of the guests. Truthfully, we didn't see a car, but we did hear one drive off. Of course, it was thundering pretty loudly about that time." She glanced at the sky. "It's a bummer about the weather. They're saying we might get hit with a hurricane. That'll blow our vacation for sure."

"Don't pack up yet. It's a freak storm in the Caribbean and is probably not coming anywhere near Florida. The media likes to scare people. It gives them something to talk about."

She laughed. "Well, they were certainly talking about you this morning. They called you a crime boss and reported that there might be some kind of mob war starting."

"Don't believe everything you hear on TV."

"Yeah, I get you. You don't really look like a mob boss—I was expecting a Tony Soprano type. You're more sophisticated. You've got a real smooth look. I bet you're a killer with the ladies."

Her eyes drifted behind Louie, her expression shifting to one of reserved caution as Holbrooke approached. Louie said, "So after you heard the gunshots, you ran out and saw my friend lying on the ground?"

"Yeah, we didn't think. We were just like … holy fuck, and rushed out there. It's a good thing we did because he was bleeding pretty bad. I called 911 immediately. Is your friend going to be okay?"

"His prognosis for recovery is good."

"Hey, that's cool. I'm glad Lisa and I were hanging. My name's Tina, by the way."

Holbrooke's arrival put an end to her talkativeness, and with a final glance at Louie, Tina returned to her group. Looking at Holbrooke, Louie said, "Detective, did you get a roster of the registered guests?"

"What are you getting at?"

"I understand Victor was knocking on one of the doors back here." He pointed at Room 38. "Can you tell me who's registered in that room?"

Holbrooke shook his head. "No, Mr. Morelli. I can't tell you anything. We're in the middle of an investigation, and I am not at liberty to share any information with you."

"Somebody is sharing an awful lot of information with the media—"

"Mr. Morelli, you're going to have to leave the premises. You're interfering with our investigation."

"Detective, I meant no disrespect. I wanted to see where Victor was shot."

"There isn't anything you can do here. We'll call you if we need you."

Holbrooke followed Louie to his car, making sure he got in before turning to confer with the uniformed cop. Louie drove to the corner, but instead of turning onto A1A, he drew up in front of the hotel, beneath their canopy. He sat there a moment, thinking.

Louie walked into the lobby. The desk clerk looked up, yawning. "Checking in?"

"No." Louie was about to ask the clerk if he could send someone to the rear courtyard to summon Tina, when he noticed two bikers having their morning coffee at a small table off the side lobby, where a breakfast bar was set up. One of the Avondale's amenities: free breakfast. Several guests were helping themselves to cereal and packaged donuts. Louie strode over. One biker was bald, with a long, pointed beard. He looked up first, blurry-eyed, and Louie directed his question to him. "Are you with the group staying in the back?"

"Who wants to know?" the man asked suspiciously.

"I'm sorry to interrupt your breakfast," said Louie. "But my friend was shot on the premises last night. I was just in the rear courtyard talking to a girl named Tina when the police asked me to leave. Do you know Tina?"

"I know you, dude," the biker said. "You're the guy they showed on TV. Yeah, we know Tina. She's Jeb's chick. We'll call her for you."

"I appreciate it," said Louie.

Several of the other guests were listening, and Louie drew up a chair, trying to remain inconspicuous. Idly, he wondered if all this publicity would affect his business. He was surprised to see that the bald biker had the latest iPhone. Speaking into the phone, the biker said, "Hey, Spoons, is Tina with you guys?"

Louie assumed Spoons said yes, because the biker continued, "Tell her to come to the lobby. Somebody's asking for her."

Looking at Louie, the biker clicked off and said, "She's coming."

The other biker acknowledged Louie with a polite nod. He wore a red bandana on his head; his wiry hair was gray, a ponytail jutting out from the back of his collar. They were both big men, with lots of ink on their forearms. Louie said, "Where are you guys from?"

"Cleveland."

"Did you have a nice ride down?"

The biker with the ponytail told him it was "sweet." They chatted for a few minutes, and then Tina entered the lobby, walking toward the table. She'd put on a man's strap T-shirt as a bathing suit cover and a pair of flip-flops, the rubber soles slapping the tile floor. "Hey," she said. "I thought that copper chased you out of here."

Louie stood. "He doesn't want me talking to you, but I didn't get a chance to thank you for saving my friend's life. One of those bullets hit a main artery. If you hadn't called 911 when you did, my friend would have bled to death." Louie gave her his card. "If you think of anything else that might be helpful, call me at this number."

"I got Detective Holbrooke's card, too."

"Well," said Louie, with a little smile. "You can call him, too. But call me first. Find out what you can about the people who were in Room 38."

Chapter Twenty-Seven

LOUIE HAD BEEN TOLD VICTOR'S prognosis for a full recovery was good, but when he arrived at the hospital, he was shocked at how bad Victor looked. Hooked up to a ventilator, Victor was heavily sedated. The tissue on his face and neck was puffy, a result of the buildup of salt in his blood. The inflammation in his lung was proving more problematic than the actual wound; he was developing pulmonary edema.

An attending physician explained the complications to Louie, who was shaken by the thought that Victor's situation was still very critical. He was in intensive care, with only Diana, and now Louie, allowed in. In the space of an hour Victor's lids fluttered open only once. He looked at Louie, but there was no recognition.

One of Nathan's guards had been posted outside Victor's door, and the Fort Lauderdale police peeked in, but after ascertaining that Victor would not be talking to them any time soon, they departed. Diana was stoic, holding up well now that the first crisis had been averted. The ventilator made a sucking sound, pumping oxygen into Victor's battered chest. The noise grated on Louie's nerves. He felt helpless, sitting there.

After an hour had passed, Louie stepped into the corridor to call Angie. He updated her, and then told her not to come to the hospital. "They're not allowing anybody in the room," he said. "There's no sense in both of us waiting here."

Louie ended the call with Angie, and went down the hall to the men's room. When he came out, his phone was vibrating, and he pulled it out of his pocket and looked at it: Rachel. He answered. "Hi, baby."

"I'm in the lobby," she said. "Can I come up?"

He thought of Diana, holding vigil beside her husband's bed. "No, I'll come down."

Rachel was waiting by the atrium elevator when Louie stepped into the lobby. She looked stressed, and it appeared she'd been crying. Her eyes were puffy. In a refreshing twist from her usual attire, she wore a gray pin-striped pencil skirt and a white blouse with cap sleeves.

Louie hugged her. Immediately, tears flooded her eyes. "Is Victor going to be okay?"

"I don't know. He's pretty bad."

"Will you tell him I asked about him?"

"He's not conscious yet."

Louie guided her toward a sitting station. The lobby was bustling, an anxious group of people converging in their path, and they walked around them. Spotting two open seats, Louie claimed them.

Rachel crossed her legs at the knee, and turned toward Louie. "You didn't call me," she said. "I had to hear about it on the news."

"I'm sorry, baby." Louie put his hand on her back and drew her against him. "I intended to call you, but I hadn't gotten around to it. You have to understand. We were here until five o'clock this morning."

Not yet ready to forgive him, she said sullenly, "I was at work when I heard."

"I didn't think you were doing much real estate these days."

"I'm not. I've been working at JoS. A. Banks."

"The men's shop?"

"Yes." She sniffed. "My boss really likes me. I already got a raise."

"Your boss must be a man." Louie thumbed away her tears, and then turned up her face, kissing her lightly on the mouth. He felt enough of a spark to recall what she'd done with that mouth on the plane ride to the Caymans, and his mood abruptly shifted.

He regarded her with a faint smile, his eyes tender. Rachel said, "When you look at me like that, you make me dizzy. I could faint—"

"Don't do that. Then I'd have you on one floor and Victor on another."

She sobered at the mention of Victor. "What are they telling you about him?"

Louie told her. She listened, and then said, "Jolene's devastated. She feels terrible. You know, they're reporting on the news that the police detained Wayne Rawlins for Victor's shooting."

Louie groaned. "I heard about it from one of the detectives just a while ago. I didn't know it had made the news. What are they saying?"

"Not a lot of details. They mentioned a 'personal issue' as a possible motive. I was stunned. I was totally oblivious, ringing up a pair of trouser socks when the news came on the radio. I was so upset my boss had to finish the sale."

"It was thoughtless of me not to call you."

Louie looked up, watching people coming and going through the lobby. Scanning the faces, Louie caught sight of Nathan. He stood, gesturing at him. Nathan spotted Louie and veered toward him.

Dressed in khakis and a blue sport shirt, Nathan was so unremarkable that it strained the imagination to think of him as dangerous. But Louie was keenly aware of Nathan's dark qualities, and he was amused when people dismissed him as inconsequential. Nathan was the type of person people saw and never noticed.

Nathan exhibited no surprise at seeing Rachel. He'd met her once before, only she'd been with Buddy Shuler then. He said hello, his dark brown eyes studying her quietly before he looked at Louie and asked for the latest on Victor.

"Not good," said Louie, who then proceeded to tell him of Victor's recent complications.

Nathan showed no emotion when Louie said, "Come with me to the Ocean Breeze Hotel. It's the last place Victor was before he got shot. I want to know why he left there and went to the Avondale."

Nathan said, "What, you're not buying the crazed deputy theory?"

"I'm not discounting it. But you know Victor. Would he let that guy get near him without even attempting to draw his gun? Look, I went over to the Avondale this morning. I saw where Victor was shot. He was halfway between his car and the building, about ten feet in either direction. The cops have a theory about somebody hiding in the bushes, and there are some tall hedges around there, but Victor was in the open, exposed. Yes, it's possible someone came out blasting, but he's got a lot of damage, Nathan. The cops didn't say, but it doesn't take a genius to figure out that Victor was shot at close range. I'm betting within three feet. So he didn't draw his weapon on whoever approached him. You hear what I'm saying?"

"Yes. And what did I tell you? With the Russians everything is complicated."

Chapter Twenty-Eight

SITTING AT MIZU CAFE'S BEAUTIFUL blue-glass bar, Louie learned nothing that he didn't already know. The hotel's owner was out of town, and his management confirmed that Victor had been in the night before, verifying that he'd left alone. The valet had a record of the time. The police had noted this last night, when they came in to make inquiries. The restaurant manager suggested Louie talk to the barmaid who had waited on Victor. Kristy wasn't due in till five, but he promised to have her call him.

In the two hours Louie was absent from the hospital, they'd taken Victor off the ventilator. He was breathing on his own, but they were giving him oxygen and monitoring the fluid buildup in his lungs. Diana reported that he'd actually been awake for some of the time—the staff had assisted him in sitting, even making him take a few baby steps, but the effort had exhausted Victor. "He asked for you," Diana said.

Susan was with her daughter, respectfully departing as Louie stepped in. Victor's nurse entered, checking his vitals. Louie sat in the chair Susan had vacated, talking quietly with Diana. She'd heard some of the news reports and was curious about the "personal" issue they'd reported as Deputy Rawlins' alleged motive for shooting Victor. She was also confused by the things the media was saying about Victor.

Since the media was essentially reporting the same things about Louie, she didn't press too hard. Louie assured Diana the police were still in the early stages of their investigation and were merely speculating. He watched Victor sleeping and checked his phone from time to time. It had been buzzing incessantly ever since the news had reported Victor's shooting during the morning rush hour. The small TV in Victor's room showed that the threat of a hurricane was passing, but a storm warning had been posted. From the window Louie observed the darkening skies, and he hoped the plane carrying Michael and Ceci, which was due in shortly, landed before the storm broke.

Louie returned calls, updating family and friends to Victor's condition. Tina, the biker chick, phoned. "Hey, Mister M, I found out that it was a couple staying in Room 38. The guy's a skinny blonde dude. The girl has dark hair and a foreign accent. Nobody talked to them. They weren't partying or anything, not even hanging by the pool."

A skinny blonde dude. Louie's mind flashed to Molinsky. He wondered if the girl was Natasha, deciding that it probably was, even though she'd feigned ignorance about the photographer. He was beginning to understand why. He also knew why Victor had been at the Avondale.

Louie thanked Tina, clicking off just as Nathan's security guard poked his head into the room. Addressing Louie, he said, "There's somebody to see you."

The guy waiting for Louie was in his mid-thirties. Wearing a royal blue T-shirt and faded jeans, he was in prime shape, with muscular arms and shoulders. He had brown eyes and cropped sandy-brown hair. Louie guessed "cop," and he was right. The man stuck out his hand. "Mr. Morelli, I'm Bernard Thompson, with the Fort Lauderdale police." He hesitated, his eyes scanning the corridor. "This isn't my case, but I'm a friend of Victor's. How's he doing?"

"They're giving us a good prognosis, but it's a rough time, and he's having some complications. Were you intending to visit—?"

"No, no. Tell him I came by, but I'd prefer not to have my presence documented. Can I speak with you?"

Louie's phone was vibrating. He took it out of his shirt pocket and glanced at it. "Go downstairs," he said. "I'll meet you in Starbucks."

Thompson was already moving off down the corridor, his Nikes squeaking on the polished linoleum. Louie's phone showed a local number, and he answered warily, saying, "Hello."

"Hi, is this Lou?" It was a young woman's voice. When Louie affirmed she'd reached the right person, she said, "I'm Kristy, the barmaid from Mizu Café."

"Thanks for calling. You know my friend, Victor. He talked to you last night?"

"Gosh, yes. It's freaky, him getting shot like that. I guess it happened right after he left the bar. Victor's a sweet man. He always calls me 'doll.' He gave me a twenty dollar tip, and he only had one drink."

"What did Victor talk to you about?"

"He wanted to know about the Russian girls, the little dark-haired one, asked if I'd seen her. You know, they haven't been coming around too long, maybe a month or two. I didn't know they were hookers. Victor called them working girls, asked if I knew about them."

"What do you know about them?"

"Not much. They weren't picking up business in here, that's for sure, although they did come in with men. Their dates, I guess. The dark-haired one—Natasha—I talked to her occasionally. She seemed a little lonely, like she needed a friend."

"Did she talk to you about anything specific?"

"Her boyfriend. She told me she was getting married, said she really loved the guy."

"Did she give you a name?"

"You mean the boyfriend? Hmm," said Kristy, "She called him AJ."

"What about the other girl—Irina?"

"Victor told me she was murdered. It's awful, but I don't recall ever waiting on her. Victor asked if I knew the bald guy, the one from Brooklyn. I have waited on him, but he gave me a bad vibe. He stays here sometimes—I guess he rents a room in the hotel."

"Did you see him last night?"

"No, not for a couple of weeks. Victor asked about him, too. But mostly, he talked to me about Natasha, asking me if I knew where she lived. I knew she was living in Sunny Isles with a bunch of other Russians—they all live there, you know. But the last time she came in she mentioned that AJ lived nearby, and she was staying with him. That's when she told me they were going to get married."

"Did she mention where?" Louie was thinking of the Avondale.

"Hmm. One of those places off the strip. I wasn't paying too much attention."

"Could it have been the Avondale?"

"It might have been."

"Thanks, honey. You've been very helpful."

"One more thing. Victor asked me to call him the next time Natasha came into the bar. About an hour after he left I was on a break, and I went into the lobby and saw Natasha stepping out of the elevator. I didn't bother to call Victor because she didn't come in the bar. She didn't look that good, either."

"How did she look?"

"Like she was sick. White as a ghost, her hair all messed."

"Did she see you?"

"No, Natasha got off the elevator and headed right out the door."

Louie's phone was beeping in his ear, indicating another call. He thought of Bernard Thompson waiting downstairs in Starbucks. He said, "Thanks, Kristy. I appreciate you talking to me."

Chapter Twenty-Nine

THOMPSON WAS SITTING AT A table in the corner overlooking the garden. A half-eaten blueberry oat bar was on a small plate in front of him, next to a chocolate smoothie. He noticed Louie eyeing the smoothie as he claimed the chair facing him. Thompson said, "It's chocolate, with banana and whey protein. Do you want one?"

Louie glanced at the line, where a small child was having a meltdown. He shook his head. "I'll pass."

Louie thought it showed entrepreneurial spirit, putting a Starbucks in a hospital. It certainly made sense commercially, as the coffee shop was doing a brisk business. Most of the tables were taken, with the overflow claiming chairs in the garden despite the threatening sky, thick with low-hanging clouds and ominous streaks of lightning.

Louie studied Thompson, saw his gaze falter and turn away. Was he second-guessing his decision to come here? He said, "I'm so sorry to keep you waiting, Officer—"

"Call me Bernie, please."

Louie smiled. "You mentioned you're a friend of Victor's."

"Yeah, I met him at the gym—LA Fitness. We press together."
He caught Louie's eye. "For a few years now."

Louie nodded. Thompson slurped at his smoothie. He said, "It's
a healthy alternative to a shake."

"That's good. You keep yourself fit."

Thompson's eyes darted nervously about, and then he reached
into his jeans pocket and pulled out a generic cell-phone. Louie recognized it as Victor's prepaid cell—identical to his own. Thompson
slid it over to Louie. "I was able to get this for you." At Louie's
inquiring look, he explained. "Victor's car was confiscated as part
of the investigation. It's in the evidence lot. I got to it first thing
this morning, before they had a chance to go over it." He breathed
a sigh of relief. "I'm glad he didn't have this one on him. I knew
about it—it's the phone he calls me on. He called me a couple of
times yesterday, too."

Louie pocketed the phone. "You saved us a few headaches."
He smiled disarmingly, hoping to put Thompson at ease. He'd
dealt with plenty of cops in his life, recalling abruptly a certain
Louisiana politician who made a name for himself battling corrup-
tion, accusing Louie of single-handedly running the entire New
Orleans Police Department. He thought of the endless payrolls,
the cops who became informers and protectors, and the ones who
eliminated Louie's rivals for the price of a child's tuition or a slice of
beachfront land. Observing Thompson's overt nervousness, Louie
knew he'd never fall into this latter category. He said, "Bernie,
what's the word on Rawlins?"

"Word is they think he did it, but they don't have a case. Rawlins
was in possession of a .357 Magnum when they picked him up. But
the gun hadn't been fired, and until we can match the .380's or find
the weapon that was fired, we don't have anything. Rawlins does

admit to tailing Victor to the Avondale. He said he was planning to confront him, but he lost his nerve and drove around the block for five minutes, returning *after* Victor was shot. Said witnesses were already on the scene when he got there, and that's when he sped off." Thompson sucked up the last of his smoothie, twirling the straw. "That's his statement and he's sticking to it. They don't have enough to hold him."

"They're releasing him?"

"They're going to have to. He's retained a lawyer. He—" Thompson gazed beyond Louie and froze, his eyes widening with fear.

Louie turned and looked over his shoulder. Not seeing anybody sufficiently alarming amongst the patrons and hospital staff in Starbucks, he said, "What is it?"

"One of the detectives from the department walked by. I saw him in the lobby just now. For a minute I thought he was going to come in here."

Louie stood. "They've been peeking in on Victor, waiting for him to wake up." He gazed levelly at Thompson. "I'll meet you in the chapel in five minutes."

Thomson skittered out. The line had gone down, and Louie purchased an iced café latte. Walking into the lobby, Louie saw that the storm had broken, and the cars pulling up in front of the hospital had their headlights on. People entering the lobby were windblown, their clothing splotched with rain. Louie didn't see Holbrooke or his partner, and he made his way to the chapel.

Thompson was in the back row on the left, glancing anxiously at the door as Louie entered. In the front pew a woman was kneeling and praying the rosary, beads clicking rhythmically. Thompson scooted over, and Louie sat beside him. Speaking in a low voice, Louie said, "I appreciate you coming here today. I know you took a risk. That means a lot to me." From his breast pocket, Louie took out his reading glasses and a pen. From his side pocket he removed his business card. Turning it over, he jotted down a number. "Victor's going to be incapacitated for a while. It's important that you keep me informed."

Thompson slid his wallet out of his back pocket and opened it, tucking the card inside the billfold. Louie said, "I need to ask what sort of arrangement you have with Victor."

"I'm not sure I follow you."

"How does Victor pay you? I want to make sure there are no lapses."

Thompson's eyes widened. "It's nothing like that," he whispered. "Victor gets me … things. Tickets to Dolphins games, theater passes, restaurant certificates. That sort of thing. Never cash."

Louie reached into his pant pocket, dug out the cash he had rubber-banded. He had twenty one-hundred dollar bills on him. He thumbed off five and handed them to Thompson. Looking at the cash, Thompson's pupils dilated. He wavered for about half a second, and then he took the money and shoved it into his pocket. Louie said, "Let me know when they release Rawlins."

Chapter Thirty

LOUIE MET MICHAEL, ANTHONY, AND Ceci in the lobby. Having waited out the worst of the storm at the airport, the new-comers arrived at Broward Medical in a limo, transferring their bags to the trunk of Louie's car before they came inside.

While Anthony oversaw this, Louie visited with his children. Michael had recently met his half-sister for the first time, and Louie was curious as to the interaction between them, approving of the protective hand Michael set on Ceci's shoulder as they walked through the lobby.

He hung back, watched them from a distance, marking the differences between them. Michael was slender and dark, his good, Italian looks so distinctive that he was never mistaken for Cuban or South American, even here in South Florida. Ceci, on the other hand, was more French than Italian, but hers was an exotic heritage, born of a diluted blend of African, Caribbean, and aristocratic French.

Mercedes had been stunning; her daughter was exquisite. Ceci's face was oval, her large, tip-tilted eyes dark and solemn. Her straight black hair was shiny, her skin tinted olive with her father's blood. She was at that magical age, her thin, childish body yielding to a woman's curves, small breasts budding beneath the folds of her pink top, hips flaring in her denim shorts.

Already, men looked at Ceci with lust, their eyes coveting her. Women viewed her with an instinctive fear, and young girls despised her. Because of this she was a lonely child, and her loneliness cut at Louie. He had the added guilt of knowing that he'd failed her, first by abandoning her to the whims of her mother, and then, after Mercedes died, sacrificing her to ensure the domestic harmony of his family. And this was his decision, not Angie's.

It occurred to Louie that Michael might be conflicted about his father's love child, but Louie was not overly concerned with Michael's feelings. He expected him to deal with it. Still, he felt a flicker of pride as he witnessed the burgeoning camaraderie between his children, particularly Michael's protectiveness, and he leaned in and kissed Michael on the cheek, patting him approvingly, and then he cupped Ceci's face between his hands and kissed her on the forehead.

Ceci seemed taller than she'd been a few weeks ago, reaching to his chin now. Her bangs had grown out, and her hair was shorter, cut just above her shoulders. She smelled like Mercedes, wearing a blended perfume of lavender and rose petals, oils and incense from her dead mother's French Quarter voodoo shop. For a moment the sense of Mercedes was strong, spiking a longing, and then Louie pushed aside his sentiment and hugged his daughter.

Her arms encircled his waist, and she leaned her head against his chest. Louie said, "Baby, I don't want to upset you, but Uncle Victor's not doing good. Maybe you should wait—"

"No," she said adamantly, drawing back from Louie and looking at him with fierce determination. "I want to see Victor."

"It might upset you to see him."

"You act like I'm a baby. Don't you know I see him in my dreams?"

"Ceci—"

"Papa Louie, I see him broken and bleeding. I can *smell* the blood. Please." Her voice quavered. "I can make him better."

She firmly believed this. Louie didn't challenge it, saw Michael's eyes widen with surprise. Brushing a damp tendril off her brow, Louie said, "Okay, baby, okay."

Anthony entered the lobby, weaving his way through the crowd. Droplets of rain clung to his dark, curly hair, and his brown eyes, sighting Louie, were warm, his dimple flashing as he smiled. Anthony was built like a Marine, and in his fitted jeans and tight black T-shirt, he turned the heads of female passersby.

Even Victor's grim-faced nurse smiled at Anthony, although she was already making noises about the number of visitors, reminding them that ICU was for "immediate family only." Victor's nurse was a middle-aged black woman and bore no resemblance to the infamous Nurse Ratched from *One Flew Over The Cuckoo's Nest*, but Louie had already started thinking of her in these terms.

Victor was back on the ventilator. In addition, he was running a fever. Louie hung back, allowing Michael and Anthony to poke their heads in. They stayed but a minute. The rest of them gathered in the corridor outside Victor's room. Here, Louie said to Susan, "Take Diana to get something to eat. I'm going to stay with Victor for a couple of hours. If his condition worsens, I'll call you."

Susan said, "I'll take her back to the hotel and make her rest. By the way, thanks for getting us the room. It makes it so much easier for her."

Easier for Louie, too, who was relieved of the responsibility of transporting them. He smiled graciously and they went out, leaving Louie and Ceci alone with Victor. Louie sat in the armchair reserved for Diana—it was still warm from her body. Unfazed by the harsh, gurgling sound of the ventilator and the tubes draining fluids from Victor's organs, Ceci stood at his bedside. When she was confident she wouldn't be observed, she unclasped her shoulder bag. Opening the flap, she extracted a small pouch, which she hastened to unzip, bringing the smell of herbs into the sterile room.

Victor's nurse came in. She had introduced herself to Louie earlier, and he'd forgotten her name. Now, looking at her nametag, he saw that it was Dora. She wore burgundy-framed eyeglasses, her eyes sharp and gleaming behind the lenses as she looked disapprovingly at Ceci. Turning to Louie, she said, "Mr. Morelli, I've made an exception in allowing you to visit but children are prohibited."

Louie said, "Ceci is Victor's daughter."

Nurse Dora's lips compressed tightly. "Mrs. DeAngelis told me her husband has no children. I'd venture to say the young lady looks like she's your daughter."

Ceci said, "Victor's my uncle, and he needs me."

Ceci's voice was a solemn whisper, her gaze direct and un-childlike as she regarded Nurse Dora, who relented slightly. "I'll allow it this one time."

Louie said, "Thank you." He looked at Victor, sedated beyond consciousness, his chest expanding as the ventilator pumped oxygen into his lungs. "Why is he back on the ventilator?"

"The fluid buildup in Mr. DeAngelis's lungs is worsening. This is a normal occurrence after such trauma," Nurse Dora assured him. She checked Victor's IV bag, made a few notations on her clipboard and departed.

Ceci took a small jar from her handbag. It contained mashed, dark leaves steeped in oil. Not being able to feed her concoction to Victor or paste it on his wounds, which is what she had intended, she contented herself with dabbing small amounts on his forehead and chin and on the sides of his throat, over his lymph glands. Then she stood over him and prayed soundlessly, her lips moving.

Mercedes had practiced a combination of Wiccan and Catholicism, and she'd taught it to Ceci. Louie did not interfere or reproach Ceci, and he sat back and allowed her to administer to Victor. Once, Victor opened his eyes and looked at her, and Louie thought there was recognition, a lucidity he hadn't noticed earlier, but the moment was so brief he doubted himself. And then Ceci's herbs made him drowsy and he slept.

He dreamed a memory. He was nine years old and dressed in his Sunday suit, the collar of his starched shirt stiff on his neck. Louie was with his father at a gambling hall, felt his father's hand heavy and warm on his shoulder as they strolled through the crowd, his father's men a few paces behind them. People stepped forward to greet them, shaking his father's hand and then Louie's. Women in low-cut dresses and high-heeled shoes cast indulgent smiles, and the uniformed policemen who provided security tipped their hats to Louie's father.

They stopped at a craps table, and one of his father's men explained the game to him. Somebody gave Louie a pair of dice, and he rolled sevens and the crowd cheered. The dealer gave Louie a one hundred dollar bill. Not until he was in high school did Louie comprehend that his father owned two hundred such casinos and that they were considered illegal. Despite this, Tony Morelli's gambling business was the number one industry in the state of Louisiana.

Louie's dream of his father transitioned to one of Mercedes, manifested by Ceci's proximity, for when he woke she was snuggled against him with her head on his chest, and he could smell his dead lover in his daughter's hair.

It took Louie a few seconds to remember that he was in the hospital, and the mechanical pumping sound he heard was Victor's ventilator. It took him even longer to understand that the hand pressing on his shoulder belonged to Angie, and that she was staring at him and Ceci with a look of absolute astonishment.

Chapter Thirty-One

CECI WAS THE CHILD ANGIE knew of and had never met. To Angie's credit she had offered her home to Louie's child when Mercedes died. They had never discussed Ceci prior to this, and it had been a bit of a surprise for Louie to learn that his wife even knew of her existence. To preserve Angie's happiness, he had compromised his duty to his daughter.

The long anticipated meeting fell short of drama, dictated by circumstance and observed by Stella, who'd met Ceci once before and had chosen not to share this with her mother. Perhaps because they were in a hospital room—Victor's hospital room—the initial awkwardness was easily overcome. "We're not staying," Angie said. "We just wanted to see how Victor was and to lend you support."

They converged in the corridor outside Victor's room, where Nathan's guard kept watch and the aggrieved family members of fellow ICU patients slumped past them on their way to rooms where loved ones lay sick. In fact, an elderly woman in the room next to Victor's had died earlier today, creating a short-lived commotion before they wheeled her out.

It was unfair to Ceci for Louie to have to justify her presence. After all, she loved Victor every bit as much as Stella or Tony or Michael did. Seeing the way Angie stared at Ceci, Louie said to her, "Baby, I realize it's awkward for you, and I suppose I owe you an apology for that. But Ceci's been having bad dreams about Victor for a while now, and it was really important for her to see him. If nothing else, I need for you to respect this."

A little while later, mingling in the lounge, Angie watched Ceci get up from the chair next to Louie's and walk to the Coke machine. She said, "Ceci has quite a presence. She's really stunning."

"Yes," said Louie.

She studied him, quietly assessing. "I'd like to know where you are planning to have your daughter sleep tonight."

"I was going to stay on the *Stella di Mare* with her and Anthony."

"That won't be necessary. Have them both come to the house. It's time Ceci got to know us a little better, don't you think?"

He looked at her, overwhelmed by her generosity. Slipping an arm about her waist, he said, "Jesus, Angie, you're so fucking beautiful."

Ten minutes later, when Angie got up to leave, she again surprised Louie by asking Ceci to accompany them, pointing out that Michael and Stella would also be leaving. But Ceci was not prepared to embrace Louie's family without him. "I'm staying with Papa Louie," she said.

Entrusting Ceci to Anthony's care, Louie rode the elevator down to the lobby with his family, walking with them to the front door where he said his good-byes. The rain had stopped and a watery, late day sun was making steam rise off the pavement. Visiting hours had peaked and more people were exiting the hospital than entering. Louie watched Michael lead his mother and sister along the sidewalk toward the parking garage. Then his phone buzzed, and he took it out of his pocket and saw that it was Chucky.

"Sorry about the downtime," said Chucky. "The storm kicked our butts, knocked out power all over the island."

Chucky inquired about Victor, and Louie gave him a quick update. After asking Louie to keep him informed, Chucky said, "I have those addresses I gave Victor, the ones you asked about."

"I'm at the hospital," said Louie. "Fax them to my office."

Louie clicked off his phone. He felt the weariness of the past twenty-four hours, and he went into Starbucks and bought a coffee, sweetening the strong brew with sugar. He wandered into the lobby and stood beneath the high, arcing dome of the atrium and sipped coffee while he thought about Victor fighting for his life. Louie was in no immediate rush to get back upstairs, and he was savoring this quiet moment when his prepaid phone rang. Sighing, Louie dug it out of his pocket and said, "Yes?"

"Sir, it's me, Bernie."

He was surprised to hear from Thompson so soon, and said, "Yes," again, automatically.

"I thought I'd let you know that they released Wayne Rawlins about an hour ago."

"Thank you, Bernie."

Thompson cleared his throat, clearly not done. "Um, sir, do you recall me telling you that Victor had called me yesterday? Well, I didn't realize he'd left me a message, but he did. I don't know if this has any relevance, but he asked me to run a criminal check on a person named Adriana McIntyre."

"What?"

This floored Louie, and he was unable to keep the surprise from his voice. Thompson sounded pleased at being so helpful. "Yes, sir," he said. "Anyway, I did run a check, and she had a misdemeanor shoplifting charge two years ago. Nothing since."

Louie thought about this for a second. "Thanks," he said. "You've been helpful."

Flabbergasted, Louie pressed the End button, returning the phone to his pocket. What had Victor learned or suspected about Adriana that led him to make inquiries about her? Louie pondered this, but before he could make sense of it, he saw Albert Seymour enter the lobby through the main doors. Seymour's goatee had been trimmed, but he still had a sloppy, unkempt look, aggravated by his lopsided, black-framed eyeglasses and baggy Bermuda shorts.

Seymour spotted Louie and made a beeline toward him. Louie took a final sip of coffee and tossed his cup into a nearby trash bin before turning to face Seymour. Looking at Louie, his eyes glinting behind thick lenses, Seymour said, "How's Victor?"

"Unconscious." Louie wasn't in the mood for Seymour. He said, "Visiting hours are over, Albert."

"Do hospitals even have visiting hours anymore? When my aunt was dying, we could go in and out at all hours. Anyway, I wasn't coming to see Victor. I was hoping to see you."

"Well, you've got me."

Seymour took his time, studying Louie. "Man, oh man," he said. "They've been talking about you on the news all day. You know, I always knew you were connected, but when I first met you, I thought Victor was the man. If half of what they're saying is true, then you're one tough son-of-a-bitch."

Sighing wearily, Louie said, "What can I do for you, Albert?"

"I want to buy my car back." Louie's brows lifted with surprise, and Seymour grinned. "I've got seventy I can give you. In *cash*. Will you take seventy, seeing as it's only been a couple of days?"

"Albert, you owe me eighty, plus interest. You told me the car's worth one-ten, maybe more."

"I can give you ninety. How's that?"

Louie nodded. "That's fair."

"How soon can I get my Ferrari?"

"Show me the money and it's yours." Louie smiled coldly. "I'm assuming you don't have it with you?"

Seymour's eyes popped. "What, I'm supposed to walk into the hospital with a bag of cash?"

"Well, I don't care what you put it in. A small satchel will do."

"You're kidding, right?"

"Look, I'm busy. Call me tomorrow, and I'll arrange a meeting."

"Don't trust me, huh?"

"Let's just say I'm skeptical. Two days ago you didn't have two dimes and were crying the blues. Now you've got ninety thousand to buy back your car. It does raise a red flag."

"Yeah, I can see how you might think like that. But I decided to go with that investor." Louie gave him a blank look, and Seymour said, "Remember, I mentioned I had an unconventional investor—an under-the-table type of thing. You didn't believe me."

"I'm not sure I believe you now."

"Oh, he's real, all right. He wants me to make a couple of low-budget films, private things." Seymour grinned. "Not for commercial distribution."

Louie gave Seymour a hard look. "It better not be kids, Albert."

"Man, I wouldn't go for that," Seymour said emphatically. "You must think I'm a sick fuck." He paused, waiting for Louie to deny this. When he did not, Seymour continued. "Some of the girls are young, but not *that* young. Besides, they don't all have papers." He sighed. "Mostly, its S&M shit."

Louie said, "Who's your cameraman?"

"Not Molinsky, if that's what you're getting at. You know, Victor called me and asked about Molinsky." He saw Louie's eyes, serious now, and he said, "Victor wanted to know how long I knew him, where he lived, that kind of thing."

"What did you tell Victor?"

"I never discussed Molinsky's personal life with him so I don't know much about him. The guy's gifted, no doubt, but he's got an ugly habit. I only use him on small jobs—you know, you get a user like that and they're only reliable until their next fix. And I have no contact for him. He comes to me when he wants work."

"And idea where he lives?"

"He has that paranoid edge and moves around a lot, but a couple of weeks ago he was having car trouble or something, and Sophie had to go and pick up the proofs he developed. He was staying at the Avondale Inn. It's a little dive off of A1A—"

"You told this to Victor?"

"Of course. But Molinsky's scared of his own shadow. There's no way he shot Victor. That's not what you're thinking, is it?"

Louie said, "Victor was shot at the Avondale. What do you think?"

Seymour's eyes widened. "Damn, I didn't know that was where it happened. The news reported that it was near the strip, they didn't mention any specific place."

Louie nodded. "What's Molinsky's first name?"

"I only ever knew him by AJ. I think its Andy or Allen James, something like that."

"What about his Russian girlfriend?"

Again, Seymour's expression registered surprise. "Man, you know more than I do." He stroked his goatee, thinking, eyes staring into space. Two women came toward them; one of them was overweight and leaning on a cane and wheezing. Louie observed her slow, agonizing gait. Looking past the women, his eyes panning the lobby, he caught sight of a man watching him. The man was in his thirties, square-jawed and suntanned, with shiny, clipped black hair and dark brown eyes. He was clean-shaven and had an athletic build, wearing black nylon running pants and a black long-sleeved T-shirt. A thick gold chain hung around his neck, supporting a large medallion studded with diamonds. For a long minute the man stared directly at Louie, and then, when he became aware that Louie had noticed him, he turned and walked briskly through the lobby. Louie marked that he headed toward the exit.

He turned to Seymour. "Did you see that man?"

Seymour was rubbing his goatee. "What man?"

Louie glanced back in time to see the man walk out of the hospital. Darkness was falling, and the glare of the exterior lights obscured his view. He looked at Seymour. "Forget it. What were you saying?"

"Funny thing you should mention that Molinsky has a Russian girlfriend. My investor's Russian. In fact, Molinsky took some dirty pictures for him. I guess that's how he came to know about me."

"Don't tell me. Your investor's name is Grigori. He's a bald guy, talks with a Brooklyn accent—"

"Nope." Seymour shook his head. "Not even close. My investor's *real* smooth. He's a sharp dresser, like you. He's got a little accent, and he's loaded, let me tell you. Came to see me with a suitcase full of money."

"Aren't you the lucky one," said Louie. "What your man's name?"

"Alexander. Goes by the name of Alexi. Said I'd understand if he didn't disclose his last name."

Louie patted Seymour on the arm. "Albert, take my advice. Return his money and let me keep the Ferrari."

Louie returned to ICU. Nobody was in Victor's room, not even Victor, and he proceeded to the lounge, where he found Anthony and Ceci sitting with Diana and her mother. Diana told him they had taken Victor to drain his lungs.

The procedure lasted about ninety minutes. During this time Louie took Ceci to the cafeteria to get some dinner. He'd hardly eaten lunch, but he wasn't hungry, barely managing a cup of watery soup. Ceci ordered a chicken-salad sandwich, pushing it away after a few bites. "Not hungry, baby?" asked Louie.

She shook her head. "It's hard to eat when you're worried, isn't it?"

"Yes."

"Victor's still here," she said. "He's not going to die."

Louie exchanged glances with Anthony, who didn't seem to be having any problems with his appetite, devouring a roast beef sandwich even though he was as fussy about his food as Louie. Thinking over the things Seymour had told him, Louie placed a call to Franco. "Can you get hold of Szarnakov for me?" he asked. "I need to talk to him."

Twenty minutes later, when they were back in the ICU lounge, Szarnakov phoned. "Louis, my friend, what can I do for you?"

Szarnakov sounded relaxed. Louie heard music in the background, wondered if the Russian was even in the country. Louie said, "Sergei, do you know a man named Alexander who goes by the name of Alexi? I don't have a last name, but he's interested in making smut movies and willing to pay a lot of money to somebody to produce them. I'm told he's a smooth operator."

There was a prolonged silence. Louie didn't hear the background music, and he wondered if the connection had dropped. Then he heard Szarnakov's heavy breathing and assumed he'd moved to a quieter location. "Alexi, you say," said Szarnakov. "This man is Russian?"

"I'm told he is. Flashes big money."

Again, there was a moment of silence. "This is important to you?"

"Yes."

"Does this Alexi have anything to do with Victor being shot?"

"I have no reason to think that."

"But you do think it, don't you?" Szarnakov chuckled softly. "I will make inquiries and get back to you."

Chapter Thirty-Two

B **Y THE TIME THEY WHEELED** Victor back into his room, it
was ten-thirty. Louie called Angie, telling her they were
leaving the hospital. In the parking garage he handed
his key-fob to Anthony, expecting him to drive as he would have
expected it from Victor. Louie sat in the front passenger seat, and
Ceci sat directly behind him.

Traffic heading north was light, and Anthony flew past the
Pompano and Boca exits, getting off on Linton, in Delray Beach.
They were tired, speaking sporadically, with Ceci dozing fitfully.
She came awake as they crossed the Intracoastal, the Mercedes
vibrating as they drove over the drawbridge's grated surface.

It was a cloudy, moonless night, the skies threatening rain yet
again. Patches of puddles gave testament to the last downpour.
As they turned onto A1A, leaving the lights of the town behind
them, the night suddenly blackened. Ahead of them the two-lane
blacktop twisted its way along the shoreline, tall trees forming a
canopy over it.

Ceci didn't spook easily, and Louie was surprised when she bolted
upright in the back seat and said, "Papa Louie, I don't like this."

"We're almost home, baby. Just a few more minutes."

The headlights of oncoming traffic provided a brief respite, and then the cars passed and darkness smothered them, broken by reflective lights at the tail end of secluded driveways, mailboxes passing in a blur. The darkness was exacerbated because it was nesting season for loggerheads, thus reducing the exterior lights on the grand residences hidden beyond the clump of trees and tall hedgerows, gated properties invisible in the night.

Scooting forward on the rear seat, Ceci reached her arm through the low console dividing the front passenger seat from the drivers. Gripping Louie's arm, she said, with a note of rising hysteria, "We can't go there."

Turning and looking at her with concern, Louie said, "What's the matter, honey? Are you nervous about coming to my house?"

She didn't answer, seemed barely to have heard him. Instead, she turned around and looked out the rear window, as though she expected to see another car. But nobody was tailing them. Glancing at Louie, she said, "It's a bad feeling. Please…let's not go there."

But they were already there. Anthony made the last curve before Louie's house, began slowing the car. Ceci's fear was tangible and completely unreasonable. She sat rigid, with her arms crossed over her chest, her eyes darting to and fro.

There was nothing to see, not yet. Louie's villa was obscured by the high brick wall, bougainvillea vines growing riotously over the top. The gate was closed. Attached to the wall posts on either side of the gate, the brass coach lights cast smoky pools of amber-tinted light. Though there was nobody behind them, Anthony signaled automatically and made a slow turn onto the driveway. Smiling reassuringly at Ceci, Louie said, "See, baby, we're home." At the same time Anthony pressed the button that activated the gate and nothing happened. He touched it again, and Louie's instincts went on full alert. He said, "Back out."

Anthony slammed the Mercedes into reverse, the front wheels rolling backward over something sharp and spiky. There was a loud pop, and the left front tire punctured, air escaping with an angry hiss. Ceci gave a strangled moan, and Anthony cussed and punched the gas, and they spun in a half circle, tires spewing gravel.

Urgently, but without panic, Louie reached into the back seat and pressed on Ceci's leg. "Get down, baby. On the floor."

He saw the whites of her eyes, her face frozen with fear, but she immediately slid off the leather and crouched on the carpet. Louie said, "Put your head down."

He drew his P250, releasing the safety before he even lifted it from his pocket. He and Anthony slid down in their seats. A heartbeat later a second tire blew and the Mercedes ground to a whining halt. Pointing at an angle the high beams exposed a man crouching in the low cover of the bushes. Spotlighted, the man sprang forward without further attempt at concealment. He was dressed in black from head to toe, his face concealed by a nylon stocking mask, the revolver in his hand glinting as he aimed it at the driver's window and pulled the trigger. Anthony ducked sideways as the gun fired. It must have had a kick, and impossibly, the shooter missed the window, his bullet striking the driver's door just below the rubber stripping. The car shuddered as it sustained the impact, rims grinding on concrete as Anthony attempted to back up the Mercedes.

There was no pause between the first and second shots, the shooter rushing boldly forward and blasting away at the driver's window. The thick glass fragmented and spider-webbed, chunks flying inward, and then the third bullet sent shards of glass flying.

Louie felt the bullet whiz within inches of his head before it tore through the padded upholstery on the door. Ceci screamed as shivers of glass rained down on her. Crouched on the floor in front of the passenger seat, Louie remained invisible to the shooter standing outside the driver's door. It dawned on Louie that he was the intended target but Anthony, sitting behind the wheel where Louie should have been, was taking the heat.

In the sudden lull, Ceci's scream fading to a sob, the emboldened assassin moved in for the kill. Concentrating solely on the driver, the shooter pointed his smoking revolver through the shattered window. He was within two feet of Anthony's head, aiming at it when Louie extended his arm, his sudden movement making the man jump so that his fourth bullet went off target, striking Anthony in the left shoulder, the impact slamming his body against the seat. Anthony howled and Louie crawled over him, gripping the P250 hard, the pistol's discharge loud in his ear as he fired through the jagged hole in the glass. Aiming upward, Louie hit the assassin in the chest, grunting with satisfaction as the man staggered and dropped his revolver. It clattered to the pavement just as Louie shot a hole in the man's throat, blood squirting as it struck. The man fell backward onto the pavement.

Louie lifted the weight of his body off of Anthony's lap. He glanced at his cousin, trying to gauge the extent of his injury. Anthony was slumped against the seat with his right hand pressed to his wound, his teeth bared as he grimaced with pain. Louie said, "I got the bastard," and looked into the backseat at Ceci, who was whimpering like a wounded animal.

Louie had no time to comfort his daughter. He reached for the door handle and touched a shard of jagged glass, barely registering the pain as he pushed open the passenger door and stumbled out, his eyes scanning the perimeter of his property to ascertain that there were no more gunmen waiting to blast him. He walked briskly around his car. The shooter was flat on his back, blood seeping from a chest wound, fingers frantically pressing against his severed windpipe as he struggled for air.

Concealed beneath the nylon mask, the face of Louie's enemy remained hidden. The eyes stared at him, glittering with fear and shock. Around the dying man's neck a solid gold chain was awash in blood, the heavy medallion attached to it canted at an angle. Louie bent and pulled back the mask and saw the face of the man who'd been staring at him in the hospital. The face of the enemy belonged to a stranger.

Louie's hand throbbed. Droplets of blood dripped onto the man's face. He was in full blown panic, gurgling sounds coming from his throat. Up at the house Louie heard the sound of a door opening, and then Angie's voice, hollering for Michael. He smelled gunpowder and blood and the moistness of the earth, the air humid and misty in the after-rain. He heard waves breaking on the beach, a siren in the distance, Ceci sobbing brokenly. Anthony talked to her, telling her it was going to be okay, and then he kicked open the driver's side door, sprinkling glass onto the driveway, and stepped out. He grunted at the effort, but he got on his feet and surveyed Louie. With his good arm, Anthony unhooked his phone from his belt, dialing 911. Three beeps, and then he spoke calmly, telling the operator that an intruder had been shot and giving their location.

But the police were already enroute, the sirens drawing closer. Louie marked his would-be assassin as an amateur, spotting his mistakes, grateful for them. He eyed the abandoned Smith and Wesson revolver, an older model .38. Not a pro, thank God.

The shooter was still alive, breath gurgling, blood bubbling on his lips. Help was minutes away, the man might make it. Louie kicked him in the side. "Who sent you?"

Michael and Angie were running down the driveway. Speeding toward Louie, the sirens wailed, piercing the night. Lights flickered on in neighboring houses. Louie estimated the sirens were half a mile and closing. He glanced back at Anthony, saw him disconnect from the 911 operator, and then he lifted his compact P250 and drove a final bullet into the shooter's heart.

Chapter Thirty-Three

FOR THE FIRST TIME IN days the sky above South Florida was clear, with only a slight haze hanging on the edge of the horizon, where the sea touched the clouds. A cargo ship shimmered, traveling north along the shipping lanes, far enough out so that it didn't spoil Louie's view.

He sat on his terrace, bathing trunks damp from his swim. For the second night in a row he'd gotten home at sun-up. Maria and Angie had made a huge breakfast, which they all fell upon like vultures before hitting the sack. Most of the family still slept; Anthony, zonked out from pain meds, in Michael's room, and Michael crashed out in the nursery. Stella was in Angie's room, having given her bed to Ceci. Angie had slept in Louie's bed—was still sleeping. Only Maria was up with Louie, bringing him a bowl of cut up cantaloupe and watermelon.

Louie had slept three hours, awakened when his attorney phoned to tell him that he'd been in touch with the Delray Beach Police, informing them of Louie's legal representation, as well as his desire to cooperate in the investigation.

Not that they'd charged Louie with anything. He was well within his legal rights, protecting his loved ones and himself. The police had questioned Louie and Anthony last night, but he'd sensed they were not satisfied and had phoned his attorney in the middle of the night. He'd called from the surgical waiting room at Delray Medical, where Anthony had been taken by ambulance and where an emergency room doctor put five stitches in Louie's hand and jabbed him with a tetanus shot. Ceci had no cuts or bruises but was given a mild sedative and sent home with Angie, who painstakingly picked glass from her hair before putting her to bed. Anthony's surgeon had removed the bullet embedded in his shoulder, repaired damaged tissue and bandaged him up. There had been some discussion about admitting him, but Anthony had refused.

Three hours was not enough sleep, but it was all Louie was going to get: The Delray Beach Police wanted him in their Atlantic Avenue headquarters at twelve o'clock sharp.

During the course of the night—between reassuring phone calls to Anthony's wife and placating ones to Ceci's adoptive father—Louie had made arrangements with Nathan for guards to be placed on his property. He was singularly alarmed that he had not done this sooner, and after the police conducted a thorough search of his property and assured him the intruder had not breached the wall, his relief had been palpable. The police established that Louie was the intended victim and that the shooter had lain in wait to ambush him. Evidence indicated he'd acted alone, as the police had scoured the area for suspicious characters. Two houses down from Louie's, a strange vehicle had been parked at the base of a neighbor's drive, beneath the heavy canopy of an oak tree. The homeowner confirmed the vehicle was not his, and the law impounded it.

The police were forthright in their questioning, regarding Louie with a modicum of distrust. It was their persistence at the hospital and their double-checking of his prior statements that led Louie to phone his lawyer and leave a message.

"No problem," said Aaron, returning Louie's call this morning. "I'm in Dubai. My biological clock is all screwed up." He then proceeded to tell Louie that the Delray Beach Police had requested a formal interview. "Your high profile, and they're being proactive so nothing comes back to bite them in the ass. It's definitely a case of self-defense and is within the guidelines of the 'Stand your ground' law. Because of this I don't anticipate any repercussions, although the prosecutor may try to make an issue out of it. The media got hold of it, so you're all over the Internet, and the speculators are having a field day." He hesitated, breathing noisily on the line, as though debating how much of his next statement to reveal. He harrumphed, and then said, "I've an inside source who tells me that the dead man is a Ukrainian national. He was here legally, on a visa. I'm not sure how they got this info so quickly, although I imagine they had a little help from the feds. The vehicle they impounded from your neighbor's driveway is leased to an elderly man in Palm Beach. It's a second vehicle, and he says he had no idea it was even missing. They're treating it as stolen."

"Jesus," said Louie.

"They worked all night on this, Lou. The county called in their specialists, dragged everybody out of bed. Palm Beach doesn't want a fiasco like the one they had in Sanford with that Zimmerman—"

"The circumstances aren't at all similar—"

"I agree. But you've got a reputation and some bozo may try to use that to his or her advantage. Which is why you have me." Louie heard the smile in Aaron's voice from clear across the globe. "If you have a problem at all, it's going to be on account of the fact that you over-killed the shooter. They know the first two shots occurred while the perpetrator was standing. It's the third shot, a direct hit to the heart while the man was already half-dead that may cause you a bit of trouble."

Ah, but that's the one that felt so good, thought Louie. He refrained from mentioning this to Aaron, who was finishing up with a tentative apology, explaining a scheduling conflict between his associates. "I'll be home in a few days," said Aaron. "If necessary, I can take over then. In the meantime, I've got a new criminal guy in my office. Just started this week. He's good—says he knows you. Name of Richard Weinstein."

"Weinstein?" said Louie. "Sounds familiar."

"Well, you can't beat a good Jew lawyer," said Aaron, who was Jewish.

Chapter Thirty-Four

SIDNEY KAISER WAS A WELL-BUILT man with burnished coppery hair and piercing blue eyes that flared upon recognition when he saw Ceci. Kaiser had once worked in the New Orleans FBI office, attached to the organized crime task force, where he'd clocked hours of surveillance on Louie and Mercedes.

He'd eventually grown disenchanted with his job, which led to him being dismissed. He then approached Louie, who introduced him to Nathan. The two men had gone into the security business together. Kaiser still looked like an FBI agent, which worked to his advantage. Today, he was in Victor's role, acting as Louie's bodyguard, and he arrived at Louie's house early, his McDonald's breakfast in hand.

After scolding Kaiser in Italian, Maria took away the McDonald's bag, allowing him to keep his coffee. She then prepared Kaiser a bacon and egg sandwich on grilled Italian bread, adding a slice of beefsteak tomato and a thin layer of pepper cheese. Kaiser was wolfing it down when Louie entered the kitchen. Maria refilled Kaiser's coffee and then made Louie an identical sandwich.

Louie was still full from the breakfast he'd devoured at six this morning. He took two bites and then pushed his plate away. Kaiser confiscated the half sandwich he hadn't touched, transferring it to his plate. Maria frowned at Louie but said nothing. He wouldn't have heard her if she had because the calls were coming in so fast that Louie's phone buzzed incessantly. He monitored ID for the callers, answering those he deemed important. He took Thompson's call, learning from the nervous cop that he could expect to see Detectives Holbrooke and Bartlett at his meeting with the Delray Beach police. Apparently, the two departments had been conferring and were unanimous in believing that whoever had shot Victor had also attempted to kill Louie. Fort Lauderdale PD was also spouting a theory, shared by their contemporaries in Delray Beach, that the shootings were mob-related.

"What happened with Wayne Rawlins?" asked Louie.

"That's another problem. They were supposed to be keeping an eye on him last night, but he eluded them. After you shot that intruder, they went ballistic, thinking it was Rawlins. They caught up with him at the Budget Inn in Delray." Thompson hesitated, and when he spoke again, his voice had a nervous quiver. "He had your home address written on a slip of paper and admitted that he'd been driving by your house."

Louie's house was sacrosanct, the place where his family lived, his refuge. He accepted this information without revealing the anger that flared in him, merely thanking Thompson before answering his next call, which came from Albert Seymour. "Man, that was some scene," said Seymour. "I saw it on the news, how you whacked that trespasser."

Louie said, "I'm really busy, Albert."

"Chill, man. I got your cash, like I told you I would. Can we meet today?"

Sam arrived shortly after Kaiser. He came expecting breakfast and sat at the table while Maria prepared it. He'd brought the *Sun-Sentinel* and the *Palm Beach Post*. In the *Post* the story about Louie was printed above the fold, next to an article about an important congressional vote. The headline read: "Alleged mobster shoots man dead in Delray Beach."

"Jesus," said Louie. "You have to read two paragraphs to learn that I was acting in self- defense."

The *Sentinel* wasn't quite as bad, printing their piece below the fold, the article titled: "Authorities Fear Mob War." The article, which Louie merely skimmed, alluded to "mob violence," and "organized crime involving alleged mobsters Louis Morelli and Victor DeAngelis."

Louie tossed aside the papers, wondering if he'd ever get his life back, missing the leisurely mornings he'd shared with Victor. At ten, the guard stationed at the gate called to announce the arrival of Mr. Weinstein. The guard said, "He showed ID and gave me a card. He says he is your attorney—"

Louie said, "Send him up."

And then the unpleasant surprise as he met Dick Weinstein on his doorstep, and now he realized why the name was familiar. With everything going on, Louie hadn't placed the "Richard Weinstein" his attorney lauded with the hippie lawyer who'd insulted him in his own building. For a moment Louie felt sucker-punched, as if he was on the downhill slide of a roller coaster. Unable to keep a neutral expression, he said, "It's you."

Weinstein was grinning like a Cheshire cat. He reminded Louie of Richard Dreyfuss, exhibiting the smug self-righteousness the actor frequently displayed in his roles on the screen. Fortunately,

Weinstein was better dressed than the last time Louie had seen him, but the pressed navy Dockers and tan sport coat still didn't quite meet Louie's approval. Weinstein's ponytail, banded tightly at the nape of his neck, sported wiry gray hairs.

Weinstein stuck out his hand to Louie, who looked at it without reciprocation, his eyes lifting to Weinstein's face. Louie said, "You look like a court-appointed attorney."

The lawyer dropped his hand. "I told Aaron you wouldn't go for me, but he said you were a reasonable man."

"I'm afraid he's a bad judge of character," Louie said facetiously.

"Look, Mr. Morelli, I'm sorry you don't like me. I admit I was a little smart with you, and I apologize. If you want me to leave, I will. But I don't think you should talk to the police without counsel."

Louie studied him a moment, his face impassive, and Weinstein said, "May I come in?"

Louie relented, opening his door and taking a step back. Weinstein crossed the threshold, pale blue eyes blinking as they adjusted to the interior light. He looked up at the vaulted ceiling, and then straight ahead at the grand colonnade, with the lime-stone floor and medieval chandeliers. "Nice," he said, "Real nice," following Louie past the formal living room and into the library where Kaiser waited in the doorway, eyes aloof and appraising. Kaiser was neatly and professionally attired in a short-sleeved white shirt and gray trousers, his sidearm holstered on his hip. He wasn't as big as Victor, but he was intimidating in his lack of personal warmth.

Louie did not introduce the men, but Weinstein nodded at Kaiser and said, "How do you do? I'm Dick Weinstein."

Kaiser acknowledged him by inclining his head slightly. Louie gestured toward the sitting area with its big leather couch and comfortable armchairs. Weinstein set his briefcase on the coffee table and sat on the sofa, glancing speculatively at Louie, who said, "Would you like coffee?"

"Decaf, if you have it."

Louie said, "Sidney," but his bodyguard was already on the move, slipping quietly from the room.

Weinstein said, "He's a little intense."

Louie shrugged. "I don't pay him to be polite."

Weinstein's gaze drifted, marking the shutters closed against the morning glare, the inlaid writing desk and sidebar, bottles glinting in the light. He reached into his briefcase and extracted a legal pad and fine-tipped marker. He said, "I came a little early because I want to get your version of events exactly as you remember them."

Louie nodded. "That's fine."

"Before we begin, I want to affirm that our conversation is protected by attorney-client privilege—"

"You don't need to explain."

"Mr. Morelli—" he looked up as Kaiser reentered the room. He cleared his throat. "May I call you Lou?"

Louie smiled. "Yes, but it doesn't mean we're pals."

"I wouldn't presume." He uncapped his marker and cast another wary glance at Kaiser. "It would be helpful if I could speak with you privately."

Louie nodded at Kaiser, who again went out of the room, leaving the door open. Weinstein said, "I was able to procure a copy of the police report, including the statements given by you and your cousin. I understand he had surgery last night. Is he going to be okay?"

"It was through the shoulder. Anthony was released this morning."

"And Victor?"

"They expect him to recover, but there have been complications." He eyed Weinstein. "The police haven't requested a formal statement from Anthony, have they?"

"No. Perhaps it is out of consideration for his injury, but it's more likely they are satisfied with his recounting. After all, he was just visiting and had only been in Florida for a few hours. No, they're concentrating on you for two reasons. One, it's obvious you were the intended target. And two, the separate shootings are indicative of something more complex. It's my opinion that the police think you know more than you're telling." He gazed at Louie with steady eyes. "Do you?"

"Yes, but I'd rather not discuss the details."

"If you hamper me—"

"Relax, Counselor. We're not going into court. If it comes to that, I may choose to confide something of the circumstances."

A noise at the door drew their attention. Angie and Isabella entered the library, Angie carrying a tray with two steaming mugs of coffee. Wearing a white sundress, her glossy curls tied back with a red ribbon, Isabella held a small plate of biscotti, which she set on one end of the coffee table before darting swiftly to Louie. She climbed on his lap and looked warily at Weinstein.

Louie introduced Angie, and Weinstein stood to greet her. Angie placed the tray on the coffee table, dividing the mugs between Louie and his guest, setting napkins and spoons beside them. Addressing Weinstein, Angie said, "Its decaf."

"Thank you."

Angie moved the plate of biscotti within reach of the attorney and looked at Louie. She said, "There's a Channel 5 van in front of the driveway."

She announced this with a note of accusation, as though Louie was responsible. He wasn't happy about WPTV's decision to put a van in front of his house any more than Angie was, but this was not the time to discuss it. Louie said, "I'm sorry it's an inconvenience, dear."

He was aware of Weinstein watching them with interest. Isabella pressed against him, demanding his attention. She'd been awoken by the commotion in the house last night, and was confused by the undercurrent of tension in the air. Ceci fascinated her, but she was also jealous, witnessing Louie's affection toward her. Now, hoping to regain the limelight, she refused to budge when Angie held out a hand to her.

Accustomed to his indulgence, Isabella rebelled when Louie said, "Go with Nonna, baby."

"No," her chin tilted defiantly, and she wrenched her hand away from Angie's. But Louie nudged her gently toward his wife, and she started to whine, but Angie was resolute, leading her from the room. Outside the door Isabella threw a tantrum, and Kaiser leaned over and shut the door, muffling the child's cries.

Louie ignored the way Weinstein was soaking it all up, reconciling the family man with the mafia prince he'd read about. Holding the coffee mug in his hand, Louie said, "You were saying?"

"Actually, it's what *you* weren't saying that we were discussing." Weinstein regarded Louie with cool deliberation. "I went over to the police station right after Aaron called me this morning. They were stumbling all over themselves trying to make sure they didn't make a mistake, doing everything by the book. They gave me a copy of the report, but they forgot to edit out the officer's comments." He opened a file with a Xerox copy on top, and, looking at the bottom of the page, he said, "Right here, the cop writes. 'Morelli calm. Just killed a man, but exhibiting no emotion except concern for his daughter.'"

Chapter Thirty-Five

WEINSTEIN CONDUCTED HIMSELF ADMIRABLY AT the interview, earning Louie's grudging respect. Louie was not surprised that the Fort Lauderdale detectives working Victor's case were sitting in, but he was a little taken aback by the presence of two FBI agents. They introduced themselves and did not speak again, content to let the Delray Beach police ask the questions. From experience Louie deduced that some of the questions had been submitted by the FBI.

The interview started amicably, with handshakes and polite greetings, discreet inquiries about Anthony's and Victor's conditions. A grim-faced captain Louie had spoken with last night was in charge. He looked a little worse for the wear, with red-rimmed eyes and jittery hands. He started the questioning. At first, it was a simple recounting of the facts as Louie recalled them. Since nothing in Louie's statement had changed, this went very smoothly.

Then they got a little antagonistic, asking Louie if he'd known or recognized the man who shot at him. Louie said, "I told you last night I didn't recognize him. He was a complete stranger to me. Have you identified him yet?"

He saw the FBI agents exchange a quick glance, the captain's eyes darting sideways. "We have not been able to do so thus far," said the captain. "We're working on it."

"What happened with Deputy Rawlins?" asked Louie.

The captain looked befuddled. "Who?"

"That out-of-control deputy from Osceola who made threats against Victor." Louie turned and looked at Holbrooke, sitting at the far end of the rectangular conference table, a mere spectator in this room. "Yesterday, you told me you felt confident that Rawlins is the person who shot Victor. You said you had witnesses who placed him at the scene."

Holbrooke gave him a flat, level stare. "In lieu of last night's incident at your house, and the lack of corroborating evidence against Rawlins, we've revised that opinion."

"I see. So you don't have any idea who the man hiding in my bushes was?"

"We're working to identify him," the captain said, skimming absently over the notes in front of him. "Mr. Morelli, it's imperative that we understand your recent activities. Earlier in the week you had a bit of trouble in Lake Worth—"

"Ahem," said Holbrooke, leaning toward the captain. "That *was* Rawlins. Lake Worth got hold of some video footage from one of the merchants. They have Rawlins on camera and know he was there at the time DeAngelis's car was vandalized. They'll be handling it."

The captain looked unaccountably annoyed. Obviously, he should have been apprised of this. He tried a different tactic. "Sir, you're rather well known in some circles. It's a fact that some of your associates are of a dubious nature—"

Weinstein said, "What kind of crap is this?"

"Mr. Weinstein, we're trying to establish the motive of a dead man. Obviously, we can't question him—"

"Perhaps you ought to ID him before you start harassing my client."

"I assure you, I am *not* harassing your client."

"You seem to have forgotten that Mr. Morelli arrived home with his cousin and daughter and was ambushed by this nut. His cousin was shot, his daughter traumatized. Does Mr. Morelli not have the right to protect himself and his loved ones, the same right that is guaranteed to every citizen of this state?"

A moon-faced detective, working the case with the weary captain, said, "Of course Mr. Morelli has that right. But it would be helpful to law enforcement if Mr. Morelli could be more forthcoming." The cop flipped his notebook, read something, and then looked directly at Louie. "Last night, you told Captain Pearson that you had no known enemies and no knowledge of who would want to kill you. Is that correct?"

"Yes."

The cop's lips twisted in a smirk. "It's a bit ludicrous to make such a statement. With your history—"

"What, precisely, do you mean by 'my history?'" said Louie. "For your information, Detective, I've never been convicted of a crime."

His words hung in the air, unchallenged. Louie wondered what they really knew about the Ukrainian national who'd tried to kill him and whose identity they were refusing to reveal. Had they connected the man to Szarnakov's disgraced bodyguard and the dead whore Irina, perhaps to Szarnakov himself? Louie knew the man's motive wasn't personal, that he was a hired hand, albeit a lousy one, and it had cost him his life. But in Louie's experience, Ukrainians and Russians worked hand-in-hand.

Needless to say, Louie wasn't sharing any of these suspicions or assumptions with the police. He remained cool and impenetrable, the aggrieved citizen who'd become the victim of a crime. And they could do nothing because their questions were based on speculation and not fact. So they thanked him for coming in to "clarify" his statement, and he walked out of the police station with Weinstein, stepping into the parking lot off of Atlantic, where the sun was burning hot and heat was shimmering on the asphalt.

Chapter Thirty-Six

VICTOR WAS AWAKE, HIS EYES focused on Louie. He tried to talk, but his throat was painfully swollen, his voice a mere whisper. His face still looked scary, all puffed with fluids. Louie set a comforting hand on his brow. "Jesus, Victor, you had me worried."

Louie noticed Victor looking at his bandaged hand, and he held it up, said dismissively, "I cut it."

He could see right off that Victor didn't believe him, his eyes darting behind Louie, zeroing in on Kaiser, standing in the open doorway. Louie said, "I beefed up security until you get back on your feet."

Victor's mouth opened but nothing came out. He rasped. Louie said, "Don't talk."

Victor's throat worked. He was speaking, and Louie bent closer, straining to hear. "Dumb punk ... hopped up."

"What?"

Louie drew back, trying to make sense of what he was saying. Victor grasped at his wrist, and Louie leaned in again, catching the word "Molinsky," but the way Victor said it, a drawn out whisper, Louie wasn't certain he'd heard right.

He looked sharply at Victor. "Molinsky," he said, "The photographer?"

Victor nodded, spoke again. Louie heard him say "scared," then "hiding." Louie said, "Are you trying to tell me Molinsky was there when you were shot?"

Before Victor could confirm this, Nurse Dora barged in, shooing Kaiser out of her path as easily as she would a small child. She glowered at Louie, indignant that he would dare disturb her patient. "Mr. DeAngelis is not supposed to be talking," she said scathingly. "I told this to the police, and I have no problem telling it to you. His vocal chords are bruised from the tubes we had to insert in his throat. He'll recover much faster and with better results if he doesn't strain them."

Victor was still grasping at his wrist, and Louie knew he wanted to keep talking, painful as it was. But he deferred to Nurse Dora and stepped back, giving Victor a look, as if to say, "What can I do?"

Louie patted Victor's hand. "She's right," he said. "It's better for you to rest."

Nurse Dora ran a thermometer across Victor's forehead, marked the result, and then felt for his pulse. Softening, she said, "Victor, we're going to take you down to X-ray and get another picture of your lungs."

Louie said, "Victor, I'll come back later. We'll talk then."

Victor gave him the thumbs up, and Louie walked out into the hallway, where Kaiser was talking with the security guard. Kaiser looked at Louie, awaiting orders, but before he could give any, Nurse Dora stepped into the corridor. "Mr. Morelli, your friend is going to make a full recovery. But he really needs his rest. Mr. DeAngelis has had way too many visitors."

"So you're kicking me out?"

"It's best for him."

"Well, you're the boss," said Louie, giving her a little smile.

Dora didn't bat a lash, and Louie said to Kaiser, "Let's go."

Louie called Seymour from the parking lot of his building on Commercial Boulevard, wondering if the Toyota Highlander parked in his spot was the Ferrari's replacement. Louie assumed it was, as Seymour affirmed that he was in, and Louie said, "Are we doing business?"

"Whenever you're ready."

"I'm at your door."

As before, the door was locked. Once again, it was Sophie who opened it. Seymour's assistant had ditched the tribal look for leggings and a tank top. Louie did his best not to look, but mounds of flesh spilled out everywhere. Sophie gave Kaiser a blank look, allowing him to enter.

Louie stepped in after his bodyguard. Offering Louie a wan smile, Sophie said, "Sorry to hear about Victor. Albert doesn't agree with me, but I think he's a nice guy."

"I'll tell him you said so."

She led the way into the studio. There was no filming today, but a couple of tech guys were sitting in the fake living room editing some footage, a cloud of cigarette smoke hanging over them. Sophie said, "Albert's in his office."

"Is he alone?"

"Yes."

Kaiser didn't like the layout, and he spent a few minutes looking around the studio. When he was satisfied, he gave Louie a brief nod, and pushed open Seymour's door, stepping back and sideways with a cop's inbred paranoia, as though he expected Seymour to shoot at them.

But Seymour sat at his desk with his sandaled feet propped on top and crossed at the ankles. A joint smoldered in the fingers of his right hand, and his head was thrown back, his face obscured by smoke. Seeing Kaiser and Louie, he exhaled loudly and brought his feet to the floor. Then he extended the joint toward Louie, who said, "Albert, put that shit out."

Seymour licked the middle finger on his left hand and snuffed out the joint, saying, "Man, it's good shit. You ought to take a hit. It'll mellow you right out."

Louie signaled Kaiser, who fanned the door back and forth a couple of times, venting the smoke, before closing it.

"You don't have to lock it," said Seymour. "No one is going to disturb us."

Kaiser smiled coldly at Seymour, and then locked the door. Louie saw Kaiser looking disgustedly at the discarded fast food bags and piles of papers and files. The vinyl chair Victor had put in front of Seymour's desk last week hadn't been moved, and Louie walked over and claimed it, lifting a stack of smut magazines off the seat.

He glanced at the magazine on top, noting that it was hardcore S&M. Skimming the pages, Louie was repulsed by the images, seeing a girl chained to a post, her ass welted. Another girl was hogtied, thighs and backside mottled with bruises. The men in the photos were hard and brutal, with thick, muscular bodies, faces concealed with masks and blacked out squares.

Grimacing, Louie let the magazines drop to the floor. He said, "Albert, this is sick shit."

Seymour shrugged. "It's Alexi's groove. He's my new investor— the man with the money, so I don't have any say."

"Your Russian pal, to whom you'll forever be indebted." Louie pointed at the bundle of magazines on the floor. "Is that the kind of garbage he wants you to do?"

"I'm budgeted for a couple of movies. Black market release, that sort of thing."

"I don't think you should do it."

"Hah, it's because of you that I am doing it. I'm broke, Lou. I'm sure you don't know anything about being broke, but let me tell you. It's tough. I need the money. And he's got tons of it, believe me." Seymour pushed back his chair and fumbled beneath his desk, came up with a black nylon book bag imprinted with the logo for Miami International University of Art and Design. The prestigious art school in Miami—somebody else had recently mentioned it to Louie, but he couldn't recall who or in what context. Grinning, Seymour slapped the bag down on his desk. "Here's your ninety thousand. I want my fucking Ferrari back."

Chapter Thirty-Seven

SOPHIE FOLLOWED THEM OUT OF the studio. Standing in the hallway, she looked plaintively at Louie. "Mr. Morelli, can I talk to you?"

She'd never addressed him by name, and now, sensing that she was nervous, Louie said, "What can I do for you, Sophie?"

"Things are getting heavy around here, if you know what I mean." She looked down at the floor, and then back up at Louie. "That new investor—this Alexi dude, he's a real creep. I told Albert not to do business with him, but he's made up his mind. Alexi brought in a chick this morning. Between you and me, I don't think she was eighteen. A pretty white girl—she barely spoke English. She was blabbering away in her own language—"

"What language was she speaking, do you know?"

"Albert says Russian." She sighed deeply, shaking her head. "That fucking pervert tied her up and whipped her, made Albert film it. I tried to stop it, but Albert told me to get out. Alexi gagged the girl so she couldn't scream. It made me sick. The thing is, I got a feeling she wasn't a willing participant." She looked at Louie. "I don't care how kinky someone is, nobody goes for that shit. I should have called the cops. I wanted to, but I was scared."

Louie nodded, understanding, his eyes connecting with Kaiser's. He said, "Sophie, how long has this Alexi been hanging around?"

"A couple of weeks." She shrugged. "That photographer Victor was asking about—AJ, he took some pictures for Alexi, paying off some drug debts. AJ doesn't have two cents to his name, but he's got a hundred dollar a day habit, and I guess he's desperate." She looked at Louie, measuring his reaction. "I heard Victor was shot by the Avondale, that's where AJ was staying. But I can tell you that AJ Molinsky didn't shoot Victor. That poor kid is scared of his own shadow."

"When was the last time you saw AJ?"

"Victor asked me the same thing. I had to think, but it was last week Friday, the day you took the Ferrari. When Victor came in on Tuesday—"

"Wait a minute. Victor was here?"

"Yeah, but Albert was out. So he talked to me. In fact, he took me to lunch, and that's when I told him about Alexi—how creeped out I was by his S&M shit. I told Victor I wanted out of here, and I asked him if he knew where I could get a job, and he told me he was going to talk to you about hiring me. Did he?"

"No." She looked dejected, and he added. "Victor didn't get a chance to discuss it with me. What kind of work are you interested in? What do you do for Albert?"

"I'm a graphic artist by trade, but that's not what I do here. I run everything, scheduling, bookkeeping, accounts payables." She grimaced. "When we're paying people, that is."

Louie thought of the bookkeeping job Adriana had vacated. He said, "I don't know what Albert pays you, but I do have a temporary position available. Come by my office tomorrow and talk to my secretary. Her name is Emily."

Sophie looked skeptical, as though she couldn't quite believe it was this easy. "Would your secretary hire a fat black chick?"

Louie smiled. "Emily knows I like blondes, so I think she'd be delighted to have you."

Sophie laughed, and Louie turned to go. She touched him lightly on the sleeve. "Thanks, Mr. Morelli. You don't know how much this means to me. I can't take another day here. When Alexi comes back—hey, he was here on Tuesday. He saw me with Victor, asked me about it."

Louie pivoted. "What?"

"Yeah, I guess I should have mentioned it sooner. Is it important?"

"It might be."

"Victor dropped me off in the front of the building, and when I came in, Alexi was upstairs in Albert's office, and he said to me, 'Was that Morelli's man, DeAngelis?' and I said 'Yes,' and he said, 'Did you tell him I was here?' and I said, 'How could I? I didn't know you were here.'"

Exchanging another glance with Kaiser, Louie said, "I don't know this man. Tell me what he looks like."

Sophie told him, "Smooth." She said he had blonde hair and dark blue eyes that sometimes looked black. He was "a handsome white dude and sharp dresser." He had an accent, but not much of one, although he'd been talking Russian to the girl this morning. A cosmopolitan type, she added. But a pervert and a creep, and he scared her, especially after today's incident.

Louie conjured an image of Szarnakov's man Dimitri. Obviously, he was using an alias. Before Louie could contemplate the meaning of this, his cheap prepaid phone rang. Patting Sophie's arm, Louie thanked her for her information and stepped away to answer his call.

"Sir, I have news for you."

Louie smiled. Thompson most assuredly had a military background. He said, "Good news, I hope?"

"No, sir. That photographer Victor asked me about was found dead this afternoon. It was a homicide. He'd been shot through the head, execution style."

"Wow," said Louie. "That's tough. Any idea who did it?"

"Not a clue. They just found the body a couple of hours ago. Molinsky's Jeep was parked in the lot of Ireland's Inn on North Atlantic—"

"Ireland's shut down about five years ago." Louie was aware of the details, having been approached as a potential buyer for the four and a half acre spread on North Atlantic between Northeast 22nd and 23rd Streets.

"The buildings are vacant," said Thompson. "There's a chain across the driveway to keep out trespassers, but this didn't stop Molinsky and whoever killed him from driving onto the property."

Louie pictured the resort, one of a dozen that had been felled by the economy, although the details eluded him. He knew the Ireland's former owners and their partners had sold it for a whopping twenty-seven million, but the new owners had yet to initiate renovations. North Atlantic was fairly residential at this site, abutted by a towering condominium on the south and a neighborhood of single-family homes on the north. Louie said, "That neighborhood is patrolled."

"Regularly," said Thompson. "But Molinsky's Jeep was pulled alongside the building. A dog walker spotted the Jeep last night but didn't investigate until this morning when it was obvious there was a dead man slumped over the steering wheel."

"Was he killed on site?"

"It appears so. Driver's window was rolled down, as though he was talking to whoever it was who popped him. Most likely he was killed last night. The crime techs' are on scene, but it'll be a while before they can piece together what happened. Molinsky was a known user, and Miami PD had issued a bench warrant on a probation violation, so the assumption is it's drug-related. In fact, if Victor hadn't mentioned his name to me, asked me to look into him, I wouldn't have bothered calling you with this. But there is one coincidence. On the surface, it doesn't seem like much—"

"What's the coincidence?"

"Molinsky was killed with a .380. That's the same caliber bullet that Victor was shot with. By itself, it doesn't mean anything. It's a common enough—"

"Can you tell if it's from the same gun?"

"Oh, no. That's only on television. All they know is that it's the same type of bullet. Without the gun, there is no way to ascertain this. You would need the actual weapon to determine that."

Chapter Thirty-Eight

LOUIE WAS DEAD TO THE world when Tony rapped on his door at five the next morning. The sleeping arrangements in the house had returned to normal, as Anthony's family had flown in and he'd moved with them to the privacy and comfort of the *Stella di Mare*. Michael was back in his room, and Stella, not wishing to uproot Ceci, had claimed the nursery.

Thus, Louie was alone when Tony summoned him, and he slipped on shorts and a T-shirt and followed his son down to the library, where Natasha sat stiffly in the center of the couch clad in black leggings and a man's white T-shirt. The T-shirt was grass-stained, and her feet, exposed in flimsy flip-flops, were gray with dust. Natasha's brown hair, smoothed by a flatiron when Louie had last seen her, was thick and unruly, ends frizzed and uneven. Her eyes were ringed with dark circles.

She was trembling with pain and exhaustion, too frightened at first to even talk to Louie, but Tony assured her he could help, and after a couple sips of Presidente Brandy, she told him Grigori had killed AJ. Against her better judgment, Natasha had gone to Ireland's with AJ. She'd tried to talk him out of going, but AJ was in desperate need of a fix. He was only days away from being admitted to the drug rehab program at Fort Lauderdale Hospital. "He was going to get better," she said. "And then we were going away to get married. We loved each other."

She wept, and they sat and let her weep. In the hallway the grandfather clock ticked, breaking the stillness. Natasha drank the brandy, lifting the cut-crystal glass with a trembling hand, a wad of tissue balled in her lap. Finally, she found her voice, revealing to Louie that after she left Franco's on Sunday night, she'd tried to warn Irina. But she hadn't been able to reach Irina, and she'd gone to AJ, hiding with him at the Avondale. At this point she never intended to go back to her old life. She was starting over with AJ. But AJ was very sick, and after a couple of days he called Grigori and arranged to meet him at the deserted resort.

Grigori was waiting at Ireland's when they pulled up, coming out of the cover of the trees. He had no car, but AJ assured her this was normal, as Grigori lived in the neighborhood. He approached the car acting friendly, too friendly. Natasha was already suspicious when a black SUV turned in and pulled alongside them. As soon as the driver stepped out, she recognized him as Szarnakov's man, Dimitri. He held a silver-plated gun to her head and forced her to step out of the Jeep. He made her get in the SUV, sitting with her in the back, his gun to her head, while Grigori shot AJ.

She started to scream, but Dimitri covered her mouth. Grigori got behind the wheel. He drove them to his house, where he and Dimitri took turns raping her. Dimitri threatened that resistance would be met with death. Irina, he told her, had resisted. He smiled when he told her this, and she was terrified that he would kill her. He told Natasha that she belonged to him now, that he owned her. The next morning he took her to the studio and whipped her, making Seymour film it. Then he drove her to a house in Sunny Isles Beach, raped her again, and locked her in a bedroom. She escaped by climbing out of a second-story window and hitching a ride to Lauderdale, borrowing the driver's phone to call Tony. Receiving the call, Tony abruptly left his family in North Carolina and drove down to rescue her.

When Natasha started her story, darkness shrouded the house, and they talked by the light of the low lamps placed strategically around the library. Now the sun was up, the streaming rays filtering through the shutters. Natasha lifted her shirt and showed Louie the vicious welts the lash had left on her back, told him of the bruises and bites on her thighs and breasts. Dimitri hadn't marked her face, not wanting to "compromise her value."

At Louie's puzzled look, she explained that Dimitri had plans to make another movie of her. She wept again, the horror of her situation sinking in. Louie could see she was flushed and warm with fever. He sent Tony to make coffee, but his fumbling around in the kitchen woke Maria, who made the coffee and started breakfast, looking curiously and sympathetically at Natasha. A few minutes later Angie wandered in. She was in her robe and slippers, her face pinched with worry as she stared at Tony and then Natasha.

At a signal from Louie, Angie cautiously retreated. Louie looked at Natasha, slumped against the arm of the sofa, and asked her if Grigori had shot Victor. Natasha turned up her face to him and shook her head. "No," she said. "It was AJ—he shot Victor. AJ was crazy scared. He thought Victor was police, coming to get him."

Chapter Thirty-Nine

NATASHA TOLD LOUIE THAT AJ shot Victor with a gun he'd taken from the room at the Ocean Breeze Hotel on Monday, when they'd gone there to look for Irina. The gun was sitting on the dresser, and AJ picked it up. Grigori had lots of guns and was always leaving them around. Natasha didn't think he'd even know it was missing. She said AJ's intent was to pawn it for cash. She never imagined that he would use it on Victor, but AJ was having a bad day. The dope, she said, "made him crazy."

They had just returned to the Avondale and were getting out of the Jeep when Victor walked into the lot. He spotted them, came right toward them. "AJ got out. I didn't even know he had the gun on him, and then all of a sudden he shoots Victor." Her eyes welled with tears. "AJ was good person, with good heart. He shoot your man because he's afraid—he believes Victor was coming to kill him. He was sick, yes." She tapped her head. "Up here."

In a panic, Natasha forced AJ back into the car. At this point she was convinced Victor was dead, and she was terrified AJ would be arrested for murder. So she had the presence of mind to lead him away from the scene. AJ still had the gun in his hand, and she put it in her purse. Not knowing what to do with it, she took a risk and drove over to the Ocean Breeze Hotel, where she left it right where they had found it. This was late on Tuesday night.

This gelled with what Kristy the barmaid had told Louie about seeing Natasha looking distressed and pale in the lobby that night. Louie did not ask for further details; he had no need of hearing them. He left Natasha to Tony's care and went into his study and made a few phone calls. When he came out, Angie was carrying a breakfast tray into the library, and Tony was standing glumly at the door.

Tony said to Louie. "When Victor got shot, I blamed myself—I shouldn't have involved you in my problems. Anyway, I was feeling guilty and confessed a few things to Gina. She knew there was something wrong with me—"

Flabbergasted, Louie said, "You confessed your infidelity to your wife?"

Tony hung his head. "I thought it was the right thing to do, the moral thing." He heaved a sigh. "Gina asked me to leave. She's planning to divorce me."

The doctor was from a local clinic. He did not advertise house calls, but he'd been recommended to Louie by his friend from Philadelphia, and he came at first summons. He was a light-skinned black man who looked like ex-military, although he was dressed casually and in athletic attire when he arrived at eight. He treated the patient in the library, leaving her with a five day supply of antibiotics and prescription pain meds. Over a cup of coffee he told Louie she needed further treatment, including psychological counseling and lab work to screen for "diseases associated with her line of work." Then he charged Louie three-hundred dollars for his house-call and left.

Nathan arrived at ten, just after Michael and Kaiser departed with Natasha. They were driving her to a woman's shelter in Gainesville, which Louie's contact in Tallahassee had arranged on short notice when he called in his favor. Conflicted, the man had stammered at Louie's request, but he did not refuse, as Louie knew he would not. When he called back his tone was cheerful and solicitous, the way politicians' voices are, and he assured Louie the girl would receive help, possibly even legal status.

Tony seemed surprised when Louie chose Michael to drive Natasha, sending Kaiser with him as a precaution, but he did not dispute his father's decision, saying good-bye to Natasha on the driveway and wishing her well. Tony was shamed-faced with Angie, who'd had him on a pedestal for so long she'd forgotten he was human. Whether from a desire to escape his mother's disappointment or a need to be helpful, Tony followed Louie and Nathan to the beach.

They sat on Adirondack chairs beneath the circular shade of a beach umbrella. They wore shorts and sunglasses and dug their bare feet into the sand like men of leisure, their voices muted by waves that crested onto the beach and nipped at their toes. Nathan, in the process of telling Louie certain facts he'd learned about Grigori Buzeczki and the out-of-control deputy from Osceola County, paused as Tony claimed a chair. Sensing weakness, he turned to Louie, as though to say, *he's your responsibility,* which, indeed, he was. At a nod from Louie, Nathan continued, and Tony sat there and listened and didn't say a word.

Chapter Forty

LOUIE AND NATHAN WENT UP to the house. Angie served antipasti with chilled Pinot Grigio and warm, crusty bread. They sat on the terrace beneath the light breeze of the ceiling fans, the ocean view before them, and ate their lunch. Stella came out and joined them. She was dressed in a gauzy white sundress with a short, flared skirt and strappy silver sandals with four inch heels. She smelled of expensive perfume, and her dark eyes were languorous as she looked at Nathan, her teeth flashing in her smile. Once Nathan set his hand on the table and she reached over and touched him, her hand lingering.

Nathan was polite though disinterested, and Louie loved him for it. But one time Stella got up and Nathan looked at her, and there was a spark in his eye that he could not conceal and made no effort to conceal, and Louie felt a pinprick of worry. After Nathan left, he drew Stella aside and said, "Baby, he's not for you."

Stella rose to the challenge, her eyes flashing. "Nathan's the only man who *is* for me," she said. "The only man I want."

"Nathan loves his wife very much. He's faithful to her."

"Well, then it's a pity he can't be more like you," she replied.

Louie didn't like her answer. His eyes narrowed. "Don't act like that with him again. Not under my roof." When Stella did not reply, Louie said, "Did you hear me?" and she moved past him and went inside the house, shutting the door loudly behind her. Angie looked sharply at Louie, and then she got up and followed Stella inside.

A few minutes later Angie's two maids emerged and cleared the table. Maria got up and refreshed Louie's wine. She nodded sleepily at him and headed inside. The maids gathered their plates and platters and discreetly disappeared. Louie was alone, the fan humming above him. Savoring his solicitude, he sipped his wine, his eyes trained on the horizon. He saw Tony get off a chaise lounge and trudge through the sand. Tony came through the gate, latched it behind him and then rinsed his feet at the shower. He turned, saw Louie watching him, and started toward him.

Tony walked slowly, his head bowed. He was unshaven, and his clothes were wrinkled. His air of defeat rankled Louie. As soon as Tony stepped onto the terrace, Louie said, "You look like hell."

Tony rubbed the bristle on his jaw. He walked to the glass door fridge and grabbed a bottle of Fuji water. He uncapped it and drank thirstily. When he was done, he wiped his mouth with the back of his hand. "I didn't get any sleep last night."

Louie shrugged. "Who did?" He took a drink of wine, held the stem of the glass loosely between his fingers. "Your mother set aside a plate for you."

"How can I eat? My life is falling apart." Tony drew back the chair on the opposite side of the table from Louie and sat. "My wife is going to divorce me."

"Whose fault is that? You're the one who decided to confess—"

"Relationships should be built on trust."

Louie sighed. "You should know by now that there are some things a man should never tell his wife."

Tony flushed, the criticism hitting home. Dismayed by his weakness, Louie said, "I shouldn't have to tell you this, but you need to understand that the words you heard Nathan and I speak today you will carry to your grave without ever revealing to another living soul that you heard them. You do understand this, don't you?"

That afternoon Louie and Angie visited Victor, bringing Ceci with them. Victor was sitting up and eating when they arrived, and Louie knew he was finally on the mend because he was criticizing the flabby piece of broiled boneless chicken the hospital had served him with a side of mushy broccoli and a cup of Jell-O. His voice was still painfully hoarse, and he spoke in whispers, making a big deal out of Ceci coming to see him and crediting her for helping to make him better.

Victor had been watching the news and reading the papers. He was dismayed that Anthony had been shot, and a bit clueless about some of the other things that had transpired. Louie filled him in as best he could, in spite of the constant interference of family and friends, not to mention Nurse Dora, who came in often, gauging the level of activity with a wary eye.

When they had a moment alone, Louie asked Victor if AJ Molinsky had shot him, and Victor said, "Yeah, dumb kid was doped up—got out of that Jeep of his and came toward me. I could see he wasn't right in the head, you know, but I never figured he'd come out blasting. The girl yelled at him to stop, but she was too late. The dumb fuck—he caught me off guard."

Victor's voice rasped. He had to stop and sip water. Louie waited until he was comfortable, and then said, "I wanted to make sure Natasha wasn't lying to me."

Victor shook his head. "She was telling the truth." Flushed from coughing, he shook his head, mystified. "I don't hold it against the punk—my fault, really. I should have known better. Don't retaliate."

"It would have been your call," said Louie. "But Molinsky's dead. Buzeczki popped him two nights ago, in the parking lot of Ireland's Courtyard."

"Tough luck," said Victor.

Knowing that the cops had been up to question Victor, Louie asked him what he had told them. Victor grinned. "Shit, Lou, I told them I didn't get a good look at the person who shot me and couldn't identify him."

They talked a few minutes, and then Nurse Dora entered Victor's room and gave Louie the evil eye. He told Victor he had to go. Bending, Louie dropped a fatherly kiss on Victor's forehead. He said, "You don't know how much it means to me to see you getting better. You run my life, you know."

Victor nodded, his eyes misting. Louie said, "I'll stop in tomorrow."

He stepped away from the bed and turned toward the door. Victor said, "You figured it out about Molinsky and his sister, huh?"

"What?"

Louie swung back to Victor, but he started coughing and Nurse Dora's head snapped up. She glared at Louie, daring him to say another word, and he went out the door and into the corridor where Angie and Ceci were waiting for him.

Chapter Forty-One

AFTER DROPPING ANGIE AND CECI at home, Louie drove to his office, arriving a few minutes after five. Since Victor's shooting, he had seriously neglected his business, and there were a few things he needed to attend to. Emily was preparing to call it quits, but she came into Louie's office to tell him how pleased she was to hear that Victor was improving. They discussed Victor's condition and then went over a few business matters, at which time Emily informed him that she had hired Sophie, but not for Adriana's position. The temp agency had sent a replacement, and it was only for another few weeks anyhow. But Sophie was computer smart, and Martin thought she'd be perfect for managing the website, maintaining the computers, and online stuff. It was all so technical and confusing, Emily said. "And," she added, smiling superciliously, "I was quite impressed that you chose an employee based on ability and not appearance. It's rather remarkable, really. Martin thought so, too."

"Well, there's hope for me yet," said Louie glibly.

"You're a good man, Mr. Morelli. It offends me when people say nasty things about you."

"Give 'em hell, Emily."

Louie's prepaid cell buzzed intrusively. Emily said, "You have a nice weekend, sir," and went out, closing the door behind her.

Louie flipped open the phone. "Yes."

"Sir, it's me, Bernie."

Thompson sounded a little hyper. Louie said, "How are you, Bernie?"

"Good, good. I'm on my way to the gym."

"That's great." There was a significant pause. Louie said, "Anything else going on?"

"You wouldn't believe it."

"Try me."

"Wayne Rawlins was found dead this afternoon."

"Really." Louie feigned surprise. "What happened?"

"I guess the guy was falling apart. You know, after they found him at the motel in Delray ... well, I didn't tell you everything, not wanting to alarm you, but Rawlins not only had your address, he had a picture of your house, and a bunch of articles he'd printed off the Internet about you. I mean, it really looked like he had evil intentions, but he hadn't done anything, per se, and Delray couldn't hold him. They contacted Osceola, and the sheriff there—Warren, is his name, and he ... well ... Rawlins worked for him, and he sent over a cruiser to fetch his deputy yesterday afternoon."

"What went wrong? Did Rawlins resist arrest or something, get himself shot?"

"Not at all. Osceola picked him up and drove him home. Rawlins lived in a double-wide on ten acres up there. Anyway, Warren took him home and ordered him to stay put, sort of like an unofficial house arrest. The sheriff said they didn't have the manpower to do a full surveillance, but they were conducting drive-by's, just to make sure Rawlins's pick-up stayed in his driveway. He was supposed to call in at eight this morning."

"I'm assuming he didn't call."

"No, and get this. When he didn't call by ten, Warren went over there. He said he knew Rawlins was cracking up, and he went to probate first thing this morning to file a petition to have Rawlins hospitalized. Said he should have done it sooner—"

Louie said, "You're not telling me what happened."

"Rawlins hung himself." At Louie's stunned silence, Thompson continued. "Yes, sir, they found him hanging in the master bedroom closet. He'd rigged it up pretty good."

"Wow. I guess he was falling apart. That's pretty extreme. Did he leave a note?"

"No."

"Any chance of foul play?"

"Doesn't look like it. Coroner says it's a suicide. I gather the place was messy, but there was no sign of a struggle or anything. Besides, the doors were bolted from the inside."

Fifteen minutes later Louie left his office, briefcase in hand. A couple of agents were putting together a deal, and Louie stopped and spoke with them. Tony had been in earlier, but the light in his office was off, confirming that he'd left. An after-hours cleaning crew was on the scene, the door to the men's room ajar as someone mopped the floor. Walking down the hall, Louie passed Victor's windowless office. Victor had an office, though he seldom used it. The door was open, the light off. There was nothing important in Victor's office, and nobody ever looked for him here, as he spent most of his time lounging on Louie's couch. On impulse, Louie halted and turned in. Entering, he hit the wall switch, and the light over the desk came on.

Louie couldn't remember the last time he'd been in Victor's office, and he was surprised to see that Victor had hung a few quality landscapes on his walls—watercolors by a local artist depicting coastal sunrises and a Miami street scene, the Pompano Beach Lighthouse at dusk. Other than the pictures there was nothing to look at. The room was furnished with a desk, chair, and two four-drawer filing cabinets. On the desk was a phone and next to it, face down, was a single sheet of paper.

Placing his briefcase on the desk, Louie flipped over the paper. Three addresses were written on the sheet in a small, precise printing that Louie recognized as Chucky's. He understood that this was the list of physical addresses corresponding to the IP addresses used in the blackmailing scheme. The first address was in Hollywood Beach. Chucky had noted that it was an apartment building, with a memo that some activity had been generated at this location. This address had been mentioned in a follow-up article the *Sun-Sentinel* ran yesterday about the young woman, Irina, who had been beaten to death, citing this apartment as her residence. The article had run because the police had not yet solved Irina's murder, and they were seeking the public's help.

Chucky noted that an address in Sunny Isles Beach was purported to have shown "some moderate activity." This made sense, as Sunny Isles Beach was home to the Russian community. Idly, Louie wondered if this was the house of horror Natasha had escaped from. But it was the third and final address, the one on NE 5th Avenue in Boca Raton that caught Louie's attention, made his breath catch in his throat, for this was the house Louie had visited when he called on Adriana.

Chucky had made a question mark next to the address. What was it Victor had said before he was shot? Something about a discrepancy Chucky had noted with one of the addresses. Sure, he'd noticed it, because Louie had asked him to find Adriana. That's why. A coincidence? Hardly. Louie didn't believe in those types of coincidences.

He recalled what Victor had said yesterday, about Louie figuring it out about Molinsky and his sister. "A twin," Margaret Peterson had told him on that day he'd visited her house. Adriana and Adam, aka AJ Molinsky, were the blonde, tow-headed children in the picture she'd shown him. And, of course, there had been the artwork, and Mrs. Peterson's boasting of her son's talents, the prestigious art school included. The last names were different because both Adriana and Mrs. Peterson had married and taken their husband's names. Lastly, the family's computer had not been working, as it should not have been because Chucky had infected all computers at the IP addresses and created what he had called "nuclear havoc."

Anger crept up on Louie, along with a sense of betrayal. He put the paper in his briefcase and snapped the lid shut. He started to walk out of the office when his phone began buzzing and vibrating. Lifting it from his pocket, Louie answered, saying, "Yes," a bit abruptly.

"Louis, this is Sergei. Is this not a good time?"

"Hello, Sergei. It's always a good time for you. How are you?"

"Very good, my friend. Elaine and I are having a dinner party on Tuesday. It's at our house on Star Island." Elaine was Szarnakov's platinum-haired mistress. "I should like it very much if you could come."

Chapter Forty-Two

THE NEXT MORNING, SATURDAY, LOUIE swam his laps, and then spent a few leisurely hours with Ceci. Gina had returned from North Carolina the night before, and Tony showed up with two of Louie's grandsons, the baby left at home with his mother. Anthony and his family arrived at noon, and Angie and Maria served grilled salmon with a green salad and a side of pasta oglio. Sitting at the table with his children and grandchildren, his eccentric daughter at his side, Louie felt blissfully happy.

Later, he said good-bye to Ceci and Michael and his cousin, all of whom were returning to Louisiana that evening. After they left, Louie and Angie took Tony's boys and Isabella for ice cream. It was dark by the time Tony took his kids home, but he returned an hour later with his overnight bag, saying sheepishly and apologetically, "It's only for a few days."

On Sunday they went to nine o'clock mass at St. Lucy's in Highland Beach. This was the mass Angie preferred, and the church—they'd become parishioners. It was no match for St. Louis Cathedral, but Angie liked the light, and the "spiritual" quality, the soft prettiness of the church. They all attended, the ladies in their summer dresses, Isabella decked in a flouncy sundress. Tony accompanied them, though he looked glum, as Gina had refused to take his call this morning.

Louie's mind wandered through the mass. He never prayed, barely listened to the homily, but his presence pleased Angie immensely, and he was glad to do this small service for her. Filing out of church after mass, Louie encountered Judge Flannery of Palm Beach County's Circuit Court. Flannery was with his wife, a too thin redhead in an ankle-length black skirt.

Flannery was a florid-faced Irishman with a middle-aged paunch and a distinguished head of silver-gray hair. He caught sight of Louie and quickly finished shaking hands with one of the ushers, moving toward Louie with an unctuous smile, his blue eyes twinkling. Louie had contributed to Flannery's re-election campaign and had met him socially on several occasions. They frequently spotted each other at church.

Giving Louie a friendly handshake, Flannery said, "Good to see you, Lou. Good to see you." The phony smile broadened. "I heard you had a bit of trouble this week."

"I'd say it's more than a bit," said Louie, good-naturedly.

Flannery nodded. "I hear you're a pretty good shot."

"I'm lucky."

People were milling about, the vestibule noisy with the buzz of countless conversations. Louie's family walked ahead of him, stepping onto the sidewalk outside of St. Lucy's. Flannery's wife was occupied with another couple, and Flannery cupped Louie's elbow and drew him aside. Lowering his voice, Flannery whispered, "I played eighteen holes with Doug Bellamy yesterday." Bellamy was the Delray Beach chief of police. Catching Louie's eye, Flannery said, "Your name came up quite a bit."

Louie's brows went up, signaling interest. Pleased, Flannery continued, "You've been in the news a lot, Lou. Everybody's talking. The funny thing is Doug swears he didn't know anything about your past, which I find hard to believe. Somebody said you nailed that intruder good, despite taking fire. Doug said you claimed not to know anything about the shooter."

"That's right, I don't."

"He was a foreigner, you know."

"I didn't know," said Louie, pretending this was news. "Was he an illegal?"

"No, he was here on an extended visa. Talk is he was as queer as they come. I guess he hung around with a couple of old queens in Palm Beach, lived off their largesse. No criminal record or anything like that. No connections to organized crime." Flannery smiled. "Doug's mystified."

"Quite frankly, so am I," said Louie, although he wasn't, not now, not anymore.

Chapter Forty-Three

TONY SKIPPED OUT AFTER CHURCH, declining brunch at the Breakers in Palm Beach with the rest of them. He did not return to Louie's house that night, nor did he answer his phone, letting his mother's call go to voicemail. He *did* call Louie early Monday morning, telling his father that he'd driven down to Miami yesterday to "visit a friend."

Louie's silence spoke volumes, and Tony said defensively, "It's *not* what you think, Dad."

"I didn't say a word. Your mother was worried when you didn't show up last night."

"I saw she called me. I didn't get a chance to call her back. Tell Mom not to worry—I'll see her tonight."

"Are you planning on working today?"

"I'll be in the office around ten."

Louie told Tony to be careful driving and clicked off his phone. Dressed for his swim, he went downstairs and found Angie in the kitchen cutting up a watermelon. Louie stood at the counter and ate a piece, eating it from the rind, the way he did when he was a kid. The melon was sugar sweet and icy cold, and the juice ran over his fingers. Tossing the rind into the trash, Louie washed his hands at the kitchen sink and then walked through the family room and stepped out onto the terrace. The maid was cleaning the tiled table with a wet, soapy cloth. She looked up and gave Louie a little smile.

Louie said good morning and walked past her and out to the pool. The sun was hot today, the sky a soft, hazy blue. Glancing out at the sea, Louie saw that it was calm and smooth as glass. He decided to do an ocean swim, slipping out the gate and trudging through sand that was already, even at this early hour, hot on his feet.

Louie waded out to his chest, started swimming parallel to shore, heading south. He swam a good distance and then started back, pausing intermittently to tread water or float, the sun beating hot on his neck and shoulders, the water warm and salty, stinging through the gauze bandage he still wore on his hand. At first Louie maintained a count, but the water felt wonderful, and his swim was so enjoyable he forgot it was supposed to be exercise.

He came out dripping, saltwater and sunlight stinging his eyes. Wiping his face with the towel he'd dropped onto the lounge chair beneath Angie's cabana, he laid the towel flat and sunned himself dry. He started to doze, then shook himself awake and went up to the house.

Stella and Isabella were in the kitchen with the dogs, his granddaughter eating a bowl of Lucky Charms, the milk in her bowl stained pale pink. Stella was sitting sideways on a chair, sipping from a glass of orange juice. She said, "Hi, Daddy," and watched with a smile as Louie bent to nuzzle the top of Isabella's head.

He moved over to Stella's chair, and she turned her cheek so he could kiss her. "If you're going to feed her sugar, you should feed her something that tastes good."

Stella said, "It's her favorite cereal."

"Where's your mother?"

"She and Nonna went to the bakery." She gave Louie a direct look. "You know Chester's coming over today, don't you?"

Louie's eyes registered surprise. "I guess she forgot to tell me. Do you know what time he's coming?"

Stella flipped over her phone and looked at the time. "In about an hour," she said."

"I want you to do me a favor when he comes. Distract your mother so I can speak to Chester alone."

Her eyes sparkled mischievously. "It'll be my pleasure. What are you going to say to him?"

"Oh, nothing too drastic. Just a gentle reminder for him to mind his manners." He walked to the counter where Stella had left the pitcher of juice. He took a small glass from the cupboard and poured it full. Stella waited for him to divulge his intentions, but instead, he asked her about the birthday party she was putting together for Angie. They discussed her plans, which had become increasingly extravagant, extending beyond the scope of immediate family. Louie finished his juice and ate a handful of cherries.

Stella said, "Daddy, do you want me to make you breakfast?"

He put his hand on her shoulder. "Not today, Princess. I have to get dressed before Chester arrives."

Chapter Forty-Four

LOUIE GLANCED AT HIS REFLECTION in the full-length mirror beside his closet. His ocean swim had deepened the tropical tan that never really left his face. Turning his head to the side, Louie smoothed his hair, noticing at the same time that he was acquiring more gray.

The closet door was open, revealing the double racks of suits, arranged by Stella—dark on one side, light on the other, the jackets and blazers grouped separately, a row of white shirts that gave way to color. Louie selected a white sport shirt, wearing it open-collared, with beige trousers and a Canali jacket with mocha-colored pin-stripes. His shoes were saddle-stitched, two-toned beige and tan.

Adjusting his pocket square, Louie turned away from the mirror. He gathered up his phones and went downstairs, accessing the back staircase so that he came down on the landing outside the kitchen, smelling Maria's chicken soup instantly. Yesterday Maria had announced her intention of making the *zuppa* and delivering it to Victor at the hospital.

The soup was simmering on the stove. Maria sat at the counter with a cup of coffee and one of Stella's Italian fashion magazines.

Stella sat with Isabella in the family room, watching the Disney channel, but she got up when she saw her father and walked into the kitchen. "Daddy, you're so handsome," she gushed. Leaning in, she whispered conspiratorially, "Chester's here. I've arranged for Aunt Vera to call with an emergency. Will that work?"

"Perfectly." Glancing out the window at the terrace and half expecting to see Angie sitting with Chester, he asked where she was. Speaking Italian, Maria told him she was in the parlor. Her tone was apologetic, as though she felt partly responsible for Angie's decision to entertain a male guest in her home. Louie gave her a reassuring pat, winked at Stella, and walked out of the kitchen.

In the parlor Angie and Chester were sitting on one of the two brocade sofas placed on either side of a marble-topped baroque coffee table. An open archway revealed the room from the colonnaded hall and Louie paused here, studying from an unobserved distance his wife and the charlatan who had swindled her. They sat within arm's reach of one another, their bodies turned toward each other, knees nearly touching.

Angie had primped for Chester, taking extra care with her hair and make-up. A rosy shade of lipstick darkened her lips and from the glossy sheen on her nails Louie assumed she'd squeezed in an early-morning manicure. Wearing a scoop-necked blue dress bordered with jade flowers, Angie presided over an antique silver serving set replete with coffee pot. Next to the tray were a plate of Italian pastry and a carafe of sparkling water with sliced lemon. In front of each of them was a half-full water goblet, a cup and saucer in delicate bone-white china with corresponding desert plates and purple satin napkins.

The surrounding room was formal, incorporating ageless Italian opulence with nineteenth-century New Orleans, as they'd furnished it with some treasured pieces, including a bronze and crystal chandelier they'd purchased from a French Quarter gallery. Covered in lace panels, the tall windows flanked a limestone fireplace, a Flemish tapestry hanging above it.

Lavender checks in Chester's seersucker jacket matched Angie's napkins, and Louie thought, scornfully, that he looked like an Easter egg with his yellow trousers and purple-plaid blazer. Thickened with hairspray, Chester's Trump-do stretched stiffly across the top of his head. He held the delicate saucer in his left hand, holding the cup to his mouth with his right hand, pinky finger extended as Louie walked into the parlor.

He smiled indulgently and stopped short of the couch, stood looking down at them. Louie said, "Hello, dear. You didn't tell me you were having company this morning."

The look on Angie's face was priceless. Since Louie's Mercedes had been towed away, she'd been having a hard time keeping track of his comings and goings. A flicker of something—alarm, perhaps anger, flared in her eyes. Her tone was measured. "Louie," she said, "I thought you had left."

Chester's reaction was a bit more dramatic. He choked, nearly dropping his cup, and just managed to set it noisily back in the saucer before a fit of coughing seized him. Angie glared at Louie and handed Chester his water goblet. He sucked in a deep breath and gulped water, then patted his mouth dry with the napkin.

Louie said, "Goodness, I hope I'm not intruding." He flashed Angie a smile. "I didn't know you were entertaining, dear."

Angie's lips compressed tightly. "I thought I mentioned it yesterday." She cleared her throat. "Louie, you do remember my friend Chester?"

"Yes, of course." Louie stepped forward and extended his hand. Chester rose, his palm as clammy as wet dough as he accepted Louie's handshake. "How are you, Chester?"

"Fine, fine." Chester let go of Louie's hand and eased his body back down on the sofa.

"Angie tells me you're a florist."

"Yes." Chester pressed the napkin to his mouth and stifled a cough.

Angie said, "Chester has a flower shop in Lake Worth."

"Indeed." Louie made a show of examining the pastry. "*Sfogliatelle*," he exclaimed. "Angie, you shouldn't have."

He sat on the couch opposite them and reached for a dessert plate, putting one of the shell-shaped puff pastries on it. He gazed at Angie, relishing her discomfort with a malicious joy. He bit into the pastry, gave a low moan of pleasure as he tasted the cream.

Angie looked mortified. She handed him a napkin, and Louie said, "Would it be too much trouble to get a cup of coffee, dear?"

Angie had set out extra dessert plates but only two cups and saucers, and Louie's request meant that she'd have to go into the dining room to retrieve a third cup. She gave him a smoldering look and got up, murmuring something about having to get it from the china cabinet. As soon as she stepped out of the room, trailing a whiff of Chanel No. 5, Louie wiped his fingers on his napkin and looked expectantly at Chester.

Chester's face reddened. He reached into his jacket pocket and produced a check, extended it toward Louie. Clearing his throat, he said, "I have a certified check for nine thousand dollars made payable to Angie."

Louie's investigative skills were pitiful—he'd counted six thousand dollars owed to his wife. Now Chester was admitting to nine, and then some. "I'm four hundred short," he said. "If you could give me another week or so—"

"I have no problem with that." Louie took the check from Chester and glanced at the denomination, ascertaining that it was indeed a certified check drawn on funds in a Bank of America account. Then he handed the check back to Chester. "Give this to Angie. It's *her* money. Besides," he allowed himself a little smile, "she has no idea I'm aware of this…transaction."

Chester folded the check in half and slid it back into his pocket just as Angie returned, cup and saucer in hand. She glanced nervously at them, and then proceeded to pour coffee from the silver coffeepot. It was part of an elaborate antique set, given to them as a wedding present from the then governor of Louisiana and used only on special occasions. It irked Louie that Angie had brought it out to use on this toad.

When the coffee was poured, Angie added a spoonful of sugar to Louie's cup and passed it to him. She then refreshed Chester's cup as well as her own. Louie finished his *sfogliatelle*, selected a Napoleon. Chester nibbled nervously on an almond macaroon. "Delicious," he said, smiling at Angie. "You shouldn't have gone to this trouble, darling."

The endearment grated on Louie. Looking out the tall windows, he observed a turquoise Thunderbird convertible parked in the mall. He could see clear to the end of the drive, where one of Nathan's men guarded the gate from beneath the shade of a canopy. Outside the front door, Louie's gardener finished soaking one of the potted hibiscus trees and moved on to its neighbor, his hose snaking across the walkway. Louie said, "Nice car, Chester. What year is it?"

"Umm, it's a 1960."

"All restored?"

"Of course."

There was no phone in the parlor, but Louie heard the extension in the library ring once, twice. A few seconds passed, the grandfather clock in the hall ticking away the time. Footsteps sounded outside the parlor, and then Stella appeared in the arched doorframe.

She looked at Louie first, a little twinkle in her eye. "Mom," she said, "Aunt Vera's on the phone. I told her you had company, but she says it's important. Can you talk to her?"

"Oh my, I hope nothing has happened." Angie got up, shooting Louie a warning glance from beneath lowered lashes, saying to Chester. "Excuse me. I had better see what this is about."

Louie said, "Take your time, dear. I'll keep Chester company."

Angie abruptly stiffened, then forced herself to relax. She looked inquiringly at Stella, who waited for her mother to pass. As soon as Angie was out of range, Stella gave Louie a wink and then followed her mother from the room.

Alone with Chester, Louie smiled coldly. He said, "Have the police spoken to you about your friend?"

Chester's expression was wary. "What friend?"

"Your Ukrainian friend. The man who tried to kill me and damn near killed my cousin and daughter."

Chester slumped forward, air escaping noisily through his nose as he realized the truth was out. "I didn't really believe he would do it," he said. "Iouri talked crazy, but I didn't think he was capable of killing anybody."

"He used your gun, Chester, didn't he? It was a .38. It's the Smith and Wesson you had in your shop, the one Victor admired."

"My God, I didn't know he took it until after ... but by then it was too late." Tears sprang to Chester's eyes. "Iouri was there the day you and Victor came. He was upstairs, listening, and he ... well, it was his idea for me to borrow from Angie, and he thought ... I guess he thought that if he eliminated you, I could get a lot more money from her." Chester's voice broke, turned to a barely controlled screech. "That morning after Victor was shot, and they were talking about you on the news, Iouri said he was going to kill you and make it look like a mob hit. He said no one would ever suspect him."

Louie's voice was like ice. "And you went along with this?"

Chester shook his head. "I didn't think Iouri was serious." He used Angie's satin napkin to dab at his brow, his eyes sliding away from Louie's. He swallowed noisily. "I didn't realize my gun was missing. Then I turned on the TV and it was all over the news that you had shot an intruder. When I didn't hear from Iouri, I grew alarmed—"

"Did you call him?"

"No. We didn't call each other. Iouri had a jealous boyfriend—an older man who supported him. He couldn't get away too often." He looked at Louie. "Our relations were secret. No one knew he was with me that morning. That's why the police haven't connected him to me."

"But they will connect him," said Louie. "You can be sure of that. Have you decided what you'll tell them?"

"No. But I'm afraid—"

"You should be afraid."

Louie said this calmly, without menace, but Chester paled considerably. He wrung his hands, twisting them together in his lap. "Mr. Morelli, please don't blame me. How can I be responsible for Iouri's actions? I swear to you I didn't know—"

Louie held up a hand, forestalling Chester's protestations of innocence. He'd heard enough. He said, "Chester, I want to protect my wife. If the police discover Iouri's real motive for trying to kill me, it'll reflect badly on Angie. Your scam will be exposed—probably in the media, too—and she'll be hurt and humiliated. I'd rather Angie doesn't know that you made a fool out of her. Are we in agreement?"

"Y-yes."

"I think you're going to have to call the police about this. Be proactive."

"I don't—"

"It'll be better for you in the long run. Tell the police you and Iouri had an affair, but that you broke it off because he was unstable. Tell them he was delusional and that he was jealous of even your casual relationships. He imagined things, even imagined that you had feelings for my wife, which you will deny, of course. Although, please do tell the police that you and Angie are friends, and that you've been here, to my house, on several occasions. You're a skilled liar—you can embellish the story, but not too much. Tell the police Iouri followed you here the last time you called on her." Louie smiled coldly. "Tell them he was completely irrational and that he threatened you."

Chester said, "I'm afraid to go to the police. They haven't exactly been kind to me in the past. I have a record, and if they find out I had a gun—"

"Was the gun registered to you?"

"No."

Louie shrugged. "Why admit to having it? Let them think it was Iouri's. After all, they are already in possession of the gun. They know he acted alone. Your job is to convince them that he was psychologically unstable and give them a motive. Can you do it?"

Chester eyed him warily. "What's it to you?"

"I want them off my back. I killed the man in self-defense, but they're hindering my activities with this investigation. I want it to go away."

"I don't suppose I have a choice."

"I'm sure it'll go better for you this way." Louie wiped his hands on his napkin. Standing, he tossed the napkin onto the coffee table. "Wipe your eyes, Chester. I don't want Angie to suspect that you're upset. And send a bill to my office—backdate it to last Tuesday, the day Victor and I stopped in to see you. The police already know I was at your shop. You can tell them I had you send flowers to my wife." He moved to the door, said softly. "And don't forget to give Angie that check."

Chapter Forty-Five

L EAVING THE HOUSE, LOUIE DROVE up to West Palm, checking on one of his developments. Now that he knew the identity and motive of the man who had shot at him, he'd given Kaiser the day off and drove himself, using Angie's Escalade. At City Place, the upscale shopping and dining area in West Palm, Louie lunched at Bellagio with a fellow investor, ordering a mixed green salad. By the time he got to his office, a copy of Chester's backdated bill had been faxed and was sitting in the pile of paper on his desk. Louie initialed it for payment authorization.

He got caught up on paperwork, discussed a few business matters with Martin, and spoke, though briefly, with Tony. His son seemed okay, perhaps a little tired. Tony was too busy to talk, although he did tell Louie he was heading home to have a serious discussion with Gina. "I don't want a divorce, Dad," he said. "I won't put my kids through that. They need me there, with them."

Louie agreed and drove home, where his family was waiting to go to dinner. Stella had initially planned to accompany them, but she'd gone with her mother to the hospital, where, she reported, they served Maria's Sicilian chicken soup, bringing in their own cutlery and arousing the ire of the nursing staff. She was happy to report that Victor ate with gusto. They'd even snuck in a couple of *cannoli,* which Victor was really appreciative of. Now Stella claimed a headache, allowing Isabella to go without her.

Having driven the ladies to the hospital and back, Sam now ferried them to Trattoria Romana. One of the perks of Sam's job was that he got to eat really well, and tonight was no exception, although he abstained from the chilled Santa Margherita Pinot Grigio Louie ordered from the wine steward—a perfect complement to the sea bass, yellowtail, and buttery pasta. Conversation at the table was deliberately light, revolving around the ladies' visit to the hospital. Everyone was pleased at Victor's progress, and there was talk of him being released from the hospital. There was no mention of Angie's early morning visitor—not that Louie expected her to discuss Chester—but she seemed a little sheepish. He pretended not to notice.

Night comes early on Florida's East Coast, even in May, and it was dark when they arrived home. They passed through the gate without issue, Nathan's night duty guard waving them in. The exterior lights were on, the motor court bathed in a soft illumination. Parked in the spot where Chester's Thunderbird had been earlier was Nathan's black MKS. Louie had not been expecting Nathan, and he felt a stirring of apprehension.

Angie said, "Is that Nathan's car?"

Louie said that it was. Sam pulled around to the front and put the car in park, and Louie got out, opening the rear passenger door of the Lincoln. Bending, he lifted a sleeping Isabella from her grandmother's lap and started toward the house, leaving Sam to assist the ladies. Shifting Isabella to his left side, Louie unlocked the front door, pushing it open and stepping in.

The grand foyer was cool and welcoming, the hall bathed in ambient light. The parlor and dining room were dark, but lamplight spilled from the open door of the library and Louie walked toward it, his heels tapping on the limestone. Isabella was slumped against his shoulder, moaning softly. Louie could hear the television in the family room—it sounded unusually loud, a Budweiser commercial blaring. Perhaps that's why they didn't hear him come in, he reflected later.

They were on the couch, Nathan reclining and Stella crouching over him, her knees bracketing his hips. It registered to Louie that they were both dressed, Nathan in shorts and an olive-green T-shirt, Stella in her white designer jeans and a black halter-top. The halter's ties were undone, and her naked breasts were flattened against Nathan's chest.

Nathan's arms were locked around Stella's waist, his hands cupping her ass. Aware of Nathan's intense devotion to his wife, Louie was stunned by this display of passion. He thought of the way Stella had flirted with Nathan on his last visit. For a second he stood there, dumbfounded, and then Isabella stirred, lids fluttering open. Angie was a few feet behind him, talking to Sam. Louie said, "Stella," and the couple on the couch broke apart.

Nathan lifted Stella off of him—both of them rising awkwardly. Stella hastily tied her top, her quick, jerky movements putting her off balance, and Nathan set a steadying hand on her elbow. When she was decent, she tossed her head, running her fingers through her locks. She gazed at Louie coolly and without embarrassment. Then she came toward him, her chin tilted defiantly, and reached for Isabella.

As though he had not witnessed the passionate scene of a few moments before, Louie said calmly, "She's heavy. I'll carry her up."

Stella brushed past him without a word and stepped into the hall, stopping to speak with Angie, her voice betraying nothing. Louie shot a warning look at Nathan, who said, "It's not what you think."

They had coffee and leftover pastry in the kitchen. Pleased to have discovered that Nathan spoke Italian, Maria conversed lightly with him. Angie poured Frangelico for herself and Maria and then fed the dogs their nightly treats. Stella did not come down downstairs.

Nathan finished his *cannoli* and then wiped his fingers on a napkin. Louie said, "Do you want more coffee?"

"No."

Louie inclined his head toward the terrace. "Let's go outside."

Nathan unhooked his cell phone from his belt and laid it on the counter. He followed Louie into the family room, watched him confiscate a bottle of black Sambuca and two snifters from the bar. They proceeded out to the terrace, where Louie set the glasses on the table and filled each one halfway with Sambuca. He handed a snifter to Nathan, then picked up the other one and tapped his glass to it. "*Salute.*"

"Cheers." Nathan raised the snifter to his mouth and took a sip.

They stood, looking out at the pool, the underwater lights coloring the water in shades of blue and green. The spa gurgled softly. The tropical air was scented with flowers, the breeze a feather's touch on Louie's skin.

Gazing appreciatively at the view, Nathan said, "I've always been surprised by the fact that you live on the ocean and not the Intracoastal. It would be much easier for you with the *Stella di Mare*. You could have deep water dockage right outside your door."

"I consider it from time to time," said Louie. "But Angie likes the ocean. Besides, there are advantages to using a marina. This way, I can come and go as I please, and entertain whomever I wish to without disturbing my family."

"As I see it, the only benefit is that you can entertain women."

"Well, that is a benefit." Louie gave Nathan a probing look, his eyes flinty hard. "What's going on with you and Stella?"

Nathan flushed. "Why don't you ask Stella? She's damned persistent," he said hotly. Then, "Aw, fuck it. My one moment of weakness and you had to walk in. I apologize—it won't happen again."

"I'm not so sure it won't." Louie knew how complicated romantic relations could be. He sipped Sambuca, felt the liquor burn his lips. "Thank you for attempting to put my mind at ease."

"It has nothing to do with you. It's out of respect for Tara. I would never betray her."

"That's what I told Stella."

"Well, she's your daughter, Lou. If you want to know the truth, Stella's a lot like you." Louie didn't say anything, and after a minute, Nathan picked up his glass and motioned toward the beach. "Time for a walk."

Removing their sandals, Louie and Nathan trekked down the path bordered with dune grass and past Angie's cabana, where Louie's grandchildren's beach toys were scattered in the sand. To protect endangered sea turtles, lights were prohibited on the beach from March through September, and the moonless night was full of shadows, the sea black beneath a star-studded sky. No loggerheads emerged from the sea while Louie and Nathan stood there, the sea warm and foamy on their feet. A few yards out a large fish jumped, making a splashing sound. Waves crested and then rolled in, swirling around Louie's shins, tugging him imperceptibly forward.

He took a step onto drier sand, studied Nathan in the dark. "Nice work with that deputy in Osceola." His eyes glittered. "I recognized your MO. I always wonder how you do it—stringing a guy up like that. You must have used a little anesthesia—a temporary knockout. Did you have help?"

Nathan shrugged. "You know I prefer to work alone."

"You're a nervy bastard."

"And you're a cold-blooded one." Nathan glanced out at sea and then back at Louie. He studied him somberly, a little smile touching his lips. "Incidentally, you don't owe me for the other one."

"Why not?" When Nathan did not answer, Louie said, "Didn't you do it?"

"He's dead, but I didn't do it. There was another operator there."

"Where, at Buzeczki's house?"

Nathan's eyes gleamed with laughter. He tilted the bulbous glass and drank Sambuca. Then he told Louie about Buzeczki's house in the solidly middle-class neighborhood tucked between A1A and the Atlantic, just south of Oakland Park Boulevard. Buzeczki's house was on the non-water side of North Atlantic and south of the quaint Earl Lifshey Park, a small spot of green at the edge of the sub where Nathan had spotted a couple of homeless kids sleeping beneath a tree on the day that he'd jogged through the neighborhood, mingling with dog-walkers, power-walkers, and erstwhile real estate agents.

Nathan had gone to kill Buzeczki Sunday evening, as the first curtain of darkness descended, when neighborhood grills were still emitting odors of roasting meat and lights shone in windows. Most of the homes in the neighborhood had been there since the sixties, although there were some teardowns and newer rebuilds. A couple of houses were vacant, abandoned by their owners and in the process of what Nathan assumed were foreclosures. The house across from Buzeczki's was under construction, the outer walls concrete silhouettes, a chain strung across the foot of the drive.

Buzeczki's L-shaped ranch was on the small side. The lawn was neatly cut, but weeds crowded the flowerbeds and the bushes beneath the windows needed trimming. A kidney-shaped pool was in the backyard, a couple of beach towels hanging on the fence to dry. Buzeczki's BMW was in the carport, an older model Malibu parked in the narrow drive.

Inconspicuous behind the wheel of a cargo van, its side panels advertising a plumbing company, Nathan cruised the dark street waiting for the Malibu's owner to leave. According to Nathan's source, Buzeczki's company never stayed past ten. It was a quarter of the hour when he drove by, his plans stymied by the bicyclist who appeared in his rearview mirror and quickly overtook the van, looping around him in the road, and then drawing to cover beneath the overhang of the sprawling willow on the corner.

It struck Nathan immediately that the bicycle had no reflective gear. It was top of the line, a Tour De France Packleader stripped of reflectors and shields. The cyclist, likewise, was dressed all in black, with a low slung helmet. He wore large safety goggles, which Nathan considered to be more disguise than necessity. He became suspicious when the cyclist circled the block a couple of times.

"Why are you telling me this?" asked Louie, cognizant of the depth of Nathan's operations without usually needing to hear the details.

Nathan said, "Let me ask you a question. When I was here last week, you allowed Tony to listen in on our conversation. Why?"

He felt the first stirrings of apprehension. He said, "I wanted Tony to understand the extent of the mess he created, and how much it was going to cost, in blood and treasure, to set things right."

"Well," said Nathan softly. "I guess he took the lesson to heart."

Louie's heart thumped. "What are you saying? You're not telling me Tony was there—"

Nathan gave Louie a piercing look. "Tony was the other operative. He's the one who killed Buzeczki. And he made some mistakes."

Chapter Forty-Six

TONY'S MISTAKES WERE FIXABLE BECAUSE Nathan had been there to fix them. They hadn't been disastrous, he said, but potentially so. Tony had one advantage—a key, given to him by Natasha, who also supplied a rudimentary layout of the house.

Coming back down the street Nathan saw the cyclist lean his Packleader against the wall of the carport. He removed a small gear-bag, buckling it around his waist like a tourist's fanny-pack as he moved briskly up to the house. There were lights on in the house, but not in the living room, and the cyclist crouched beneath the picture window and peeked in. When he straightened, head turning to scan the street, Nathan saw Tony's face in the hazy light of the carport.

He drove past the house so as not to alarm Tony, came back around only to find that he'd gone inside. Nathan parked the van at the foot of the drive, pulled on a pair of long, rubber gloves, and stepped out—a bearded, shaggy-haired plumber with a ball-cap, loose-fitting shirt, and cargo pants. He carried a toolbox, complete with a commercial-grade snake and pipe wrenches.

The front door was cracked open, revealing a scuffed stretch of hardwood flooring. A burgundy leather sectional took up most of the space, with a long, low coffee table set in front of it. A sixty-inch flat panel television was against the wall. Thankfully, the TV was not on, although music was playing somewhere in the house—a soft, mellow jazz. The picture window was without blinds or draperies, and Nathan, leaving his "tools" on the porch, stepped in cautiously.

Light came from the adjacent kitchen, where the fixture above the sink revealed shapes and shadows. It also showed that there was nobody in the kitchen or dining area, which led onto a patio by means of a sliding door. This door was closed, and verticals were snapped shut over the glass. A couple of dinner plates were standing in a drying rack next to the sink, empty bottles of Rolling Rock lined up on the ledge.

Nathan released the safety on his Glock and crept into the house. The jazz was smooth and smoky, notes dying out long enough for Nathan to hear the sound of water hitting a tiled wall before it transitioned to another song. But now, above the music, came the harsh, startled cry of a man, and then the unmistakable thwack, thwack, thwack as a small caliber handgun discharged in rapid succession. A violent crash ensued, followed by a loud bang. A second later Tony raced into the living room.

Nathan caught him from behind, smothered him in a bear hug, felt his wild surge of panic, and hissed, "Stop. It's me, Nathan," holding him tight until the words penetrated and Tony quit fighting. The goggles hung loose around his neck, but his helmet remained on his head. His eyes were wild with fear and adrenalin. On his hands were sporty, waterproof racing gloves, fingertips padded with silicone.

Speaking in a whisper, Nathan said, "Did you get Buzeczki?"

"Yes, yes, he's dead. Let's go."

"What about the girl?"

"What girl?"

Nathan said, "We're going to clear the house, room to room."

The hallway was short, with two rooms on one side and two on the other. The bathroom was obvious, the water still drumming, shower curtain pulled loose, and Buzeczki collapsed against the back wall, the tile behind him streaked red and a line of pinkish water trailing toward the drain. He'd been shot in the chest and blood was seeping from the wound. His eyes were open, staring. He blinked once, and Nathan said, "Shoot him again, in the head."

Tony shot him. Buzeczki's naked body jerked and went still, his head lolling against the wall, a red spot appearing in the center of his forehead. Nathan pivoted into the hallway, whipped open the door to a small bedroom that had been converted to an office, saw that nobody was in the room, and spun forward.

The music was coming from the master bedroom, where a bed-side lamp cast a pool of light over a king bed with rumpled, black satin sheets, a coverlet trailing onto the floor. Nathan crashed into the room like a combat soldier, saw the combination radio/CD player on the dresser, and heard Ella Fitzgerald's voice coming through the speakers. A glass of white wine was on the nightstand, a lacy brassiere crumpled on the floor.

Tony crowded Nathan, cringing as he flung open the closet doors. The blonde was huddled in the corner beneath a row of hangars that had been pushed violently apart. One hand was poised over the keypad of her cell-phone, the other clutching a Walther PPK. She was naked except for a pair of red panties. She gave a startled squawk, looking at them with enormous eyes, lifting the Walther in a quick, jerky movement.

Nathan kicked the gun out of her hand before she could steady it, sent it skittering across the floor. She screamed once, holding her palms out in a gesture of surrender. She started babbling in Russian. Nathan turned to Tony. "Use your gun."

Tony looked horrified. "I … I can't," he said. "She's not part of this."

"She's seen us." Nathan reminded him. "She can sound the alarm before we reach the door."

Tony hadn't felt any misgivings about killing Buzeczki, but the girl made him stupid. Holding the gun on her, he could not bring himself to shoot. Sensing his weakness, the girl pleaded for life. Stricken, Tony looked at Nathan. "I can't do this."

Nathan took the pistol from Tony and shot the girl between the eyes. Her scream froze in midair, her head slamming against the closet wall and bouncing forward. By all accounts she was dead, and Nathan handed the gun back to Tony. "I didn't want to introduce another weapon onto the scene," he said.

Tony was staring at him in shock. He gave a strangled cry, as though he was in pain, and for an awful moment, Nathan thought he was going to lose it. He checked the girl's phone—she'd been in the act of composing a text. He looked at the log, breathed a sigh of relief when he saw that she hadn't succeeded in sending it.

Nathan dropped the phone onto the floor and hustled Tony from the room. He did a quick sweep of the house, checking under beds and in closets, finding only a cat. They left through the front door, closing it after them, but leaving it unlocked. Nathan collected his tool box. He said, "Tony, get your bike and put it in my van."

He didn't start the van until after Tony hauled in the bike and climbed in after it, shutting the cargo door as quietly as he could. Nathan backed out slowly, unhurriedly, and turned south because two houses north of Buzeczki's an elderly man was walking two bowlegged schnauzers. They got out of the sub without incident. Turning onto A1A, Nathan asked Tony where his vehicle was.

Tony was too stunned to say anything, and Nathan prompted. "You didn't bike down from Delray Beach?"

"I'm parked on the strip, in front of the beach."

Nathan had bottled water in the van, and he gave one to Tony, who uncapped it and drank thirstily. Nathan drove to the Fort Lauderdale strip, the beach coming up on their left. Traffic was light. Tony took off his helmet, ruffled his hair. Nathan said, "Do you have a change of clothes in the car?"

"I have a pair of jeans in the backseat."

"Put them on over your bike shorts as soon as you get in the vehicle. I want you to drive down to the Walker. Don't make any stops. When you get to the Walker, park in the garage. Take Tara's spot. I'll tweak the video so that your arrival time shows two hours earlier, giving you an alibi if it should ever come to that."

Tony said, "What about your alibi?"

Nathan smirked. "I'm on an incoming flight from Tel Aviv. I'll be clearing customs in a couple of hours."

Nathan made the turn around, cruised slowly northward on A1A, where vehicles were parallel-parked on the right side of the boulevard. Tony pointed at his Range Rover.

Nathan said, "When you get to the Walker, go into the lounge and get a drink, order some food. I want you to be seen. Hell, go into the office and do some paperwork. But don't get a room—that will clock arrival time." He looked at Tony. "Is your father's condo available tonight?"

"I don't have the keys."

"Regardless, go to the Venezia Tower. I have a key to the unit adjacent to Louie's. Sidney's living there—he'll be glad to give you the guest room."

Tony drew a deep breath. He said, "Nathan—"

"Do you think I wanted to kill the girl?" asked Nathan. "It's a fucked up operation because you're an amateur. You had no business being there."

Stunned and more than a little sickened by Nathan's tale, Louie looked at his friend with shock. "Jesus Christ," he said. "What in the hell was Tony thinking?"

Chapter Forty-Seven

LOUIE SAT ON THE COUCH in his Miami condo and put his elegantly shod feet up on the coffee table. It was Tuesday evening, and he was dressed for Szarnakov's dinner party or almost dressed—his off-white, shawl-collared dinner jacket was still on its hanger, hooked to the door of the bedroom closet.

Louie had abandoned the bedroom to Rachel, who'd brought four dresses and was still trying to decide which of the four she would wear. This included four different pairs of heels, several evening clutches, and a dozen pair of earrings. She'd laid them all out on the bed, their respective shoes on the floor beneath them, and asked Louie to choose her outfit. He'd pointed to a slinky red number. "I kind of like this."

"Hmm. That's my least favorite."

"Wear whatever you want, baby. They're all beautiful."

Escaping to the front room, Louie poured Scotch into a glass and drank it neat. Using the remote control he turned on Channel 6, where the local news was starting. Louie checked his phone, listening to his messages and then returning a call from a man who'd called earlier when he was "indisposed," confirming an appointment for tomorrow.

The glass doors were closed, showcasing the view of South Pointe Park and Fisher Island while blocking the heat, leaving the condo pleasantly cool. Recessed lights in the kitchen highlighted the granite countertops, another recessed light above the bar shone down on the bottles and cut-crystal glasses.

They'd driven down early, stopping for a light lunch on Los Olas before swinging by the hospital to visit Victor. Arriving at the condo, they'd gone directly into the master bedroom, and now, mellow from sex and the nap that followed it, Louie savored his malt whiskey, raising the glass to his mouth as Jackie Nespral, anchoring the NBC affiliate WTVJ, said the words, "grisly double murder in Fort Lauderdale."

Abandoning his leisure, Louie sat upright, feet on the floor, and leaned forward as the screen shifted to show a reporter standing in the street across from Buzeczki's house, the camera panning the formerly sedate neighborhood, invaded by police and emergency vehicles. A crowd of curious onlookers had gathered.

The screen split to show Nespral in studio and the reporter at the murder scene. In response to Nespral's questioning, her associate was reporting that a maid had discovered the body of a man and a woman late this afternoon. Both victims had been shot, in what the police were describing as "execution style." And no, the police hadn't released the identity of the victims. The investigation was still in its early stages, although a medical examiner at the scene was said to have proclaimed that the victims had been dead for at least one full day, quite possibly two.

Neighbors were purported to be "stunned," and in full cooperation with the Fort Lauderdale police. The reporter said, "Jackie, this is a quiet neighborhood, and now, for the second time, it's been rocked by murder. If you recall, a man was shot to death in a vehicle in the parking lot of the now vacant Ireland's Inn just last week. Police aren't saying, but there is speculation that these two murders are connected. The homeowner has not lived in this house long, but there is a rumor that he is connected to organized crime."

Chapter Forty-Eight

BOAT TOUR OPERATORS ON BISCAYNE Bay were quick to point out the homes of the rich and famous. If the guides were to be believed, every big name movie star, rapper, Hollywood mogul, and billionaire basketball player had a house on Star Island. They never mentioned Russian oligarchs or their mistresses, and if they pointed out the sprawling three-story Moorish mansion with the octagonal turrets, they invariably named it as the home of a famous pop star.

But the pop star's house was the smaller, less pretentious one next door to Szarnakov's. Louie knew this for fact, as the pop star was one of several dozen people milling about on Szarnakov's terrace that evening. Notable personages included an aging British rocker and a seven-foot two retired NBA player and his pretty wife. The garden was full of busts and alabaster statues. Designed to mimic Neptune's pool at the Hearst Castle in San Simeon, the enormous pool was tiled turquoise and black, with gold flecks that glittered in the dusky green light. Moving silently amongst the guests was an army of white-gloved waiters bearing silver trays laden with fluted glasses of Dom Perignon and plates of caviar.

The celebrities tended to stick together, occupying a linen-draped table at the side of the pool, and causing a star-struck Rachel to stumble and grab at Louie's arm. To her credit she managed not to point. But Rachel was intimidated by the size and opulence of the house, with its white marble floors, coffered ceilings, and museum-quality art. Szarnakov's mistress, Elaine, a former British Airways flight attendant, was equally impressive with her aloof, elegant bearing and icy blonde beauty. Guests included middle-aged and elderly men of a business and money-class, many of whom spoke English badly, with pronounced Russian accents. Their escorts were literally that—escorts, but they were invariably blonde and beautiful and very young.

In greeting, Szarnakov placed his hands on Louie's shoulders and kissed him on both cheeks, Russian-style. He took Rachel's hand and lifted it to his lips. His bodyguards trailed discreetly behind him, a dozen other security personnel moving indiscriminately amongst the guests. Noticeably absent was Szarnakov's man, Dimitri, or Alexi, as Louie had come to think of him. Szarnakov's cousin Cyrus was introduced. He was a thick-necked, bullish young man with glazed eyes, a pimp, but of no account. He'd denied knowledge of any blackmailing scheme to Szarnakov, who believed, and more importantly, protected him.

For the first time since he'd met her, Rachel exhibited self-consciousness. "My God," she whispered to Louie. "I used to be a dancer and now I work at JoS. A. Bank—"

"You don't have to work there, you know. You don't have to work anywhere. I'll take care of you."

"You already take care of me better than any man ever has." She lifted her hand and fingered the ruby-and-diamond cocktail ring Louie had slipped on her finger earlier. Admiring the ring, Rachel said, "You're going to spoil me rotten, aren't you?"

Louie set his hand on her hip, gave her an affectionate smile. "You look beautiful tonight. I'm glad you wore the red dress for me."

The pop star, who did indeed own the unpretentious palace next door, sat directly across from Louie at dinner. Her companion was an Italian designer from the Abruzzi region. He was a young man, very good looking, and very gay. He admired Louie's jacket, and they chatted in Italian, lapsing back into English when Louie's Sicilian dialect failed to impress him.

The pop star was wearing one of his dresses, which Louie thought hideous, but maybe it was just that the entertainer's body was malnourished to the point where she could be considered anorexic. She had a gift for showmanship and a lack of any real talent, and Louie was singularly unimpressed with her act onstage and off.

But she knew who he was. "You're the man who took a bullet for Josephine Moore," she said. "I was in Cannes with Josephine last August. She told me all about you."

Louie had indeed been shot while escorting the actress Josephine Moore. They'd been coming out of Franco's when it happened, and he was the intended target, but Josephine hadn't known this. Kaiser had shot the supposedly "crazed" fan, and Louie had convalesced quite nicely, his wounds being non-life-threatening. A couple of years had passed, but Louie had kept in touch with Josephine, whose career had catapulted since then.

In reply, Louie said something charming and complimentary toward Josephine, and the pop star studied him a moment, head tilted to one side. "Hmm. You're an interesting man," she said. Her gaze flickered to Rachel. "And something of a bad boy, I'm told. Not that I abide by convention, mind you."

The baby lamb chops on the pop star's plate were said to be "fabulous" and "divinely sumptuous," but she barely ate anything, excusing herself soon after. Louie thought the food was mediocre, although he told his host it was good. But what did Russians know about food?

Louie talked to the gay designer and a Jewish financier who sat on his left. Dinner was a bit long, and Louie was glad when it ended. People strolled on the terrace or gathered on the loggia, where an orchestra was playing and couples slow-danced.

Rachel was sipping at another glass of Dom and Louie was accepting a glass of single malt whiskey from an elegant bartender when Szarnakov and his mistress came upon them. Putting a slender bejeweled hand under Rachel's elbow, Elaine said, "You must come with me. I want to show you my Picasso."

Rachel looked at Louie, and he gave her a little wink and watched her walk off under Elaine's charge. Sensing the diversion was calculated, he turned inquiringly to Szarnakov. The Russian's face seemed curiously blank, but the hand he set on Louie's arm trembled with repressed excitement. "I promised to show you my wine cellar," he said, though he had promised no such thing.

Escorted by Szarnakov, Louie walked through a sumptuously appointed room, passed through an elegant salon, and stepped into a lengthy corridor. They entered an office furnished with rich, dark woods and a thick carpet, with a large window overlooking the garden. But they were not to stay in this room. Indicating a side door that led to a back hall, Szarnakov said, "Come."

They were alone, absent of bodyguards or household staff. Stopping in front of a heavy oak door, Szarnakov removed a key from his pocket and unlocked it. He stepped in, held the door open for Louie, and then closed it after him, bolting it from inside. They were in the wine cellar, as evidenced by a distressed brick-paved floor and shelves lined with bottles. Accent lighting highlighted some of the racks, but now Szarnakov flicked a switch and recessed lights came on, illuminating the bottles, bright enough so that Louie could read the labels closest to him without his glasses.

The cellar was chilled, set to a perfect temperature for the vintage. A vaulted oak barrel ceiling disguised the modern functionality of the cellar. Two trestle tables occupied the middle ground, the cellar being long and narrow. Crates of unopened wine were stacked in one corner. Overall, it was a very nice cellar, at least a thousand bottles, if not more. Louie nodded approvingly at his host. "It's very impressive, Sergei."

They walked the length of the cellar. Szarnakov breathed noisily, though his mouth. His breath smelled of garlic; he wore a black dinner jacket, flawlessly pressed. The bright lighting did not flatter Szarnakov—his pockmarks were pronounced, the blackheads on his nose visible. His pitch black hair was heavily gelled and stiff as a raven's wing. Beneath his beetling brows his gray eyes burned with a sudden intensity that made Louie draw up short and look at him.

Szarnakov said, "I have something else to show you, Louis."

The hand Szarnakov set on Louie's forearm trembled slightly, but his grip was firm. "This way," he said, leading Louie to a steel door set in an opening between two racks. Another key unlocked this door, the bolts sliding ominously in the cold stillness of the space. Observing Louie's hesitation, Szarnakov said, "Louis, I do not forget that you are my friend and a guest in my house. But I have somebody here you might like to see."

Louie met Szarnakov's gaze, acknowledged his sincerity with a nod. Logic warned that he was entering into a potentially volatile situation, but he felt no personal danger from his host, and when Szarnakov pushed open the door, Louie followed him through it and stepped onto a small, iron-railed platform. A long flight of steps descended down into a brick-walled tunnel, adequately lit by a row of ceiling bulbs, so that Louie could see clear to the opposite end of the tunnel, where an identical set of steps ascended.

The house's superior climate control did not extend into the tunnel. Following Szarnakov down the stairs, the musty heat rose up around them. The tunnel smelled of damp and stone, but the concrete walkway seemed relatively new and was swept clean. Spider webs were tucked into corners, but even these were kept to a minimum, as though they were regularly brushed or sprayed away. Hearing the distant sounds of the party from overhead, Louie realized they were walking beneath the terrace and toward the water, where he'd noticed several boats tied to the dock earlier.

Their footfalls sounded loud, echoing off the walls. Ever the officious host, Szarnakov walked slowly, looking back to see how his guest was managing. "The tunnel is original to the house. In the old days they used to bring the rum in from Puerto Rico—they called them rumrunners, yes?"

"Yes," said Louie. "Bootleggers. Is the house that old?"

"Rebuilt in the fifties, after a fire. When I got the property, this tunnel was bad—the walls were falling in. But I had it fixed. It's a good escape, no?" He pointed toward the ascending staircase. "It leads to the boathouse. Did you see my new fishing boat out there?"

"I noticed a few boats."

"Yes, yes. My fishing boat is the SeaVee—"

"The 390 series with the quad outboards," said Louie. "Sure, I noticed. It's a beauty."

"It's a very fast boat. I like my fishing boat better than the big yacht I keep in Cyprus. It's nice to be on the water, makes me a free man."

They were ten feet from the ascending staircase. Szarnakov gestured to a padlocked steel door set between the bricks. "We go in here." He extracted another key from his pocket and fit it into the hasp. "When I bought the house, this was walled up with cement. I had them blow it open."

"What is it?"

"A small space. Storage, I think, for the rum. Or pirate's treasure." He chucked softly. "My men found human bones in here, but it's bad luck to move the dead, so we left them in the dirt."

Szarnakov removed the padlock and kicked open the door. It crashed noisily onto a side wall. Immediately, a foul odor emerged—a dead space, like a tomb, stinking of rot and human waste, the odor of urine and blood. The space was a black hole, impenetrable to Louie's sight, even with the tunnel lights overhead. Szarnakov reached in, and fumbling for the wall switch, he flicked it upwards, and the small dungeon came into focus by way of a dangling bulb, revealing rusty, red-bricked walls slimy with mold.

The space was roughly the size of a walk-in-closet. A man was chained to the back wall, held upright by his arms, which were suspended above him. He was stripped to his briefs, which were crusted with blood and vomit. His entire body, particularly his chest, arms, and shoulders, and most certainly his back, was lacerated with welts, the skin flayed open, exposing tendons and muscle. Dimitri's face, surprisingly, was untouched—a handsome face, even now, when he was dying and his lips were cracked with thirst and his body contorted with pain. His golden hair was matted with blood and sweat, shiny in the heat, the black soil floor muddied beneath his body.

Dimitri was half dead, his dark blue eyes blinking against the light, flickering with fear as they moved from Szarnakov to Louie and back. His body twitched spasmodically, causing the chains to rattle. A long guttural groan was wrenched from him.

"It was from your lips that I learned he was a traitor," said Szarnakov. "When you called me and asked, do I know a man named Alexi—a man with money—I knew it was him. Alexi is his birth name. When it became dangerous to use his real name, he changed it to Dimitri. But now, when he cheats me, *betrays* me, he calls himself Alexi."

The confined space was stifling. Louie felt the sweat start beneath his collar, break on his brow. The heavy meal, just digesting, soured in his stomach. Tasting bile in the back of his throat, Louie reached into his pocket and drew his handkerchief. Pressing the folded silk to his nose, he tried to blot the stench, but it was overpowering, and he took an involuntary step backward, turning his neck so that he could breathe the cooler, fresher air in the tunnel.

Gesturing at Dimitri, Szarnakov said, "He likes to whip little girls so I give him the whip. It is fitting punishment for a pig like him."

"Yes," said Louie. "I see."

"I wanted you to see him so that you would not doubt me when I say he is gone. I gave this man my trust, and he violated it. He stole from me, made me a fool in front of my people. Your situation was the one that revealed his lies, but when I began to look, I found other deceptions and thefts greater than you can imagine. So now I will kill him and make his death a gift for you."

Szarnakov unbuttoned his dinner jacket and reached inside, extracting a small automatic; a Ruger, thought Louie, thinking that it was eerily similar to the gun he was carrying. It might have even been the same model. Dimitri groaned again, the sound fading to a whimper as his eyes caught sight of the gun. His cracked lips opened, tried to talk, and expelled a weak, gasping breath.

Szarnakov took two steps toward Dimitri, saying, "Traitor," and spitting in the dirt at his feet. He said something in Russian, damning Dimitri just before he raised his arm, placing the Ruger's squat barrel to the space between his eyes.

Instinctively, Louie ducked into the tunnel, sidestepping the door as Szarnakov fired. One shot—loud in the enclosed space— but muffled beneath the earth. Louie's ears rang. He stepped back into the room. Dimitri hung limply from his arms, a black hole in his forehead, brain matter splattered onto the wall behind him. His bowels let loose, and the smell was death itself, choking them.

Szarnakov slipped the gun back into his jacket, and turned to Louie. Leaving the light on, he exited the death hole, shutting and padlocking the door behind them. They walked quickly through the tunnel, climbed the stairs, and entered the wine cellar where the frosty air washed over them. Szarnakov bolted the door, touched Louie lightly on the arm. "In that famous movie, *The Godfather,* they have that line about killing somebody being business, not personal. You remember?"

"Yes, of course."

"You and I… men like us… we understand what that means, don't we? We understand it too well, I think. But Dimitri, tonight, this was personal."

They refreshed themselves in the garden, at a small table near a tinkling fountain, where the lush beauty stirred tenderness in Louie's heart and the sweet, seductive fragrance of the flowers chased the stench of Szarnakov's dungeon from his nostrils.

The ladies joined them, Rachel visibly more relaxed than she'd been earlier. She'd been given a partial tour of the house, which included the prized Picasso, and she was animated and slightly drunk. Guests milled about, paying their respects to their hosts, the thick-faced and heavy-bodied guards blending into the background. Looking across the property, Louie sighted the boathouse adjacent to the docks, thought of the tunnel and the dead man, wondered which one of the hulking guards would be assigned the unpleasant task of disposing of the body, for Szarnakov had assured him that Dimitri would be "fed to the fish" before daybreak.

Louie felt nothing for Dimitri. He was unmoved by his death, if not actually relieved by it, and a bit skeptical of Szarnakov's motive in staging it. Louie's revulsion was merely physical—he'd detested the smell and heat and had been offended by it. But it was nice to know Dimitri was dead, and Szarnakov was right in surmising that he'd wonder if he hadn't seen it for himself. Louie had been a little put off by Szarnakov's liberal use of the term "men like us," because Louie adhered to an antiquated code where the families of your enemies were not fair game and the innocent were to be spared and protected, whereas the Russians were renowned for their brutality and ruthlessness, a quality that made Louie uneasy.

Szarnakov, obviously, saw no moral disparity, judged Louie his equal. Believing himself to be better, this did bother Louie, but not to the point that he dwelled on it or gave it more than a passing thought. He was more amused by Szarnakov's need for his approval, and the fact that he'd been made a sort of honorary guest, sitting with Szarnakov and his lady. To anyone who approached their table, Szarnakov would wave at Louie and say, "Allow me to introduce my good friend, Louis," and Louie would shake hands and exchange pleasantries.

Just as Louie was contemplating taking leave of his host, Szarnakov gestured to his butler, who came over at a clip. He issued orders in Russian, then told Louie and Rachel that he had a nice surprise for them. Five minutes later the butler returned with a black bottle, void of any label. The butler handed it to Szarnakov, who looked at it, and gave it back, saying, "Open it." To Louie and Rachel, he said, "I honor my good friends with champagne."

They watched as the butler, whose steady, cautious hand succeeded in popping the cork without spilling any of the sparkling wine, returned the open bottle to Szarnakov, placing it within reach of him as an attendant set four silver-stemmed antique glasses on the table. Louie observed that this thick-glassed bottle did not in the least resemble the pretty bottles of Dom Perignon he'd seen poking from the servers' ice-buckets all evening.

Louie waited patiently while Szarnakov filled each glass. Setting the bottle down, Szarnakov did not yet distribute the glasses, but took his time, studying them, and then saying, with great solemnity. "This is a most precious vintage, one of the rarest champagnes in the world. It is a 1907 Heidseick, lost to the sea in a shipwreck soon after it was bottled. It was recovered off the coast of France in 1997. There are less than two hundred bottles in the entire world. I was fortunate to be able to acquire one. Now, I wish to share this precious champagne with my friend."

Szarnakov distributed the glasses, first to Louie and Rachel, and then to his lady, keeping one for himself. Lifting his glass, Szarnakov proposed a toast to "friendship."

Louie clicked his glass to Szarnakov's and drank, the sweet champagne tickling his tongue like a lover's kiss, cleansing his palate and washing away the aftertaste of poorly prepared food and the ungodly stench of the murdered man's blood.

Chapter Forty-Nine

N THE MORNING, LYING ABED with Rachel, they watched the morning news, which replayed last night's story, with the added fillip of identifying photos of Grigori Buzeczki, a native of Brighton Beach, and the murdered girl's complicated Russian name, which the anchor badly mispronounced. The Fort Lauderdale police were said to be "pursuing leads." Evidence strongly suggested that the murders were connected to organized crime within the Russian community.

"We certainly had our fill of Russians last night," said Rachel. "Some of them did look a little scary, now that I think about it. Do you think any of them could be connected to that type of crime?"

"I wouldn't know." Louie deliberately lowered the volume with the remote control. Rubbing the side of Rachel's cheek with the back of his hand, he gave her a gentle smile. "Have a good time last night?"

"God, are you kidding? It was awesome. I didn't dare take pictures, so I'm not sure anyone will ever believe me when I tell them who was at the party. I can't believe it myself—sitting down to dinner with rock stars and celebrities. High society—"

"Pretty low, if you ask me," said Louie. "You're better than all of them. You shouldn't equate money with class. Aren't I proof of that?"

"I happen to think you're a pretty classy guy." Rachel stretched leisurely, like a cat. "It's amazing—all that champagne and I don't even have a headache. Do you think Sergei's girlfriend was lying when she said that the Heidseick was two-hundred and seventy-five thousand dollars a bottle?"

"He made such a ceremony of it I think she was pleased to be able to tell you."

"But two-hundred and seventy-five thousand dollars a *bottle*? For one bottle of champagne? That's insane."

"I agree."

"To tell you the truth, I feel guilty I drank it."

"Don't feel guilty." Louie glanced at the digital clock on the nightstand. He reached for his phone. "Baby, I have to make some calls. Do me a favor and go next door and tell Kaiser to get me the newspaper."

She slipped out of bed, stood there naked. "I can get you the paper in the lobby. Why is Sidney next door?"

"He lives there."

"No kidding." Rachel lifted her arms above her shoulders and stretched again. "God, I love a good fuck in the morning."

Before Louie could reply, she moved toward the bathroom, calling back over her shoulder. "I'm going to make you breakfast."

"Go next door first. Tell Kaiser to be ready at eleven. I have a meeting at the Marriott on Biscayne Bay. "

Louie started his calls while Rachel was in the shower. First to Angie, then to Victor, who casually mentioned that he was watching the news without revealing exactly what reports he'd seen, but it was his way of letting Louie know that he'd seen the one that mattered. He also told Louie the hospital was discharging him—he was heading home today and was scheduled to start physical therapy tomorrow.

This was great news, and it got better when Louie called Anthony, who was recovering so nicely he was at the gym. But there were a few things in New Orleans that needed Louie's attention, and Anthony wondered aloud how long it would be before Louie would be in town. "Not long," said Louie, knowing he'd have to get there within the next few days.

Louie phoned Ceci, but she was pouting, and he ended up speaking with her adoptive father. Next, he placed a call to Emily and got brought up to date on a few business matters. Then it was his turn to shower. When he came out, he could smell bacon frying, but he lathered up, started his shave. He was halfway through when Thompson called him.

Thompson said, "Sir, I have news for you. There was a double murder at a home on North Atlantic—"

"I saw it on the news," said Louie. "They released the homeowner's name as Grigori Buzeczki."

"Yes, that's the man. I wanted to tell you that we recovered a gun in the house. It's a Walther PPK, fires a .380. Ballistics tells us this was the same gun that was used to shoot Victor. If you recall, there was a spent shell at the scene. Incidentally, it's also the same gun that was used to kill Adam Molinsky. There's a definite connection. In fact, we've learned that Buzeczki—"

"Wait a minute. You're telling me that the gun that killed Buzeczki was the same gun that was used in Victor's shooting—"

"No, no. You misunderstand," said Thompson. "Buzeczki and his girl were killed with a different caliber weapon. That gun has not been recovered. What I am saying is that Buzeczki was the shooter in both Victor's case and this other one in which Molinsky was murdered. The Walther was Buzeczki's gun—he was proud of it, showed it off a bit. So it's believed Buzeczki was the shooter—we've found our man. Unfortunately, he's dead, and we can't question him."

Louie thanked Thompson and clicked off. Anxious to finish shaving, he nicked himself on the chin and was forced to slow down. Rachel came in to announce that breakfast was ready, but the smell of frying bacon had been replaced by one that was decidedly less pleasant, a smoky, burnt smell permeating the condo. Louie said, "Did you burn the bacon?"

"I've got a fresh batch going. Bacon's not always easy. I'll use the microwave—it turns out better."

He looked skeptically at her. She shrugged. "It's not a big deal. I'm a good cook. You'll see."

Louie noticed that she was wearing one of his sleeveless undershirts with a pair of yellow jean shorts that were so short they looked like panties and excluded the possibility that she was actually wearing any of these. She saw him looking, and lifted her brows in inquiry, but he turned away to dab at his nicked chin. He said, "Give me a few minutes to get dressed."

He took twenty, dressing in a lightweight suit and then calling Tony, which was the call he'd wanted to make all along. Tony was in the office, getting ready to go into a real estate closing. His voice sounded normal. "Everything okay?" asked Louie.

"Sure, everything's fine." Tony mentioned some business he was attending to, gave Louie a brief rundown. Then he volunteered that he and Gina had had a serious discussion and were "working things out." Without going into detail, Tony said that Gina had forgiven him, understanding, in part, her culpability in leading him to make the kind of choices he had.

"So we're good," he said. "We're going to make it."

"That's great news." Casually, Louie asked Tony if he'd heard from Natasha.

"She called to thank me and tell me she was doing well. She's going to be enrolling in a cosmetology course. She's getting better, too, you know, physically and mentally. I guess they're providing her with counseling, and they're going to help her get legal status."

"Good."

There was a question in Louie's voice. Tony said, "I'm cool, Dad. We're friends. Nothing more."

"That's good, because I want you to call her. I don't know if you saw the news, but there was a shooting in Fort Lauderdale—"

"I read about it in the paper," said Tony coolly.

"Then you're aware that Grigori Buzeczki was killed?"

"Yes."

"Natasha needs to talk to the police—clear up a few loose ends for them. With Buzeczki dead, she has nothing to fear."

"What about that other man, the one who beat her and filmed it? He may retaliate."

"At this point, he's immaterial."

Tony let this sink in, smart enough not to question it. "Okay, I'll call her."

"An Officer Thompson will be contacting Natasha. Assure her that he will be a gentleman. It's time for her to identify the players. Make sure she understands that she has nothing to fear—nobody will come after her. She's safe now. But the police need to know what happened to her and to her friend Irina."

Rachel poked her head into the bedroom. "Louie, your breakfast—"

Holding the receiver away from his mouth, he said, "I'll be there in a minute." To Tony: "I have to go."

"Will you be in the office later?"

"Tomorrow."

Louie said good-bye and placed a quick call to Thompson, gave the earnest young cop Natasha's name and something of her situation. Told him where to find her. Then he went to have his breakfast, which he knew was going to be awful.

Chapter Fifty

WHEN LOUIE ARRIVED HOME AT six o'clock that evening, Judy Garland was singing. The source was his television, transmitting the long dead star in black and white for the sole entertainment of his mother-in-law, who was resting on the couch in the family room. She greeted Louie as he came in, and pointed toward the terrace, where he saw Angie and Isabella sitting at the table.

Doubled-up seat cushions elevated Isabella to an acceptable height. She was hunched over, concentrating on some kind of scratch-off game, scribbling furiously. Angie sat at the end of the table, her chair at an angle, legs stretched out in front of her, ankles crossed. She held a small pink book, which Louie realized was not a book at all, but a decorative cover for her electronic reading device.

Louie's wife and granddaughter looked up as he stepped out the door. Isabella exclaimed, "Papa," while Angie said, "Oh, you're home."

Angie was closest, and Louie dropped a quick kiss onto her brow before bending to kiss Isabella, who flung her arms around his neck, giving him her sparkly-eyed smile. "How's my little princess today?" asked Louie, smooching her cheek.

She giggled. "I made you a Hello Kitty card."

"You did?"

"Uh huh." She held up the card, shiny black along the edges, but in the center a glittering orange kitty had been revealed by scratching off the top layer.

"Wow," said Louie. "You did this by yourself?"

"Yep."

"Amazing. I'll treasure it." He gave her another kiss, ruffled her silky black hair, curling softly around her face. He turned to Angie. "Did you eat?"

"I was just going to go in and make Isabella some fish-sticks."

"Fish-sticks."

Isabella giggled at his tone. Angie sighed. "Louie, she likes them. Don't you, honey?"

"Fish-sticks and macaroni and cheese. Yum. It's my favorite."

To Angie, Louie said, "I'm hungry. Let's go to Tramonti."

"Well, that does sound better than Van de Kamp's frozen fish sticks. I'll have to get cleaned up. Me and Isabella both. She'll have to come with us. Stella's not here." At Louie's look of inquiry, she added. "Stella had a date."

"What?"

Angie laughed. "Don't look so stunned."

"Who did she go out with?" he asked stiffly, dreading the thought that it might be Nathan.

"It's not Nathan," said Angie, surprising him. She caught his eye. "Do you think I didn't notice how she looks at him?"

Louie was too relieved to comment. After a minute, he said, "Who is the guy?"

"A friend introduced them. His name is Ricardo. He sells boats somewhere on the Marina Mile. He told me the name of the place, but I don't recall."

"What is he, Cuban?"

Angie rolled her eyes. "Half-Cuban, his father's family. They've been here since the Revolution. Ricardo looks a little like Marco Rubio, but not so pudgy in the face. He's around forty, I think. Divorced."

"That's too old for her."

Angie stood, extended her hand for Isabella. "Come on, sweetie, let's go get cleaned up. We're going to dinner with Papa." She turned toward the door. "I'll invite Mama; she always likes to go out." Then, under her breath, she said, "Louie, sometimes you are absolutely ridiculous."

Chapter Fifty-One

THE NEXT MORNING LOUIE MET the man from Philadelphia for breakfast at Marlee's Diner. After a pleasant exchange between friends, he drove to the office. Here, he found Tony at his desk, negotiating a deal on the phone, and Louie waited patiently, eyeing the pictures of his grandsons that Tony had on display.

Tony ended his conversation and hung up, looked inquisitively at Louie, who said, "Let's get a coffee."

Tony got up and reached for his iPhone. Louie said, "It wouldn't hurt to leave that here, give your old man a few minutes."

They walked to the coffee shop, where Tony ordered two coffees and one cinnamon scone. While Tony was paying, Louie carried his coffee outside, sat at one of the small tables with the green-canvas umbrellas. He looked at the fountain, the water from the smaller, upper basin overflowing into the lower. A couple of fat robins were washing themselves in the lower basin. Two young women, employees of the ad agency on the third floor, sat on a bench on the other side of the fountain.

Louie heard the whoosh of the revolving door and turned, watched Tony walk toward him. Tony set his coffee and scone on the table and drew back a chair. "I'm surprised you want to sit out here. It's a little hot."

"It's more private."

Tony met his gaze, and then glanced away. He ripped open a packet of sugar and stirred it into his coffee. Louie studied him a moment, thinking how handsome he was with his clean-cut good looks, his thick hair curling in the heat. He waited for Tony to look at him, and when he did, Louie said, "Where did you get the gun?"

Something flickered in Tony's eyes. He set down the stick he'd been stirring his coffee with and said coolly. "I asked Nathan not to tell you."

"Did you think he wouldn't?"

Tony sighed. "I figured you knew yesterday, when you called me. I could hear it in your voice."

"Where did you get the gun? It's not one of yours, is it?"

"For God's sake. You must really think I'm stupid. Do you honestly believe I'd use a gun that I own?"

"I'm not sure what you would do in a situation like this. Please tell me."

"I got it from Anthony."

"Anthony."

"Yes, our cousin, Anthony. He gave it to me when he was here, told me it was cold."

"You discussed your plans with Anthony?"

"I didn't discuss anything with Anthony. I merely told him I might need a gun—that's all. He gave it to me, and, as far as I know, Nathan took care of it. I let him dispose of it."

"He did." Louie sipped his coffee. He didn't really want it, had had enough at breakfast. He looked at his son. "You really took a risk, going into that house. What were you thinking?"

"It was my responsibility. If I hadn't let myself be blackmailed, Victor and Anthony would have never gotten shot. I started the mess—it was mine to clean up."

"Jesus, Tony, what if he had shot you? Going into a house like that without backup—it took balls. It's not my style—"

"No, you have someone do it for you. Someone like Nathan."

"Nathan has his own way of doing things. I don't question him because he's very good at what he does. But for you to take this upon yourself..." His voice trailed off. He looked up, met Tony's level gaze. "I don't know what to say. You really put yourself at a disadvantage. What if somebody saw you?"

"I was careful—"

"Not that careful. Nathan saw you."

"Yes, but that worked to my advantage. Besides, Nathan was right about the element of surprise. I caught Buzeczki completely off guard."

"You could have been killed. For God's sake, what if you had been caught?"

"I was ... am ... prepared to live with the consequences." He caught Louie's troubled expression. "I'm sorry, Dad, I'm not perfect."

"Jesus, Tony. I never asked for you to be perfect. You put that burden on yourself. I only want you to be happy. As it is, the police are crawling all over that neighborhood. Someone could still come forward. It scares me to think about it."

"Honestly, I'm not worried. They're looking for a Russian—"

"Don't do anything like this again. Promise me."

"Dad—"

"Consult with me first, okay? You can talk to me. Trust me a little, Tony. I have some experience in these matters."

"Yeah, I guess you do." Tony's voice quavered, and he lifted his coffee cup, drank a mouthful. He said tightly, "I feel awful about the girl."

"You made a decision. You have to live with it." Louie gave Tony an intense look. "No guilty confessions to your wife or a priest. It's your secret now, your burden to carry."

"God, no. Don't worry. I can handle this. I *will* handle it."

There was a glimmer of moisture in Tony's eye. He blinked rapidly, turned his head away. Louie got up and put his hands on Tony's shoulders, clasped him in a hug. "You're my son," he said. "I love you. I don't want anything bad to happen to you. Don't ever be afraid to come to me with a problem again. Do you understand me?"

Tony nodded his head against Louie's chest, like he had when he was a kid. He wiped his eyes with the back of his hand. Louie kissed him on the cheek, and then he stood quietly by his son, his hand on his shoulder, and watched a dove swoop down into the courtyard and land on the rim of the fountain.

Chapter Fifty-Two

THAT AFTERNOON THE DELRAY BEACH police informed Louie that they'd identified the man who had ambushed him on his driveway. They gave his name as Iouri Kharkiv, and added that he was a Ukrainian national. They'd had a tip from a citizen as to the late Mr. Kharkiv's motive, and it seemed, unfortunately, to be connected to Mrs. Morelli. When Louie expressed shock at this, the officer assured him that Angie was not in any trouble, although they would like for her to come into the station to clarify a few things for them.

Louie engaged Dick Weinstein for this, and then he went home and told Angie the police wanted to talk to her, relaying what the officer had told him and adding that he suspected her "friend" was quite possibly Chester. "But let them tell you his name," he said. "For all we know it could be someone else."

Angie looked suspiciously at him. "What do you know?"

Louie denied knowing anything, and when they arrived at the police station, meeting Weinstein there—who consulted with Angie in the parking lot before going inside—the police made it clear they wished to speak to Mrs. Morelli without Louie. So he sat in the reception area and read the sports section of the *Palm Beach Post*, and then an article in a tattered old copy of *National Geographic* about elephants.

He hadn't finished the article when Angie and Weinstein emerged with the detective, who shook their hands, thanking Angie for coming in. The detective gave Louie a cordial nod. Angie looked at Louie, and then quickly looked away. Louie said, "Is everything okay, dear?"

The detective said, "Yes, sir. Everything is fine."

They went out to the parking lot, Louie and Angie with Weinstein, who was wearing his ponytail and sandals. Louie glanced distastefully at his feet before looking at his face. "What happened in there?"

"Nothing drastic. Everything really is fine. Mrs. Morelli was a little stunned to learn that a friend of hers, Chester Morgan, was not quite the person he presented himself to be. Certain incidents came to light, and the police had a few questions, mainly about Mr. Morgan's character and some of the relationships he has with other people. There was a direct connection—a romantic relationship between Morgan and Iouri Kharkiv—the man you killed. It appears Kharkiv had illusions about Morgan and Mrs. Morelli." Weinstein glanced apologetically at Angie. "They think Kharkiv's motive was some kind of misplaced jealous rage. The police have a theory, based upon Morgan's statement, that Mrs. Morelli might have been the original, intended target. Apparently, Mr. Morgan presented himself to the police and volunteered this information, telling them Kharkiv was mentally impaired. They needed Mrs. Morelli to corroborate and confirm a few pertinent facts. That's all."

Louie glanced at Angie, who refused to meet his eye. He offered his hand to Weinstein, thanked him for being available on a moment's notice. They got into Angie's Escalade, Louie holding the passenger door for her and then climbing behind the wheel. He adjusted the air vents and backed out. He was turning onto Atlantic when Angie said, "Did you know about Chester?"

"Did I know that his real name was Fred, and that he served time for fraud, and that he was gay? Yes," said Louie. "I thought he was getting too cozy with you, and I had him checked out."

"Oh my God. Why didn't you tell me?"

"If I recall, I *did* tell you, and you accused me of having unpleasant motives. Jealousy, mainly."

"Did you know I loaned Chester money?"

"No," said Louie cautiously. "How would I know that? How much did you loan him?"

She said, "Of course you knew. How could I be so stupid? The police asked me if I had given Chester money, and I said no, that I had not. But I lied. They looked like they didn't believe me. Did I say the right thing?"

"Yes."

"Oh, Louie, I'm so humiliated." Her voice cracked. "They wanted to know if I was sleeping with Chester. 'Have you had sexual relations with Mr. Morgan?' they asked. I could have died. 'Absolutely not,' I told them. 'Our friendship was purely platonic.' I knew nothing about his personal life, and that the honest to God's truth. I was a naïve, trusting fool."

Angie started weeping, fumbling around in the console for her travel packet of tissue. "I almost got you killed," she said. "You and Ceci and ooohh...poor Anthony." She wailed. "They asked if I had a reason to want you dead...as if I was a part of this thing...oh, it was horrible. To think they actually suspected me—I was stunned by the question and Mr. Weinstein—he's a nice man, Louie—he told them they were out of line. They apologized but said they had to consider all possibilities because Kharkiv was dead and they'd never really know what was in his head, and I guess...I guess they don't trust Chester."

Chapter Fifty-Three

T WAS MEMORIAL WEEKEND. LOUIE flew to New Orleans with Angie, Stella, and Isabella. They stayed in their house on the lake and spent the weekend visiting with family and friends. On Memorial Day, Louie visited his parents' graves in Metairie Cemetery, and then Michael drove the family across the causeway to the north shore of Lake Pontchartrain where they attended a barbecue on Anthony's horse farm in the piney woods north of Covington.

Throughout the weekend Angie's mood alternated between shame and defiance, and when she decided to fly back to Florida on Tuesday, Louie voiced no protest. He devoted the rest of the week to his business interests, which included a luncheon in Baton Rouge and a golf outing with the mayor of New Orleans. He took Ceci to dinner, went fishing with Michael, and advised Anthony on a couple of difficult situations.

On Thursday afternoon Louie was sitting in Anthony's office at Crescent City Coffee when he received a call from the FBI. They knew he was in New Orleans and asked when he planned to return to Florida. Louie told them he would be home on the weekend, and the agent said, "We'd like to talk to you regarding your friendship with Sergei Szarnakov. Can you come to the Federal Building in Miami on Tuesday at ten o'clock?"

Louie was tempted to say no, but he knew this would piss them off. He told the agent he would be there, and the man said, "Good. You may bring counsel."

Like he was going to walk into a federal building without a lawyer. Were they kidding? Louie said, "Certainly," responding in kind to the agent's cordial parting, and then hanging up.

Louie immediately called his attorney, but Aaron said, dismayed, "Next Tuesday? They're not giving you much notice, are they? I hate to tell you, Lou, but I'm having surgery on Monday. It's nothing serious, but I'm going to be out for a few days. I know you've been keeping Weinstein busy. Would you feel comfortable with him handling this?"

"Do I have a choice?"

"I'll call him for you."

"Don't bother. I've got his number in my phone."

Angie was still acting sheepish when Louie arrived home Saturday night, but they didn't have time to discuss Chester. They had a social engagement on Sunday, after which they were too fatigued to do more than watch TV and go to bed.

On Monday morning Louie did his swim, emerging to find Victor waiting with his newspaper and coffee and fluffy, scrambled eggs with diced sweet peppers and toasted Italian bread. Louie compared this breakfast to the one Rachel had served him with its rubbery bacon and doughy bread. He'd asked her, incredulous, if it was Wonder Bread, and she said, "No, silly, it's the Publix brand."

Louie eyed Victor, who'd lost half his muscle weight and was using a cane to walk. "Are you up to doing this?"

"What am I going to do, Lou? I've got to start living again. I've got physical therapy three afternoons a week. The rest of my time is yours."

"What does Diana say?"

"This morning she said 'good riddance.'" Victor guffawed. "Another week of me lying around the house and we'd be heading for divorce court."

Louie said, "Well, to tell you the truth, Victor, I'm damn glad you're back. I haven't had a decent breakfast in weeks."

He sat at the kitchen table, fragrant steam wafting from the plate Victor placed in front of him. Then he unfolded the *Sun-Sentinel* and saw a grainy sketch of Dimitri. The caption below the picture read: "Police seek suspect in brutal Fort Lauderdale slayings."

The accompanying article reported that the police had not formally identified the suspect in last month's double murder, although he was known to use the name Alexi and/or Dimitri. Buzeczki's neighbor had seen the suspect at Buzeczki's house the day before the murders, and was able to report that some sort of argument had ensued. Alleged to have been involved with organized crime, Buzeczki was an associate of the suspect, who appears to be the ringleader of a nefarious gang of Russian and Eastern European criminals.

> *Working on tips, police have determined that the suspect is a member of the Russian Mafia and a known sex trafficker. An unnamed source led police to a residence in Sunny Isles Beach where six women were being held, some as young as seventeen. All of the young women are Russian and are*

believed to have been brought to this country by international sex traffickers.

As a result, criminal sexual activity is being investigated at a Hollywood Beach apartment, as well as at several local massage parlors. A raid on a Fort Lauderdale film studio yielded pornographic materials—some of a bizarre and sickening nature—and has led to at least one arrest.

The investigation is ongoing, but Detective Thompson of the Fort Lauderdale Police says that this was not a random crime, and citizens should not feel threatened. The victim, Grigori Buzeczki, has been positively identified as the shooter in the recent murder of one Adam Molinsky, who was killed execution style in the parking lot of an abandoned property on North Ocean Boulevard. The suspect is also being sought in connection with this crime.

According to Detective Thompson the motive for Adam Molinsky's murder appears to be drug-related. Molinsky was a known drug abuser and is believed to have owed money to Grigori Buzeczki and the suspect.

"It's complicated," said Detective Thompson, whose ingenuity in cracking the case has earned him a promotion, "but we're discovering that the recent rash of crimes in Fort Lauderdale is directly connected to this gang, including the savage murder of a young woman whose body was found in a drainage ditch last month. It is unfortunate that Grigori Buzeczki is dead, but we've learned that he was a very dangerous man, and our suspect is considered even more so."

Chapter Fifty-Four

WHEN LOUIE ARRIVED AT THE office, Adriana was sitting in the chair next to Emily's desk. Surprised to see her, Louie stopped short, his eyes sliding inquisitively to Emily, who made a face, indicating that she was as clueless as he was.

As soon as he came in, Adriana hopped upright, smoothing the wrinkles in her denim skirt and shifting the bamboo handle on her straw bag from her right hand to her left. She wore no make-up—perhaps just a touch of nude gloss—and appeared wan and pale. Her golden hair was as shiny as ever, and she wore it in a low ponytail. Her top was a simple navy T-shirt, totally unpretentious.

Glancing nervously at Louie, Adriana said, "Can I see you?"

"Sure." Louie offered her a polite smile and opened his door, stepping aside so she could precede him.

He hadn't been in his office in days, but everything was orderly, a lingering trace of lemon cleaner in the air. On his desk was a stack of files and pink message slips. His phone light was blinking. Louie indicated the visitors' chairs in front of his desk, and Adriana sat on the edge of a chair, resting her handbag on her lap. Louie walked behind his desk. He said, "Can I get you anything?"

She shook her head. "No, thank you. I can't stay."

Sitting, Louie studied her, saw the smudge of shadows beneath her eyes, felt her grief like a physical presence. He waited for her to speak, and she cleared her throat, and said, "My brother died."

"I'm very sorry for your loss."

"He was my twin—Adam. My mother told you about him." Louie nodded, and she drew a deep breath, swallowed nervously. "Adam was murdered. You may have seen it on the news. His name was Adam... Adam James Molinsky. His friends always called him AJ." Again, she caught her breath, steeled herself. "Adam was killed in the parking lot of the old Ireland's Inn in Fort Lauderdale."

"I did see it on the news," said Louie tersely.

"Adam had problems. He got involved with drugs... and he... well, his life fell apart. My mother and I were trying to get him into a detox and rehabilitation program, but he was resistant to getting help. He always needed money, and I... I was so bitter and angry at what my husband did to me that I helped him."

"How did you help him, Adriana? Did you give him money?"

"No." She shook her head. "I had no money to give. Kevin took all my money, and I was dead broke. But I thought of a way to make him some easy cash. He—" she pressed her lips together, looking down at her lap, and then back at Louie. "He had a girlfriend, and she... well, she worked in the sex trade, an escort. Natasha is Russian, and she owed money to the men who had brought her to this country, and she and Adam—they really thought they could make it together if he got clean. And she was determined to get away from that life. She told me that some of the girls she knew were involved in blackmailing men, and I suggested that she and Adam extort money from her clients by filming them." Seeing the way Louie's eyes hardened, she said, "I mean, most of those men are well off and could spare an extra thousand here or there. And it helped Adam to get by."

"I'm sure it did," said Louie coldly. He recalled Victor telling him that the original extortion gig had been implemented by Buzeczki. But Natasha had admitted to Victor that she and Irina and an unnamed friend had started their own blackmailing business. Louie had assumed Natasha was protecting AJ, and that he was the "friend." Now he realized that Natasha was also protecting Adriana, and he felt a slow, burning anger.

Adriana sighed bitterly, her eyes darting to the windows behind Louie, where she gazed absently out at the courtyard. Then she looked directly at Louie, and her eyes welled with tears. "I didn't take into account the caliber of the men Natasha worked for—their utter ruthlessness."

Louie said, "You don't have to tell me the rest. I know they blackmailed Tony. Whose idea was it?"

Adriana looked down at her hands, made a steeple with her fingers. "When I started here, I casually mentioned where I was working, and it came out that Tony was a … uh … client … and I … I had access to the personnel files and provided his address. Adam was a genius with the camera, and he positioned it—" She bit down on her lower lip, and then took a deep breath. "They brought Irina in on it, confided in her, and that was why those men killed her. Her and Adam, and maybe even Natasha. She's disappeared."

Louie said, "Natasha's in a safe place, out of the life." At Adriana's inquiring stare, he explained. "After your brother was killed, she called Tony. We helped her."

"Oh, my God." She dropped her head into her hands, her shoulders shaking as she cried silently. "I'm sick about what happened—so ashamed. I'm not like this … I'm a nice person, but I was harboring so much hatred toward my ex that I detested men, especially men who were cheating on their wives, and I ..."

She gave a harsh sob, struggling to compose herself, and Louie got up and grabbed a box of tissue from his credenza and set it down in front of her. Adriana pulled several tissues from the box and blew her nose.

She sat silent. Louie said, "Please continue."

"After Tony paid, it seemed so easy. You were supposed to be the big prize ... I was going to get half ... but after we were together that first time, I knew I couldn't go through with it." She looked at Louie, her eyes streaming. "You see, I was supposed to put a recording device in your stateroom, but you touched something in me, and I ... well ... that's the real reason I quit my job. I couldn't bear seeing you or Tony, knowing what I had planned."

When Louie didn't say anything, she sniffled and used fresh tissue to wipe her eyes. "Dick Weinstein told me not to mess with you. He saw us that night, remember, when you dropped me off in front of the building. Adam was out there in his Jeep—he'd stopped by to see Dick, who was handling his case for him. I guess Adam kind of hinted that we were planning something because Dick called me that night and emphatically told me to stop whatever it was I was doing. He said that you were not the type of man to fool with. He was right, of course, because the minute you started asking questions, Irina was killed, and then Adam—" she gulped noisily, drew a ragged breath. "Victor got shot, too. It was Buzeczki who shot him—that's what the police told me. They think Victor was going to that motel to meet Natasha."

Louie knew, as Adriana did not, that it was AJ who had shot Victor. Based on the fact that Victor had been shot with Buzeczki's gun, the police assumed he was the shooter, and Natasha—protecting

AJ even in death—had not told them otherwise. Louie said, "Why are you telling me this?"

"I just couldn't live with myself anymore. I feel enormous guilt about my brother and that other poor girl, and I ... Anyway, I wanted you to know. You see, I went to the police on Friday and turned over my brother's files. His computer crashed, but he had data stored on memory sticks, and I ... I'm so sorry."

"Did you give the files to the police?"

"Yes. All of them except for one. I have it with me." Adriana opened her purse and brought out a small envelope. The envelope was not sealed, and she cracked it open, extracting a device that to Louie's untrained eye resembled a slender key fob. Handing it to him, Adriana said, "The video of Tony is on here. I didn't give it to the police out of consideration for him and you."

"That's decent of you." Louie turned the thing over in his hand. "Is this the only copy?"

"Yes. Adam was the one who kept the files. He had a laptop, but that went bad, too. And since Natasha frequently borrowed it, they were careful not to store too much on it for fear it would fall into the wrong hands."

"I see," said Louie curtly. Then, "Did you tell the police you were involved in this thing?"

"No. I told them that I found the flash drives in my brother's closet, which is the truth, and that I had no idea what Adam was up to, but thought it might be relevant to their investigation."

There was a long moment of silence, and then Louie's speaker buzzed and Emily's voice came through the intercom, reminding him of an appointment. Looking dispassionately at Adriana, Louie said, "You can go now."

She made a fist, clutching balled up tissue. "I was hoping you might find it in your heart to forgive me."

"I'm not a priest. What I think is immaterial."

She stood, hugging her arms to her chest. "There's no chance for me, is there?"

Louie's eyes flickered; he felt nothing but contempt for her. He said coldly, "Like I said, you can leave now."

Chapter Fifty-Five

ONE OF THE FBI AGENTS was a woman. Her name was Lorraine Watson, and she confounded Louie because she was attractive in a cool, professional way. She wore a black pantsuit with a white blouse and pearl-stud earrings, her light brown hair clipped in a barrette at the nape of her neck. She exuded confidence, giving Louie a ballsy, no-nonsense look through the rectangular lenses of her frameless glasses. Her eyes were brown.

The feds had flown in big-shots from Washington, assembling the "experts" in a conference room in the Miami field office. Interspersed amongst the Beltway elites were the local grunts, of which Lorraine was one, as she announced that she was "attached to the South Florida bureau of operations."

It was a room of suits and mingling aftershaves, with undertones of breath mints and the chalky smell of powdered coffee creamer. The suits were varying shades of blue and gray, with one lone rebel wearing an ill-fitting tan suit. Louie himself wore navy, but the blend of cashmere and silk, not to mention the European cut of his jacket, set him apart from his interrogators. They eyed him like sharks as they claimed seats at the long conference table, although it was made clear from the outset that the head honcho—a black man named Henry Towson—would be asking the questions.

Towson's gravelly voice made Louie suspect he was a smoker. He had a hard demeanor, addressing Louie as "Louis," with exaggerated politeness. He introduced himself and his team, but made no reference to the grunts at the opposite end of the table, who might have been stenographers for all Louie knew, as they presented themselves as note-takers, legal pads on the table in front of them, nodding courteously, if not curiously, at him.

Most of Towson's team was attached to an organized crime task force, although at least one man was with an "anti-terrorism unit." And the tan-suited rebel with the receding hairline and brown-framed eyeglasses was not FBI at all, but CIA. Louie knew this not because it was told to him, but because he'd met this same man at Ruth's Chris Steakhouse when Nathan showed up for lunch with him several months back. Nathan had introduced him as Paul, with no last name given. The acronym CIA was never mentioned, nor was there any discussion of what Paul's occupation might be, but the fact that he was hanging with Nathan was faintly suggestive.

Paul, Louie recalled, had ordered a medium-rare porterhouse. He'd had at least three glasses of VO and water and had left without bothering to thank Louie for the meal. Today, the VO was replaced by black coffee in a Styrofoam cup. Tipping the cup to his lips, he gazed at Louie without revealing that he'd ever seen him before.

Louie and Weinstein were seated at one end of the long table, with Towson directly across from Louie. Garbed in a conservative blue suit, Weinstein had surprised Louie by showing up this morning minus his trademark ponytail. He'd left Palm Beach at sunrise, beating most of the traffic and arriving at the Miami Marina while it was still relatively early.

Weinstein had come to the marina because that's where Louie was, sitting at breakfast in the dining room of the *Stella di Mare* when Weinstein boarded. One of the crew brought him to Louie, who sat at the table wearing his crisp white shirt and navy trousers, his tie and jacket not yet in place. His understated Swiss watch was clamped around his wrist, and, as he did for formal or important functions, he'd put on his gold wedding band.

But the woman in Louie's cabin was not his wife, and Weinstein's gaze shot to Rachel, prancing around the galley in her pink terry-cloth shorts and low-cut tank top. He'd looked a little nonplussed, and Louie stood to greet him, shaking his hand and telling him he looked nice, and then Victor, walking stiffly into the dining room, had surveyed the lawyer and said, "You cut off that ragged ponytail for Lou. That's nice."

Weinstein said, "Actually, my wife wasn't too crazy about it."

Louie waved Weinstein to a chair, and Victor said, "Doll, set a place for Dick," and then he'd served them baked ricotta with spinach and tomato. A blended dark roast with real cream and guava *pastelitos* from a Cuban bakery on Bird Road were set out for dessert, but Louie abstained from the pastry for fear he'd be uncomfortable during the meeting.

Sweetening the muddy coffee the FBI served him with a packet of sugar, Louie thought longingly of that earlier blend Victor had brewed—a superior Colombian bean distributed by Crescent City Coffee. Weinstein had remarked at how good it was before getting down to business and asking Louie if he was aware that it was a crime to lie to a federal agent.

Towson said the same thing, saying it indirectly, using words like "fraudulent information" and "intentional deceit." Louie pondered the hypocrisy—he could be imprisoned for lying to them, but they willingly lied and employed deceit to entrap their victims.

They ruined lives by exploiting trivial matters because the FBI was a kiss-ass organization, and the road to promotion lay in their conviction rate. Furthermore, Louie was one of the few people to have ever escaped their snare, and they detested him for it.

Voodoo and trickery was the teaser in the *Times-Picayune's* headline when the grand jury failed to indict Louie, the article insinuating jury tampering without having actual proof of it. At any rate the feds' case crumbled, and Louie walked out of the Federal Courthouse in New Orleans a free man. His victory had resonated throughout the underworld, given him star status.

With an unctuous smile, Towson looked at Louie through the lenses of his metal-framed eyeglasses and told Louie that he was being given full immunity for his cooperation in the government's ongoing investigation of Sergei Szarnakov. One of Towson's minions read the actual case numbers—and there were several—disclosing the legalese for Weinstein, who nodded accordingly. Then they informed Louie that their conversation would be taped, and one of the agents pressed a button on a recorder and repeated some of the information already put forth.

Towson asked Louie if he understood, and he said, "Yes." He looked down the table and saw Agent Watson observing him. He made eye contact, giving her a little smile, which she responded to immediately, her icy demeanor softening as she returned his smile, and then the agent sitting beside her shot her a pissed-off look, and she quickly averted her gaze, a low flush tinting her cheeks.

Observing, Towson's eyes narrowed. He began by asking Louie basic questions, such as where he had first met Szarnakov and when. Was it true Louie had sold him a warehouse on the Miami River? Since the transfer of property was public record, Louie surmised that Towson knew that this was indeed true, and he answered affirmatively. These general questions continued for some time, and Louie was starting to get bored when Towson said, "What's your opinion of Sergei Szarnakov?"

Surprised, Louie said, "Does my opinion matter?"

There were a few snickers from down the table. Expression tightening, Towson said, "Not to me, no." His eyes were hard, and it occurred to Louie that Towson's dislike of him was personal. Towson amended, "Szarnakov is considered a lone wolf. Not a very sociable man beyond his inner circle. He throws lavish parties and disappears before his guests assemble." His eyes lingered on Louie's, baiting him. "It's unusual that you and he should become such good friends. He doesn't trust many people but he seems to trust you, Louis."

Louie said, "I doubt that my relationship with Szarnakov could be defined as friendship. We're acquaintances."

"You were his guest of honor at a recent party." Towson said this deliberately, watching for Louie's reaction, disappointed when there was none. "Szarnakov introduced you as his 'very good friend,' and proceeded to serve you and Rachel Richards a three hundred thousand dollar bottle of champagne. How do you explain this?"

Louie was not surprised they knew this. He had been seen at Szarnakov's party and understood immediately that the feds had somebody on the inside. He wondered how much they knew or suspected and felt the first stirrings of discomfort. He said, "I imagine Szarnakov was trying to impress me. I didn't think too much of it."

"Hmpf." Towson eyed him warily. "How was the champagne?"

"I found it a little sweet, but then, I'm not big on champagne."

"Did you know the price?"

"Not when I drank it. He told us it was a rare 1907 Heidseick, recovered from a shipwreck. Szarnakov's girlfriend revealed the price a little later."

"She told you?"

"Actually, she told my friend Rachel."

"What do you know of Elaine Howard?"

"Not very much," said Louie. "Szarnakov told me he met her in England, and that she used to work for British Airways."

"Were you aware that she was married when she met Szarnakov?"

"No," said Louie.

Towson smiled coldly. "Her husband was killed in a boating accident shortly thereafter."

His tone insinuated that the so-called accident was no accident at all. Louie said, "I know nothing of this."

Towson turned to the bald agent who sat on his right, and the man flipped open a legal file and slid a black and white 8x10 photo across the table to Louie. Towson said, "You know this man?"

Looking at the picture without picking it up, Louie nodded. "Yes. That's Dimitri."

Towson snorted. "His real name is Alexi Markovitch."

"I didn't know that. He was introduced to me as Dimitri. Szarnakov referred to him as his business advisor."

Towson looked at Louie, as though assessing whether or not he was telling the truth. "Where did you meet him?"

"Franco's."

Towson blinked. "The nightclub in Miami?" His brow furrowed, and Louie realized that in tailing Szarnakov, they must have missed this. Then he touched his forehead with the heel of his hand, and said, "Ah, yes, you own Franco's, don't you?"

"I have a controlling interest. Szarnakov likes to frequent the nightclub. I met him and Dimitri there a few weeks ago. It was on a Sunday. We had drinks." He met Towson's gaze evenly. "It was the first and only time I met Dimitri."

"He wasn't at the party?"

"No."

"You're sure?"

"I'm positive. I didn't see him."

"Did you ask where he was?"

Louie allowed himself a faint smile. "Why would I? Szarnakov's choice of guests was none of my business. He had some celebrities and sports stars there. Do you want to hear about them?"

Somebody down at the other end of the table chuckled, but Towson glared, not appreciating Louie's wisecrack. He came back, dug the knife a little closer to the bone. "You and Szarnakov disappeared for about thirty minutes during the party. Where did you go?"

"He showed me his wine cellar."

Towson allowed this comment to hang in the air. He looked down at his notes. "Anything else?"

"Excuse me."

"Did he show you any other rooms?"

"His office, a long hallway. He pointed out some paintings and artwork."

"What about the tunnel?"

"Tunnel?" Louie's brows came together. "I don't know anything about a tunnel."

"You're sure?"

"I did not see a tunnel, Agent Towson," said Louie calmly. "I'm not denying that one may exist. The house is old and quite large. Szarnakov told me that it was used as a drop off point by rumrunners in the twenties."

Towson scribbled something on his legal pad. Without looking at Louie, he said, "How was the wine cellar?"

"Impressive. It was very well stocked, well over a thousand bottles. Szarnakov employs a sommelier."

"Was the sommelier in the cellar with you?"

"No."

"So you were alone with Szarnakov?"

"While we were in the cellar, yes."

"Anything significant stand out?"

Louie glanced at Weinstein, who said, "Agent Towson, you're getting redundant. Please define 'significant.' Mr. Morelli is not a mind reader."

Towson sighed irritably. "We have an unimpeachable source who tells us that Markovitch was brought to Szarnakov's mansion the night before the party. Our source informs us that Markovitch was taken to a dungeon-like room beneath the wine cellar and tortured. We've been led to believe that Markovitch was killed sometime during the party or shortly thereafter. It's been told to us that Szarnakov murdered Markovitch and had him dismembered." He smirked. "Quite possibly while Mr. Morelli was savoring his quarter-million dollar glass of champagne." He looked at Louie with piercing eyes. "What can you tell us about this, Louis?"

Weinstein held up a hand, forestalling Louie's answer. He said, "I'd like to confer with my client in private."

One of Towson's aides escorted them to a small office. Conscious of the fact that he was probably being filmed and recorded, Louie said, "Dick, I don't know what the hell Towson's talking about. I know Szarnakov about as well as I know you. I've met him socially on a few occasions. He invited me to a party, offered me a glass of champagne."

"They wouldn't have called you here if they didn't believe they could build a case against Szarnakov."

"Come on. They've concocted some kind of BS story or put the screws to somebody who's feeding them false information. What the hell… a dungeon? You've got to be kidding me."

"So you deny any knowledge of this?"

"Jesus, whose side are you on?"

"I'm sorry. I didn't mean it like that. I just…Towson seems pretty damn sure of himself. Like they really do have a source."

"I'm sure he *thinks* he has a source. But consider it. I don't *know* Szarnakov that well. We're acquaintances. Hypothetically, even if he did kill his man, why would he involve me? It doesn't even make sense."

Back in the conference room Weinstein reiterated Louie's position. But Towson continued to needle Louie, asking him about the "business dealings" he had with Szarnakov. Louie said, "I don't do business with Szarnakov."

"What about the warehouse deal?"

"I sold him property. I didn't even handle it—I gave it to somebody in my office. It was a straightforward deal."

"What about Victor DeAngelis?"

Louie said, "What about Victor?"

"Was he involved with one of those escorts Szarnakov's gang was peddling?"

"No."

Towson snickered. "I think you're lying."

Weinstein said, "Agent Towson, you called my client here to ask about Sergei Szarnakov. Mr. Morelli has told you what he knows."

Towson said, "He hasn't told me shit." He gave a signal, gesturing to the agent who was operating the recorder to kill it. He looked at Louie, his eyes hostile. "You know what I think, Louis. I think Victor DeAngelis was playing around with one of those young escorts Szarnakov's gang was smuggling in. Some of that group had a little blackmailing business on the side. They tried to blackmail DeAngelis, didn't they? That's why he got shot. And you went to Szarnakov to cut some kind of deal."

Louie said, "I'm afraid I don't know what you're talking about."

Towson said, "This meeting is concluded. Get the fuck out of here."

Chapter Fifty-Six

THEY DROVE BACK TO THE marina, where they found Victor napping on the deck of the *Stella di Mare*. He roused himself, making Louie a drink. He asked Weinstein what he wanted, and the lawyer said, "Ah, hell, make me a Bombay and tonic. Do you have it?"

Victor said, "Sure."

They went inside, where the air conditioner was blasting. Looking around, Louie said, "Where's Rachel?"

"I gave her some money and sent her shopping."

Weinstein guffawed. He set his briefcase on the coffee table, admiring the burnished woods and posh furnishings. Louie removed his jacket and loosened his tie. He said to Weinstein, "You might as well get comfortable."

Weinstein draped his suit jacket over the arm of the couch and sat. He checked his messages and made a quick call. Victor brought over his drink, and he nodded his thanks. Taking a sip, he exhaled loudly. His eyes sought Louie, sitting opposite him in a white leather chair. "How much of what they said is true?"

Louie shrugged, "You know the blackmailing part. Except it wasn't Victor they blackmailed, it was my son Tony. I asked Szarnakov to look into it."

Weinstein's eyes got big. "Jesus Christ," he said.

Louie said, "It was your girl Adriana who fed them the information on Tony."

"Why is she *my* girl? You're the one who slept with her. And I didn't *know*, so please don't look at me like that. I *suspected* and told Adriana and Adam to knock off whatever it was they were planning." He sighed heavily. "That's why Adam was killed. It wasn't drugs at all."

"I imagine he was killed because he cheated the cheaters." Louie savored a mouthful of Scotch, swallowing it slowly. "I needed a drink."

"You were as cool as a cucumber in there." Weinstein rattled the cubes in his glass, took another drink. "Everything I read about you in that book was true, wasn't it?"

"I didn't read it so I couldn't tell you. You'll have to ask Victor, he read it."

Weinstein looked at Victor, who'd taken a seat in the chair next to Louie's. Victor said, "Are we on client-attorney confidentiality here?"

"Absolutely."

"Except I'm not your client, am I, Counselor?" Victor's eyes twinkled. "I guess most of it is true. The book, that is. *Gulf Coast Mob Dynasties,* right?"

"I knew it." Weinstein glanced at Louie. "What about the tunnel?"

"What about it?"

"Come on. Does it exist? It sounded like fiction in there."

Louie laughed shortly. "It exists."

"Did you see it?"

"I'm going to decline to answer that one."

Weinstein got drunk. He crashed in the spare stateroom, waking at dawn the next morning. Louie's steward took pity on him and made him a Bloody Mary. In fact, Louie's steward made them all Bloody Marys while Victor prepared omelets with crumbled bits of the Spanish pork sausage, chorizo, and sweet red peppers. Showered, eyes bloodshot and hands trembling, Weinstein restored himself and departed. After he left, Louie's crew sailed the *Stella di Mare* out of the marina and set it on a northeasterly course for Bermuda.

Louie sat on a sun-bed beneath a shade awning with Rachel as his captain steered the Hatteras through the traffic on the shipping lanes. They passed Fisher Island, ferry boats already cruising. On the portside the Venezia Tower glimmered like a gem, the Miami skyline pink in the morning light. For a quarter of an hour there was organized chaos, gulls swooping and screeching, the engines of deep water vessels rumbling on ingress, foreign tankers gliding into port alongside cruise ships, with small water craft chugging behind them.

The air was golden, the sea varying shades of blue and turquoise. They slipped by South Pointe Park, and then South Beach was portside, the track of sand fading as his captain increased their speed, the sea foaming at the stern. The day was hot, the wind warm on his face.

Before land slipped from view, Rachel moved to a neighboring sun-bed, one without a shade. She wore a thong, her ass-cheeks slick with oil as she turned them up to tan. The bow sliced gracefully into the sea, the engine hummed. The first mate's wife, Linda, brought Louie a San Pellegrino and a glass of ice, setting it on the small table beside him.

Sensing that Louie wanted to be alone, she retreated back to the cabin. Fifteen minutes later Victor emerged and claimed a seat on the wide cushion next to Louie. Glancing at Rachel, who appeared to be sleeping, Victor said, "She's going to burn."

Louie said, "I'll wake her in a few minutes." He reached over and patted Victor on the arm. "You look tired. You overdid it yesterday."

"I called the clinic. They set up a couple of therapy sessions in Bermuda. I'll have to check in with a doctor in Hamilton."

"Do what they say." Louie sipped his mineral water, his eyes gazing at the horizon.

Victor said, "What's wrong, Lou? You worried about the feds?"

"Hmpf." Louie gave a snort. "You know, I don't give a damn what happens to Szarnakov. He means nothing to me. Whatever business he had with Dimitri or Alexi or whoever the hell he was had nothing to do with me. It doesn't affect me in the least. But of all the things I've done in my life—and you, of all people—know what those things are, I'm afraid this is what they're going to get me on."

"What are you thinking?"

"Somebody close to Szarnakov got pinched and talked. Or the feds had an informant there all along. Either way, they know I was down in that tunnel with him."

Chapter Fifty-Seven

LOUIE GOT HOME THREE DAYS before Angie's birthday party. He'd been gone a week and had missed the actual day, and he could tell she was miffed. Before leaving he had advised Angie that he would be gone for a few days, but when he walked in wearing his boating attire, his face and arms freshly tanned, it was obvious he'd been at sea.

Angie said, "You look like you were on vacation."

"I had to go to Bermuda."

Something in the way he said this discouraged further questioning. Eyeing him suspiciously, she said, "How's Victor?"

"Much better. He was able to rest. It did him good." He saw the way she was looking at him, and he slipped his arm about her waist and kissed her on the cheek. "Look, I'm sorry I wasn't here for your birthday. I'll make it up to you."

"You always do, Louie."

She said this with sarcasm, but that night, coming upon him in the sitting room, her tone was cautious. "Stella invited Ceci and Robert to my party this weekend, but Ceci doesn't want to come."

"She's not comfortable in crowds. Don't take it personal."

"I didn't. I just thought it would be nice to have her here."

Angie bit anxiously on her lower lip, and Louie said, "Is something worrying you?"

"Huh. That's what I was going to ask you. What's wrong, Louie?"

He was sitting on the loveseat, readers perched low on his nose as he looked over an offer on the building he had for sale in Pompano, the one he'd recommended to Brian Chapman weeks ago. Chapman had scoffed at the idea, but now he'd come back with a solid offer from his buyers, and Louie turned the contract sideways on his lap and scrawled his signature on the bottom. He dated it and looked up. "Nothing's wrong, baby."

He was in his robe, the lamp throwing a circle of light around him. The French door to the balcony was ajar, admitting humid air and the smell of rain. Angie pattered over to the door and closed it. She was barefoot, wearing striped cotton pajamas, loose, ruffled hems cuffing her calves. Angie latched the deadbolt and turned to face Louie. "Ceci told Stella you were having a bad time. She said you were in some kind of trouble. Are you?"

Louie capped his Mont Blanc and set it on the coffee table. He tossed the contract onto his briefcase and patted the space beside him. Angie walked over, and he held out his hand to her, drawing her down beside him. "I didn't tell Ceci anything," he said. "I talked to her a few days ago. You know she's intuitive. She picked up on my mood, which wasn't good at the time. I'd spent the whole morning being grilled by a bunch of FBI agents—"

Angie stiffened, turning to look at him. "What are they questioning you about? I thought we were done with the FBI years ago."

He sighed. "They never really go away."

"Does it have anything to do with my situation?"

"Your situation?" Louie was startled. "What situation is that?"

"You know, that thing with Chester. It's been eating at me."

"God, no." He laughed. "I haven't even thought about that." Gently, he rubbed his knuckles along the side of her face. "This is something different."

"Does it have to do with your business?"

"Not at all. This involves a Russian man I know—"

She gasped. "It has to do with Tony and Natasha, doesn't it?"

"Indirectly." Her eyes widened with alarm. Seeing this, Louie said, "Don't worry, Tony's not in any trouble. But the FBI thinks I have knowledge regarding a man they believe was murdered." He read suspicion in her eyes. "Don't look at me like that, baby. I didn't do anything."

"Did they subpoena you?"

"No, they offered me immunity if I told them things about this man, but I didn't tell them anything they wanted to hear, and now they're angry with me."

"You should have told me about it sooner."

"Jesus, I don't want you worrying. You worry too much as it is." He touched the back of her neck, applying pressure to the kinks he discovered there. "You're all tense." After a few minutes he drew his hand back, patting her gently on the shoulder. "Why don't you pour us a nightcap, baby? The brandy will do."

Chapter Fifty-Eight

THE MINUTE LOUIE WALKED INTO Rachel's condo, he knew there was something wrong. Rachel liked to set a mood for sex, with candles and soft music. On the few occasions on which he'd come to her condo, she'd answered the door wearing sexy lingerie.

Today, Rachel didn't even answer the door. It was Jolene who admitted Louie, directing him to the living room where Rachel sat slumped over on the couch. In Bermuda Rachel had spent a small fortune on lingerie, purchasing an intricately beaded corset with a matching garter belt and suede pumps with five inch-heels. This morning, when Louie called Rachel and advised her he'd be over at three, he'd told her to wear her new outfit.

Louie had spent the better part of the day imagining Rachel in her lingerie, and he was disappointed to see her in wrinkled cut-off jean shorts and a white T-shirt. Rachel wasn't crying, but a mound of balled-up tissue was on the coffee table and her eyes were suspiciously swollen. A glass of watered-down lemonade was sweating, leaking all over the latest issue of Vogue.

Louie looked at Rachel and then at Jolene, his brows arching with inquiry. Jolene gave him a wan smile, shrugging apologetically. She, too, wore jean shorts, showcasing her muscular legs. "How's Victor?" she asked.

"He's doing great."

"Tell him to give me a call, when he's up to it," she said. "Tell him I'm moving down here permanently. I got a job at JFK Medical."

"Good for you," said Louie, who couldn't care less. His eyes shifted to Rachel, who was dabbing at her eyes with tissue.

Jolene said, "Rach, I'm going to Publix. Are you sure you don't want me to bring you anything else?"

Rachel sniffed. "No, just the frozen fruit bars. Raspberry, if they have them."

"Sure thing." Jolene walked into the kitchen, where she grabbed her handbag and a set of keys from the table. Keys dangling from her fingers, she said, "Bye, Louie. Be sure and tell Victor I asked after him."

Jolene left through the front door, closing it hard behind her. For a minute there was a pronounced silence, as though all the energy in the room had been sucked out of it. Louie stepped to the couch and stood, looking down at Rachel. "Baby, what's wrong? Did something bad happen?"

"Oh, Louie, my life is awful."

Rachel flung herself down on the sofa and, burying her face in her hands, she began sobbing. Sensing that something life-altering had occurred, it dawned on Louie that, not only was he not going to see Rachel in her garter belt and stockings today, there was a good chance he would never see her in them again. Setting a hand on her back, he said, "Tell me what happened."

She sobbed loudly. Louie let her cry, stroking her back, and after a few minutes she roused herself, reaching for the box of Kleenex on the end table. Snatching several, she blew her nose loudly, and then looked at Louie. "I have to have a hysterectomy."

"What?" The minute she said it, he knew it was a deal breaker. She knew it, too. Her eyes welled, and she attempted to turn away from him, but Louie caught her in his arms and held her. "Are they sure?"

She nodded against his chest. "They did a bunch of tests. Remember, I told you I had to go to the doctor right before we left for Bermuda?" At Louie's nod, she continued. "I've been having a lot of cramping with my periods. I have a couple of ovarian cysts they've been keeping an eye on. The cysts are getting bigger. They're benign, but they test for some kind of precancerous malignancy, which really means that if I don't have a hysterectomy, I'll get cancer. Not only that—because I test high on this scale—I won't be able to take hormones. I'll be slammed into menopause immediately."

It was one thing to have a post-menopausal wife. A girlfriend with hot flashes and schizophrenic mood swings would be a nightmare. Louie said, "It can't be that bad."

"It's awful news, Louie. Just awful. I'm only forty. Now I'm going to get fat and old—"

"I think you're being a little extreme. It could be worse, it could be cancer. At least this way they can forestall any problems—"

"Oh yes, I know. I should be grateful. But I'm not. I'm angry. It's so unfair," she wailed. "I was having such a great time with you—"

"We can still have a great time."

"Don't patronize me. You don't want a dried up old maid."

"Don't be silly. You're a beautiful girl—you've got lots of good times ahead of you."

"You're just saying that to be nice." She reached for her watery lemonade. Lifting the glass to her mouth, she took a couple of small sips. "I was afraid it was going to come to this."

"Baby, lots of women have hysterectomies. My wife did, and she's fine."

"Yeah, right. See what I mean? When was the last time you had sex with Angie?" She looked at him, saw the hard truth in his eyes, and said, "The Latin word for hysterectomy means 'female castration.' I'm being castrated. How horny do you think I'm going to be?"

Louie laughed softly. "Baby, you're being extreme. Maybe you ought to think a little more positively about this?"

"I'm being realistic." She swallowed a mouthful of lemonade and set the glass down. "I've been doing my research. I know." Rachel looked directly at him. "I won't be able to be your girlfriend anymore."

"Why don't you have your surgery and make that judgment afterward, when you're not feeling so emotional?"

"Hah, after surgery it'll be six weeks before I can even *have* sex. It's not like you're going to wait around for your girlfriend to recover."

"You're selling yourself short. I don't know if you realize this, but I'm having a great time with you. You're been phenomenal, baby." He drew her against him, gave her a light kiss. "When is your surgery?"

"Monday morning. I could have waited a few weeks, but why be miserable? I might as well get it over with." She took his hand, lined her palm up against his. "I talked to George—"

"Who?"

"You know, my manager at JoS. A. Bank? Remember, I told you about him?"

Louie didn't recall that they had ever discussed her boss. He said, "What about George?"

"Well, I quit the store to go to Bermuda, but I called George up today and asked him if I could have my job back after my surgery, and he ... well, he was really understanding. He told me he wants to date me, and that it doesn't matter to him that I'm getting older. He wants to settle down, and I'm thinking maybe I should give him a chance."

Chapter Fifty-Nine

VICTOR WAS SITTING ON THE big leather couch in his great room, looking at a recipe book. He was wearing his workout clothes—long gray shorts, a blue, short-sleeved Nike running shirt, white cotton socks and gym shoes. In front of Victor's couch was a black marble-topped coffee table. On the table was an issue of *Men's Health,* the remote control to the sixty-inch flat screen that was pinned on Victor's wall, and a tall plastic glass half-filled with a chocolate and banana protein shake. Louie knew it was banana because he could smell it.

"I'm back to my regular workouts," said Victor, looking at Louie as Diana led him into the room. "I quit therapy."

"Was that wise?"

"I talked to my doctor. He said it's okay as long as I don't do any heavy lifting. I got tired of those therapy sessions. I had some snippy little gay guy coaching me like Richard Simmons. I couldn't take it anymore."

Louie hitched up his trousers and sat on the couch that was set at an angle to the one where Victor was sitting, forming an ell. His gaze drifted to the triple-wide door-wall, overlooking Victor's patio and pool. Victor's house was on the Intracoastal, his thirty-eight footer at an angle on his boat-hoist, and Louie could see the tall masts of a sailboat gliding northward.

Victor said, "When did these queers start becoming proud of being queer? The guy was showing me pictures of his boyfriend."

Diana was wearing white shorts and a sleeveless red top. Looking at Victor, she rolled her eyes in exasperation. "I hope you were nice to him."

"Of course I was nice. I gave him my recipe for pesto sauce, didn't I?"

Having greeted Louie with a perfunctory kiss, Diana nonetheless seemed a little off, and now, when Victor asked her to get Louie a Pellegrino, she cut her eyes at him and turned abruptly, the rubber soles of her flip-flops slapping the hardwood floor as she crossed through the dining room and into the kitchen. She retrieved the bottle from the refrigerator, took down a water glass, and brought them to Louie, placing them on the coffee table within arm's reach of him.

Louie gave her an easy smile. "Did your mother leave?"

Diana softened. "She flew home yesterday. She wanted to stay longer—she hates the thought of missing Angie's birthday party—but my aunt got sick and she needed to get home." Diana looked at Victor. "I'm going to get my nails done."

"Okay, swell."

"I need some money."

Victor pulled a rubber-banded wad out of his side pocket. Snapping off the rubber band, he said, "How much?"

"A hundred." He looked up at her, and she said, "I'm getting my feet done, too."

He peeled off a couple of bills. "Here's two. Treat yourself."

"Thanks, Victor." Diana took the money, stooped to give him a kiss, and then said, "Bye, Louie."

She retraced her steps through the dining room. They heard her go out through the laundry room and into the garage, the electronic hum of the door lifting as she stepped out. Seconds later the side door closed. Louie looked at Victor, "She's got an attitude."

"You think?" Victor stirred his shake with his plastic straw, sucked down about an inch of it. "Diana's stewing over things—all that shit they printed about me in the paper when I got shot. She's got the same damn theory the feds have, that I was going to the Avondale to meet a hooker. Jesus, sometimes I'm sorry I got married. It's a hassle trying to keep a woman happy."

"Tell me about it." Louie poured mineral water into his glass, brought it to his lips and drank.

Louie then proceeded to tell Victor about Rachel needing a hysterectomy. By the time he finished telling, Victor was sucking air at the bottom of his glass. "It's a bummer, Lou. Rachel might be overreacting, but she's got a point, doesn't she? I mean, if a chick's not feeling sexy, how good of a blowjob are you going to get?"

This was about as accurate a summation as any, and Louie laughed. He passed along Jolene's message, and for a few minutes they commiserated about women. Then, on a more serious note, Louie said, "Albert Seymour came to my office this morning. He got popped for making those smut movies for Dimitri. Lauderdale arrested him. I don't know the details of the charges—at this point it's the State of Florida. I got a feeling it could get a little heavy, although he was able to make bail."

"Why'd he come to you?"

"He needs cash. I bought his car back." He caught Victor's look. "I did it totally legit—had Emily call the bank and make up a cashier's check. I sent Carmen to the Department of Motor Vehicles to transfer title and ownership."

"How much did you pay Seymour?"

"Eighty thousand."

Victor nodded. "Did he want more?"

"Seymour always wants more. But I told him beggars can't be choosers."

"So now you own a Ferrari."

"Yes, except that I don't exactly want one. I was thinking of gifting it to you. In fact, if you recall, Seymour signed the title over to you a few weeks ago. I didn't bother to change it."

"Why not give the Ferrari to Michael or Tony?"

"Michael doesn't need to be hot-rodding around in a Ferrari. And as for Tony … well, I'd rather give it to you. You can sell it for cash—it'll give you a nice little bonus."

Victor nodded. "Thanks, Lou."

Louie took his two phones and set them on the coffee table. He got up and walked to the door-wall, sliding it open. "Let's go outside."

They walked on the stamped concrete walkway, past Victor's stainless-steel outdoor kitchen and kidney-shaped pool with its dolphin mosaic on the bottom and past a ribbon of green grass, until they reached the Intracoastal, where a wooden bench, facing east, offered them a place to sit. The seawall was directly in front of them, a metal-rung ladder leading down to Victor's narrow dock, his boat in hoist, hull elevated above the choppy water.

It was a hot day, but the sun was obscured by a thick cluster of clouds. Marine traffic on the Intracoastal was light, only a few fishing boats passing. Across the wide canal, visible between the houses opposite, vehicles navigated the curves on A1A. The air smelled like water and grass and a trace of diesel fuel, exhaust sputtering from an outboard on one of the trawlers.

Louie said, "Seymour was all nerved up. He's scared to death— he's dropped ten pounds. He kept bringing up the thirty grand we muscled him on, telling me he was aware of it and that he'd pay me back—he wouldn't forget a friend, that kind of bullshit. I told him I'd send him a 1099 at the end of the year so he could declare it as income." Louie crossed his arms, watched a noisy speedboat chug by. "That son-of-a-bitch was wired. I'm pretty sure of it."

Victor sighed. "You gotta figure the feds offered him immunity, same as they did you with Szarnakov. But Seymour's not you, Lou. He'll tell them what he knows, and then some. The only thing is: What does he know? Your business with him was legitimate."

"Seymour's a pain in the ass, but I know where he's coming from. He's hustling to make a buck. I really don't want to put a hit on him, but he's making me uncomfortable. If he's talking to the feds… hell, you know how they misconstrue everything. That bastard Towson will manufacture evidence to get me."

"What do you want to do, Lou?"

The sun streamed through the clouds, instantly ratcheting up the thermometer ten degrees. In the sunlight, Victor's hazel eyes looked green. Louie said, "Seymour's got family up north, doesn't he?"

"His mother's on Long Island. He goes up every Independence Day for some kind of reunion."

"That might work. The fourth is only a couple of weeks away now, isn't it?" At Victor's nod, Louie said, "Find out if he's going— have Chucky take a peek, see if he's booked on any flights."

"Sure thing." He studied Louie, eyes narrowed. "What are you thinking?"

"I can't take any chances, so it'll have to be an accident."

"You want me to set something up?"

"No. I'll call my contact in New York. It's in his backyard. He'll know what to do."

Chapter Sixty

EVERY TIME LOUIE ATE AT Villagio he admired the marble-slab bar, with its design of jade and bronze and varying tints of green and amber. Louie liked it enough that he was considering a similar type pattern for his own kitchen, but Angie didn't want to be bothered with the mess of redecorating.

Sitting at the bar with Victor on Friday afternoon, Louie eyed the thick chunk of gleaming marble. It was a slow sports day—rain up and down the East Coast had delayed most major league games—and the television mounted in the cabinet above the bar was showing horse racing. One half of the double door leading onto the side terrace was open, admitting a steady flow of warm air that was quickly sucked up and dispelled by the air-conditioning.

Even on a hot day in June most of Villagio's diners opted for out-door seating. Some of the tables in the dining room were occupied, with the bar being the least desirable place to sit for the midday crowd, which was comprised of Boca's usual aging population with a smattering of families and business people. Situated on a busy corner in Mizner Park, overlooking the fountains on the boulevard and walkways, it was an ideal spot for shoppers seeking respite from the fashionable boutiques lining both sides of the thoroughfare.

Louie and Victor frequented Villagio, as it was conveniently located to his office and one of the few Italian restaurants open during the lunch hour. The food was always good, and the prices were reasonable by South Florida standards. The bar was their preferred place to sit. It was open to the dining room, with a view through the glass walls onto the patio. People drifted in and out on their way to the restrooms and hostess station.

Louie was halfway through his Amalfi salad when a woman stepped in from the side patio. She was slender and slim-waisted, with straight, light brown hair worn in a center part and tucked behind her ears. She wore a raspberry-pink V-necked lace top with cap-sleeves, a matching beaded necklace, and snug-fitting white Bermuda shorts. Her sandals were sensible low-heeled wedges, ideal for walking.

She was attractive enough to command looks from both men—discreet, civilized glances—and then Louie looked into her face and almost choked on his shrimp. It was Agent Watson, Lorraine Watson, if he remembered correctly. She was staring directly at him, flushing slightly as his eyes met hers.

Louie dabbed at his mouth with his napkin, dropped it on the bar next to his plate, and stood. "Agent Watson, what a surprise."

She extended her hand to him, and he took it, his hand grazing hers without actually shaking it, his eyes on hers—brown, with flecks of gold. Her makeup was non-existent, or what Stella called "understated," just enough mascara to accent her eyes, nude lip gloss, and a warm tint to her cheeks that may or may not have been put there intentionally. The eyeglasses she'd worn at their first meeting were gone, replaced by the glint of contact lenses.

Louie introduced Agent Watson to Victor, whose eyes widened upon hearing her title. Victor shook her hand, his expression neutral. Louie's lips curved in a smile. "Are you on duty?" he asked.

"Yes." She looked horrified. "I mean, no."

His smile deepened. "Undercover, then." His eyes looked beyond her, scanning the restaurant for one of her comrades. "You must be on assignment, unless, of course, I'm your assignment."

"No, no, it's nothing like that," she said. "I took a personal day."

"Coincidence then," said Louie, lightly and teasingly, even though he did not believe their meeting was coincidental.

"Well ... sort of."

She looked a little flustered, and Louie said, "You don't have to tell me."

"No, I don't have to tell you anything, Mr. Morelli. But since you think I have you under surveillance, I'll admit that I was curious."

"Curious about me?" he jibed. He couldn't help it—she was making it so easy.

"No," she said. "You're an open book." Her gaze held his, and she laughed softly. "I was curious about Villagio. I had to be over this way, and I've never been here. I remember reading in your file that you occasionally come here for lunch, and one of my coworkers told me that you only eat at the best places. So I figured it had to be good."

"It is," said Victor.

"Are you alone?" asked Louie.

"Yes."

He liked the easy way she admitted this. His eyes flickered to Victor, who said, "Doll, you don't look like any FBI agent I've ever seen."

Agent Watson's eyes opened wide at the term "doll." She laughed again. "And you, Mr. DeAngelis, are a lot less threatening in person than you are on paper."

She let this hang in the air a moment. Louie and Victor exchanged a look. Just then a businessman whom Louie knew walked into the bar. He wore a gray suit and had his phone in one hand and a folded newspaper in the other. He started toward a chair, saw Louie, and came over to say hello. Pumping Louie's hand, he said, "It's a nice day, isn't it? I hear it's supposed to be a spectacular weekend."

"I hope so," said Louie. "I'm entertaining a hundred people tomorrow."

"What's the occasion?"

"My wife's birthday."

The man's eyes slid to Agent Watson. He looked back at Louie. "Have a nice weekend, Lou. You too, Victor."

He nodded at Agent Watson, walked down the bar and claimed a spot. Louie turned to the agent, saw the way she was studying him. His eyes connected with hers. "Agent Watson, would you like to join us for lunch?"

"Yes, but I don't want to sit at the bar. It's too conspicuous." She glanced nervously about. "And don't call me Agent Watson. Lorraine will do."

They resettled themselves at a round table in the corner of the bar, where the glass walls met. With the aid of a busboy, the bartender brought over their food and drinks. Victor, having finished a bowl of *pasta fagioli* and a meatball topped with ricotta, ordered linguine with oil and garlic.

Louie said, "You're not hungry today, are you, Victor?"

"My appetite's coming back."

Agent Watson surprised Louie by ordering a glass of Chardonnay. She studied the menu. "I don't know what to get," she said. "I don't eat too much Italian food. I don't want anything garlicky or spicy."

"Where are you from?" asked Louie.

"Dayton, Ohio."

He smiled. "Don't they have Italian restaurants in Dayton?"

"Yes, but the only Italian restaurant I ever liked was Olive Garden. I always get their chicken parmesan."

Victor looked appalled. "Doll, if you go to an Italian restaurant and they serve you a dish loaded with garlic that means it's no good. Garlic is supposed to be used subtly, to enhance flavor. It should never be over-used—that's the first sign of a bad cook."

Louie said, "Take it from Victor."

Agent Watson ended up ordering *agnolotti*, which was round pasta, in this case stuffed with ricotta and spinach. While they waited for the food, they talked, Watson volunteering that she'd been in Florida a year and a half. She was single, never married, and somewhere in her mid-thirties. She worked long hours.

"Except for today," said Louie.

"Yes, this is nice. When I get home at night, I'm usually too tired to go out."

"I'm glad you happened to stop by." She looked at him, looked away. She picked up her wine and took a small sip. Setting her glass down, she again looked at Louie. This time, there was no mistaking her blush.

Louie said, "Are you going to tell Agent Towson you had lunch with me?"

She shook her head. "No, I think I'll keep this one to myself."

"I can't imagine Towson would approve. I sensed his dislike of me was rather … personal. He's a man who takes his job seriously."

Agent Watson smiled. "That's one way to put it. He's furious now, too—especially since his whole case against Sergei Szarnakov and his *associates*," she paused, her look implying that Louie fell into this last category, "just blew up in his face."

"It did?" said Louie, glancing at Victor, suspicious of her motive for relaying this.

Detecting his tone, she looked at him with surprise. "Didn't you hear the news?"

"What news?"

"Szarnakov and his girlfriend, Elaine Howard, were killed yesterday."

"I didn't hear that," said Louie.

"CNN and Fox are both reporting it. It happened on Cyprus. It was a car bomb. It took out Szarnakov, two bodyguards, and Elaine Howard. To be honest, no one at the bureau is grieving for Sergei Szarnakov. But Mrs. Howard is a loss."

Chapter Sixty-One

N THE SPAN OF A single day Louie's house had been transformed. A peaked, white tent ran the length of the side garden, where a platform was being erected for the Big Easy band Stella had arranged for Angie's party. On Friday evening two band members were present, inspecting their stage. A dozen relatives were lounging about the terrace. Most of the relatives were Angie's, but Louie's sister and brother-in-law had arrived on the same plane as Anthony's family. Michael had also flown in, bringing with him a blonde who worked as a cocktail waitress in a Bourbon Street club.

To Louie's practiced eye, the blonde looked like she did more than serve drinks. She set Angie's teeth on edge. "Please tell your son that *that girl* is not sleeping in his room with him," she said to Louie. "You think he'd have more sense than to bring a girl like that home. Hmpf. She came downstairs in a thong. Mama almost had a heart attack."

Standing in the kitchen, Louie had a clear view to the poolside lounger where Michael's girlfriend was relaxing with a silver flask in one hand and a lit cigarette in the other. Her breasts were outstanding, held in place by a black bikini-top. She wore cutoff jean shorts. Louie said, "She's not wearing a thong now."

"No, Michael told her she had to change. She pouted about it, too. Now she's out there getting drunk."

A party tray of pizza and a platter of half-cut subs were on the counter. Stella was in the dining room, going over last minute details with somebody from the catering company. Out on the terrace Isabella and a young cousin were taking turns pushing a doll carriage. Tony and Carmen were in the pool with Tony's boys and a couple of young cousins, and Gina sat poolside, bouncing Louie's youngest grandchild on her knee. It was the party before the party. Louie said, "Don't worry, baby, I'll talk to Michael," and then he went out to greet his relatives.

At sundown, Louie was sitting on the terrace talking to his brother-in-law when Nathan called. Louie had eaten poorly, leaving a slice of undercooked pizza on the plate in front of him and eschewing the sub altogether. Some of the relatives—the ones toting young children—had departed and a few more were preparing to leave. Inside the house Angie and her sisters were in the throes of a heated discussion. A few of Michael's buddies had dropped by, his girl had traded her bikini for a skimpy dress, and they'd all taken off.

The night was sweet and warm and still, the potted palms motionless, hibiscus gleaming pale in the twilight. Nathan said, "I just landed at FXE. Meet me at D'Angelo's Pizza in Lauderdale."

FXE was Fort Lauderdale's executive airport, the one Louie most frequently used. By his calculations D'Angelo's Pizza was three and half miles from the airport. Louie said, "Give me about thirty, forty minutes."

It took Louie forty-five minutes to get to D'Angelo's, but he traveled fast, considering it took him ten minutes to get out of the house. Then he swung by the marina in Boca and picked up Anthony, who was staying on the *Stella di Mare* with his family. The cousins walked in half an hour before closing, when the place was winding down. Three tables were occupied, and a few couples sat at the bar.

Nathan sat alone at a table for four. He was eating a slice of pizza with anchovies and oregano and did not bother to get up or shake their hands. A bottle of red wine was on the table, the wine glass in front of him half full. He looked at them through eyes that were glassy with fatigue, indicated the pizza, and said, "Help yourself."

A fresh-faced young waiter came by. He introduced himself, ready to go into his spiel, and Nathan said, "Bring a couple of plates."

Nathan appeared to have been traveling as a businessman. Flying into FXE, he was wearing a conservative gray suit and maroon-striped tie. But his skin was swarthier than ever, and he hadn't shaved today and probably not yesterday either. Louie said, "Where you flying in from?"

"New York." He swallowed a mouthful of pizza, wiped his fingers on his napkin, and said, "I flew out of Rome this afternoon." He looked at Anthony. "I see you recovered nicely from being shot. Nothing to it, is there?"

Anthony said, "I'm sore in my shoulder."

"Give it a few weeks."

The waiter dropped off fresh plates and glasses. Louie poured wine for Anthony and himself, topped off Nathan's glass. He watched Nathan reach for another slice of pie. "Didn't get any pizza in Rome, huh?"

"I didn't get any food in Rome. I was only there two hours."

"And before that?"

Nathan laughed, his eyes flickering with a ghostly glimmer. "I was in the Mediterranean, on an island east of Greece and west of Lebanon."

"Jesus," said Louie, comprehension dawning. "How did you—"

"You don't get to ask. Let's just say that I persuaded some individuals who were planning an operation on that order to implement their strategy by moving it up a few weeks. I pointed out to them that their target was likely to fall into the wrong hands and thus complicate matters." He drank from his glass of wine, looked at Louie's expression, and grinned. "You're very fortunate you had a friend in the room with you on that day you were questioned."

Louie thought of the lone CIA agent at Towson's meeting. Twirling the stem of the wine glass between his fingers, he said, "I wasn't sure he was a friend."

"To tell you the truth, he was more concerned about the target betraying sensitive information to your ambitious acquaintances. Even Russian oligarchs talk, you know. I gather there was some important information our friend preferred not to share with his compatriots. Based upon this, my associates believed it was to their benefit to expedite matters."

Louie was too dumbfounded to speak. Nathan took a bite of pizza. He chewed noisily, with hunger that had not yet abated. Glancing at Louie, he said, "Elaine Howard was the snitch. She's the one who fingered you to the feds."

Chapter Sixty-Two

THE ONLY LIGHT IN THE sitting room came from the recessed light set above the bar. But this was perfect for spotting the bottle of Prosecco Angie had left on the counter. Louie uncorked the bottle and took two long-stemmed glasses down from the shelf. He filled both glasses with the dry, sparkling wine.

The French doors were opened, letting in the balmy night air, scented with jasmine and roses and the fragrance of the sea. Out on the balcony Angie sat on the cushioned love-seat in an off-white silk negligee and matching peignoir with lacy sleeves and gleaming satin slippers. She looked up as Louie came through the open door with the wine. She smiled and patted the space beside her, scooting over so Louie had ample room to sit. He handed her a glass and then set his on the low glass-topped table Angie had been using as a hassock, and, claiming the offered space, he slipped his arm about her waist. "Happy, baby?"

Barefooted, Louie still had on the cream-colored trousers he'd worn for Angie's party, topping it with a midnight blue silk robe, belted loosely at the waist. Though he'd had a busy day, he wasn't tired, but felt instead the energy that comes after hosting a successful party. Seeing the sparkle in Angie's eyes, Louie knew she shared this feeling.

Angie leaned her head against his shoulder. She'd taken her bath—she smelled of creamy French soap and expensive body lotion. "I had a wonderful time, Louie. It was such a beautiful party. I won't ever forget it. Thank you."

Louie smiled. "Thank Stella. She planned it to be special for you."

"It *was* special, although I think my best present was seeing Tony and Gina reconciled and happy."

Louie concurred. He had to smile at the ease with which Angie had re-elevated their oldest to favored status. They discussed Tony's improved relations with Gina, and then they talked about the party, for which Stella had gone all out—lobster and pink champagne with prime rib and baked oysters, with a dozen side dishes and a dessert table that had ruined the diets of every woman in attendance. Despite the elegant décor and the succulent food, it was an informal affair and guests moved between the beach and the terrace, playing bocce while their kids swam, and then dancing to the combination of jazz, blues, and big band era music. Nobody got sloppy drunk, although one of Angie's brothers-in-law was passed out on the couch in the library.

It was two weeks till the 4th of July, but somebody to the south of them had gotten a jump on the holiday and provided a spectacular fireworks display. The party broke up soon after the show ended. Now, looking out to sea, Louie saw a bottle rocket burst over the beach somewhere due north, the cascading shower eliciting an appreciative gasp from a spectator who sat on the terrace in the company of Michael and a dozen young people—all that remained of the guests. Bits and pieces of their conversation drifted up to Louie and Angie, their voices muffled by the soothing sound of waves cresting onto the beach as well as the gurgling of the spa and the gentle slap of water hitting the pool's tiled walls. One girl laughed; bottles clinked. A crescent moon was high in the sky.

Angie said, "I saw you talking with Stella's friend, Ricardo. What did you think of him?"

"You were right. He's a great guy. I'm glad she has a friend, but I don't think it'll last."

"Why?" Angie turned her head to him. "Is it because of Nathan? Do you think she's in love with him?"

"I suspect she might be. Too bad for her—he's very devoted to his wife." Louie sighed. "Nathan sent his regards, but it's just as well the Roths couldn't make it." He lifted his glass and took a sip of Prosecco. It was dry and cold. He thought of what Nathan had said last night. *Tell your wife I left her present in Cyprus.* He smiled to himself, touched Angie gently on the shoulder. "Baby, that FBI thing has been resolved. I don't want you worrying about it anymore—that threat has been removed."

"Resolved, how?"

Louie didn't say anything, and Angie said, "So they're not investigating you anymore?"

"I suspect they'll always be investigating me in some capacity or another. But this thing with the Russians is over."

Angie twirled the stem of her glass between her thumb and forefinger. She gazed tentatively at him. "Over, for good?"

He kissed her on the top of her head. "Yes, baby, for good."

"Thank God. I was so worried. I'd hate to have to lose you now, after all these years." She set her glass on the table and resettled her head on his shoulder. Louie rested his hand on her hip. They sat like that for a few minutes, listening to the sounds from below. Some of the young people were getting up—chairs were scraped back. Loudly, Michael's girlfriend said, "I want to go swimming."

Angie's mouth pursed, but she didn't say a word. A few of the group turned and went into the house, and about half remained sitting, Michael amongst them. An ocean breeze gusted in, making the palm fronds quiver and rustle and the surface of the pool dimple. Out of the blue, Angie said, "Do you still love me?"

"How can you even ask me such a thing? Of course I love you."

"You don't ever say it anymore."

"Do I *need* to say it?" Angie blinked tears and Louie bent his head and kissed her between the eyes. "What's the matter with you? After everything we've been through, how can you doubt my love? I know I'm not a perfect husband, but my affection for you is constant."

The moon dipped behind a cloud. Out at sea ships moved silently, their silhouettes revealed by their lights. Michael's blonde got up and pattered barefoot to the edge of the pool. She wore a short black dress, which she pulled over her head and dropped to the ground. Beneath the dress she had not bothered with undergarments and now stood completely naked. Gleaming in the pale light, her body was spectacular.

Angie's mood was spoiled. She sat up huffily and hissed, "The little slut."

The blonde stepped into the pool. "Ooh, this is great," she called out, summoning another young lady, who quickly shed her shorts and blouse, and jumped into the water in panties and skimpy bra. Plunging into the deep end, the newcomer lost her bra—it floated to the surface—and the blonde snatched it, started twirling it around her finger while her girlfriend shrieked in protest. She tossed it to the group on the patio. One of the young men caught it, and laughter erupted.

The guys were on their feet and moving toward the pool. Michael's buddies went in, clothes and all. Louie took a final drink of Prosecco and then stood, holding out his hand to Angie. "Come on, baby, let's go to bed."

She looked ruefully at the pool, where her own son was jumping into the water in his underwear. "Shouldn't we say something?"

Louie smiled. "Let them have their fun."

Angie got up, smoothing her hair, gown billowing in the breeze. She held her wine glass in her right hand and set her left on Louie's forearm. "I want to ask a favor of you."

There was a hint of something serious in her tone, and he looked at her, his brows arched. "What favor, baby?"

Angie said, "I want you to do something about Chester."

Louie's eyes met hers and then moved away. Shrieks and laughter abounded from the pool, and Louie looked at the young people, saw Michael standing waist high in the shallow end with his arms around the naked body of his girl. They were kissing. He said lightly, "I don't remember. Did we ever go skinny-dipping?"

Angie's fingers closed on Louie's arm. "Listen to me, Louie. I'm serious. I've been thinking ... Chester's on heart medication. You could make it look natural, couldn't you?"

Louie's eyes flickered in the dark. He didn't say anything, merely looked at her, and Angie said heatedly, as though to persuade him. "He humiliated me."

"My dear, of course he humiliated you. Why do you ask me such a thing?" Louie took the glass from her hand and set it on the table. He nudged her toward the door. "Let's go inside, leave the night to the young people."

Angie held back, gazed intently at him. Tears stood in her eyes. "Louie—"

He took her hand. "Let it go, baby. He's dead. Didn't you know?"

Books in the Louie Morelli series

Louie Morelli's Mistress
Stella di Mare
Louie Morelli's Daughter
The Prince of Mafia Princes

To subscribe to Patricia Bellomo's blog, or to be placed on a mailing list to receive updates about new releases, visit her website and select the contact button:

www.patriciabellomo.com

Thank you for buying this book. I hope you enjoyed reading it as much as I loved writing it. As always, I'd love to hear from you. Please contact me via my website.

Patricia Bellomo

www.ingramcontent.com/pod-product-compliance
Lightning Source LLC
Chambersburg PA
CBHW071151020726
47502CB00002B/374